CORNHUSKER DREAMS

CARA PUTMAN

ALSO BY CARA PUTMAN

ROMANTIC SUSPENSE
Beyond Justice
A Wedding Transpires on Mackinac Island
Love's Prize
Deadly Exposure
Trial by Fire
Dying for Love

HISTORICALS
Canteen Dreams
Sandhill Dreams
Captive Dreams
A Promise Kept
A Promise Born
A Promise Forged
Where Treetops Glisten
Shadowed by Grace
Stars in the Night

GUIDEPOST MYSTERIES
Timeless Treasures (Patchwork Mysteries)
Squared Away (Patchwork Mysteries)
Work In Progress (Mary's Bookshop)
Mixed Motives (Mary's Bookshop)
Mason Jar Mayhem (Sugarcreek Amish Mysteries)
Blessed are the Cheesemakers (Sugarcreek Amish Mysteries)
To Have and to Hold (Sugarcreek Amish Mysteries)
Novella to come (Sugarcreek Amish Mysteries)
By Air and Sea (Mysteries of Martha's Vineyard)

CANTEEN DREAMS

To Willard and Audrey Kilzer, my grandparents and members of one of the greatest generations, and to Jesus for blessing this dream.

ACKNOWLEDGMENTS

A book is never written alone. While this book was awarded the ACFW Book of the Year for Short Historical in 2008, I still wanted to finesse and fine tune it. Many thanks to Lacy Williams and Andrea Cox for helping me get it ready for its second take at book life.

Also many thanks to Jim and Tracie Peterson for encouraging this idea and then giving my first book a home. This was the beginning and it's amazing to think that as I edited this I'm also writing my twenty-fifth book. It's incredible to think I've written twenty-five books in nine years.

This story is dear to me because it marries a story from my hometown, North Platte, Nebraska, with an adaptation of my Kilzer grandparents' love story. There is something about the World War II generation and the way they rose to the demands of their time that inspires me. Add in my grandparents' love that survived 65 years and set the standard for me, and it's a story that captures my heart. I hope it captures yours, too.

CHAPTER 1

DECEMBER 6, 1941

*S*he hated attending dances alone.

The hardwood floor of the train station thumped with the beat of couples jitterbugging. A record hissed and popped as it circled around a player. The slight distortion gave the swinging rhythms of Glenn Miller and His Orchestra a unique sound. Audrey Stone watched the couples dance from her spot on the side of the room. She should step over and start a conversation with someone.

"Hi, Audrey."

The deep voice startled her. She spun toward it, her hand clutching her throat. As she looked up into Graham Hudlow's square face, she wanted to throttle him. "Graham, you scared me. Don't you dare sneak up on me again."

His expression fell before he set his jaw. "Audrey, would you dance with me? You know you'd rather be dancing, even if it's with me."

She considered him as she weighed the correct response. They'd grown up together since he introduced himself by pulling her pigtails in school. He'd pursued her since they were in junior high, but his bookish looks and orderly personality held no appeal to her. While she didn't want to encourage him, one little dance couldn't hurt. And it would certainly relieve the boredom of the night. She inclined her head in a slight nod. "I think I'd like that."

She placed her hand on his arm and allowed him to lead her to the dance floor. The shuffle of dozens of couples on the floor beat a rhythm in time with the strains of "Chattanooga Choo Choo." She followed Graham as he guided her into a vacant slot on the floor. Seamlessly they joined the others.

"You look beautiful tonight." He eyed her, shoulders hunched forward as if already defeated.

Audrey wanted to believe his words but knew they couldn't be true. "Graham, you say I look beautiful when I clean stalls in my grandparents' barn."

"Well, you do."

"A woman cannot look beautiful in that setting and you know it. And when you say I do, it cheapens the words now." Audrey felt his shoulder stiffen under her hand as she spoke. She slipped another six inches between them as they continued to dance.

"You are the most difficult woman I know."

"You don't know enough women, then, Graham." *And stop following me everywhere.* As the song faded to an end, Audrey stepped away from him with a slight smile. "Thanks for the dance, Graham. I enjoyed it." Audrey fanned her warm face with her hand. The heat told her that her normally china perfect skin had flushed a bright pink.

She stepped away as Graham switched his attention from her to locating a new partner. Audrey scanned the laughing couples and looked for a friendly face to approach.

Lainie Gardner swirled past in a whirl of swinging skirts. She winked at Audrey over the corner of Roger Wilson's shoulder and then returned her full attention to him with a coquettish laugh. Audrey grinned at her friend. Lainie, always determined to be the belle of the ball, hadn't rested since she arrived forty minutes earlier. Instead, she flitted like a firefly from dance to dance, each time with a new partner. Her exotic, dark coloring and energy attracted the men, while Audrey felt like a common sparrow in contrast.

"Why on earth did I let her talk me into coming?" Audrey shook her head as she watched Lainie. She knew better—Lainie was the life of most parties, while Audrey wanted to enjoy for a moment and then be alone. Walking to the dance by herself hadn't exactly gotten her in the mood either.

Audrey smoothed the peplum of her navy gabardine dress with her fingers. She'd bought it because it made her feel beautiful despite her petite build. She'd even tried to flip her short reddish curls to look like Kate Hepburn's. And the only one who had noticed was Graham. "I might as well be mucking stalls for all the notice anyone has given me."

The scent of pine boughs filled the air and mixed with the potpourri of perfume the women wore. Overwhelmed by the fragrance and number of people in the room, she moved toward the door. Stepping around a couple as they entered the station, she inhaled a lungful of fresh, December air. She wrapped her arms around her waist and looked toward downtown North Platte. The familiar piercing of a train's whistle pricked the night, and she smiled. North Platte, Nebraska, saw more than its fair share of trains as a hub for the Union Pacific Railroad.

A shiver shook her frame. "Time to get back in there and warm up."

Audrey walked through the crowd until she spotted Lainie with another young man. She struggled to release the feeling her best friend had abandoned her, but it took immense self-control. With a sigh, she accepted fate and returned to the food table. A cup of punch would quench her thirst as she waited for a dance. She picked up the delicate cut-glass cup, then startled when someone bumped her shoulder. Drops of punch sloshed over the edge of the cup and onto the white tablecloth. More drops splashed the front of her dress.

"Please don't stain." She groped for a napkin and quickly patted her bodice where the red punch dotted the fabric.

"Excuse me. Is there anything I can do to help?" The tenor voice didn't belong to anyone she knew.

Heat flushed Audrey's face as she brushed the last drops off. "I'll be fine. Thank you."

"Could we start over? Would you dance with me?"

Audrey drew in a deep breath and ordered her face to mask her frustration at the spilled punch. She turned to meet the stranger's gaze. The more she looked, the more he seemed vaguely familiar, like someone she might have walked by downtown or at an event. A blush crept up her cheeks, but she couldn't tear her gaze away.

"Hello." A hint of laughter touched his brown eyes. They were flecked with a hint of gold. And he towered over her, since he stood at least a head taller than her slim frame.

"Hi." Audrey tried to gather her thoughts, which had completely abandoned her.

"So may I have the honor of a dance?"

She shook her head slightly to clear it, then stopped when his smile faltered a touch. "I would enjoy a dance, but first you have to tell me your name." Why couldn't her voice be steady at a time like this?

"Willard Johnson, at your service." He raised his eyebrows and flashed a rakish grin at her, one that would make Clark Gable proud.

Her heart stopped in the best way possible, and Audrey willed it to resume beating in a regular pattern. Willard Johnson. The name belonged to the son of a rancher who lived ten miles north of North Platte. Any girl who'd been lucky enough to spot him usually followed his name with a pretend swoon. She couldn't believe that, with all the gals who would gladly dump their dates to dance with him, he stood in front of her.

She extended her hand to meet his. As he pulled her onto the floor, Audrey saw Lainie gesture broadly from the arms of her latest partner. Unable to understand the words Lainie mouthed, Audrey shrugged and prepared to enjoy the dance.

One dance melted into another as they spun around the room. "You must dance with more than the cows on your ranch, Mr. Johnson."

As his deep laugh rumbled past her, the heat climbed in her cheeks. Had she really spoken the words? "I'm sorry, I meant that ..."

"Oh, the cows and I dance with regularity. I don't have too many partners on the spread, but I'd trade them all for another dance with you." He pulled her a little closer as the music stopped, the record was replaced, and then Bing Crosby's voice serenaded with a cackle and pop of the old phonograph.

As Audrey settled in for the dance, Lainie bustled up. "Come on, Audrey. I need your help taking tickets at the door."

Audrey pulled back from Willard and looked at Lainie. It had been at least thirty minutes since someone manned the door. Audrey nodded and stepped back from Willard. "Okay. Thank you, Mr. Johnson. I really enjoyed our dances."

And I'd enjoy getting to know more about you, too. With relief, she realized she'd thought those words. Lainie hustled her away before he could respond. Audrey looked over her shoulder at him with a smile as Lainie dragged her toward the door.

"What on earth are you doing?" Her friend's temper exploded like fireworks.

"What do you mean? Are you the only person who can dance when a man asks?" Audrey's voice rose until those around them turned to look at her. Humiliated by the attention, Audrey lowered her voice. "Lainie, I'm sorry, but I don't understand why you're mad at me."

"Willard Johnson came with Betty. You know she treats each man who takes her out like she owns him."

"It won't last long. He'll get tired of being owned and move on like the rest."

"No, this is serious. Betty believes they'll get married soon." Lainie looked at Audrey with desperation. "You can't let her see you with him."

"Fine. How can one dance harm anything?"

"It wasn't one dance, and I saw your face. Don't get attached. She'll make things miserable for both of us."

Lainie's words rang true. Her sister Betty Gardner held a grudge unlike anybody Audrey knew. And she could create the most unusual reasons to carry one.

"Come on, Lainie. This is nothing like the time we mixed hair dye with her shampoo." Both grimaced at the memory of the punishment their fathers had inflicted. Audrey's grimace turned into a giggle at the memory of Betty's perfect blonde hair streaked with black. "Lainie, we danced a few times. That's all, I promise. Nothing more will happen."

* * *

WILLARD LEANED against the wall and smiled as Lainie pulled Audrey across the floor and outside his grasp. Betty had trained Lainie well. If only he could convince Betty he only wanted a friend for his rare nights in town. Her tentacles suffocated him in his attempts to claim him. Women like her were the reason he usually refused Roger's attempts to drag him to dances. Go to one and next thing you knew, some gal was convinced you're days from watching her walk down the aisle. Who had time for nonsense like that? Nope. He'd enjoyed twenty-four years of freedom and saw no reason to change that for the likes of Betty.

Across the room, Audrey's voice rose in pitch before it fell to a whisper. He wished he could hear what she told Lainie. Audrey hadn't said much while they danced. He hadn't either. He'd been taken by her light steps and grace. He smiled at the image of the sun coming over the hills on the ranch lighting her hair on fire.

He considered her from a distance and decided Audrey might make the extra effort to get to church in the morning even more worthwhile. Father hated wasting gas and wearing out the tires to drive to town and church. Instead, he gathered the family in the great room with any hired hands who cared to join them. After a hymn or two, Father asked one of the kids still at home to read a chapter of the Bible before everyone discussed it. Willard enjoyed this new Sunday morning ritual, but missed the peace that flooded him when his voice mixed in worship with those of dozens of other people in the congregation. He also longed for the meaty sermons served weekly by Pastor Evans.

If he could combine the trip to church with a visit with Audrey, it would be well worth it.

"Hey, buddy." Roger Wilson's voice jolted him from his thoughts. "Ready to go?"

"Yep. Let's grab the girls and head out."

Willard scanned the crowd as they gathered Lainie and Betty. No matter where he looked, he couldn't find Audrey, and his shoulders slumped at the reality. After a round of good-byes and putting on heavy wool coats, Willard, Betty, Roger, and Lainie piled into Roger's Packard. The trip to Betty and Lainie's house took minutes since they lived straight down Sixth Street with a quick left on Elm. Pleasure filled Willard as he realized he'd enjoyed the short drive. Betty wasn't so bad when she didn't plaster herself to a guy's side like she owned him.

Willard helped Betty out of the car and then walked both girls to the door. Lainie slipped in the door, but Betty stood on the porch looking at him.

Betty leaned toward him and her lips tipped in a smile. "Come here, Willard. I don't know what you think you're doing." Her eyes turned hard as granite as she stared at him. "But I don't like being invited to a dance and then left while you dance with a kid."

Willard stepped down a step and reached out to steady her when she shuffled off balance.

"You didn't miss a dance all night, Betty."

Her lips curled into a pout, and she turned toward the front door. "Good night."

The sound of the door slamming echoed in the stillness, as Willard returned to the car.

"Betty invite you in?" Roger twisted to look at him.

"Yep." Willard heaved a sigh.

Turning the car toward home, Roger opened his mouth then closed it.

"Hey, keep your eyes on the road."

Roger grimaced as he drove out of town on Pine and toward the ranch. "Okay. So what are you thinking?"

"What do you mean?"

"That was a mighty big sigh you heaved. You're lost to the world since you danced with Audrey Stone."

Willard considered his words as the car jostled along the gravel road. "You might slow down before we shake right off the road. She's lovely, isn't she?"

"Beautiful, but that's exactly what I mean. You went to the dance with Betty. You're not supposed to notice the other girls."

"Like you didn't. I can count on two fingers the number of times you danced with Lainie, and she was your date."

"But here's the difference. Lainie and I knew we'd dance with others. She needed transportation, and I fit the bill. Betty thinks you're more serious than you do."

"I know that, but there's nothing I can do about it."

11

"Be careful. Audrey is Lainie's best friend. If you hurt her, I'll hear about it. And Lainie is a lot like a broken record when she focuses on something."

Willard rolled down his window a crack. The frigid air slipped into the car and cleared his head. "It's getting mighty hot-winded in here. Drive. I'll worry about who I visit tomorrow after church."

Roger shot him a worried glance and then relaxed. "She has the most incredible hair, though."

Willard smiled as he remembered Audrey's cloud of soft curls. "Yes, she does."

CHAPTER 2

DECEMBER 7, 1941

*T*he morning sun peeked through the curtains too early Sunday morning. Audrey cracked her eyes open, then threw an arm over face and groaned. She needed to get up or she'd walk to church. All she wanted to do was roll over and fall back into the dream. It had been delicious. Willard Johnson held her close as they spun around the floor to a love song crooned by Bing Crosby. She leaned into his tall form and let him lead her. As the music faded, he whispered into her ear, but she couldn't hear a word as she disappeared in his chocolate eyes. This dream deserved to be relived. She pinched her eyes closed, but the image had evaporated in the sunlight.

Sticking her toes out the side of the comforter, Audrey tested the air. Her breath curled in front of her when she blew, but quickly disappeared. Good. Someone had lit the kerosene stove downstairs. With a leap she dashed out of the bed and grabbed her robe. Throwing it around her shoulders, she hurried into the hall and to the bathroom.

Ten minutes later she headed down the stairs, dressed in her favorite navy suit, hair bouncing against her shoulders. If she hurried, her younger brothers might leave her a scrap or two for breakfast. John and Robert were sixteen and fourteen but ate enough to make anyone think at least four young men lived in the house. On Sundays Mama had to flip pancakes for fifteen minutes straight to fill their stomachs.

As she rounded the corner into the kitchen, Dad stomped in with a swirl of frigid air. "Come on, everyone. Grab your coats and head outside before the car dies. I've got her warming up out front."

Dad grabbed Mama's coat from the rack and he gently shrugged it around her shoulders. With a small pat, he looked in her eyes and kissed her. Audrey envied them their strong affection. Some days she wondered if she'd find someone who would cherish her the same way Dad loved Mama. Today the face of Willard Johnson accompanied the thought and shimmied at the edge of her sight.

"Come on, slow poke. Looks like you danced too much last night." John jostled her out of the way as he dashed out the door with a holler.

"Brothers." Audrey knew his enthusiasm wasn't for church but for the chance to see Nancy Tagalie. She grabbed her coat and slipped into it before Dad could leave without her. This morning she wouldn't risk walking to church.

As they chugged to church, she burrowed between her brothers to stay warm.

A pointed elbow shoved into her side woke her up when they arrived at church a few minutes later. She frowned at Robert as she rubbed her side. Why did boys feel the need to use brute force? Her brothers and male students were cut from the same cloth. Both baffled her.

Audrey trailed her family up the stone stairs of the First Christian Church. She loved to soak in the beauty of the stately brick building that had joined the North Platte's skyline a couple of years earlier. The detailed circle of stained glass underneath the spire radiated color. Its stillness quieted her heart as she prepared to worship.

She entered the foyer and stumbled when someone tapped her from behind. Turning with a frown, she looked into the face of Willard Johnson. "Oh. Willard. I didn't expect to see you here. Do you attend services here?"

"It's been awhile. It's been too long since my last visit. It's a pleasure to see you again."

Feeling her Dad's stare, Audrey nodded her headed and turned to follow her family to their regular pew. For as long as she could remember, the Stone family had sat in a pew on the left side a third of the way from the front. They used to fill the pew when Grandma and Grandpa had joined them. Now her grandparents sang along from heaven.

She stood and sang "Praise God, from Whom All Blessings Flow" with the congregation. As she did, she counted her blessings. While war raged around the globe, she and her family enjoyed peace and safety. While they weren't rich, they lived in a comfortable house and didn't lack for anything. She even had a good job at a small school in town. She loved approaching Dad once a month with her contribution to the family income. God had gifted her more than she needed or deserved, and she breathed a prayer of thanks.

* * *

WILLARD HOPED his father wouldn't ask him details about the sermon when he got home. After stumbling into Audrey Stone, he'd focused on nothing but the back of her head. Roger elbowed him to signal when to stand and sing. Williard shook his head, amused at his intense reaction to her. He'd never felt this way about anyone, especially so fast. Usually he could state with pride he was immune to any girl. For some reason Audrey affected him differently. He had to learn why. And he vowed he would.

As the pastor blessed the congregation and dismissed them, Willard headed toward Audrey. He wanted to invite her to join him for a soda at the drugstore Friday night before he returned to the ranch.

"So what now?" Roger looked at him with a smug grin.

"You know exactly who I want to talk to."

"I do, but I also see someone else headed our way."

Willard followed Roger's gaze. His brain froze when he saw Betty Gardner headed in his direction. Instead of her thin form, it seemed the grasping legs of a tarantula reached for him. If she caught him, he was as good as dead. "I didn't know she attended here."

"If you'd asked, I'd have told you, but you've had a single focus since last night."

Rubbing his hand over his head, Willard accepted the truth. "Guess I have. I'll catch up with you at the car." He stepped out of the pew and headed in the opposite direction of Betty. He hoped she hadn't seen him look her way. He knew with certainty if she had, he'd pay for it.

After sidestepping people clustered in conversations, he finally reached the foyer. He looked around, but couldn't see Audrey anywhere. She'd disappeared while Roger distracted him. Willard groaned and returned to the sanctuary.

Roger sidled next to him. "You should check the fellowship hall, Romeo."

Willard slapped his forehead in mock relief. "You're brilliant. Thank you for saving me from myself, friend." Willard turned his head from side to side, looking for a doorway that might lead to the hall.

"You don't remember where it is, do you?"

"Guess it's been too long since I've been here." He followed Roger to the hall. He scanned the crowd in the room but didn't see her anywhere. His shoulders slumped and he shoved his hands in his pockets. Somehow she'd slipped past him.

"Come on, buddy." Roger headed toward the door. "Let's get back to the ranch before Betty corners you. Maybe we can catch the Giants and Dodgers game on the radio."

Willard looked at his watch. If they left now, they'd return to the ranch in time. "All right. Dad will like the company. I'll find Audrey another time. Maybe she's a figment of my imagination anyway."

"Sure she is." They laughed as they exited the church and found the car.

Forty minutes later they settled into the great room at the ranch house. While Roger lived in the hands' building, he spent most of his non-work hours in the great Room with Willard. An immense stone fireplace—a mosaic of stones his father had hauled in from the corners of the ranch—dominated one wall of the room. It had a voracious appetite for wood, but kept the space warm even on the coldest days.

Roger grabbed the checkerboard and settled at the small table in front of the fire with Willard. The chairs creaked as they sank onto them. The sweet scent of spiced cider filled the air as Willard's mother brought each man a steaming mug.

Father gently fiddled with the knob on the radio, his ear pressed against the radio's speaker, as he tried to pick up the football game. He fumbled up and down the dial and grumbled when he couldn't find the game after several minutes. Reluctantly, he settled on NBC's broadcast of *Sammy Kaye's Sunday Serenade*. "Guess we'll have to wait for updates, boys. So, tell me about Pastor Evans' sermon."

Willard grimaced and waited. He dreaded Father's sharp words when he learned how unfocused Willard had been. He studied the checkerboard intently. The silence stretched, and Willard knew Father had a bead on him. *Come on, Roger.* He kicked Roger under the table to help him along. When he looked up, Roger wore a big grin that shifted into an innocent look.

"It was a moving sermon on service, Mr. Johnson." Roger jumped two of Willard's checkers and slammed his checker at the edge. "King me. Pastor Evans challenged us to stretch our definition of service. We can serve no matter where we are and what we do."

"Sounds like a good one."

"Yes, sir."

Relief flooded Willard when he snuck a look at Father and saw his eyes take on the faraway glow they wore when he focused on the radio. After a few minutes Father settled back in his chair. He picked up the latest issue of the *North Platte Daily Bulletin* and read it with intense focus.

Willard studied the checkerboard and carefully countered each move Roger made with a checker. He couldn't afford to let Roger jump two pieces at a time if he wanted to win. The mantle clock ticked loudly in the quiet room. At one thirty, the soft strains of music were interrupted when the radio crackled to life with a news bulletin.

"From the NBC news room in New York: President Roosevelt said in a statement today that the Japanese have attacked Pearl Harbor ... Hawaii from the air. I'll repeat that, President Roosevelt says that the Japanese have attacked Pearl Harbor in Hawaii from the air. This bulletin came to you from the NBC news room in New York."

Willard's stomach fell as if he'd swallowed a heavy stone. The announcer's words echoed through his mind. There must be a mistake. How could the Japanese have reached Hawaii? It simply couldn't be true. No bomber had the range to sneak up undetected like that. But as dread covered his heart, he knew it must be possible. Otherwise, it wouldn't be on the radio. This wasn't like Orson Welles' broadcast of the "The War of the Worlds," was it?

"Did he say Pearl Harbor? What about the *Oklahoma*?" Father's soft words echoed through the quiet room.

The radio's noise retreated as Willard turned toward his father. The man hadn't wanted Andrew to join the Navy. Willard's younger brother had marched forward with exuberance. He'd see the world, kiss the foreign girls, and return home with enough tall tales for a lifetime. A Japanese attack hadn't figured into his plans. This couldn't be how his life ended.

"Father. Look at me. Are you okay?" Willard forced his voice to be strong. He willed himself to move to his father's side. Shake color back into his face. Yet he remained chained to his chair.

"Did he say the Japanese bombed Pearl Harbor?" The blood continued to drain from Father's face until it turned pasty white. "Surely, they've made a mistake."

"He could be wrong. Anyway, it's Sunday. Andrew was off the ship looking for a church. We'll hear from Andrew. I'm sure he's fine." Willard looked at Father. Everything had to be fine. The news must be wrong. Or the Japanese had killed Father's favorite son, and Willard knew he'd be a poor substitute.

CHAPTER 3

DECEMBER 8, 1941

The shouts of Audrey's second graders engrossed in an intense game of dodge ball reverberated through the Franklin School gymnasium. She knew if she raised her eyes, she'd see Billy Kuhlman winging the ball at top speed toward another boy's stomach. It didn't matter how often she told him to stop, he aimed there. She should reprimand him but didn't have the heart. How could she tell him he erred when she wanted to throw something, anything, as hard as she could against a wall? Wanted to stand outside and fling questions at the sky. Instead, she stared at the industrial desk she sat behind, seeing nothing, yet seeing too much.

Her mind painted pictures of bombs exploding, ships sinking, flames burning, men screaming. The radio bulletins echoed through her mind. They hadn't stopped since Lainie called yesterday afternoon. Last night Audrey couldn't walk away from the radio and had endured the programs to catch periodic updates. With a few simple words, her world tilted on its axis. Her mind cried for answers, but a sleepless night spent tossing and praying produced none. At breakfast she'd devoured the newspaper until she'd read every slim detail of the Pearl Harbor articles.

Where are You, God? How could You allow this to happen? Audrey tapped her pencil against the metal table in an endless beat that matched the pace of the doubts threading her mind.

The doors crashed open, and she looked up to see the fourth and eighth graders rush into the room. Now the students required her full attention. Otherwise, someone could lose an eye as balls and jump ropes flew around the room. She should stand and participate with the students. Instead, she sat as her breath caught in her chest. What would happen to these children? Especially the boys? Audrey wondered how many would defend their country before events overseas played to an end. The children continued to play, and she forced herself to wait. She circulated through the mix, examining their faces and envying the second graders their ability to play and learn as if nothing had happened. She feared the questions the older children would voice. How had their world changed? Would brothers and friends enlist or the draft expand? Could Japanese bombers find their way to Nebraska?

Silence echoed from heaven. God seemed so distant and removed. She hated His silence when she needed His assurance most. Nebraska boys had probably died on some of the ships. The papers didn't list casualties yet, but they would. Her heart clenched at the thought—knowing would be worse than the queries.

After circling the room, she returned to her desk and instinctively picked up the pencil. A hand settled on hers and calmed the tapping. She jumped and then looked up into the kind, weary eyes of Principal Vester.

"Miss Stone, I need you to help gather the children in the cafeteria by eleven thirty this morning. I've decided they will hear President Roosevelt's address to Congress. They may not grasp the importance of his words, but I want them to hear them."

"Yes, sir." Audrey looked away as the pain in his eyes seared her heart.

"Are you all right, Miss Stone?"

"Honestly, no." Audrey carefully placed the pencil on the table before she started tapping it again. She gazed at the children. "But I'll manage for them."

An hour later Audrey helped calm the 237 students gathered in the cafeteria. They filled the room to capacity. The din of voices and chairs scraped along the floor caused the room to vibrate with noise. After a sharp whistle from the football coach, the children quieted to a dull roar. Principal Vester strode to the front of the assembly.

"Students, in a few moments you will hear the voice of our President. Can someone tell me his name?"

"FDR," piped up Janey Thorson. The second grader already had a reputation as a know-it-all.

"That's right. Can someone tell me what those letters stand for?"

"Franklin Delano Roosevelt," sang out several children with loud enthusiasm.

"Who doesn't know that?" One of the older kids snickered. Audrey wished she knew which one so she could corner him later.

Coach Wellington waved his arms back and forth and caught the principal's eye. Principal Vester pivoted back toward the children and slammed his hands together. "All right, students. It's time to listen."

Coach cranked the volume on the radio as high as it would go as the principal retreated to the side. A microphone propped in front of the radio crackled, and silence descended on the hall in waves of retreating sound. In the quiet, Audrey marveled at how well the President's voice rang across the country to North Platte. She held her breath as she concentrated on his words.

"Yesterday, December 7, 1941, a date which will live in infamy, the United States of America was suddenly and deliberately attacked by naval and air forces of the empire of Japan. The United States was at peace with that nation ..."

Audrey released her breath as she stood against the wall and kept an eye on her charges. The events in Pearl Harbor might impact the President, but he controlled his emotions instead of allowing them to dominate him. Across the room, Gladys Farmer pulled a handkerchief out of her pocket. Her oldest son had enlisted in October. What questions raced through Gladys's mind as she listened to the President? The older boys' eager expressions telegraphed their desire to enter the fray and take on the Japanese. The President's warm tone pulled her attention back to the speech.

"… Hostilities exist. There is no blinking at the fact that our people, our territory, and our interests are in grave danger.

"With confidence in our armed forces, with the unbounding determination of our people, we will gain the inevitable triumph—so help us God.

"I ask that the Congress declare that since the unprovoked and dastardly attack by Japan on Sunday, December 7, 1941, a state of war has existed between the United States and the Japanese empire."

War. Audrey knew no options existed, but she had clung to the hope the President held secret plans that would render war unnecessary. Since yesterday she'd feared war marched on the horizon toward the United States, but to hear the words made her terror concrete.

As the announcer came back on the radio, Principal Vester resumed his post at the front of the assembly. "Children, the broadcast is over. I am sure you will want to discuss it with your parents tonight. Please pull out your lunches, and we will bless the food." Heads around the room bowed, as the children waited for the go-ahead to eat. "God, be with our leaders today. Give them wisdom. Comfort those who mourn. And help us each to find our part to play in this new chapter in our country's history. Bless the food. Amen."

Audrey collected her lunch from the floor where she'd set it earlier. Settling down at a table with the other teachers, she opened her bag and picked through it. Her stomach rebelled at the smell of peanut butter and the thought of eating anything. She rolled the bag back up and tucked it out of sight. A sigh boiled up from the depths of her soul.

The quiet conversations around the table stopped as her tablemates looked at her.

"Are you all right, Audrey?"

Audrey thought before she answered Lydia Sparrow. Lydia flitted from topic to topic and never failed to repeat each tidbit to every person she met. As Audrey considered her co-workers gathered around the table, she wondered if any of them felt adrift.

"I don't know. I'm upset by everything that's happening. I pray the children don't start asking questions I can't answer." Audrey paused and decided to voice her thoughts. "I'm furious that innocent people died yesterday. How many more will die while I sit here and focus on meaningless activities?"

Coach's glasses balanced precariously on his crooked nose as he watched her. "Don't waste your energy worrying. There's nothing you can do to change anything."

"You're probably right. But I don't like that answer and don't think I can sit by."

"Well, it's not as if you can join the military." Lydia looked at her with horror etched on her face at the thought. Audrey could tell she'd given Lydia her tidbit for the week: Have you heard Audrey Stone wants to join the military?

"Maybe not. But there has to be something I can do." She stood, retrieved her lunch, and marched to her classroom.

The afternoon passed slowly. The minutes ticked by, and Audrey relaxed as none of the students broached the topic of the President's speech. When the bell buzzed, the children grabbed their coats and dashed out the door before she could remind them of the spelling quiz the next morning.

Audrey followed her students out of the school at a more sedate pace. She allowed her mind to wander as she walked north on Dewey toward Wahl's Drugstore. Today she definitely needed a cherry Coke from its fountain. As she pushed open the door, the bell announced her entrance.

"Hey, Audrey. How was school today?" Lainie waited for her on a stool at the fountain.

"Let's just say I'm glad this day is over." Audrey sat on the stool next to her friend and unwound her scarf from around her neck. She slid off her coat, and then ordered a cherry Coke with extra cherries.

"Don't turn around now, but your Prince Charming enters."

Audrey turned to look, and then Lainie shoved her in the ribs. "I told you not to look."

"That's a set-up and you know it. Besides, Willard Johnson is not my Prince Charming. I hardly know the man."

"Based on the look on his face when he saw you, you will."

Audrey shrugged and accepted her Coke. Though she'd never admit it, she knew exactly where he stood as he walked toward her. "Please tell me he isn't headed this way."

"Oh, but he is. Should I leave now?" Lainie grinned at her.

"Don't you dare leave me." Audrey formed her mouth into what she hoped passed for a composed smile and turned toward Willard. "Good afternoon."

"Audrey."

"Would you like to join Lainie and me for a Coke?" Audrey cringed as Lainie's high heel connected with her shin.

"Afraid I have to rush back to the ranch, but I'm glad to see you. It saves me a trip. Would you join me for a movie Friday night? I'd very much enjoy spending the time with you."

Audrey nodded her head, speechless that Willard Johnson had not only asked her to dance, but now asked her on a date.

"Great. I'll pick you up around seven. Have a nice day, ladies."

"Did he ask what I think he did?" Audrey shrieked as he exited the store.

"He did, and you agreed. What on earth will I tell Betty?" Lainie dropped her head onto her crossed arms. Then she peeked up at Audrey with a twinkle in her eyes. "You know you'll have to raid my closet to find anything decent to wear."

CHAPTER 4

DECEMBER 12, 1941

*P*erfume soaked the air in Lainie's room. Audrey and Lainie took turns squirting fragrances on their arms, the pillows, anything that held a scent.

"We really need to crack a window before the perfume knocks us out." Audrey stood with a giggle and staggered across the room. She stretched out her arms and swayed from side to side. With a prolonged sigh, she toppled onto the bed. "I … can't … make … it, Lainie. Save me from fume suffocation."

"I bravely accept the assignment, ma'am. I promise to do my best to save you from a death filled with beauty." With a quick salute, Lainie marched to the window and pushed it open.

Frigid December air flowed through the gap beneath the pane, dissipating the sweet mixture of perfumes until only the scent of lilacs remained. Audrey slowly sprayed a bit more. "This has always been my favorite scent. It reminds me of the large lilac bushes that sat on Grandpa and Grandma's farm. Do you remember hiding under the branches and pretending we had a secret house there?"

"Oh, and the tea parties our brothers couldn't invade."

"Why do I feel like those simple days are gone?"

"Because you overthink everything. You act like the foundation of the world shifted on Sunday. Maybe in some places, but not here. North Platte will never change. It'll always be a wanna-be town."

"A wanna-be town?"

"You know. A spot that always thinks it's more or better than it is. We're really nothing special."

"I don't know. It's growing every day. Dad says it's tipped twelve thousand residents. And we're here, so that makes it unique." Audrey stood and walked to Lainie's walnut wardrobe. She pulled open its doors with a swoon. "I feel festive tonight. It's almost Christmas, so why not begin the celebration now."

"You may feel festive, but you've also caught a drama bug." Lainie rolled her eyes. "Yes, you can wear my red velvet dress. All you had to do was ask. No melodrama necessary. You'd look better in the green one."

"No thanks. I want to see what it's like to have fun with one of the best looking men in the county, and red is the best color for fun." She pulled the scarlet dress out of the wardrobe and twirled in front of the mirror as she held it in front of her. She stopped and stepped closer to the mirror. "Maybe you're right. This makes me look like I've been on Lake Maloney too long in a rocking boat." She grimaced and replaced the red dress with quick movements and pulled out a rich green satin dress. As she danced around the room, she stroked the fabric and held its cool softness to her cheek. "This is perfect. You don't think it's too formal, do you?"

"Of course not. You only get one first date with a man like Willard Johnson." Lainie laughed and stood to join Audrey in her dance. "We've got to get you out more if you get this excited about one date."

"It's not just a date. It's an evening with Willard Johnson, a mature man. He's no boy, and I will savor each moment. Especially since he'll come to his senses soon enough."

"And return to Betty. That would make life easier for both of us. You'd better run if you're going to get home and changed before Willard picks you up. Otherwise you'll be wearing that old thing."

Both girls looked at Audrey's flour bag dress and winced. "See you at the theater."

Audrey flew the mile to her house. Her heart raced at the thought that in minutes Willard would arrive to pick her up. She winced at the ways her dad and brothers might chase him away. Her family could be as madcap as Jean Arthur's in *You Can't Take It With You*, only Audrey never quite fit in with hers. And she prayed Willard would accept her family as readily as Jimmy Stewart's character had accepted Jean's.

In ten minutes Audrey stood in front of her mirror, ready to leave for the theater. What was the best way to make an impression on Willard? Betty would know since she had much more experience in capturing a man's attention. Should Audrey wait in the front room or would that look too eager? Or should she delay in her room, so she could make a grand entrance down the staircase, and risk leaving Willard alone with her family?

* * *

WILLARD PULLED onto East Fourth Street and squinted as he tried to read street numbers through the darkness. The long day had worn him down, and he hoped he wouldn't regret scheduling a date this evening. His father and he had bounced over the hills on the ranch, dumping hay in mounds for the cattle. The almanac predicted snow next week. Father always prepared for the worst, and

Willard's muscles ached from every bale he'd thrown as he pulled up to the Stone home. As tight as he was now, tomorrow he'd be stiff as a zombie.

After opening the car door, Willard got out and headed up the sidewalk to the house. The first floor and one second floor window blazed with light. Bracing himself, he marched up the steps and knocked on the front door. Moments stretched while he waited. He shoved his hands deeper in his coat pockets in an attempt to still and warm them.

Finally, the curtain to the front window parted, and he saw a man peek through the pane. Knowing he must be her father, Willard wished he'd met him around town. It was easier to take a man's daughter out if he was comfortable with you. He fixed a smile on his face and pulled his hands out of his pockets as the door squeaked open.

"Good evening, son." The man eyed Willard as he stepped aside to let Willard enter. "Come on in. Audrey's somewhere around here. I'm sure she'll be down shortly."

That must mean the light upstairs shone from her room. Willard extended his hand. "Sir, I'm Willard Johnson. My father owns a ranch north of town …"

"Yes, yes. I know your father well. It's a pleasure to meet you."

"Tell him your name, dear." A middle-aged woman walked up and smiled at Willard. "I'm Ellen Stone, and this is my husband, Thomas. Please come in and have a seat in the parlor."

Willard allowed Mrs. Stone to lead him down the hallway. He glanced up the staircase to see if he could catch a glimpse of Audrey. When he didn't, he continued into a small room on the right of the hall. The rich aroma of burning oak logs filtered through the room from the fireplace. He quickly unbuttoned his coat and removed his gloves as heat from the flames penetrated them.

In front of the fire, two young men stretched out on the floor with a checkerboard. Did Audrey have brothers? As he watched them move the pieces, Willard realized he knew only the bare facts about Audrey Stone. Tonight he wanted to learn much more. Even in his short exposure to her at the dance and church, some spark about her captured his attention. He didn't know if it was her wit or her captivating smile. All Willard knew was he wanted to study her.

"Here, Willard. Have a seat. These young men are our boys. John's in the sweater and Robert's beating him." Mrs. Stone motioned toward the young men, who glanced up long enough to grin.

"So what are your plans, Willard?" Mr. Stone examined Willard as his body relaxed onto the small, carved Victorian couch.

"Well, we'll go to a movie, and if it's not too late, have a soda or milkshake at the drugstore."

"Oh, that's fine. But I'm really interested in your life plans. Where are you headed?"

Willard's mouth suddenly felt parched like someone had vacuumed it dry. He swallowed hard and tried to gather his thoughts. Where was Audrey? A guy shouldn't have to answer questions like this on the first date.

"Thomas. Give the boy a chance. You don't need to interrogate him right now."

Way to go, Mrs. Stone. Willard forced his lips into the shape of a smile. "Things are kind of uncertain right now. Until Sunday, I'd planned to stay and help Father run the ranch. Now I'll have to wait and see."

"Fair enough. Glad you don't plan to run off and enlist tomorrow. Audrey's a sweet girl, and I won't have you toy with her heart."

"Father won't even discuss me enlisting until we hear from Andrew. We haven't heard anything except that his ship was bombed in the attack."

Mrs. Stone inhaled sharply as her hand flew to cover her mouth. "Your poor family. We'll keep him in our prayers."

"Thank you, ma'am." Willard hoped it wasn't too late for her prayers to matter.

* * *

AUDREY HEARD MUFFLED voices float up from the parlor. She looked in the mirror one last time. "Well, this is as good as it gets." She smoothed down the green satin and picked up her handbag. After slipping on her shoes, she headed down the stairs. She lingered in the hallway a moment and eavesdropped on the conversation. Taking a breath, she entered the room.

"Hello, Willard. I see you've met everyone."

"Hello, Audrey." The words practically whistled from his mouth.

A blush rose in her cheeks. "We'll be back after the show, Dad."

"Take the time to grab a milkshake if you want, sweetheart." Why was dad winking at Willard? Definitely not a good sign.

She allowed Willard to settle her coat around her shoulders and walked smartly to keep up with his long stride. Once they were settled in the car, he turned to her. Under his intense gaze, her hand fluttered to her throat.

"I thought we'd see *Shadow of the Thin Man* if it's all right with you."

Audrey looked at him, questions filling her green eyes.

"Don't tell me you haven't seen the *Thin Mans?*"

"There's more than one?"

Willard grinned in the darkness. "You're in for a treat, then. William Powell and Myrna Loy are the stars and my favorite cinema duo. They play a husband and wife team that solve impossible crimes before the police know what's happening."

"If they were really impossible, they couldn't be solved."

"Maybe, but you'll see what I mean." The car slid into the theater's parking lot, and he found a parking spot for them. After he got out, he walked around to the passenger side and opened Audrey's door. "Mademoiselle, we've arrived."

Audrey accepted his help climbing out of the car. "Why, thank you, kind sir. Let's go see *The Shadow.*"

"That's *Shadow of the Thin Man.*"

"Isn't that what I said?" They laughed together and rushed through the cold to the theater.

Willard led Audrey to the open ticket window and plunked down two nickels. "Two tickets for *The Shadow.*"

Almost two hours later they walked down the street to Wahl's Drugstore. The movie surpassed Willard's promises. Audrey rubbed her ribs where they felt strained from laughing, yet the mystery had kept her guessing till the end. As they entered, Audrey saw several couples ahead of them in the line for sodas and shakes.

After a few minutes Audrey and Willard approached the counter. "What would you like?"

"Would you share a banana split with me? I love them, but can never eat an entire one." Audrey crossed her fingers as she waited for his answer.

"Is this a test of my devotion? Sure, I'll share one with you. But next time we split a chocolate malt. Those are my favorites."

Audrey stilled at his words. Apparently, she hadn't scared him off yet. Her heart raced at the thought. "I'd be glad to share a malt next time. I'll find us a table." She walked away before he could hear the pounding in her ears.

She sat down and twirled her purse in her fingers as she waited for Willard. After a few minutes he joined her at a small table as far away from the door as Audrey could find. He handed her a spoon, and they dug into the split with relish.

Audrey licked her spoon and looked into Willard's eyes. "I don't know why, but banana splits have been my favorite since the very first one I had. Maybe it's because Grandpa Stone was with me. He made everything extra special."

"Andrew and I used to get chocolate malts when Father gave us some change for working on the ranch. It wasn't often, but we enjoyed our tradition."

Audrey watched Willard and wondered what to say. She'd heard rumors Andrew had served on the *Oklahoma*. "Have you heard from him this week?"

He stared at the long-handled spoon he held. "No. And it's the most helpless feeling in the world. Mother and Father both act like he's already gone. I want to argue with them, wipe the sorrow from their faces, but I can't. They're probably right."

His shoulders fell as if weighted by a shroud of grief. Audrey reached across the table and touched his hand. "I'm so sorry, Willard. I wish there was something I could do to help."

He held her hand like it was a lifeline. "Please pray. I keep telling myself there's hope until we get a telegram that confirms our fears."

"Then what?"

Willard released her hand and stacked their spoons in the empty dish. "I don't know."

CHAPTER 5

DECEMBER 17, 1941

 he cold penetrated Audrey's coat as she walked home from school. Her thoughts tripped back to her night with Willard, but even those didn't stop her shivers. It was only three forty-five in the afternoon, but the dusky sky cast a shadow as if twilight had settled on the town. How she hated this time of winter when everything grew dark and still long before she wanted the day to end. As she trudged through downtown, she decided to stop in Wahl's long enough to warm up and see if Lainie was having a Coke.

The tinkle of the bell announced her arrival as she pushed on the door. The bell was yet another sign that, while the world might pivot on its axis with one event, some things never changed. It had jingled and jangled its way through her childhood, and it would still hang there when she brought her children downtown someday.

"Audrey. Hurry up."

At the sound of Lainie's voice, Audrey pulled herself back to the moment.

"Come back here. I've got news." Excitement bounced through Lainie's words.

Heading toward the soda fountain where Lainie perched on a stool, Audrey hoped the news was as good as it sounded.

"Hurry, hurry." Lainie patted the stool next to hers. "I'm so glad you stopped in. I didn't know how I'd get the word to you if you didn't."

"Slow down, Lainie. You could always try the phone." Audrey chuckled as her friend bounced on the stool. Then she unwound her scarf and slipped off her mittens. "I promise I won't rush off until I hear your news. What's up?"

"The boys'll be back tonight. Company D of the National Guard will come through town on the train. Do you know Rae Wilson?" As Audrey shook her head, Lainie rushed on. "Well, she works here at the drugstore. She's six or seven years older than we are, but a good sort. Anyway, she's going to be there since her brother commands the unit. It sounds like others will, too. Let's go home and gather apples and things in baskets to share with the boys when they come through."

"Lainie, catch your breath before you hyperventilate. I think it sounds like a great idea, but when are they coming through?"

"We're not really sure. Some people have waited all afternoon at the station, but now it sounds like the train'll arrive around five. Come on. We can make this Christmas for them. Will you meet me there?"

"Sure." Audrey shrugged, not understanding Lainie's excitement. "Guess I'd better hurry home and see what Mama has that'll work for the boys." Audrey wound her scarf back around her neck, and then pulled on her thick mittens. "I don't suppose it'll warm up before tonight."

"No, silly. I'll see you soon." Lainie stood and dashed to the back of the store. Her energy and enthusiasm overwhelmed Audrey at times, but Lainie certainly kept life from getting dull.

The next hour evaporated as Audrey and Mama searched the pantry for treats to lift the spirits of the men who made up Company D. Most were from North Platte, so that automatically made them boys that needed their care. As they loaded two baskets with apples from Grandpa's small orchard and a few oranges, Audrey eyed them warily.

"These are wonderful, Mama, but I don't think I can carry both of them to the train station alone." She tentatively lifted the handle on one and realized it was doubtful she could carry even one of them.

"Don't worry. I'll send John and Robert with you, and they can come back right away. The empty baskets should be easy to carry back, though I'd feel better if you got a ride home. It could be pretty late when you're ready to come home."

Audrey rolled her eyes at the thought of her brothers escorting her to the station. The nine-block distance dictated she needed their help to transport the treats. "I suppose that'll be okay, but I'll need to leave soon. I don't want to miss the train after all this work getting ready for it." She went to her mother and gave her a quick hug. "Thanks for letting me do this, Mama. I'm useless lately. It feels good to do something that will help with the war, no matter how small."

"I know, honey. Go tell your brothers it's time to leave."

Audrey darted up the stairs to her brothers' bedroom. "Boys, Mama says you get to help me take some baskets to the station. We need to leave in a minute, and I'll meet you downstairs."

John and Robert looked up from their homework. John grinned at the break from his assignments, while Robert bounded to his feet. He liked any excuse to get outside. She doubted they'd remain eager when they hefted the baskets.

She swooped into her bedroom and ran a hairbrush through her shoulder length curls before she pulled them back with a ribbon. Dusting some powder on her face, she decided she looked fine for the ten minutes the boys would sit at the station.

Five minutes later, Audrey and her brothers pulled on their coats and bundled up with hats, scarves, and mittens. Her brothers playfully moaned and groaned about how heavy the baskets were and how she used and abused their labor. She grinned back at them. They weren't bad eggs, even if they were so much younger. And at times like this, they were useful to have around.

As they approached the depot, Audrey stopped short. Hundreds of people milled on the station's platform. She'd expected ten, maybe twenty, people to wait for the train. "Wow. This is bigger than I thought. Guess lots of people wanted to do something."

John looked around and stood taller as he spotted a group of high school girls clustered on one corner of the platform. "Where would you like us to put the baskets, sis?"

"Over by those girls will be fine. You can even say 'hello' if you like." Audrey stifled a smile at the eagerness she knew he tried so hard to hide. Life wasn't easy at sixteen. She'd gladly slid to the other side of the teen years. At fourteen, Robert remained oblivious to the attraction girls held. John's fascination was more than enough for one house.

Audrey scanned the crowd for familiar faces. In one this size, she usually saw several she knew. There. Across the platform, Dr. Edwards stood with his wife. Their son served in the Guard unit, so she wasn't surprised they'd turned out with gaily wrapped presents tucked under their arms. Pastor Evans chatted with the Edwardses as he guarded a basket at his feet. She kept looking, but didn't see Lainie anywhere. A horn tooted behind her, and she whirled around.

Roger and Lainie waved at her, then they stepped out of his Packard. The man loved to drive and must have limitless funds for gasoline. Audrey wondered how he did it since he lived miles out of town on the Johnson ranch. Audrey stilled when Willard stepped from the car's backseat. Images of their closeness as he'd held her hand over the banana split quickened her heart. Lainie ran up to her and smothered her with a big hug that pulled her back to the moment.

Audrey returned her hug with a squeeze. "I've looked all around this crowd for you. I had no idea so many would be here."

"Me either. Isn't this grand? Won't the boys be surprised when they arrive?" Lainie's words bubbled out in a rush.

"Yes. I wonder how long we'll have to wait." Audrey dug her thin watch out from between her coat sleeve and mitten. It read four fifty. "If we wait too long, this will turn into a really cold night."

Roger tucked Lainie against his side with a flourish. "I'll keep this one warm."

Lainie slapped him on the arm and slid away with a giggle.

Willard stepped up with a box of candy and basket of cookies. "Hi, Audrey."

"Hey. How did you get to town so quickly?"

"Mother got the call from Doc's wife and sent us with a few dozen of her fresh cookies."

"He and Roger each ate one on the drive over." Lainie rubbed her hands together. "I wish we had some coffee to help with the cold. The train has to get here soon, or we'll be hundreds of icicles when the boys arrive."

"Shhh." Audrey cocked her head as she listened for a whistle to pierce the air. "I think I hear it."

A slow murmur swept over the crowd as people passed the word that the train drew near. Soon the sound of heavy wheels rolling along the lines reached across the still night. A small cheer went up as mothers and fathers pushed forward on the platform to look for their sons in the windows when the train pulled into the station. The excitement dimmed as people walked up and down the length of the train, but saw no familiar faces.

"Hey, what company are you boys with?" Dr. Edwards yelled up to a soldier.

"Company D, sir. Kansas National Guard."

A disappointed groan hung over those gathered.

Audrey sensed the frustration of parents who wanted to give one last hug to their sons before they were sent somewhere overseas.

"Oh, this is so sad." Lainie leaned into Roger as he put an arm around her.

Willard turned toward Audrey and shrugged as he hefted his basket. "Mother won't be too happy if I return her cookies."

"Well, what are we waiting for?" A soprano voice filtered over the murmurs.

Audrey turned and scanned the crowd, searching for the person who spoke up.

"I don't know about you, but I'm not taking my cookies home."

Lainie elbowed Audrey as a young woman stepped forward with her basket. "That's Rae Wilson."

Rae stepped toward a window and held up her basket. "Hey, soldier. Merry Christmas."

Those assembled on the platform came to life as they followed Rae's example. They pushed their shoulders back, shrugged off their disappointment, and walked toward the train. Baskets were passed through open windows to the boys. Willard hefted several for those who couldn't reach the windows. A few even boarded the cars and walked their gifts down the aisles. Shouts of "Merry Christmas" filled the air. Audrey went with her brothers to one of the cars where no one else had made it. The gratitude of those young men, some of them younger than she was, warmed her more than any coffee would have.

Fifteen minutes later, Audrey waved as the train pulled out of the station. Soldiers hung off the sides of the train and waved back, many with apples clenched in their teeth.

"Wow." Lainie stepped next to Audrey. "That was something."

"Yes." Audrey squeezed Lainie, and then linked her arm with Lainie. "Thanks for telling me about this. I'd better find John and Robert, so we can head home. You think we made a difference today, Lainie?"

"Maybe. They're sure handsome in their uniforms, aren't they?"

"Lainie!" Audrey shook her head as she walked toward the parking lot with her best and slightly crazy friend.

Behind her, John chortled loudly. She turned to chastise him, in time to hear Robert chime in.

"They're so dreamy." He mocked as he batted his eyelashes at her.

"Go on, you two. I'll catch up." Audrey turned to Lainie and gave her a quick hug. "See you tomorrow." She watched Lainie join Roger at his car.

Willard approached her with a lopsided grin. "Glad we made it."

"Yes. It's probably not the first train of soldiers we'll see."

"No." His gaze turned inward as he stood there. Audrey waited a moment for him to say something, but he seemed lost in his thoughts.

"Well, I'd better catch up with my brothers. Night, Willard."

He searched her face. "Night, Audrey." He spun on his heel and headed toward the car.

She watched him and waved as the car pulled out of the parking lot. In the distance a train whistle sighed a warning to the North Platte residents. Another train headed to town. Audrey looked to the west and strained to see the glimmer of the engine's light. Only house lights reflected off the rail lines.

"I wonder how many soldiers we'll see through town before the war is over. Lord, let us help them on their way. And bless the boys from Kansas tonight."

"Come on, Audrey."

She opened her eyes and smiled. Time to head home and fill Mama in on the excitement.

CHAPTER 6

DECEMBER 18, 1941

*W*illard groaned when his door shook from a pounding.

"Time to get moving, son. The cows are waiting."

Not even a hint of morning light slipped through his drawn curtains. He grabbed the clock from the side table and wanted to throw it across the room. He wished Father'd sleep past four o'clock even once.

"I'm coming." *Just stop pounding.* He kicked the covers back and rolled out of bed. As the cold air rushed over him, he grabbed his coveralls from the chair and pulled them on. A shiver shook his shoulders before he hustled down the stairs to the warmth of the kitchen.

Father handed him a mug of steaming coffee. "Here you go, Willard. Today we'll head to the north acreage after milking. See if we can't check on the pregnant cows."

Willard inhaled the hearty aroma of his coffee and blew on it before taking a careful sip. Father looked ready to tackle anything the day would throw their way, whether Willard wanted to join him or not. Might as well surrender to the inevitable. "All right. Where do you want the hands today?"

"They'll check fences on the east parcel and throw hay where it's needed. Weather's got all the signs of another cold, hard winter, and we need to prepare." The intense expression in Father's brown eyes softened as he turned his gaze to his wife.

Willard hoped his father's prediction was wrong even as he knew he'd never be caught unprepared. That ran counter to his careful nature. "All right, Pops." By the look on his father's face, the rare use of a nickname must have startled him. Willard suppressed a grin. "Let me grab a bite."

"I don't know, sonny boy. You may have dawdled too long upstairs." Father slapped him on the shoulder, pushing Willard forward from the force. "I'll head to the barn, start the truck, and then get to the milking. Don't dawdle."

As Father strode onto the porch, Willard hurried to the stove. "Got any more pancakes, Mother?" He kissed her cheek as she slapped him lightly on the chest. Heat from the stove had flushed her round cheeks a warm red.

"The stove's no place for you. Sit down, and I'll have some for you in a minute."

"I don't think Father wants to wait while I sit, even if it's 'cause I'm eating your great pancakes."

Mother turned back to the stove and deftly flipped the pancakes that dotted the griddle. She tucked behind her ear a strand of blonde hair that had escaped her loose bun.

Willard grabbed his coat from its perch on the coat tree in the corner. After shrugging it on, he picked up a couple of pieces of fruit from the bowl on the counter and shoved them in his pockets. After she slipped the flapjacks onto a plate, Willard scooped several up and rolled them. "Thanks, Mother." He took a bite from one of the pancakes as he wrestled with the door.

"Don't forget your coffee."

Willard looked from the thermos she held to the pancakes coiled in his hands. Shoving another roll into his mouth, he grabbed the thermos and mumbled, "See you later."

She patted his cheek. "All right, chipmunk. Be careful."

His breath curled in front of him as he stalked toward the barn. Willard hoped the truck's temperamental heater worked today, otherwise the day would pass by shivers rather than minutes.

The truck hummed in the barn, casting a circle of heat around it. Willard searched for Father and found him settled on a stool next to a cow, milk streaming into a pail.

"Hop to, Willard. We don't have all day." Steel filled his voice with determination. "Daylight'll be here before we're ready if you don't get to work."

Willard sighed and crammed the last pancake in his mouth. After snuggling up next to the other cow, he teased the milk from her udder until he'd stripped her dry. He hefted the pails and hiked back to the house, while Father backed the truck out of the barn.

The cab of the truck bordered on warm when he climbed in. He pulled the door shut and settled back. A second later he jerked forward as Father pushed the truck into gear and they rolled out of the barn. The truck scaled the hill leading from the ranch before Father turned onto a rutted track.

A contented grin tweaked Willard's lips as he watched the sun crest the sandhills. While he might hate rising before the sun, it always seemed worth it when he got to greet it. Andrew had never felt that way. Instead, he rushed into the Navy as soon as he could enlist. Visions of unseen panoramas pulled his heart away from home. Heaviness trickled through Willard at the thought. *Why'd Andrew have to leave, Lord? Couldn't the ranch be enough for him, too?*

They were similar in so many ways. Each had the strength to throw a calf to the ground and pin it in an instant. Life on the ranch gave them physical strength in abundance. But where Andrew's eyes roamed the horizon, Willard couldn't imagine leaving the vastness of the ranch. Nowhere else could he watch the spectacular sunrises that painted the skies here. The ragged hills were filled with beauty to him. He liked to imagine the Creator's paintbrush flying across the landscape with varying colors as the seasons changed.

Moments like this were what made life complete. As peace strummed into his soul and replaced the heaviness, his thoughts returned to heaven. *Thanks for another day I can praise You, Lord. But feel free to raise the temperature a bit. It's mighty cold down here.*

A smile escaped as his attention centered on the vibrant colors lighting the sky.

"What's tickling your funny bone this morning, son?"

"Nothing much." Just the thought Audrey's hair matched the yellow melting into red. He shook his head. Since Saturday night, she'd invaded his thoughts at the strangest times. No other woman intruded when he was in the middle of praising God for His creative work. Although, now that he thought about it, His creative work included Audrey Stone. The thought of learning more about that very special creation made him want to break into a hymn of praise.

Instead, he hid his grin and tipped his hat over his eyes. Might as well catch a few winks until they reached their destination.

* * *

AUDREY STARTLED awake as a train whistle pierced the morning's silence. She rolled over and read her clock. Seven ten. If she didn't hustle, her students would beat her to school. The image of how her classroom would look after twenty-one second graders had unsupervised time in it catapulted her out of bed. Soon she rushed down the stairs, tying a red ribbon in her shoulder-length curls.

"Morning, honey." Mama turned from the stove and gave Audrey a kiss. "You should take a look at the *Daily Bulletin* this morning."

"I really don't have time, Mama." Audrey searched the kitchen for anything quick to cram into her growling stomach.

"Sit, read it, eat a few pancakes. I've got your favorite maple syrup set on the table."

"All right." Mama knew she couldn't resist her favorite sweet treat, but what could be so important she had to read it before she left for school? Audrey grabbed the paper from the table, but didn't see what made Mama so excited as she scanned its articles. She settled into a chair and drizzled her pancakes with syrup. Turning back to the paper, she slowly flipped through it. "I don't see anything."

"There's a story on page one and a letter on page two. You made some kind of impression last night at the Depot."

"Oh." The word squeaked between Audrey's lips as she flipped back to the second page and found the letter. "Rae Wilson was busy last night." She scanned the letter and a flutter of pride climbed her neck. "Listen, Mama. 'Smiles, tears and laughter followed. Appreciation showed on over 300 faces.' She wants to start a canteen here. Mama, I want to be part of that. It would be a wonderful way to participate in the war effort. Think of all the troop trains that will stop in

North Platte between now and the end of the war." Audrey imagined all the Union Pacific trains that chugged through town before the war. Surely that number wouldn't diminish.

"Calm down, hon. I think it's a great idea, too. I remember helping my mother get food ready for the canteen during the World War. It's a great way to be part of the war effort here."

Audrey shoved another bite of pancake in her mouth and followed it with a swallow of milk. "I'll talk to Lainie about it after school." Looking at her watch, Audrey stood and grabbed her coat. "I'll have to fly to get to school on time."

"Wait a moment. Some man called for you last night right after you left. Did I give you the message?"

Audrey stopped buttoning her coat and looked at Mama. "What was his name?"

"Willard." Mama's brow furrowed in concentration. "The man who took you to the movies?"

"Willard? Are you sure, Mama?" Audrey tried to stifle a squeal of delight. "That's even better news than the letter." She danced around the table to her mother and gave her a quick kiss. "Have a wonderful day."

"Must be great news to garner that reaction." Mama smiled at her. "You'll have to fill me in after school. Keep the kids in line today."

Audrey smiled as she walked to school. Her mama's parting line never changed. As she strolled the same streets to the same school she did every weekday morning, her heart sang. Willard Johnson had called for her! That, coupled with the prospect of a Canteen, opened a new horizon for her. She spun a circle on the sidewalk with her arms thrown into the air. "Lord, I'm so excited." She stopped and giggled at the thought that people might watch her crazy dance of joy, but she simply didn't care. "You can use even me, can't You? If there has to be a war, please help me do my bit."

* * *

AFTER SUPPER AUDREY's family gathered in front of the parlor fireplace. The heat from the fire radiated into the corners of the room, while the hiss and spark of the logs provided a musical backdrop. Audrey ran her hands up and down her arms in an effort to ward off a lingering chill that had sunk into her bones during the walk home. She curled her legs underneath her as she settled onto the couch with a stack of papers. Time to see if her students understood the finer points of double-digit addition. As she worked her way through the pile of papers, she fought the desire to pull a blanket over her lower body and settle in for a nap. As her eyelashes brushed her cheeks and her chin tapped her chest, her brothers careened down the stairs and raced into the room.

"John. Robert." Dad's sharp voice stopped the boys in their tracks. "What on earth are you doing? You don't live with a herd of elephants last I checked."

"Good thing, too, since elephants wouldn't tolerate them." Audrey mumbled under her breath, but Dad heard her.

"Careful, young lady. They aren't perfect, but as long as you are a member of the household, you're stuck with the rascals." A twinkle in his eyes softened his tone.

Audrey sighed and collected the scattered math sheets before settling back against the couch's cushions. Boredom stayed far away while her brothers thumped around. The sound of the phone ringing in the hallway grabbed her attention. Robert pushed John into the living room doorway as he raced to grab the phone first. She clamped her hands over her ears to muffle the din they made as they wrestled for it.

"Boys." Mama stood from her chair and looked at Dad. "I have no idea what's gotten into those two."

"They'd better work it out before I have to do something about them." He shook his head and reached for the *Bulletin*.

Audrey straightened her stack of papers and tried to ignore the racket. She'd scheduled parent-teacher conferences on Friday, and couldn't complete the report cards without the quiz scores. "Focus, kiddo."

Even as she said it, Robert tore back into the room.

"Audrey. Phone's for you. It's a boy." He exaggerated the last word.

Could it be Willard? Her heart raced at the thought though she tried to reason with it. Surely he'd moved on to someone else by now. No amount of straight talk could convince her heart to ease back to its normal rhythm as she darted into the hallway. She grabbed the earpiece from John as she knocked him to the side with her hip. Taking a deep breath, she turned her back on the foursome watching her.

"Hello?"

"Audrey? This is Willard."

She leaned into the telephone table as her knees melted. He'd really called.

"Audrey? You still there?"

"Yes. How are you?" She swallowed in an effort to force the tremble from her voice.

"A little tired. It's been another long day. But I called to see if you had plans tomorrow night."

Audrey's fingers slipped on the phone. Tightening her grip, she smiled as butterflies exploded into flight inside her. While unsettling, it was the best feeling she'd experienced. Willard Johnson wanted to spend another Friday night with her. "Just an evening at home. Would you like to do something?"

"I thought we could go to the dance at Jefferson Pavilion or catch another movie."

The memory of spinning in his arms flooded her. If she still felt this way two weeks later, she'd be wise to avoid entering the circle of his arms. "How about a movie?"

"Works for me. We can pick the flick then."

"What no *Thin Mans*?"

"Not unless you want to watch *Shadow* again."

"We'll see what our options are. Thank you, Willard. I'll see you Friday."

"Night, Audrey. Sleep well."

As Audrey hung up and turned to her family, she couldn't wipe the smile off her face. Less than twenty-four hours until she'd see him again. She waltzed past her brothers and doubted addition would hold her attention after the call.

CHAPTER 7

DECEMBER 21, 1941

$\mathcal{T}$he choir sang "Just as I Am," yet Willard hardly heard. His mind remained thousands of miles away as he worried about Andrew. With each day, it grew harder to sleep at night. Visions of what had probably happened to his brother filled what little sleep he managed.

Sailors had survived the sinking of the Oklahoma. But if Andrew lived, why hadn't they heard anything? Surely, he would have sent a telegram to ease Mother's and Father's minds. Andrew did everything by the book and rarely disappointed. That's why he'd thrived as a sailor.

Willard's family filled the pew this morning. Father said they needed fellowship with other believers at such a time. Willard wished their clan didn't take up so much room as the armrest rammed into his side. Pastor Evans stood and walked to the rostrum. Willard vowed to glean something from the sermon rather than focus on Andrew or his favorite girl.

His mother shifted slightly next to him. When she noticed him looking at her, she patted him lightly on the leg. She'd aged several years over the past two weeks. The not knowing could kill her. Surely, God in His mercy would give them an answer so they could grieve or rejoice.

Despite his resolve, Willard scanned the pews in front of him, looking for shoulder-length reddish curls that poked under a felt hat. He sensed her near and longed to see her. The day since their last night out had passed slow as a stubborn bull. Audrey wouldn't slip away this morning if he could help it. He hoped she didn't want to slip away. He still needed to talk with Betty, but today he'd simply avoid her. She must understand he'd moved on, since he hadn't called or spent any time with her recently.

"Let us pray." Pastor Evans's booming voice grabbed Willard's attention.

Father, help me focus on You during the service. Help me. Help my family. Help Andrew, wherever he is. Willard struggled to believe God knew and cared about Andrew.

"Today our text comes from Mark 4:35-41. In it, Jesus performs a great miracle by calming the storm. Many of us find ourselves in a storm we can't control."

Willard nodded his head. A storm had overtaken his life. He would capsize if help didn't come soon. He listened, desperate for a lifeline.

"As I've pondered what God has for each of us, this passage made it clear. In the midst of whatever storm we find ourselves in, whether man-made, war-made, or self-made, Jesus stands in our rocking lives and says, 'Peace, be still.' To the waves in our lives, He says the same thing He did thousands of years ago. And those waves must obey as surely as they did then. We may not be removed from the battle, but we can walk in peace. Peace despite our circumstances."

The minutes flew as Willard inhaled the message. He wanted to believe peace waited even when everything was unclear. As the pastor closed with a prayer, Willard prayed silently. *Lord, give me Your peace. Speak that peace into my restless heart.* He waited, hoping the peace would come. When it didn't, he shook his head. "Guess I can't expect a miracle every day."

"What did you say, son?" His mother leaned closer as they stood.

"Nothing. Hoping some peace finds me."

"I know. Me too." She pasted a smile on her face and stepped into the aisle. "Tell your father I'll be in the fellowship hall when he's ready to leave."

Willard searched the crowd for Audrey's face. There. She stood beside her family's regular pew. It might as well bear their name. When she looked toward him, he waved. Her smile warmed him through. He controlled his pace as he walked up the aisle to her.

He reached down, and then squeezed her hand. "It's been too long since I've seen you, Audrey."

"Why, Mr. Johnson, it's been one day since the movie. I'm sure you barely had time to miss me."

"No, ma'am. Every moment is too long when I miss you."

Audrey's face blanched, and she looked over his shoulder instead of at him. Willard turned hoping something behind him had caused her reaction.

"There you are, Willard. You've been a stranger."

His stomach dropped at the sound of Betty's voice. He'd forgotten all about avoiding her. "Hi, Betty. How are you?"

"Better now that I've caught up with you."

Caught. That word said it all. He imagined her tentacles wrapped around his neck, choking the life from him. How could he feel so differently about Audrey?

"So where've you kept yourself?"

"Doing the usual." *Just haven't wanted to see you.* Why couldn't he speak the words and be done with her? "You know Miss Stone don't you?"

"Hi, Betty." Audrey looked like she wanted to be anywhere but ensnared in this conversation.

"Hello, Audrey." Ice poured from Betty's words like water from the North Platte River.

"Willard, it was nice to see you again. I really need to go find my family. Bye, Betty." Audrey grabbed her small purse from the pew and walked away before Willard could stop her.

"Betty, why did you do that?" Willard didn't attempt to hide his frustration.

"She needs to know you're taken." She licked her reddened lips lightly, and then smiled at him. "Why don't we walk down to the King Fong Café for a quick lunch?"

"Even if I wanted to, I can't. The whole family drove into town, so I have to leave when they're ready."

"Surely Roger can drive you back."

"I'm not interested, Betty. I'm sorry, but my family is more important right now."

"Your words would be different if Audrey asked rather than me."

"You're probably right. But I don't want to be with you, and my family needs me to go with them." He looked around the sanctuary and noticed no one stood near them. "Betty, you're a nice woman, but I'm not interested in anything more than friendship with you. If you want more, you should spend your time with someone else."

She raised her hand, and he braced himself for whatever she would do. She stopped and flung a coquettish smile his direction.

"If you think you're the only man in this area, you are sorely mistaken, Mr. Johnson. Don't deceive yourself into thinking I'm interested in you. Good day." She turned and flounced down the aisle and out the sanctuary doors.

Willard hoped she'd taken her tentacles with her. He prayed she wouldn't create a way to make Audrey pay for his actions.

* * *

AFTER A LATE LUNCH Willard wandered into the Great Room. His father sat in his leather chair and fiddled with the radio dial in an attempt to bring the outside world to the ranch. Willard walked over to the wall beside the fireplace. His kid sister Margaret had tacked a large map of the world on it, determined to track what happened on both fronts of the war. As he examined the pins she'd poked in the map, he focused on the Pacific Theater. He set his jaw and straightened his back against the stab of pain from the sight of the Hawaiian Islands.

He turned from the wall and tried to force the questions from his mind. The questions about whether he'd be allowed to serve it needed? Would he get to play a role in the larger conflict if it reached the United States? The unknown encircled him like a cloud, robbing even the illusion of peace.

"Do you have a moment, Father?" Willard leaned against the stone mantel.

His father turned from the radio and looked at him. "Sure, son. What's on your mind?"

Willard grabbed a baseball from the mantel and rolled it through his fingers, back and forth between his hands. "Can we talk about Andrew?"

Father looked away. "There's nothing to discuss."

"Yes, there is. Father, I'd like your blessing to enlist. I want to do my part, and that can't be done from here. And ever since Andrew, you won't even talk about the war, let alone me serving."

Even before the words escaped Willard's mouth, his father shook his head.

"You know I can't give my blessing."

"You mean you won't."

"If I wouldn't bless Andrew's enlistment, why do you think I'd give you my permission?"

Willard closed his eyes. Andrew had insisted he'd enlist with or without their father's blessing. Willard heard the argument as if it occurred in front of him again.

"Dad, my number will be called soon. If I enlist, I can pick the branch I serve in."

"I won't have it. No son of mine will join a moment before required. This isn't our war." Father turned his back in an attempt to end the discussion.

"Maybe not yet, but that'll change, Dad. And I'm going to be part of that. So give me your blessing, or I'll sign up anyway. It's what I'm supposed to do." Willard couldn't remember a time before when Andrew stood firm like that.

"I need you here, son. There's too much work to have you leave."

"Dad, I want to do what you ask, but I can't. Tomorrow, I'll join the Navy ..."

Twelve months later, Willard wondered if Andrew still lived. He'd looked ready for anything in his uniform, taking to his training like a fish to water. All his letters home had glowed with the adventure of traveling the world. Hawaii had been an exotic contrast to the sandhills of Nebraska.

The woody smoke from the fire reminded Willard how far he was from Hawaii. "Did you hear the sermon, Father?"

His father looked at him over his small reading glasses. "I probably heard more of it than you did. I wasn't distracted by a cute redhead."

Willard acknowledged Father's words with a smile and then strode across the room toward him. "I haven't had any peace since Pearl Harbor. Maybe if I enlist, I'll be doing my job. I can't stay here and wait."

"I respect that, but I need you here. I can't run this ranch by myself. The spread's too big."

"Let the other kids help. There are three of them who can work."

"No. They're all girls and still in school. I'm not saying no forever, but I am saying no for now. I need you too much."

Willard wanted to argue. It took all he had to hold his tongue in check. He tossed the ball higher and higher trying to channel his energy on something productive.

"Give it a bit, Willard. We can reevaluate in the spring."

"Yes, sir." Willard grabbed his coat from the rack by the back door. He resisted the urge to slam the door shut behind him and walked across the yard. He kicked at snowdrifts as he muttered. He puffed his breath out and inhaled slowly.

Father, I want to honor my earthly father. But I can't do it right now. I am so mad. Show me what I'm to do in this war. It can't be staying on the ranch. A feeling he refused to call peace settled on his heart. "I'll try to wait on you, Lord."

He fingered the ball he'd shoved in his coat pocket. He couldn't wait until spring arrived to do his part.

CHAPTER 8

DECEMBER 22, 1941

A car rattled up the long driveway toward the ranch house. Willard and his father looked up from their work patching a piece of fence a steer had torn down the night before. The steer hadn't hobbled far with barbed wire wrapped around its front feet. Willard shielded his eyes against the sun that bounced off the snowdrifts.

"Car look familiar, Father?"

"Nope. Guess we'll have to walk down to the house and see what they want."

They carefully wrapped the extra barbed wire and grabbed the tools before heading down the hill. One time Willard had left tools on top of the snow. When he'd gone back to get them they were gone, and he'd waited until spring melted the snow to recover them.

Willard inhaled sharply when he saw Bob Salmon step out of the car. He could only be here to deliver a telegram. Willard reached out to steady Father when he stumbled on the path to the yard. Willard struggled to breathe as he prayed the car's appearance didn't mean what his heart told him it did. Maybe they'd found Andrew. He could have been injured or lost his memory. He had to be alive. Willard refused to consider other realities.

"Willard, go get your mother. Please keep her in the house until I come for her."

He examined his father, usually so sure and strong, observed the pallor of his face. "Are you sure? Do you want me to stay with you?"

"No." The word rattled sharp and heavy with pain. "Go protect your mother."

Willard glanced at the car, saw Pastor Evans unfold his pudgy frame from the vehicle. Pastor Evans hesitated, then strode toward them with Bob. The uniformed man stopped when he stood ten feet in front of them. He slowly removed his hat from his head and held it in front of him.

"Go." Father gasped and reached his hand to clutch at his heart.

The one-word command crushed Willard's hope. He wanted to push back time, change what his father would hear. Ignore the envelope clutched in the officer's hand. Alter the fact Andrew had enlisted with the Navy. Instead, all he could do was obey. "Yes, sir."

Willard stumbled into the house, stopped at the kitchen window, and parted the curtain to watch the scene unfold. Pastor Evans stepped up to Father and put a hand on his shoulder. He said nothing, lending support. Willard winced as Father's knees buckled, and Pastor Evans kneeled beside him, pulling his father into a bear hug as tears ran down both their faces. Father, a man of strength, broken.

"Willard? Did somebody pull into the yard?" His mother bustled into the kitchen, dust rag clutched in her hand, scarf tied over her hair. "Willard?"

He tried to wipe the fear from his face, but she'd already seen it. Her steps stilled, and she stared at him, searching for information.

"What's wrong, honey?"

"I don't know that anything's wrong."

Her free hand climbed her throat. "Your father. Is anything wrong with him? Please tell me he's okay." She threw herself into his arms.

"He's fine, Mother. He's fine." Willard turned so she couldn't see over his shoulder to the yard. "He asked me to come in and wait with you while we see what our visitors want. He'll be in shortly." He awkwardly rubbed her back.

"What aren't you telling me, Willard Josiah Johnson?"

"I honestly don't know, Mother. You'll have to wait for Father."

She pushed out of his embrace and slammed open the back door. She hustled down the steps and ran to join Father as he and Pastor Evans lurched to their feet. "Tell me what is wrong." She screamed into the still air. "Is it Andrew? Tell me ... tell me." Her words trailed into broken sobs as Bob looked on uncomfortably.

Willard frowned, knowing time would make this more commonplace for the officer, though he doubted it would grow easier.

With a nod to Pastor Evans, Bob got back in his car and turned the vehicle around in the yard. In moments any indication he had visited were gone, other than the broken sobs of the group huddled on the lawn. Father clutched Mother in his arms, the envelope tossed to the side on the ground. Minutes passed, but Willard didn't care how little or how much evaporated. Father gently protected her and walked her up the stairs and into the house.

"I'm going to lay your mother down, let her get some rest." His voice ground to a halt. He cleared his throat. "Pastor, if you can wait a minute or two, I'd be grateful. I need to talk to you about what happens from here."

"Certainly, Robert. I'll do anything I can to help you and Evelyn at this time."

Willard watched his parents disappear through the door. He turned to Pastor Evans. "If you'll excuse me, I'm going to check the livestock. I'll come back in a bit and drive you to town."

He staggered to the barn, the truth crushing him with its harshness. While he had stayed home in safety, his younger brother had become the casualty of an undeclared war. Fire burned through Willard's veins. He wanted to throw something, looked for anything to hurl against the sky. A message to heaven that all was not right in the world. An innocent, young man had fallen too soon. Willard fell to his knees in the hay, feeling the dust rise around him.

"Why, God?" His yell startled a cow in a stall. "Why? It's not right and it's not fair. You should have taken me, not Andrew. Why, God?" He fell facedown in the hay as he wrestled with God for answers that refused to come.

An hour later Willard sat awkwardly next to Pastor Evans as he drove the truck up the hill and away from the ranch. His anger boiled below the surface. He glanced sideways at the pastor, afraid he could detect the furnace ignited that afternoon.

"How are you, Willard?" Pastor Evans's eyes reflected sadness mixed with kindness.

"To be honest, I'm real angry, Pastor. Real angry. God could have stopped this, but He didn't. Is that the way to take care of His faithful children? Andrew's never done anything wrong. Nothing worthy of a death penalty. But that's what the Japs gave him."

Pastor Evans sat quietly and let the silence build between them. Finally, when Willard couldn't take another minute, Pastor Evans spoke. "God did not abandon Andrew, and He has not abandoned your family, Willard. I wish I could tell you I understand why God allows the things to happen that He does, but I can't. I have a list of questions I would love to ask Him when I get to heaven. But let me tell you something I know with certainty." He turned in his seat and looked at Willard with an intensity Willard couldn't ignore. "This is something I'd stake my life on. When I get to heaven, all these questions I'm collecting here on earth will be answered with one look in Jesus's face. And that has to be enough right now, because I don't always get the answers I seek."

"See, Pastor, those words are hard to hear right now. I don't want to wait for answers till I get to heaven. My family's in pain now."

"It is. But your family won't be the sole one that experiences this pain. It will get much worse before it gets better. Let the sure hope we have in Christ build a bedrock of faith in your life. It's the only way to survive a storm like the one your family has entered."

Willard pulled up in front of the church and idled the truck as he waited for Pastor Evans to leave.

Pastor Evans looked at Willard and touched his shoulder. "Willard, your family needs you to be strong. Your parents want to delay a memorial service until they receive Andrew's personal effects. They're holding on to a thread of hope even as their hearts break."

Willard swallowed hard around the sudden lump in his throat. He refused to show any weakness, because if he started, he feared he wouldn't be able to stop collapsing.

"Willard, I will pray that God guards you and leads you at this time in your life. I will also pray for your family. God will go through the fire with you as He did with the three Israelite boys in the furnace. Don't turn from Him."

"I'll consider all you've said, Pastor."

"Do more than consider it. Pray about it. Turn to Him, and He will meet you." Pastor Evans stepped out of the truck and closed the door.

Willard put the truck in gear and drove away as fast as he could. Pastor Evans's words bounced like rubber balls around his mind. They weren't what he wanted to hear. He wanted to be mad, to cling to his anger. To know he was still alive. He pulled into Munson's Texaco Station and waited as the attendant put five gallons of gas in the truck. That would be enough to get him to the ranch and back to town a couple of times. The family would need it in the coming days.

Then he'd call Audrey. See if she could spend a few minutes with him. Maybe in her presence he would be able to see that life could go on. Even as it tilted on its axis.

CHAPTER 9

DECEMBER 22, 1941

"I'm home." Audrey rushed through the house to the kitchen, but found it empty. She wanted to dance around the kitchen and celebrate. School was closed for two weeks for the Christmas break. "Mama? Where are you?"

"Back here, hon."

Audrey followed the voice to the dining room, shaking snowflakes out of her curls as she walked.

"How was your day?" Mama stood beside a chair, folding laundry with quick hands.

"Well, I managed to keep Petey Sedlacek out of the principal's office, so that's an improvement."

"That's good." Her mother looked up and smiled at Audrey. "Looks like you found a blizzard on the walk home."

"It's a lazy snow. It trickles out of the clouds. I love days like today." She gave one last shake to her curls and then kissed Mama on her smooth cheek. "I don't suppose you have any hot water ready?"

"The tea bags are next to the kettle. Are you going to the Canteen meeting tonight?"

"Yes, ma'am. 'Let's do something and do it in a hurry!' Rae hasn't wasted any time, has she?" Audrey watched her mother work for a minute, then plopped a tea bag in a mug before filling it with hot water. As Audrey leaned against the table, she considered all the practical experience her mother could add to the Canteen. The love and cookies she would dispense to every soldier who walked through its doors. "I wish you'd joined us Wednesday night. Seeing those boys in

49

uniform was inspiring. We're really at war, and think of all the servicemen who will travel by UP trains."

"I think a canteen's a great idea, hon." Mama stilled Audrey's hands where they picked at crumbs left on the tablecloth. "I wish I could come tonight. Be sure to tell Rae and the others that I'll help however they need."

"Yes, Mama." Audrey squeezed her mother's hand. "It will be nice to look at all those uniforms."

"A nice change from second graders." Mama raised her eyebrows as she looked over the neat stacks at Audrey. "Well, before you swoon too much, you can carry this pile up to your brothers' room. Your tea should be ready when you get back downstairs."

Willard filled her thoughts as she carried the clothes upstairs. Did the snow make life on the ranch harder? They might live in the same county, but in many ways they existed worlds apart. She'd always experienced the convenience of town. Would life on a ranch isolate her, or would she find the open space liberating? Of course, it depended on who explored the fields with her. If a certain rancher with eyes the color of rich chocolate rode beside her, she couldn't imagine anything else she'd need. A blush crept up her face as she realized the implications of her thoughts.

"What's got you looking like a tomato, sis?" Robert grinned like the Cheshire cat as he watched her from his bed.

"It's nothing. Get back to your homework, troublemaker." It couldn't be anything. Her stomach twisted because she had no right to imagine any kind of future with Willard. Whenever her dreams about the future took over, reality whispered from the corner of her mind who she was. The daughter of a railroad employee held no hope of keeping the attention of the son of a prosperous rancher.

"For nothing you sure look like you've gone far away." John grabbed the clothes from her hands.

Audrey shook her head as she left the boys' room. "You still have a thing or two to learn about women."

A knock pounded the front door. She flew down the stairs. "I've got it, Mama." She took a moment to catch her breath and then opened the door. She stilled at the sight of Willard slumped against the doorframe. "Come in. Let's get you something to drink. Are you all right?" Her words rushed in a flood.

He pushed through the doorway and she took his arm and eased him toward the kitchen. "The Navy visited the ranch today." He sighed and ran a hand across the top of his head. "I'm sorry to stop without calling, Audrey, but I had to see you."

Audrey froze and turned toward him. "I don't know what to say, other than I am so sorry. Here, let's sit in the parlor for a minute." She took his hand and led him toward the couch.

He cluthed her hand like he couldn't let go. Slowly, he sank onto the couch, her fingers dwarfed in his grip, but she didn't mind. Instead, it warmed her even as her heart broke for him. She sank next to him wishing she knew how to comfort him.

"I've never seen my Father broken like that. He is the strongest man I know. But it's like his most precious possession was taken. And I can't fix this."

"I know."

"How can this be God's will?"

"I don't know, Willard. I'm so sorry."

He leaned his head against the back of the couch and then looked at his watch. "I have to get back to the ranch."

"You're welcome to stay for supper, Willard."

"No. I need to get home, see how I can help." He let go of her then rubbed his face. "I needed to see you. See that there are still good things in my life." He lurched to his feet and offered her a hand.

They walked to the door, and Audrey searched her mind for something to say that would matter, that would help ease his pain.

Willard stared into her eyes for a long moment. "Thank you for the haven, sweet Audrey."

"I'll be praying for you."

He nodded, then ducked out the door, back into the snow.

* * *

WILLARD LINGERED in her thoughts through dinner and as Audrey pulled on her coat and stepped outside. The flakes that trickled from the sky stacked half a foot high as she hiked through the drifts. She had eight blocks to walk before she reached the Sedlaceks' home and Canteen meeting. As her breath curled in the air in front of her, she decided she should have accepted Lainie's offer of a ride. Silence marred only by the crunch of her footsteps surrounded her as she hopped from foot to foot through the drifts.

Fifteen minutes later she stomped her feet in the doorway of Mrs. Sedlacek's home.

"Come in out of the cold." Mrs. Sedlacek reached for Audrey's coat as Audrey shrugged out of it. "Your cheeks look all rosy. There's a fire stoked in the parlor. You'll find the other ladies there enjoying the heat."

Audrey followed her hostess and waved at Petey when he stuck his head around the kitchen door. She stepped into the parlor and marveled at the group of women. Did she belong in a meeting populated by doctors' wives, pastors' wives, and other established women? She was completely out of her element. Lainie waved frantically at her, and Audrey smiled. No atmosphere could stifle Lainie.

After walking across the room, nodding at Mrs. Evans and Dr. Edwards' wife, Audrey joined Lainie on a piano bench in the corner. "What on earth are we doing here?"

"Exactly what you've bellyached about. We'll get involved in the war effort. Isn't this exciting?" Lainie threw her arm around Audrey's shoulder and squeezed.

"Pinch me to let me know this is real. I really don't belong here, you know." Audrey jumped and rubbed her arm when Lainie pinched it. "You didn't have to do that."

"Just doing what my best friend asked." The twinkle in her eyes warned Audrey not to push back. "The fact your dad works for Union Pacific instead of a bank or a school doesn't mean anything. And if I know you, you'll work harder than any three women put together."

Hearing the words, Audrey vowed she would. She might not have extra money, but she could contribute energy and time to the effort.

The two settled down when Rae Wilson called the meeting to order.

"Thanks for coming, everyone, and to Mrs. Sedlacek for making her home available to us. The women of North Platte can contribute something big to the war if we work together. We saw the need Wednesday when we met the train filled with Kansas boys. A canteen'll make the community proud and boost the morale of our boys in uniform."

Mrs. Edwards raised her gloved hand. "How often do you plan to operate the canteen? Do you plan on certain days each week?"

"Why limit ourselves? Let's open it every day. Each soldier who stops in our town should be greeted by a friendly face and warm cup of coffee."

Audrey's mind flooded with the image of serving coffee to troops as the discussion flowed around her. A glow of excitement flooded her at the scene. She could play a role! Ideas pinged back and forth across the room, the speakers talking on top of each other in their enthusiasm.

In short order, Rae organized the chaos into small committees to tackle the concerns. One group huddled on a small Victorian couch and plotted how to spread the word and get donations of food and money. Another group clustered at the fireplace on straight-back chairs to discuss locating volunteers. A third group gathered in the dining room to discuss the logistics. After wandering among the groups, Audrey settled with the fireplace group when she saw Lainie in the thick of it.

"Let's meet the trains on Christmas." Lainie bounced up and down on the chair, wound tight with nervous focus. "The boys shouldn't be alone on a holiday."

"Can we be ready in time?" Audrey ticked off the days on her fingers and wagged them in front of Lainie.

"Of course. It's not like we'll have a full meal for them. But we can have baskets of candy and apples to pass on the trains."

"I bet I can even talk the Cody Hotel into loaning us coffee cups so we can pass out something warm." Mrs. Evans made a note on her pad of paper. "And I'll talk to someone at the station about how to get electricity to make the coffee."

"We can do this, Audrey. You'll see. There's no time like the present to start."

"Well, what can I do?" Audrey tried to keep her hands still in her lap.

"Have your dad talk to the Union Pacific bigwigs and see if we can get some-place to store our things between trains. We can work on everything else as we get started."

Audrey smiled. Surely Dad would be happy to help with that little part.

An hour later, Audrey and Lainie walked out arm in arm, Audrey almost as excited as Lainie. "We're really going to do it. I can't believe we start in three days. We have so much work to do."

"We'll start slow. Nobody expects anything yet, but wait till they see it." They chatted about all the details on the drive home.

"Here we are. See you tomorrow, Audrey."

"Thanks for the ride, Lainie. Night." Audrey plowed up the sidewalk, her mind racing with everything that had to happen. If it was in her power, the Canteen would open for the first trainload of soldiers on Christmas.

She raised her arms to the sky and turned a stumbling circle on the sidewalk. *Thank You, Father, for a role to play.*

CHAPTER 10

DECEMBER 25, 1941

*A*fter two days filled with activity, Christmas arrived much too soon. Audrey looked at the small clock perched on the mantel and stopped fidgeting. Her thoughts traveled to Willard and his family. She wondered how they were doing their first Christmas without Andrew. Then she thought about everything she needed to do at the Canteen. If her brothers didn't speed up unwrapping their presents, she wouldn't get to the Canteen before noon. Mama had agreed she could spend the day there, but Dad insisted she stay through the reading of the Christmas story.

The fire warmed the parlor as it did every Christmas. This morning after the gifts were finally unwrapped, everyone would gather in front of the fire and listen to Dad read the first two chapters of Luke. He liked to say he saved the best gift for last. Usually, the tradition melted her heart as she thought of all Christ had given to become her Savior and wondered what Mary felt when she learned she would bear the Messiah. Today, all Audrey could think about was walking to the train station on Front Street as fast as she could. She might even talk her brothers into hauling the heavy, loaded baskets for her.

Audrey smiled at the thought of those baskets filled with treats for the troops. She had walked door to door through her neighborhood asking for contributions of fruit, candy, and homemade cookies. Multiple trips to her neighbors had filled her arms with loads of goodies. Even this morning, a couple of families brought more offerings. What pleased her most were the letters accompanying many of the plates and baskets. Whether the soldiers knew it, the residents of North Platte planned to adopt them. At least her neighborhood did.

Finally, John ripped open his last package. A bright-red scarf, socks, and mittens tumbled into his lap.

"Well, I believe the tree is bare." Dad lumbered to the floor and made a big show of pushing aside the tinseled tree's lower limbs. "Did I miss anything?"

"Over there." Robert played the role perfectly with the right tinge of excitement in his voice. "Look to the right, Dad."

The man scratched his graying thatch of hair and shuffled onto his hands and knees. He reached under the tree and made a show of tipping the tree off its stand with his broad shoulders. John and Robert each grabbed a foot and pulled back with exaggerated groans.

Mama hid a smile and pulled the final package from its hiding place. "Here you go, dear."

Brushing the tinsel from his head, Dad chuckled and reached for the package. "Thank you. Audrey, would you like the honor of opening the final gift?"

"All right." Audrey pulled her thoughts from the Canteen and reached for the rectangular package. She pulled a last piece of silver tinsel from behind his ear before accepting the ribbon-trimmed box. Snapshots from the years flashed through her mind as she considered it before carefully removing the bow, and then folding back the paper. In her lap sat the family Bible that first belonged to Grandma Kate. She traced the letters on the cover, feeling the heritage of faith passed through the generations now resting on her and her brothers. "Dad, look. It's the greatest gift of all. The wisdom of God resides in these pages and points us to Him and to Jesus, the reason we celebrate."

"Let's pray." Quickly, each head bowed, and he prayed. "Father, we are humbled by who You are and all You have done for us. Protect our boys in uniform wherever they are. Show us how we are to serve You in the coming year. Thank You for the bountiful blessings You bestow on us. May we grow closer to You and look more like Your Son each day. Thank You for sending Him as the greatest gift of all. Amen."

Audrey reached up to swipe tears from her eyes. She had so much to be thankful for this year.

"Time to gather 'round for the Christmas story. Audrey, may I have the Bible?"

Reverently, she relinquished the book. Dad took it and settled into his easy chair beside the fire. Twenty minutes passed as he read the story aloud. The fire popped and hissed in the background, as he played the roles. Mama smiled as she watched her children in a semi-circle on the floor in front of their dad. Audrey wished she could capture the image and remember the moment forever.

"'And Jesus kept increasing in wisdom and stature, and in favor with God and men.'" Dad closed the Bible and looked each child in the eye. "My prayer for each of you in the coming year is that you increase in wisdom and stature. That you find favor with men, but most important, that you find favor with God."

"Amen," Mama breathed from her chair. "All right. Time for you kids to get your coats and hats on. Boys, you get to help Audrey cart everything to the Cody Hotel."

"Ma, it's too cold out there."

"All the better to keep you moving and out of trouble, John. It's little enough for you to do to help others. Now get moving." She swatted him gently on the behind as he reluctantly left the warmth of the fire.

Ten minutes later the three tumbled into the snow. Audrey laughed as she struggled to keep her balance under the tower of packages she carried. John wore a determined expression as he pulled the wooden sled tied down with baskets and boxes. Robert walked behind to steady the sled and carried one large picnic basket.

"We three kings of Orient are." She started the song.

Robert jumped in. "Bearing gifts we've traveled so far."

"Street and sidewalk, sled and walking, traveling oh so far." John quipped.

"Oh, oh." The blocks passed quickly as they sang carols. A train whistle pierced the day, and Audrey resisted the urge to quicken her steps. The sled had tipped only once, and she wanted to keep it that way. None of the contents had disappeared in the snow thanks to the rope and John's knots. Audrey hoped Mrs. Foust's prize-winning spice cookies weren't breaking into crumbs.

"Wait here, okay." Audrey gave John her packages and quickly climbed the steps to the Cody Hotel and then looked around the lobby for a familiar face. Seeing none, she approached the clerk at the desk. "Can you tell me where I find the ladies with the Canteen?"

"I ain't seen them for a while. You should look over at the station." Before she could thank him, he had returned to reading the *Saturday Evening Post* that rested on the counter in front of him.

Pushing open the front door, Audrey looked for John and Robert. They leaned against the wall of the adjoining building.

"Hurry up, sis. It gets real cold when we aren't moving." John stomped his feet and rubbed his mittened hands together.

"The clerk suggests we head to the station. Let's see who we find there." Retrieving her packages from the top of the sled, where John had stashed them, Audrey led the way. After crossing the street and walking to the back of the station, they arrived at the platform. It bustled with so much activity they all stopped and stared.

Audrey had expected people, but the platform contained the activity of a beehive. Complete chaos reigned as soldiers milled with townspeople. The moment the conductor blew his whistle, boys in uniform dashed back to the train, but not before grabbing one last apple or package of candy. Audrey thought she'd collected enough to feed a small army. Now she hoped it lasted for one train. As the soldiers boarded, she spotted Rae Wilson on the far side of the tracks.

"Wait here. I'll be back as soon as I know where we should put all these boxes and baskets." She wound her way through the dispersing gaggle and approached Rae. "Miss Wilson, I don't know if you remember me or not."

"Of course, you're Audrey Stone. Thanks for coming to help. As you can see, we need you."

"If all the trains are like that one, I understand why. My brothers helped me carry down a bunch of donations from my neighbors. It's mostly fruit, candy, and cookies. Where do you want us to put it?"

"Is any of it hot?"

"No." Audrey wondered if she'd somehow let Rae down by not bringing hot food. "I thought it'd be easier this way."

"It certainly will be. We don't have any electricity or running water here. I'll take care of that later. You can take your things to the maintenance shed we're working from. The next train won't arrive for about thirty minutes we're told." Rae turned as someone else yelled her name from across the platform. "You'll have to excuse me while I see what other emergencies have popped up. Thanks for coming."

Audrey watched Rae walk away, hands shoved deep in her coat pockets while a scarf tied around her head kept her bobbed hair contained. Rae wore a determined expression as she marched off to confront the next need.

"Hey, Audrey. We're getting cold over here."

Sounded like she had her own set of emergencies. From John's tone she doubted her brothers would stay and help. "Okay, kids. Pull that sled over to the shed, and you can head home and get some hot chocolate. Drink a cup for me, okay?"

The afternoon flew by and melted into evening as the trains rumbled into the station for a quick stop. Most stayed less than twenty minutes. Occasionally, the train stood in the station longer as it was refitted to make it over the Rocky Mountains.

After Audrey watched the controlled frenzy with the first few trains, Mrs. Sedlacek gave her a basket, and Audrey worked as a platform girl. She helped coax the boys off the train so they'd get treats. If a soldier couldn't get off for some reason, she brought the treats to him.

As the trains pulled out of the station, she waved and yelled, "Merry Christmas. God bless you." Prayers for the safety of the men she'd met flooded her mind as she helped prepare for the next train. By midnight she joined an exhausted group of women in a huddle on the platform. Each breath frosted the air.

"We'll serve the next train with the few things we have left. Then we'll call it a night." Rae looked around the group. "I'll be here tomorrow and would appreciate any help. We'll need lots of people to help until the word gets out."

Audrey raised her hand. "I'm happy to help during Christmas break."

Several other women quickly agreed to return as well.

"All right, let's send these next chaps off with a Merry Christmas and then get some sleep. The work is beginning."

When Audrey fell into bed, she couldn't remember a time when she was so bone-weary. She'd worked hard, but she'd relished the opportunity to cheer the boys. *Thank You, Lord, for the opportunity. Use me. Let me be Your hands extended to these boys.*

With a satisfied sigh, she curled up under the comforter and slept with dreams of what the morning held dancing through her mind.

CHAPTER 11

DECEMBER 31, 1941

A muscle in his jaw tightened as Willard bounced a ball back and forth between his hands. Tonight he got to see Audrey, something that hadn't happened enough during her break. She'd thrown herself into the burgeoning Canteen and spent every spare moment there. She seemed to enjoy it, but for reasons he couldn't explain, he didn't like driving there to catch a moment with her. Train after train loaded with troops filled the station with men who walked a step taller when they reboarded.

In thirty minutes he and Roger would leave to pick up Lainie and Audrey. He wanted to spend all the time with her he could. Get to know her and what mattered to her. He sighed and threw the ball against the headboard. That wouldn't happen if he didn't get to see her apart from the station. Tonight they'd ring in the New Year. Start something fresh together.

He stepped to the walnut wardrobe next to the door and opened it. He pulled out a clean shirt and rehearsed the words he wanted to say in his mind. "Audrey, no one knows what tomorrow holds. Maybe the crazy Japs'll find a way to fly across the Pacific and reach Nebraska." No, that wasn't quite right. He didn't want to scare her into loving him.

"Audrey, we live in a world gone mad. I love spending time with you. I don't want to wait and see if we have time to get to know each other. Times are too uncertain to waste another minute."

No, that wouldn't work either. *Lord, I don't know what to say to her. You know my heart. Give me the right words at the right time. She's so special.*

As he knotted his tie, Willard thought about her smile. It upped the wattage in a room every time she flashed it. From the first moment she graced him with a smile, his world seemed brighter, clearer. He wanted that every day, not just those times he got to town and found her. They might have known each other only a month, but he couldn't lose her to a uniform at the station.

Willard looked up as a knock pounded his door.

"Are you ready, Willard? We've got to get moving, or we'll be late." Frustration laced Roger's voice. "You're as good looking as you'll get."

"Yeah, I suppose you're right." Willard opened the door and took in the blazer Roger wore. "I didn't even know you owned one of those."

"I'm full of surprises. Now let's get going. We don't want to make the ladies mad."

Roger socked him in the arm and then pulled him down the stairs and out the door. They walked to the car and soon flew across the oiled back road to the highway.

Willard clenched his teeth as they slid toward town. "Hey, watch out for ice."

"Don't worry." Roger swerved the steering wheel back and forth, causing Willard to grab for any handhold he could find. "We'll get there safe and sound —and I'll even make sure we're on time."

Willard sighed with relief when they hit North Platte in one piece. One day Roger's driving would kill him, but anything was better than being stuck on the ranch. They skidded to a stop at Lainie's house before Roger ran up the walk to get her. Willard stilled when Audrey came out with them. Her green coat reflected her eyes even from a distance. A quiet elegance and control he admired but she didn't seem to recognize radiated from her. She took his breath away. If only she felt a fraction of the same emotion for him.

Willard slid from the car. He hurried to the other side and opened the back door for Audrey. Then he walked back to the passenger side and sat beside her.

She slipped next to him and snuggled close. "Hi." Her word sounded like a contented purr.

"Hey. How'd your week wrap up?"

"It was busy but wonderful. I've never done anything so meaningful. To see the boys' faces when they arrive at the Canteen and the change when they leave. It's absolutely amazing to me."

"You've spent a lot of time there. Why? It's your break, isn't it?"

"Yes." She looked past him as if watching a scene play through her mind. "It's hard to explain. But the soldiers drag off the trains like the weight of the world and its questions burden them. Fifteen minutes later they race to catch the train before it pulls out of the station. During that time, they get hugs from North Platte's mothers. We give them simple fruit and candy, but they act like we've blessed them with treasure. I can tell them how much I appreciate what they're doing in the Army or Navy." Her gaze focused on him, and he shifted under the weight of her scrutiny. "I haven't felt safe many places since Pearl Harbor, but surrounded by those boys willing to die to keep us protected, I do. Meeting their trains and thanking them is a small act I can do to say 'thank you.'"

Willard listened to her recount stories from the Canteen, and a flash of envy created by the image of boys in uniform assailed him. It was something he needed to analyze later. Audrey looked at him when he shrugged his shoulders in an effort to dislodge the emotion.

"Are you okay?" Her eyes reflected concern as she shifted to gaze at him.

"Yeah, just thinking. But I want to savor tonight and ringing in the New Year. I haven't seen enough of you."

"Well, before December 6, you didn't know I existed. I think we're doing pretty good." She teased him with a twinkle.

Willard reached up and chucked her under the chin. "There's never enough time to be with you." She stilled at his touch and turned completely serious.

"There's no need to rush things, Willard. We're young with plenty of time."

"I don't know. Everything feels topsy-turvy." He pulled her back against him. "But I want to enjoy every moment I have with you."

After circling the Pawnee Hotel a couple of times, Roger gave up and parked several blocks up Dewey Street. Willard smiled as Audrey tremored with excitement when they approached the Pawnee.

"I've never attended an event in the Crystal Ballroom. I've heard it's magnificent."

"You'll love it. I've been there for wedding receptions. It's nice, but my mother talks about it for days." He hoped it made the same kind of impression on Audrey. He watched her face as she stepped into the large room. It was the sole space of its scale in North Platte. The hotel towered above the rest of the skyline, and the inside was in a class all its own.

"Oh, Willard, look at the ceiling." Audrey pointed up at the six chandeliers dripping from the ceiling. "I've never seen anything like them. This is wonderful."

* * *

AUDREY CAUGHT HER BREATH, then reminded herself to exhale and breathe again. This night had the touches of a fairy tale. Willard opened another world for her when he brought her to the Pawnee. She'd walked by it for years. It sat in the middle of downtown across the street from the Fox Theater and a few blocks from the station. Sure, she'd entered the building a couple times to meet friends at the Tom Tom Room for tea. But she'd never seen the inside of the Crystal Ballroom.

She looked around and saw North Platte's finest citizens, turned out in their best, ready to enjoy the evening. There'd even been a coat check where a young woman who was vaguely familiar. Maybe that's where she should spend the evening. She'd have something in common with that girl. Audrey didn't think she could say the same for the others in the room.

With effort, Audrey stilled her wringing hands and forced her shoulders to lower.

"Are you okay?"

Audrey looked up into Willard's brown eyes. She tried to smile. "I will be. I'm sorry, I feel a bit overwhelmed, I guess." How could he understand when these were the people he'd grown up with? She'd never felt so out of her element until Willard danced into her life.

"Come on. I know how to make you forget about yourself for a bit." He led her across the room toward the rostrum, where a band warmed up their instruments. As they approached, the bandleader launched the group into swinging tune.

The evening passed quickly with frequent stops for punch and hors d'oeuvres. Each time a man in uniform entered the room, Audrey sensed Willard follow each man's progress across the room. The room filled, and Audrey pulled him from the claustrophobic dance floor. "Willard, let's go find a place we can talk for a bit."

He looked at her with a quirked eyebrow for a moment, but agreed. "Let's try the Tom Tom Room. If it's open, we can sit there for a bit."

"All right." Audrey inhaled deeply and then they made their way down the stairs and entered the less crowded lobby.

"You don't like crowds, do you?"

"Not really. After spending most days surrounded by my class plus an additional two hundred or so students, the last thing I want to do is pass time with a crowd of strangers."

"Then why are you so committed to the Canteen?" Willard led her to a couch in the corner of the lobby and then sat down beside her. "I would think all the people in and out of there would make you uncomfortable."

"They need me. And I need them. It's one way I can do something important for the war effort." Audrey shifted on the couch so she could look at Willard. She searched his face and was surprised to see a distance there that hadn't existed when they sat down. "Talk to me, Willard."

"There's nothing to say." The words squeezed past a jaw that looked clenched.

"This is a fine kettle of fish. In the car you tell me you don't see enough of me. Why would I spend more time with you when you stonewall me when we are together? Let me get to know you. It's not enough to simply have a good time."

He shifted his jaw back and forth. "I'm not even sure what I think right now, Audrey. I'm at a crossroads. Father needs me on the ranch, but I want to enlist."

"Why? If your father needs your help, it must be important."

"I can't explain it. I have this drive to be part of the fight."

A blast of frigid air flowed over them when a boisterous group exited the hotel. Audrey shivered and watched the laughing couples stumble through the snow. The silence stretched but wasn't uncomfortable, just long. "Thank you for trying to explain, Willard." She studied him, taking in the planes of his face that had sharpened since Andrew's death. "You are a good man. I've seen glimpses of who you are, and I like what I see. I enjoy being your friend and want to know you better."

The door swung open again, and he glanced at it. He turned toward her and leaned closer. "There's so much I don't know about you, Audrey. But I want to."

Audrey's cheeks flushed warm under his gaze, and she shifted on the couch. Her heart raced and she looked for a way to break the intensity building. Chilled air brushed her neck, and she stood. "I think I need a cup of punch. Would you escort me upstairs?" She barely paused to see if he would follow. At the moment, she was too flustered to wait for him.

* * *

WILLARD WATCHED her walk away and smiled. He knew she felt what he did even though all the words he'd practiced to move them toward a commitment had abandoned him. He two-stepped to catch up with the woman who brought color into his life.

"Audrey, wait."

She halted but didn't turn his direction. He imagined her cheeks flaming even brighter than they had a moment before.

"I'll tell you all kinds of stories about me and the ranch. I want to introduce you to every part of my life." He touched her shoulder gently, and she shivered, then turned toward him. His heart stopped when she looked at him with twin tears hanging from her eyelashes. He reached up to brush them from her cheeks as they fell. "I didn't mean to make you cry. Audrey, I think I love you. I'll do anything you want, including let my family tell you every story they can create about me."

The flush fled her cheeks, and she became as still as a fence post. Would she faint? This wasn't the reaction he'd expected.

"Let's go upstairs and get you that punch." He offered his arm and smiled when her hand fluttered onto it. She looked up at him, her eyes as big as his baseball. "Breathe, honey." The last word slipped out before he could slam his lips shut. *Now I've done it. If I didn't scare her off before, I did now.*

"All right." Her lips twitched into a slim smile. "You are full of surprises, Willard. And I would very much like to hear all those stories and learn about your life."

He tried to disregard the fact that she'd ignored the words *I think I love you* as they walked upstairs. When they reentered the ballroom, the bandleader had gathered everyone around the rostrum. "When the drum rolls, we'll start the countdown."

Willard and Audrey hurried to the back of the crowd. At the signal, they joined in with the others. "Three ... Two ... One ... Happy New Year!" A cheer erupted in the hall and made the chandeliers bounce on the ceiling.

Willard pulled Audrey to him, saw her look questioningly into his face. "Happy New Year, sweet Audrey." He carefully leaned down, considered kissing her full lips, then brushed his lips against her soft cheek. "May we have many more together."

CHAPTER 12

JANUARY 10, 1942

*A*udrey rolled over in bed and stifled a groan. She hated to admit it, but she was exhausted. School had started again on Monday. After corralling twenty-one second graders all day, she headed to the Canteen most nights. Rae Wilson had talked Mr. Jeffers, president of Union Pacific, into giving them access to the old lunchroom with its kitchen. Over the last ten days, the volunteers had turned it into a functional space for serving the servicemen.

When she wasn't at school or the Canteen, Willard invaded her dreams. Had he really said "I love you"? The "I think" certainly added a caveat to the phrase, but no man had said those words to her except Dad. The converging forces in her life made it impossible to tell up from down. And her fatigue made that worse.

Word about the Canteen had spread, and new volunteers appeared each day. It wouldn't be long before Audrey knew she wouldn't be needed every night. But right now, the Canteen needed as many hands as possible to manage the number of trains rumbling through town. On an average day, more than three thousand troops walked through the Canteen. Thinking the number made Audrey want to roll over and hide her head under the pillow.

Today she would spend the morning hunting for donations. She had taken all but one bushel of apples from Grandpa's orchard to the Canteen. Mama would give her the last apple if she asked, but before she did, Audrey wanted to allow other people to get involved. Let them experience the joy of serving.

She looked forward to spending the morning under the open sky rather than crammed in the lunchroom with hundreds of strangers. At the end of each night, the accumulation of crowds overwhelmed her, though working inside the station was warmer than serving as a platform girl. Maybe she'd ask to be a platform girl for a train or two to get a break from the lunchroom crush.

After getting ready and eating a quick breakfast, Audrey corralled her brothers and headed outside. John and Robert covered one side of Fourth Street while she walked down the other. After two hours all three had sleds loaded with food offerings. Several women also asked Audrey how they could volunteer. She gladly handed them small fliers with information. Then they stomped into the kitchen with cheeks rosy as the apples piled in a basket on the table. Mama had hot chocolate ready, and Audrey sipped the beverage gratefully.

When she could feel her fingers again, she looked at her watch and then jerked to her feet. "Time to head down to the Canteen. Can you boys bring the sleds down?"

John and Robert looked at each other and started to shake their heads. As they caught Mama's glare, they turned the shakes into nods.

"I guess we can do that." John reluctantly stood and retrieved his coat from its hook. "Mama, can't this wait? My gloves haven't dried out yet."

"Take Dad's. He won't mind. Robert, you can use mine." Mama pulled a basket up from its hiding place beside the stove. "Here's another basket to add to your stash, Audrey."

"Mama, do we have enough food? You've already sent so much."

"We'll be fine. What else are the boys supposed to eat if we don't offer them something?" Mama pushed the basket to John and turned back to the stove. "Tell Rae I'll be glad to help during the day next week if she needs. The Ladies' Aid from our church is about organized, too. We plan to break into groups and have one group a week volunteer as long as they need us."

"I'll be sure to tell her." Audrey walked over to Mama and gave her a quick kiss on the cheek. "Thank you for all you're doing, Mama."

"Pshaw. You'd better head out or they'll wonder where their most faithful volunteer is."

Audrey shrugged into her coat and pulled on her gloves. She followed John and Robert down the steps and watched the boys pick up the ropes attached to each sled. They waved at Mama, walked downtown, then pulled the sleds down Walnut, followed by a turn onto Front Street.

"Finally." John grumbled. "This walk doesn't get any shorter."

"No, it doesn't. Think how much it would mean to have strangers serve you if you were on a train chugging across the country and didn't know a soul."

"Yeah, I know. Do you really think it makes a difference?"

"I know it does. Why don't you stick around for a train or two and see for yourself? We always need help filling the coffee cups." Audrey smiled as John and Robert agreed to stay and help. She'd seen other boys work the coffeepots. Even these two couldn't mess it up too badly.

From the moment the code phrase "I have the coffee on" buzzed through the building, she pointed them toward the coffee and watched from her station at the magazine table. In the course of one train, John's demeanor went from resignation to curiosity. By the second train, she knew he was hooked. The "thank yous" and other expressions of gratitude had penetrated even his cool air. That's what she loved about the Canteen. It took a ton of hard work and effort, but the reward came quickly.

When the third train rolled into the station, she walked the platform with a basket of fruit and candy and encouraged the boys to step off the train for the duration of the stop. "Come on inside, gents, and get a hot cup of coffee and a sandwich."

"How much does it cost?" A deep voice yelled over the din.

"Nothing, soldier. It's North Platte's gift to you. But you have to come inside to accept it. Kind of like God's love, you know. It takes a step of action on your part." Cheers followed her as the men stood and shuffled off the train.

She smiled at a man in his Navy whites. "How long you been on the train, sailor?"

"Two days. Boarded in San Diego and won't get off till we hit Chicago. Then I get to transfer to another train that'll take me to Virginia."

"Sounds like quite the adventure."

"Not as big a one as waits me when I join my ship in Virginny."

"Well, head inside and get some hot coffee. God bless you."

The sailor didn't wait to respond. The tinkle of piano keys through the open door seemed to draw him as he two-stepped into the Canteen.

* * *

WILLARD STROLLED down the sidewalks of downtown North Platte. Father had sent him to town for extra supplies since the Almanac predicted another storm would hit town in a day or two. Since he'd already made the trip to town, Willard decided to look Audrey up and see if she'd have dinner with him. When he'd stopped by her home, her mother had informed him she was out, which meant she had a shift at the Canteen. Though, come to think of it, she seemed to have a shift at the Canteen anytime the doors were open and her day at the school had ended.

He turned onto Front Street and walked the block to the station. A train whistle pierced the afternoon as he approached the station. The coffee must be on.

Taking a deep breath, Willard shoved his hands into his pockets and hunkered deeper into his corduroy coat. He'd wait till this train had left to let Audrey know he'd come to see her. She'd be too busy for the next twenty minutes to do more than smile at him anyway. He leaned against the station's wall and watched Audrey exit the building carrying a basket lined with a colorful cloth. It overflowed with apples and a few oranges. Where on earth had she found oranges? She wore a bright, perky smile, her green coat that accented her eyes, and a navy skirt that peeked from the bottom of the coat. She looked beautiful, and all the men would notice.

As the train pulled into the station, Audrey and the other platform girls waved widely to the men. He watched the weary soldiers lean out the window at the sight.

"Come on off that train, guys. You've got twenty minutes to enjoy North Platte's hospitality."

Audrey climbed the steps to board a car where none of the men had made a move to disembark. A minute later she debarked, laughing with several of the soldiers following her. His heart clenched with each smile she flashed a

67

uniform. He followed her group into the canteen. People crammed the large room, so he stayed right inside the doorway and watched Audrey move with a sailor toward the piano. A young soldier, who didn't look like he could be more than eighteen, made the instrument sing. Audrey tilted her head toward the sailor, then nodded. She placed her half-empty basket on the floor near the piano and stepped back. Her head bounced in time to the music and then she started to jitterbug with the sailor.

Willard watched a moment before turning and abruptly leaving the building, swinging the door wildly behind him. He stormed to the edge of the platform and stepped to the sidewalk, ready to hike back to the truck. He had to find a way to enjoy the changes in the soldiers when they left the Canteen rather than focus on Audrey.

"All aboard!"

The words stopped him as the soldiers flowed out of the Canteen in a frenzied mass. Two minutes later the last straggler boarded the train, and it pulled out of the station. Audrey and many of the volunteers followed the boys out and stood waving on the platform. When Audrey turned to go back inside, she saw him. A big smile split her face, and she ran to him.

"Willard. How long have you been here?"

"Long enough." His harsh tone stopped her short. He rubbed his hand across his head.

"I don't understand. What do you mean?"

"I saw you flirting with the soldiers and then dancing with a sailor." He leaned into the wall.

"Is that all? Of course I did. That sailor was scared and missing his girl. He asked if I would dance with him to help take his mind off things. I said, 'Certainly.' And I'd say it again. He was a different man when we stopped. It didn't mean anything to me, but it meant the world to him. Don't tell me you're so small that bothered you." Indignation flashed from her eyes, and she practically dared him to tell her she'd read him correctly.

Willard looked down and kicked a snow clod with his foot. "Can you blame me for wishing you were with me instead of him?"

"No. But remember, you don't own me. And I did nothing wrong, so don't even attempt to make me feel bad. It won't work."

"I'm sorry, Audrey. My reaction was wrong, and I don't like it. I know you're doing good work here. Can I make it up to you? Come have supper with me. I have to head back to the ranch before long, but at least we could see each other for a bit."

She opened her mouth, but nothing escaped.

"Ladies, I have the coffee on." Mrs. Sedlacek bellowed.

Audrey looked toward the door. "That's my cue. If you want to wait thirty minutes, I can meet you at the Tom Tom Room. Otherwise, we'll have to try another night."

"I don't get to town every day. You know that."

"True. But I also know Roger comes every weekend on Friday, usually Saturday, and most Sundays, too."

"This is Saturday, and I'm here." He fought to keep from yelling his frustration.

"I know. And I'm here for another thirty minutes. When this train is gone, I'll meet you at the Tom Tom Room." Audrey reentered the building without waiting for his reply.

He watched her leave, and weariness rooted him to the spot. If he went home now, he'd hear his mother's stifled sobs and the unnatural quiet of his sisters tiptoeing around the house. It was as if joy had evaporated from the home with the confirmation of Andrew's death. No matter how hard he prayed, peace eluded him and his family. How could a person find peace when the death was so meaningless?

"Hey, Willard."

He looked up at Roger's voice. "Ready to head back?"

"Yep. I promised your Dad I'd get this stuff in tonight. He's convinced we'll have another blizzard, like the New Year's Day one wasn't enough for him."

Willard grimaced. "That's Father. Always over-prepared. Sure we can't wait another half hour until Audrey gets off?"

"He called the pharmacy while I was there to make sure I was coming back right away." Roger shrugged and looked at the Canteen. "Did you see Lainie in there?"

"I only had eyes for one gal. If Father's calling, he must need us. I'll just try to catch Audrey's eye and let her know I can't stay. It's probably best anyway. I can't talk my way into trouble if I'm not here."

Roger grinned and shook his head. "She does tie your tongue up. Let's get out of here."

Willard hustled into the Canteen and looked around for Audrey. Finally, he spotted her flying out of the kitchen with a tray stacked high with egg salad sandwiches. "Audrey?"

She looked up, and he stopped to soak in her smile. "Roger just told me we have to head back to the ranch now. I'm sorry. Can we grab lunch tomorrow after church?"

Audrey set down the tray and brushed a curl out of her eyes. "I'd like to but need to check with my family." She stilled as a train whistled into the station. "Time to get back to work."

"I know. Sorry about tonight."

"I understand." She gazed at him a moment before bustling back to the kitchen.

As she left, he felt an emptiness that told him he was a goner where she was concerned.

CHAPTER 13

JANUARY 16, 1942

*W*illard looked out his bedroom window and watched Father stagger to the barn. Grief continued to place a heavy imprint on his vibrant body and slow his steps. Willard picked up his baseball from the night table and ran it back and forth through his fingers. Willard had tried to come up with another way to do his part but couldn't. It was time to talk with Father again. He couldn't spend another day watching but doing nothing.

He turned and walked out of the room, down the wooden staircase, and across the frozen yard. Willard flipped the ball in the air. As it descended, he imagined the bombs that had fallen on Andrew's ship and made it his grave. When he entered the barn, he paused and let his eyes adjust to the gloomy interior. Dust particles played in the thin sunrays that pushed their way through ice-crusted windows. Barn cats scampered in the hayloft, but their noise couldn't muffle his father's heartache.

Willard strode across the floor of the structure that smelled of sweet hay and earthy manure. The office sat at the far end, with walls that didn't quite reach the ceiling. As he approached, Willard heard Father scream questions and then saw him sitting in the desk chair, face buried in his hands, shoulders shaking from raw sobs.

"Why, Lord? Why did You take our Andrew? I don't understand why he died. How could You allow this?"

Watching him from the doorway, Willard's impotence congealed in his stomach. He struggled to breathe around the lump in his throat and the questions that mirrored his father's. He carefully cleared his throat and grew more concerned when Father didn't look up and acknowledge his presence.

71

"Father? I need to talk to you about something."

"Go away, son. I can't handle anything right now." The words groaned past taut lips.

Willard looked out of the room. Should he wait since this wasn't a good time? No. He straightened his shoulders. He had to do this now. It would never get easier. He shoved his ball in his coat pocket and cleared his throat again. "I'm sorry, Father, but I can't wait. I have to do something other than sit here on the ranch and grieve. Andrew's gone. And tomorrow I'm going into town to enlist."

His father's head jerked up. Grief-drenched eyes bored into Willard's. Father's jaw squared and his face flushed.

"Like it or not, Willard, you work in an essential occupation. The board won't take you, and I refuse to encourage you in this folly."

"Why won't you understand I have to do this? They killed my brother."

"Vengeance is God's. Willard, don't let hate consume you. Grieve, but don't turn it into hate." Father looked down at his hands, then back in Willard's face. "I love you, son. But if you proceed in this pig-headed enlistment, you will not have my blessing or my help. Your mother needs you right now, and so do I." He stood and moved past Willard. "It's time to go back inside. See what help your mother needs."

He wiped his face with calloused hands and walked through the barn without looking to see if Willard followed. Willard watched him and fought the urge to throw his ball through the window.

* * *

A FRESH SNOW blanketed the ground, turning the streets of North Platte from a dingy grey to a glistening white. Audrey curled her hair and wondered if she'd be ready before Willard arrived. Stealing a glance at her alarm clock, she dropped the brush and reached for some powder. Ready or not, he'd pick her up in fifteen minutes. She couldn't control the smile that curved her lips at the thought of spending time with him.

The Canteen had overflowed with sailors and volunteers when she stopped by on her way home from school to help prepare for the Open House scheduled for the next day. A group of women from Stapleton bustled about the lunch-room and platform trying to keep the coffeepot full and the table loaded with sandwiches and fruit. Because of their presence, the North Platte regulars got the day off. The Canteen may have opened three weeks earlier, but the day passed strangely empty when she didn't spend time encouraging the soldiers.

This afternoon Rae had quickly shooed her away when she spotted Audrey. As she walked home, Audrey'd anticipated the evening with Willard. It seemed longer than a week since she'd seen him.

Looking out the window, she watched Roger's headlights pull to the curb. Pinning her hat in place, she dashed down the stairs and to the door.

"Night, everyone."

"Don't be too late, Audrey." Dad yelled from his spot in front of the fireplace.

"We won't be." She grabbed her coat and scarf and slipped into them then opened the door. On the front porch she bounced into a solid wool coat, and the rough fabric scraped across her cheek.

A low chuckle vibrated against her head. "Now that's quite a welcome."

She looked up into Willard's face and laughed. "Isn't this how you're always welcomed? We like to bowl our guests off their feet. But since we're both still standing, let's get out of here before we're trapped in an endless game of Pitch."

They ran through the cold air to the car and slid into the backseat.

"Thanks for the ride, Roger."

"No problem. Consider me your faithful taxi driver." Roger winked at Audrey through the rearview mirror. "Where to, ma'am?"

"I think you'd better ask the lovely lady sitting next to you."

"Lainie?"

"I really want to see *Mr. & Mrs. Smith*. North Platte has finally joined the rest of the world, and it's showing here. To the theater, Jeeves."

Roger flashed a mock grimace at Lainie and then they rumbled down the brick street to the theater, chatting and laughing. While they stood in line for their tickets, Willard loosely held Audrey's hand on his arm and guided her through the Friday night crowd. His nearness caused her heart to skip, and she wondered at it.

"Penny for your thoughts."

"What?" Audrey looked at Willard, and heat climbed up her neck.

"Tell me what you're thinking. I'll even give you a dime for your thoughts."

"Oh." Her right hand fluttered to her throat, while Willard tightened his hold on her left. "I'm enjoying the evening with you. That's all."

"For some reason, I'm not convinced that's it."

"Well, be a gentleman and let it rest." Audrey scolded him with her best schoolmarm tone. It worked with second graders, so surely it would chastise him.

"Why should I?" A glint of pure mischief dared her to answer him.

Audrey's heart stopped as she considered the ramifications of answering him with complete honesty. No, she couldn't bare her feelings like that. He hadn't earned the right to it yet. "Because you want to spend more than tonight with me."

"All right. What would you like to discuss?"

"How is your family doing? We've been praying for all of you."

Willard stiffened beside her, and she sensed him erect a wall between them. "I suppose we're doing as well as expected, thank you." The line shuffled toward the attendant, and Willard purchased their tickets. "Your show awaits. Let's find some seats."

Audrey strained to keep her face placid. How could she be angry at him for surface comments when that's all she had willingly given him? She quickly forgot her frustration when Willard brought her a Coke and some popcorn. The movie turned out to be a fun comedy of errors that had her rolling with laughter. As they stood to leave, she turned to Lainie. "Wow. I didn't expect a screwball comedy from Mr. Hitchcock."

"Yep, it was good, wasn't it?"

Roger rolled his eyes, then tucked his hands under his chin and batted his eyes at Willard. "It was good wasn't it?"

"Dreamy. That Robert Montgomery is such a dreamboat." Willard pretended to swoon into Audrey.

"Oh, come on, boys. Don't be so silly." Audrey pushed Willard away from her.

Willard straightened and threw her a boyish grin. "You know you were thinking it."

Audrey caught Lainie's eye and saw her fighting not to laugh. She looked away, but laughter bubbled up anyway. "All right, you clowns. I think you owe us girls a soda."

"Nope. Roger, you'll have to buy me a malt to pay for that terrible acting." Lainie pulled him down the street toward Wahl's. Willard and Audrey followed at a slower pace, moving with the flow of people shopping on a Friday night.

Willard looked at a family sitting in their car and then turned to Audrey. "Did you know that, when I was a kid, we often came to town on Saturday nights to people-watch?"

Audrey shook her head. "I didn't know you then. Was that the only reason you came to town?"

"Mother and Father would do some shopping. If Andrew and I had completed our chores for the week, Father would give us each a quarter to spend. We'd usually try to see a movie and get a Coke. We'd hoard the rest for candy."

"Your father was more generous than Dad. He gave us fifteen cents. You rich ranchers." Audrey stilled as she watched his expression fall. "What is it, Willard? I was only joking."

"I know. But I would give the entire ranch to have Andrew back." His voice cracked with raw emotion. "Father won't even discuss me enlisting. How can I make him understand I can't stay on the ranch? I can't pretend everything is okay."

Audrey looked around downtown through the crowds of people. Somewhere there had to be a quiet corner where they could talk without strangers overhearing.

"They all know."

"Who, Willard? Know what?"

"Watch them, Audrey. Everybody looks at me with pity. Don't they understand my family won't be alone? Unless the Japs and Germans are stopped, other families will suffer, too."

"Come on. Let's see if the Tom Tom Room is slow. It's getting cold, and I don't get to wear pants like you." Audrey steered Willard across Dewey and toward the tracks. A few minutes later they stamped the snow from their feet in the Pawnee Hotel lobby. Audrey pulled him through the lobby to an empty table in the tearoom. "Two hot chocolates, please." When the waitress left, she grabbed Willard's hands where they rested lifelessly on the table. "Look at me, Willard." Several seconds passed while she waited for him to comply. "You and your family will get through this. God is walking beside you even in this pain." She tipped his chin with her finger. "Tell me why you want to enlist."

"I have to do something. I won't sit and wait. I've spent my life on the ranch, and now I have to go be part of this. It's bigger than I am. And I ... I have to do it."

Audrey considered him carefully. His emotion surprised her, though she supposed it shouldn't. She searched her mind for something to say, but could think of nothing that would erase his pain. "I wish you'd stay."

Willard shook his head and pulled his hands from hers as the waitress approached. She placed their hot chocolates on the small table. "Can I get either of you anything else?"

"No, this is great." Audrey rubbed her hands together against the sudden chill from Willard's distance.

"If you change your mind, I'll be right over there."

"Thanks." Audrey picked up her cup and blew down into the whipped cream. "Have you prayed about enlisting, Willard?"

He looked up, then back at his hands. With slow movements he picked up the mug and sipped before returning it to the table. "God didn't answer my prayers about Andrew, so why keep trying?"

"Maybe He answered, but it wasn't what you wanted."

"If God told me to, should I enlist regardless of what Father says?"

Audrey frowned. "I don't know. But if you really feel like you are supposed to enlist and you've prayed about it, then I suppose you should. Though I don't like to say that."

"Why?"

"Because we've spent time together." Pain sliced through her heart at the thought of him stepping out of her life.

"Audrey, I want more than friendship with you. You are a special young woman, and I don't want to wonder if some soldier is going to sweep you off your feet. Or if I enlist, that somebody from here in town will snag your heart."

Audrey chewed on her lower lip and considered how to respond. "The soldiers are only in town for a few minutes. It's hardly long enough to do anything more than say 'hello' and smile." She shrugged. "We haven't known each other very long, Willard."

"It doesn't matter. We have the rest of our lives to learn every detail about each other."

Her hands clutched her purse in her lap. Could they really be discussing the possibility of forever? Her head spun at the thought of what he implied. "You know how to move things along. Our friendship has developed so fast. We don't need to rush into anything."

Willard nodded and stared into his mug. "That's not the answer I'd hoped for."

She watched him a moment. *Lord, what can I say to ease his pain?* "Willard, let's take this day by day. I can't imagine life with you off fighting in Africa or the Pacific."

His shoulders slumped as he slouched in the chair. "I don't know what I'm supposed to do."

Audrey placed her hands on the sides of his face and urged him to look at her. "Willard Johnson, you are a good man, and you will find your way through this. And I will be here to help you." *And love you.*

CHAPTER 14

JANUARY 21, 1942

*W*illard jerked in his seat as the train rattled toward Omaha. The close air caused his stomach to churn. What had he done? With each whistle that announced a stop, he fought the urge to get off the train and explain he'd made a mistake.

Monday morning he'd driven to the draft board's office at the National Guard Auxiliary. He'd walked in determined to leave with an assignment on the next train. They'd given him a ticket for the second. Now the determinations of the examining doctors and a final review by the board would determine his steps. Standards were loose. All the talk about farmers and ranchers being essential to the war effort on the home front could evaporate in an instant. Originally, Willard's hope had focused on that. Now rocked by the train, he prayed for direction and peace.

Yesterday Mother and Father received Andrew's few personal effects and scheduled his memorial service for Friday. The image of Willard walking into the room on his two-week enlistment leave dressed in a uniform tamed his grief. He could do something about Andrew's death and the war that raged across the African deserts and Pacific front.

Maybe he could join the Army Air Corps and take to the sky. His spirit jumped at learning to fly and the complete freedom of bouncing through the clouds. What a rush to see the countryside disappear beneath his plane. And surely Audrey's eyes would reflect the twinkle of the pilot's wings on his shoulders when she saw them.

The officer traveling with Willard and the other men stood as the train slowed at the next stop.

"All right, men. We've reached Omaha. Everybody off."

The mishmash of men stood and stretched. Willard recognized a few of the men from North Platte, but many were strangers. As he walked down the narrow aisle, the man behind him tapped him on the shoulder.

"My name's Leroy Jackson."

"Willard Johnson. Nice to meet you."

"You played on the North Platte High baseball team, didn't you?" Leroy's orange hair stuck up all over his head and matched the freckles that dotted his face. His skin was the pale white of someone who didn't work outside, unlike Willard's tanned face and arms.

"Yeah. That was a while ago, though."

"My brother played on Brady's team, so I watched you a few times. You're quite a pitcher."

"Thanks. I loved playing." Willard unconsciously reached in his pocket for the ball he'd left at the ranch.

"Can understand why. Wonder what kind of tests we'll git run through today."

"I don't know. My brother didn't have to do much when he enlisted, but that was before the war. I have a feeling it's different today."

"Yep, lot's changed since Pearl Harbor."

Willard looked at Leroy. He had no idea how much had changed. Willard lowered his head and ignored the rest of the words that babbled from Leroy's mouth. As he stepped off the train, an officer pointed him toward a waiting school bus painted a dirty beige. He climbed aboard and settled in an empty seat, with Leroy next to him.

"So why are you here, Leroy?"

"My number came up. Besides it'd be nice to see part of the world. I've never been farther than Kearney before." The fear in Leroy's eyes contradicted his words' excitement.

"That's why my brother joined."

"Did he get to see the world?"

"More of it than if he'd stayed on the ranch." Willard pulled his baseball cap bill firmly over his forehead. Leroy took the hint and yakked with the nearest guy, across the aisle. Willard watched the narrow downtown buildings turn into open blocks through the bus's windows. What had he gotten himself into?

Seven hours later, after he'd been poked and prodded in places he didn't know existed and in the company of at least a hundred men, Willard wandered back to the bus and waited for the others. He'd passed the physical tests, so nothing should restrict him. He'd return to North Platte, the local board would review his file, and then he'd receive an assignment. It was that simple. He prayed his parents would forgive him.

Nobody said anything when Willard dragged through the door early the next morning. His mother flipped flapjacks at the stove, while Father stood at the coat rack pulling on his heavy scarf and gloves. He leaned into Mother and kissed her on the cheek before he walked outside. Willard watched him stride past without a 'hello' or acknowledgment. His chest tightened as he hung up his coat.

"Don't be too hard on him, Willard. He doesn't want to lose you." His mother's whisper barely reached his ears.

Willard turned toward her and caught himself on the edge of the table. Two tears shimmered down her cheeks. His heart clenched at the pain those represented. "I'm sorry, Mother." The sentence squeezed past the constriction in his heart. "I had to do something."

"I know, son. I know." She turned from the stove and placed a plate of steaming pancakes on the table, then slid a small pitched toward him. "Here's some warm maple syrup. Sit down and eat. But consider how you can make things right with your father. I can't bear the thought of you separated like this. It's too hard after Andrew." She patted his hand, wiped her eyes with her apron, and then returned to the stove.

Willard took in her words but couldn't respond. Before he could think of the right response, his sisters flew down the stairs, loud as a herd of young calves.

"You're here." Twelve-year-old Lettie threw herself against his chest. "I'm so glad you're back, Willard. Father didn't say a word while you were gone."

Ten-year-old Margaret and slim Norah looked at him with big eyes, then descended on the stack of pancakes.

"Slow down, you two. Father and I will need some breakfast, too."

"You mean you haven't eaten all ready?" Norah butchered the words around her mouthful of pancakes. At eight years old, she still lacked key manners.

"No. Shouldn't you be at the bus stop by now?" While Norah turned to look at Mother for confirmation, Willard swiped her plate and took a big bite of pancake. The other girls giggled while Norah glared at him. Willard laughed, ruffled her hair, and then took another bite. Norah reached out to reclaim her plate, ready to fight for what was hers.

Mother leveled a look at Willard. "Norah, no need to fight for your food. Here's a plate of fresh pancakes."

Willard raised an eyebrow. "Thanks for breakfast, Mother. I'm going to see if Father needs any help."

She nodded without looking at him. Willard prayed for wisdom as he walked across the yard. He should have prayed before he ran out and enlisted like Audrey had suggested. Now all he could do was live with the consequences and try to make things right.

He pushed into the barn and waited for his eyes to adjust to the dim light. "Father? Do you need any help?"

"Yes, but obviously not the kind you're willing to give." His words floated from under the hood of the pick-up.

Willard walked over to join him. "Now what's that mean?"

"I need you to stay and help run the ranch. But you have other things planned for yourself." Father stepped back from the truck and slammed the hood down. He reached in his coveralls pockets for a rag and wiped the grease from his hands.

"I'm sorry you feel that way. I took all the tests yesterday and report to the board tomorrow. That's when I'll learn where they put me." As his father continued to study his hands, Willard wished he would make eye contact. "It's done. I'm sorry you're angry at me, and I hope you'll forgive me, but I had to do this."

"You are a pig-headed young man. No one forced you to do any of the things you did this week."

"Don't forget I'm twenty-four. I can do what I please. But I don't want our relationship to change."

"It's too late for that. When you disobeyed and went to the board, everything changed." Father shoved his rag back in its place. When he looked at Willard, betrayal marred his face.

Willard staggered backward as if Father had punched him. *God, what have I done?* "I'm sorry you feel that way. I'm going to get some sleep." Willard lurched from the barn. The back door slammed shut behind him when he entered the house. His sisters watched him with mouths hanging open, but he didn't care. Once he climbed the stairs and entered his room, he threw himself on his bed. A little sleep and everything would be better. It sure couldn't get worse.

The tension in the house didn't ease, and Willard eagerly climbed in the pick-up with Roger Friday morning. One more day at home and he'd go crazy. Roger would pick up supplies while Willard kept his appointment with the draft board. Then they would join his family at Andrew's memorial service.

"This is it, Roger."

"I hope you know what you're doing. I've never seen your dad like this."

"I know. But this is the right thing. I have to do something. This town is filled with trainloads of men who are doing something for the war. That's all I want, too." Images of Audrey working the Canteen slipped into his mind. "Do you think she'll miss me?"

"If she loves you, but I'm not sure leaving now is the best thing."

Willard snorted. "Suddenly you're a Romeo?"

"You know it." Roger waggled his eyebrows at Willard and then turned back to the road. "What's the real reason you're doing this?"

"I—" Willard swallowed against the lump in his throat and tried again. "Andrew died, and I have to fix it somehow."

Silence stifled the truck for a mile. Roger cleared his throat as he drove into town. "You know you can't replace him, right?" He didn't wait before continuing." How long do you think you'll be?"

"I'm not sure. An hour maybe."

"I'll get the supplies and run by the grocery for Mrs. Johnson. I'll plan on meeting you at the drugstore, okay?"

"Sounds good."

As the truck pulled up to the Federal Building at Fifth and Pine, Willard hopped out of the truck. After thumping the hood with his fist, he waved to Roger and dashed into the building. The letter he'd received at the end of the testing had told him to report to the first-floor conference room. He glanced at his watch and saw he was a few minutes early. It didn't matter, he'd go find the room. Always better to be early rather than late.

Ten minutes later Mrs. Potts, the board secretary, ushered him into a room where a panel of three men waited for him. He nodded to Mayor Dent and acknowledged the other two men, who were strangers to him. After he took a seat, the Mayor got the meeting started.

"Willard, thanks for coming in."

"Glad to. I'm eager to serve." Willard leaned forward in the chair, ready to take his orders and move out.

"We appreciate that, Willard, and you did a fine job on all the tests. Passed even the physical, and you'd be amazed at the boys who can't, for whatever reason." The Mayor settled back and laced his fingers across his ample belly.

A sense of satisfaction grew in Willard. This was it. He'd made it and soon would be issued a uniform of his own.

"But, you see, while we all know you'd make a fine soldier, we can't let you go."

Willard shook his head, trying to clear his ears. Surely, he hadn't heard the Mayor correctly.

"Willard, you're a rancher. That's on the essential occupations list, and your father has asked that you be exempted. We will honor his request and won't draft you or let you enlist. Your family has given enough for the war."

A sound like an engine roared in Willard's head. His father had gone behind him to prevent his serving? "I'm ready to serve. Mayor, I want to do my part."

"I understand, but your part, young man, is to help produce the food this country is going to need if we're to win. Your exemption is granted. That's all."

Willard sat in the chair, too stunned to move. "There must be a mistake. I want to serve my country."

"You will, but you'll do it from here."

The two men sitting with Mayor Dent nodded agreement.

The edges of his world collapsed inward. Willard fought the sensation he was stuck in a room with tall walls that moved toward him. They'd trapped him. He had to stay on the ranch.

CHAPTER 15

JANUARY 23, 1942

The familiar tinkle of the bell above the door at Wahl's echoed as Audrey walked through the door. Her gaze darted around the large room until she saw Lainie waiting at the soda fountain for her. Audrey slid between shoppers before she reached the counter and sat on the stool Lainie cleared of her coat and purse.

"Wow. I haven't seen it this crowded since Christmas."

"Someone told me the store got an extra shipment of sugar and word spread quickly. You missed seeing the ration books fly around in here."

"Maybe we'll have to meet at the Tom Tom Room next week." Audrey's thoughts strayed to the crowd at Andrew Johnson's memorial service. The church had overflowed with people offering support to the Johnsons. She'd longed to hug Willard, let him know she cared, but the crush of people had forced her back.

"Wasn't that funeral just awful? Andrew was so young." Lainie pasted a pretty pout on her lips, making Audrey laugh.

"I can't shake it. Mrs. Johnson looked so frail. I can't imagine what it would feel like if something happened to John or Robert." Audrey shuddered. Before the war wrapped up, one or both of them could be called to serve. And Willard couldn't wait to serve. Her thoughts cycled back to Willard.

He hadn't called since Tuesday, when he'd let her know about Andrew's service before telling her the draft board was sending him to be tested. The conversation had been quick since his family had many people to call about the service. Lydia Sparrow and the newspaper had filled in the details. She'd attended the service with her parents and prayed for God to comfort Willard.

He'd sat sandwiched between his sisters, but she'd longed to sit next to him and console him. Tell him how sorry she was about everything. She picked at the folds in her skirt as she wondered how he'd held up under the strain.

"Lainie calling Audrey." Lainie tapped her fire-engine-red nails on Audrey's arm.

Audrey jerked and looked at her, eyes wide. "I'm sorry, Lainie. Did you say something?"

"Who me? No, I prefer talking to myself to wasting breath on you. What's up?"

"My mind's caught on a merry-go-round." She looked up to see the soda jerk standing in front of her. "A cherry Coke, please."

Lainie cocked an eyebrow and then shook her head. "Maybe we'll see Willard and Roger. They breezed through downtown earlier. Willard looked like a walking storm, so I stayed out of his way."

Silence settled over them in a thick fog. As it turned uncomfortable, Audrey searched for a new subject. "I got the strangest letter yesterday. Some GI wrote me a letter and said he got my name from a popcorn ball he grabbed at the Canteen. I have no idea what he meant."

Lainie laughed. "That's nothing to worry about. A couple of weeks ago, some of us made the balls at the Canteen and inserted names and addresses of the gals working. Someone must have added your name to a ball."

"It wasn't Betty, was it?" Audrey smiled as she pictured Betty tucking her name in a ball in the hopes it would distract her from Willard. "I suppose I should write him back."

"There's no harm in writing. I don't think Betty did it, but why not form plan B in case things don't work out with Mr. Storm Cloud."

Audrey clenched her hands as she fought to understand what her heart wanted. "He's entitled to be stormy on a day like today. He's got a good heart, and he's got to be the handsomest man I know. Especially those brown eyes."

"Eyes like chocolate."

"Hmmm. A nice, rich river of chocolate." Audrey sighed at the sadness that filled them now. "But I won't marry the first man who talks to me, war or no war."

"Then I suppose you're not interested in the fine-looking rancher walking your way."

A blush ignited Audrey's cheeks, and she vowed next time she'd grab a stool that allowed her to watch the door. How did Willard always find her when she was having a Coke with Lainie? Slowly she swiveled on the stool. Each argument for why she wasn't ready to run and marry the first man who talked to her fled her mind as her gaze met his. The dark shadows under his eyes couldn't hide the way they sparkled when he looked at her. She wondered if she did the same. Did she deceive herself that she felt nothing for Willard?

"Hello, Audrey. Lainie." He smiled at Audrey then nodded to Lainie.

Audrey studied him, saw fatigue and something she couldn't identify weigh his smile down. The spontaneous enthusiasm he'd carried when they'd met had vanished. Every action and feeling seemed a chore he performed because life required it.

"Willard, how are you? With the service and everything?" Audrey faltered.

"We're surviving. I hate to interrupt, but, Audrey, do you have some time right now? Maybe we could go walk for a few minutes."

Audrey hurt for Willard and the traces of a broken heart lingering in the lines on his face.

Lainie swept her fingers toward them. "Go on, you lovebirds. I'll catch up with Audrey later."

Audrey hugged Lainie, then stood and pulled on her coat, with Willard's help, before following him from the drugstore. The frigid air slapped across her face and threatened to steal her breath. She inhaled against the cold and turned into Willard's shoulder to shield her face from the wind. "Is it March yet?"

"Not quite. Anything special happen in March?"

"We might get a break from the deep-freeze, and it's my birthday month. Each year I wait to see if the daffodils will open in time for a birthday bouquet. Then I know spring is around the corner."

* * *

WILLARD FILED THE INFORMATION AWAY. He'd ask Lainie for the exact date, but now he knew what to give her. He'd talk to the florist at Helen's Flower Shop and order daffodils in case the weather didn't cooperate. He hadn't planned to see Audrey, but after Andrew's memorial service concluded, he longed for an escape. The grief threatened to choke him if he'd stayed at the church one more minute. Audrey was the perfect distraction from everything wrong in his life.

They strolled the block to the Pawnee Hotel, comfortable with each other and with no urge to rush into conversation. Willard hardly noticed the brick buildings that lined the street leading to the Sixth Street Grocery and the train tracks.

Audrey cleared her throat but kept her gaze on the sidewalk in front of her. The disappointments and heaviness of the week threatened to capsize the shaky boat of his life, and her steadiness loomed like an anchor that could still the rocking waves. Just having her by his side reinforced how desperately he needed her.

His steps slowed till he stopped. She looked at him, questions across her face. "Audrey, I've had the ugliest week of my life."

She nodded but stayed quiet, not rushing to fill the lull with words. He looked through the window into the Tom Tom Room. Patrons filled the tables he could see, so Willard steered them toward Molly's Café across the street. He relished the feel of Audrey tucked by his side, but didn't want to force her to stay outside a moment longer than needed.

"Ready to tell me about your week?" She didn't give up easily.

He barely heard the muffled words. Tell her the truth or gloss over? The truth. He needed to see how she'd handle it. "It's been long."

"More than the service?"

He opened the door and followed her into Molly's. The brick walls made the narrow storefront feel cozy rather than crowded. He directed Audrey to a table by the fireplace and pulled out her chair for her. After he seated her, he settled in a chair and found her locked on him. "I went to enlist on Monday."

She nodded slowly and then looked into his eyes. "I take it things didn't go well."

"Oh, I passed all the tests they threw at me, but seems I'm essential here and Father made sure the board labeled me that. There are hundreds of ranchers in western Nebraska, but I'm too essential to draft. Even when I practically begged to serve." He drummed his fingers on the tablecloth.

She reached out and stilled his large fingers with her small hand. "I'm sorry, Willard. And then to have Andrew's service today...I can only imagine how hard it's been." Compassion radiated from her.

He fought the lump in his throat. He didn't want her compassion. He needed her to see him as a man. A man worthy of her love. He'd been ready to tell her about the memorial service, but bit back the sentence off rather than risk more sympathy.

The door opened and a gust of air blew into the café. Audrey looked from him to the door and smiled. Willard turned to follow her gaze and froze. A sailor strode into the café, bringing images of Andrew and the memorial service with him.

"Willard, are you okay?" Audrey watched him carefully.

He shook his head and then focused on her. "Audrey, go out with me tonight. We'll see a movie or find a dance. I miss you and want to think about the possibilities of the future."

A rosy color climbed her cheeks, but she didn't look away. "Okay. Meet me at the Canteen in an hour? I promised Rae I'd swing by and help get everything reorganized. That shouldn't take long and then I'll be free to spend the rest of the evening with you."

"All right. I'll be there at six."

Audrey nodded. "Today was a day that tries the soul of any teacher. I never thought I'd get Petey Sedlacek to settle down to his studies."

Willard listened to Audrey's story while fighting the image of Andrew's battered body each time his gaze landed on the sailor seated at the table behind Audrey. The waitress brought them cups of coffee and a slice of pie they shared. Willard drank his coffee black and listened as Audrey talked.

After a bit Audrey looked at her watch and stood. "I'll take care of my responsibilities at the Canteen." She leaned over and brushed his cheek with her lips. "See you soon."

Willard nodded but couldn't respond. Her spontaneous kiss had stopped his world. With the faintest touch, his heart began to hope again. Maybe she felt more for him than friendship. He pulled enough coins from his pocket to cover their coffee and pie and placed them on the table with a small tip. He had an hour to kill before he collected Audrey from the Canteen. Pulling on his coat, he headed out to find Roger and fill him in on the new plan. Roger wouldn't mind the excuse to spend more time in town and catch up with Lainie or one of the other gals on his list.

At five forty-five, Willard strode down the sidewalk toward the Canteen. He'd arrived a few minutes early, so they could grab a quick bite, probably back at Molly's, and then go find a dance with Roger and Lainie. Roger had promised not to kill them, and the stars would put on a brilliant display in the cloudless sky.

A train whistle blew as he crossed the street toward the station. The sound of brakes thrusting against iron wheels grated across the air.

Willard sighed at the realization that Audrey would work until this group departed even if she'd just gone to help organize. He could watch her work her magic. Then he noticed the soldiers coming off the train. This group of boys looked different from the others he'd watched disembark as they sprinted to the station without prompting. Many walked with a swagger. Word must be circulating that North Platte offered something special.

The hair on the back of Willard's neck stood on end as he watched one group approach Audrey and a couple of other platform girls. He took a few steps toward the group, watchful of the soldiers' movements. Audrey backed up to the wall, but smiled. She and the other girls talked with them. One of the soldiers leaned into Audrey, and she flinched away from him.

"That's enough." Willard propelled himself through the crowd and pulled back his right arm as he approached. He tapped the soldier on the shoulder with his left hand. As the man turned toward him, Willard threw a right hook into his nose.

A hand grabbed his coat collar. Spun him around. He pulled both fists up to his face to protect it. Ignored a tap on his shoulder. Punched the nearest soldier. Winced as pain exploded under his right eye from a solid hit. Swung out at anyone he could reach. Connected with a solider with corporal stripes. Fell to his knees as someone sucker-punched him in the kidneys. Looked up. Saw Audrey reach for him, screaming something he couldn't hear. Roger rushed to her side. Pushed the soldiers back. Roger and Audrey hauled Willard to his feet. Pulled him around the corner of the station. Willard looked up at Audrey, stumbled back at the emotion on her face. Fear and concern vied for control of her features. She opened her mouth. Closed it. Opened it again.

"You have a lot of explaining to do, Mr. Johnson."

Willard flinched. She'd called him Mr. Johnson. Definitely not a good sign.

"And don't expect to spend any time with me until you can defend your actions. Furthermore, don't bother coming near the Canteen. I'm sure you'll be banned after that little performance."

He watched her turn and dart away.

"She can't get away from me fast enough, can she?"

Roger shook his head. "You've really done it this time, Willard. Wait till your father gets a look at your face."

CHAPTER 16

JANUARY 23, 1942

*A*udrey fumed as she stalked back to the other girls on the platform. "Of all the nerve. What does he think he's doing?"

Cora Black laughed and handed Audrey her basket. "Willard Johnson is as jealous as any man I've ever seen."

"You must be wrong, Cora." Confusion flooded her mind. He didn't have any reason to be jealous. She'd never done anything to harm or cheapen their friendship. "If he cared about me, surely he wouldn't make such a spectacle of himself. I'm going inside." Audrey forced herself to walk rather than run into the station. She fought the urge to pull on her coat and escape through the back exit. Everybody would talk about the fight as soon as the train left. Gossip made her stomach clench. She looked for a way to keep busy and distract herself. Seeing a group surrounding a long kitchen table making mountains of sandwiches, she set her basket to the side. "How can I help?"

Mable Evans looked up from the table where she peeled hardboiled eggs for egg salad. "We're fine, Audrey. You should go home and get some rest. We're ready for tomorrow, the trains leaving, and you're working too hard. Take care of yourself so you can help the boys."

The starch drained from Audrey's backbone at the words. Exhaustion and confusion replaced her careful composure. Maybe she could escape the gossip after all. "Thank you, Mrs. Evans. I'll see you tomorrow."

"The weekend's covered, dear. Don't come back until Monday."

Audrey tried to feel glad, since she had tests to grade before Monday. Yet, two days away from the Canteen made her wonder what she would do with herself. Maybe she shouldn't have chased Willard off after all.

* * *

As ROGER'S car bounced over the last hill before coasting into the ranch, Willard groaned. His entire face radiated pain, and he didn't know if his back would be the same anytime soon.

"Those soldiers didn't stand back and take it, did they?"

"No. What was I thinking?"

"Honestly, you weren't. In all the years I've known you, I've never seen you do something like that. You're the level-headed one, remember?"

Willard gingerly touched his eye. It was swelling fast. "I know, and after this experience, I hope that doesn't change. The whole world seems upside down right now."

"I doubt fighting will right it. Especially with Audrey. Did you see the look she gave you? Not a pretty one, bud." Roger whistled between his teeth.

The sound pierced Willard's throbbing head, and he moaned. "What will I tell Father?"

"I'd plead the Fifth. But if that doesn't work, how about admit the truth. Tell him you're insanely jealous of men in uniforms because they can serve and spend a few minutes at the Canteen. So you laid into one that looked cross-eyed at your girl. I'm sure he'll love that." Roger swerved to avoid a pothole and pulled to a stop in front of the house. "You're too smart to do dumb things like this."

"Could you save the sarcasm for a day that I'm able to counter?" Willard opened the passenger door and rolled out of the car. "Maybe I'll be lucky and can sneak up to my room."

"Why would that make you lucky, son? And what did you do to your face?"

At the sound of his father's deep voice, Willard considered running but knew he wouldn't get far. He tried to square his shoulders, but couldn't straighten his back against the fist imprinted in it. "I guess I lost my temper, Father."

"Actually, I think he lost his sanity. Temporarily." Roger ducked and grinned as Willard considered walloping him for the comment.

"We'll talk about it later, but let's get you inside and see what your mother can do about your eye. It's going to turn some bright colors for you."

"Traitor." Willard whispered it over his shoulder and then followed his father into the house.

* * *

AUDREY FOUGHT her anger as she marched the blocks to her house. Who did Willard Johnson think he was? The last thing she needed was for him to serve as her protector. Guard her from what? The soldiers and sailors who streamed through North Platte on the trains? Young men she'd see for roughly twenty minutes before they left again for distant battlegrounds. His actions bordered on possessiveness, and she refused to stand for it.

"I won't let some man push me around." She wanted to shout toward his ranch and pound them into his thick skull. "What do I do, Lord? I'm so humili-ated." She wanted to hug the emotion to her and use it as a shield to shield her heart from Willard. But it was too late. Sometime during the past two months, he had crept under her defenses. Now, tonight, she hated how vulnerable that made her.

She dragged up the steps to the front door. She considered sitting on the porch swing and moping, but the night was too cold. Instead, she walked in the house and headed upstairs.

"Audrey? Is that you?" Dad called to her from the dining room. "We're sitting down to eat. Come join us."

Audrey stopped on the stairs. Even though she wanted to crawl onto her bed and wallow in her mixed-up feelings, she turned around and entered the dining room.

"What happened to you?" Leave it to John to be blunt.

"Nothing."

Mama bustled in from the kitchen with an extra place setting. "I thought you might stay downtown with Willard or Lainie."

"That's what I thought too, Mama. But plans changed."

"Let me know if you want to talk about it later, out of the ears of all these men." Mama winked at her and returned to her seat at the foot of the table.

"Thank you, but I'm all right. I'm a bit tired, so it's probably a good thing I'm home tonight. I have schoolwork to catch up on before Monday."

The meal passed quickly, with conversation flowing in all directions. After cleaning up, everyone gathered in the living room to listen to the radio. Audrey carried down a stack of spelling tests and worked on them while half-listening to the background dialogue. As time dragged, she wished she were anywhere but curled on the couch. Why had Willard behaved so out of character, with the manners of a bull?

* * *

THE DAYS DISSOLVED into each other as the snow slowly melted from the sidewalks in town. Audrey missed Willard with an intensity that shook her to the core. He hadn't called or tried to find her in town. His actions at the canteen filled her mind with questions. At the end of each, she missed him. When Lainie asked why she didn't do anything about the distance between them, Audrey shrugged. What could she do? They'd both seen red when they'd parted. He had probably decided she wasn't worth the effort and moved on to the next girl. There were certainly enough willing victims lined up in North Platte.

Audrey spent every spare minute at the Canteen. The mornings flew as she taught reading and English, her afternoons filled with math, science, and history, and then she walked as fast as she could to the train station. She'd tuck her book bag under a table in the kitchen, toss her coat beside it, and wander into the lunchroom. With the phrase, "I have the coffee on," the large room would pulsate from barren to overflowing with people. Now that there were others to work the platform, Audrey manned the magazine or coffee table until a soldier would pull her out for a quick dance in front of the piano. Often the dance led to the soldier telling her about his girl back home. She stashed stamps in her pocket to stick on the letters home those soldiers handed her. On the walk home, she'd drop the letters off at the post office and pray an eventual safe return home for the writer.

Prayers for the uniforms tripped off her tongue almost without stopping, yet she couldn't bring herself to do the same for Willard. She wanted to, but couldn't find the expression to address the rift between them. Instead, she walked alone through the sharp nights and hoped for an end to their separation.

* * *

AFTER A QUIET MORNING, Father hauled Willard out to the barn to work on a tractor. Silence stretched until Father stepped back from the tractor and wiped his hands on a rag. "Son, are you ready to explain what happened in town yesterday?"

Willard examined the engine, unable to meet Father's eyes. Willard didn't know where to start. He'd never possessed a temper before Andrew died. Life required too much energy to make it worthwhile. Now he slogged through time with anger weighing him down. "I don't know how to, sir."

"Look at me."

Reluctantly, Willard faced his father.

"This isn't who you are. I know it. And I think that gal you travel to town to see knows it, too. But that doesn't justify your actions."

"I know."

"You have got to control your reactions. Since Andrew's death, you haven't acted like yourself." Father shoved the rag back in his pocket. "Son, this has been difficult for all of us." He swallowed hard and then looked at the ground.

"Father, I'm not sure what came over me, but I won't let it happen again."

"I know you won't. Your mother and I raised you to be much more than that display. Now let's get back to work so we're ready when the weather breaks."

The hard work on the ranch failed to sidetrack Willard from the Audrey-sized ache in his heart. His body healed from the punishment he'd received, but had he ruined things with Audrey? She fit the hole he hadn't known existed until she'd danced into his life. How had things gotten so messed up? An ice storm Saturday night kept Willard home with his family Sunday. The rest of the week saving stranded cattle occupied him. Thursday he and Roger delivered hay and feed to the shelters scattered around the fields.

"So are you going to do something about it?" Roger heaved a bale of hay Willard's direction.

"About what?" Willard caught the bale, then brushed straw from his jacket. Roger needed to leave him alone.

"You know exactly what I mean. Are you going to avoid town and church for another week, all to evade Audrey?"

Willard puffed out a breath as he counted to ten. Then he counted to ten again. Next time he'd head for twenty from the beginning. "Why are you so committed to me fixing things? Maybe there's nothing to remedy."

"Not from what I hear. You both sidestep each other, because neither one of you will admit you were stupid. You should have never started a fight." Roger raised his hand to silence Willard when he started to interrupt. "And Audrey's convinced you need to take the first step. You're both working too hard to dodge the issue. One of you has to act like the adult here."

"And you think I'm the one who needs to?"

"You are the one who tossed the first punch."

Willard hurled his hands up and stomped past Roger. The realization he couldn't get far without the truck stopped him. "So what do you want me to do? Waltz up to her front step and sweep her off her feet?"

"I'd try taking her to lunch after church. You have to do something other than circumvent her the rest of your life. North Platte isn't that big."

"Sure. I'll call her up, and I'm certain she'll race to meet me at Wahl's for a soda. Sounds like a winner of an idea. Let me know what else you think I should do, Sherlock. I'm sure it'll be great." Willard wanted to bite his tongue off. Where had all that venom spurted from? "I'm sorry, Roger. I'm out of line. I know you're trying to help, but we'll have to figure this out on our own."

"Then I suggest you get to figuring before she disappears. She won't wait forever, and some soldier will be smart enough to snatch her up before she's taken."

Willard hung his head. "I know. That's the problem."

CHAPTER 17

JANUARY 30, 1942

*A*udrey slid Grandma's figurines and delicate china cups lined up in rows in front of the prized plates from the china hutch one by one as she dusted its never-ending surfaces. After a full week at school and the Canteen, Audrey didn't have the patience to deal with them, but the moment supper ended, Mama had handed her the dust rag with a stern look.

"This is awful." Audrey threw down the rag and stomped her foot. "Why does he have to be such an idiot?"

Mama walked into the room and frowned at her. "I'm not sure who you're referring to, but you've got a long way to go on the dusting. It'll be an inch thick before you get done at the rate you're moving."

"Sorry, Mama. I really would rather do anything else tonight." Audrey's lips curved down in a pout.

"We all feel that sometimes, but chores remain forever."

Audrey forced her frown into a smile as she picked up the rag from the floor where she'd thrown it. "I know. I'll get back to work." She finished dusting the surfaces then carefully lifted each piece back into position. She stifled a sigh that rumbled from her toes up her throat. This night would never end.

Mama moved through the room and stopped when she reached the doorway. "Mrs. Evans called earlier today. Tomorrow the church youth group is skating on the south fork of the Platte River. Mrs. Evans asked if you could chaperone. I told her you'd be delighted."

Audrey groaned as thoughts of standing outside and freezing while young couples zipped around the ice flashed through her head. "I'm working at the Canteen, Mama, like every other Saturday this month."

"It won't fold if you take one day off. And you told me yourself volunteers have flooded there since the Open House two weeks ago. Give them a chance to serve. You know you won't do anyone any good if you work yourself to death. Besides, I promised Mrs. Evans, so you'll go." Mama left the room with a firmness to her gait that telegraphed no arguments would stand. Like it or not, Audrey would chaperone.

"Guess I'd better borrow some long johns," Audrey muttered.

Early the following afternoon Audrey followed her brothers to the church. Everyone would meet in the parking lot and caravan the few miles to the river. As she walked, Audrey controlled the urge to waddle. With thick wool socks on her feet and long johns tucked under her skirt, she felt far from glamorous. "Kate Hepburn wouldn't look like this."

"Yeah, sis. She'd wear pants." John snickered at her as he strode along in his dungarees. He insisted they were comfortable and even offered her a pair, but Audrey couldn't imagine feeling feminine dressed in them.

The parking lot overflowed with young people standing around cars when they arrived. John and Robert quickly found their friends and left Audrey standing by herself, searching for the other chaperones. When she found them, she realized she was easily twenty years younger than them and the lone single woman. What on earth had Mama been thinking? This promised to be a long afternoon.

Mrs. Evans exited the church and quickly organized the group into carloads. "Whichever car you ride in to the Platte is your ride home, so keep track of your driver. If they leave without you, you might find yourself stranded. Have a good time, everyone, and make sure you're back before dark."

As she slid onto the backseat of an older Model T, Audrey scanned the group to see if her brothers had rides. When she couldn't find them, she settled against the car next to Rebecca Key and placed her ice skates in her lap. "They're old enough to take care of themselves," she whispered to herself.

"What was that, Audrey?" Graham Hudlow looked at her through the rear view mirror.

Audrey blushed when she realized he'd heard her. Of all the luck, she couldn't believe Mrs. Evans had paired her with Graham. Somehow she'd missed him in her earlier scan. He'd been scarce since the dance in December, and every time she saw him, he'd given her the cold shoulder. "Nothing, Graham. Let's get going. I'm sure the kids are eager to skate."

The town of North Platte sat between the two forks of the Platte River. Today the group would skate on the south fork if there was enough ice. A couple of men from the church had checked out the ice the previous day and deemed it thick enough. Audrey wouldn't believe it until she saw the ice for herself. Since the Platte was an inch deep and a mile wide, as locals liked to say, if the ice cracked under someone's weight, nobody had far to fall. Still she'd feel better once she'd been on the ice and tested it for herself.

When Graham pulled up to the Platte, kids from the church spilled from cars and onto the ice. Their excited shouts filled the air as some sank to sit on rocks to put on their skates. Audrey watched them, unable to find energy to mirror their enthusiasm.

"Are you going to join us on the ice, Audrey, or stand and watch the fun all afternoon?" Graham's voice held a challenging edge to it that stiffened Audrey's spine.

"I'll be along in a minute, but first I'm going to check the ice." It only took a moment of skating to assure herself that the ice would hold. Then she settled against a rock to watch the kids to note how comfortable they were with the ice and each other.

Graham circled back around. "You ready?"

"I need to watch a bit longer." She couldn't explain that skating with Graham felt like a betrayal.

"If you're ever ready to join the fun, let me know."

Audrey settled onto a rock after carefully arranging her coat beneath her, grateful for the thick, warm sweater and blouse. The day felt fairly balmy for this time of year. She slowly laced her skates as d the group break into pairs. Loneliness settled on her, and she wished Mama had left her alone. When she'd delayed as long as possible, Audrey stood and hobbled over the uneven ground to the river's edge.

As soon as she stepped onto the ice, Graham joined her. "Can I offer you my arm, Audrey?" His eyes mirrored eager hope.

She bit her lower lip and looked up at him. What harm could come of skating with him? "All right. Be a gentleman, Graham."

"I always am, mademoiselle." The afternoon shadows lengthened as they skated. Audrey watched for any couples that tried to wander off by themselves, but the kids behaved. The sun's disappearance cooled the day, and a shiver danced up and down her frame.

"Looks like it's time to get you back to the car."

Audrey nodded as her teeth clacked against each other. "The others are ready to head back, too. Can you gather our riders?" She climbed off the ice and headed to his car without waiting to see if he'd comply. As another shiver shook her shoulders, she longed for a warm blanket and mug of hot chocolate.

When Graham walked over, he had Robert and John in tow. "I thought I'd drop you off at your house instead of going back to the church. Don't worry, Audrey, the other kids have rides."

She nodded and watched the fields fade into town. When Graham pulled up to their curb, the boys bounded out of the car with quick thanks. Audrey opened her door, but stilled when he placed a hand on her arm.

"Join me for dinner this Friday?"

She froze at his words. Did she want to say yes? And what about Willard? Her mind race as she considered what she needed and how to avoid hurting either of these men. "I really don't think I can on Friday. I'm sorry, Graham."

"How about the following week?" He leaned forward like an eager puppy.

At his hopeful expectation, she didn't have the heart to say no. "Okay."

"I'll call with the details. Thanks, Audrey. You won't be disappointed."

As Graham pulled away, she wasn't concerned about whether she would be disappointed. Instead, her thoughts centered on Willard Johnson. Would he care that she had a date with someone else? Her heart wished it was so, while her head said nothing could be further from the truth. That simple realization bruised her heart.

CHAPTER 18

FEBRUARY 8, 1942

*P*eople crowded the church lobby and spilled down the lobby steps when Willard and his family arrived for the morning service. A cloying mix of perfumes threatened to suffocate him in the tight space in the vestibule. He squeezed around a small gaggle of older women chattering and then into the sanctuary, eyes focused straight in front of him. Maybe if he concentrated he wouldn't look to see if a redhead occupied her usual pew. He fought to quiet the war in his heart, but failed. He sank onto a back pew and bowed his head. *Father, I don't know how to get out of this mess we're in. Help me.*

A finger tapped his shoulder. Willard opened his eyes and looked into Betty Gardner's face.

"Hey there, cowboy. I hear you're alone now. Maybe I should give you one more chance." Her painted lips curled into a pretty, red smile.

He paused and wished he could say yes. Spending time with Betty wouldn't solve his problems with Audrey, though. A new thought darted across his mind, and he stilled. Maybe Audrey would understand why he had acted the way he did at the Canteen if she saw *him* with somebody else. This might be the ticket out of their mess.

"I can join you for lunch. Where would you like to go?"

Betty's eyes danced with delight and a touch of triumph. "We can decide where to go after church. See you then."

Willard watched her leave and wondered why he didn't feel anything. An empty deadness filled his chest, the spark Audrey created in him absent. The choir took its place at the front, signaling the service would start soon. He couldn't spot Audrey anywhere. His pulse raced at the thought that lunch with Betty might be wasted. What if Audrey didn't see them together? He couldn't have lunch with Betty otherwise. Willard cringed as his thoughts registered. What depths he had fallen to, all for the sake of pride.

Mother slid into the pew next to him. "Are you all right, Willard?"

"I will be. What are we doing after church?"

"We'll head back home as usual. Why?"

"A friend wanted to have lunch, but I forgot Roger didn't come to town. We'll have to catch up another time." Willard tried to keep relief from coloring his face. Now he had a reasonable excuse to cancel lunch.

"Are you sure?"

"Yep. I'll go tell her now." Willard avoided his mother's sharp gaze as he stepped from the pew. He couldn't see Betty, but Lainie Gardner sat halfway across the sanctuary. He walked toward her, hope squaring his shoulders. "Lainie, do you know where Betty is?"

"No." Lainie's expression hardened. "How could you do this to Audrey? She'll be crushed when she finds out."

He shrugged and turned to look for Betty. "I doubt she'll even notice. She doesn't seem to miss me much right now."

"You are the biggest fool I know, Willard Johnson. If you play with Betty to get at Audrey, you'll have three angry women knocking on your door. I completely misread you. To think I thought you were good for Audrey." She turned her back on him and tossed her hair over her shoulders.

Lainie's words stung as they hit their mark. He wanted to believe they didn't reflect him. He had more honor than she gave him credit for.

"Why are you waiting? Go find my sister and break my best friend's heart. I'm through with you."

He turned to leave and nearly knocked Audrey off her feet. She stared at him, mouth gaping. She turned and hurried away from him. "Audrey. Wait."

The stares of the nearby parishioners bored through him. He hardly noticed as he dashed after her. "Wait. You don't understand." He reached her as she pushed open the exit. "Stop, Audrey. Let me explain."

She stopped, the door cracked as she held it. "Like you've explained the brawl you started at the Canteen? Like you've explained the fact you haven't called or stopped by to see me in two weeks? Maybe this will surprise you, but I don't need you. If that's how you're going to treat me, go find Betty and good riddance." Audrey trembled as she spoke. Her eyes that usually twinkled with joy now sparked with anger and hurt.

Willard fought the urge to pull her to him and calm her.

He raked his fingers through his hair. His gaze darted around the lobby as the sound of the choir singiing "'Tis So Sweet to Trust in Jesus" slipped from the sanctuary. He brought his focus back to her before she disappeared. "Audrey, I'm so mixed up and mad at me right now. Don't ask me to explain. I couldn't if I tried. Maybe it's all because I feel things with you I've never felt for anyone else."

Audrey stared at him, her crossed arms telegraphing she didn't believe him. "That's real helpful. Makes me feel all warm and gushy inside. Next time, try something original, like the truth."

Willard watched the fire dance in her gaze. He'd never seen Audrey this worked up and stood transfixed. As he replayed her words, his head began to roar. He'd laid his heart on the table, and she accused him of lying. She couldn't be worth the trouble and the pain. As she turned to leave, he grabbed her elbow.

"I spoke the truth. If you're unwilling to accept them, there's nothing I can do about that."

Audrey shook his hand off. He watched her leave and made no move to stop her.

Lainie stood behind him, lines etching her face into a mask of disgust. "You are something else, Willard." She shook her head and frowned. "You're letting the best woman in town walk away."

"Better than you, Lainie?" Willard smiled in an attempt to distract her.

"What a waste of a good-looking man. Guess you've spent too much time talking to cows. Wooing a woman is a bit different." She pushed past him and followed Audrey outside.

Willard watched Lainie chase Audrey. How had things spiraled out of control so fast? He had walked over to tell Betty he wasn't interested in lunch. Audrey's anger at him burned brighter than it had before. "Women." He snorted and stomped back into the sanctuary.

* * *

AUDREY COULDN'T STOP the tears that poured down her cheeks. She brushed them aside as quickly as she could before they froze to her face.

"Audrey."

She kept walking despite the concern in Lainie's voice.

"Talk to me, Audrey."

"I want to be alone." She snuffled and swiped more tears away, angry at herself for letting Willard hurt her. She sucked in a breath and tried to staunch the flow.

Lainie caught up, took one look at Audrey, and threw her arms around Audrey. "Oh, honey. He's not worth it. He's some rancher who thinks he's God's gift to women."

"But it looked like he was my gift, too."

* * *

AFTER THE SERVICE, Betty waltzed up to Willard. "Ready to go to lunch?"

Willard sensed her tightening a noose around his neck with that one question. He rolled his neck in a small circle and tried to shake the rope.

"Willard, are you ready?" Haughtiness dripped from her words as she stared at him.

"Actually, I tried to find you before the service to let you know I can't go after all."

"Why not? I went home and changed for the occasion."

He took in her red pout, relieved he didn't need an excuse. "Roger didn't come in this morning, so I have no way to get back to the ranch if I stay. I'm sorry, Betty."

A cloud marched across her face.

"Have a great week, Betty. Sorry I can't make lunch."

Rather than wait to receive her wrath, he turned away. As he walked, he realized the woman he wanted to spend time with was a redhead he angered each time he saw her.

CHAPTER 19

FEBRUARY 12, 1942

*B*y Thursday her second graders needed a break—even the ever perfect Janey Thorson. Audrey stared out the window and wished the calendar would magically flip to the last day of school.

"Okay, kids. It's time for recess."

The kids jumped up and raced to put their coats on.

"Line up. Janey gets to lead today."

Janey proudly walked to the front as the other kids jostled into place behind her. As Audrey prepared to open the door so they could walk to the playground, an older student entered the classroom and handed her a note. She thanked him and tucked the note in her pocket.

"Let's see how quiet we can be."

The kids tiptoed down the hall. When they turned the corner and rammed the door to the playground, the children shouted in glee. Audrey smiled and wished she possessed their ability to find simple pleasures every day. She stuck her gloved hand in her pocket and pulled out the note. At its simple message, she stilled. "You're needed at the office." Noticing Mrs. Mulligan across the playground, she motioned back inside. When Mrs. Mulligan nodded and waved her toward the door, Audrey ducked inside and jogged to the principal's office.

"Hi, Doris." Audrey stopped when she saw a bouquet of red roses sitting on the desk. "Those are gorgeous."

"Hello, Miss Stone. I'm glad you think so, since they were delivered for you."

Audrey gawked from the flowers to Doris.

"Go on. Take them. Someone wants you to enjoy them." Her smile melted the hard freeze that settled in Audrey's limbs.

Audrey grabbed the flowers and walked out of the office with her nose buried in the fragrant petals. She placed them on her desk and pulled out the note before rushing back to the playground. Once there, she read the note. "I'm so sorry about Sunday. Please do me the honor of having lunch with me on Valentine's Day. I'll call for you at noon if it's all right. Willard." She closed her eyes before reading it again. Her eyes hadn't deceived her.

As soon as her last student headed for home, Audrey pulled on her coat. She cradled the vase filled with roses in her arms. The roses' sweet fragrance tickled her nose during the walk home and brought a smile to her face. She swept up the stairs and into her room. The bouquet looked perfect on her vanity in front of the mirror.

"What a pretty bouquet."

Audrey looked up to see Mama standing in the doorway. "Willard sent them. He wants to take me out on Valentine's Day."

"Sounds like he's trying to say he's sorry."

"That's what his note says. I think I'll let him tell me in person on Saturday." Audrey followed her mother down the stairs and stopped at the hall table to call Willard. She couldn't stop the rush of excitement that flooded her at the thought of seeing him again.

* * *

FRIDAY EVENING AUDREY considered her reflection in the mirror on her vanity and fingered a rose. She must have lost her mind when she'd told Graham she'd have dinner with him. He would pick her up in twenty minutes, and dread filled her.

Graham. The man who thought she looked beautiful mucking stalls. She knew what to expect from an evening home with her family. Graham Hudlow was a completely different matter. He'd had a crush on her for years, and while good-looking, he did nothing to make her heart race. Every time she thought of him, Willard's face and their lunch tomorrow played across her mind. If she wasn't careful, she'd go crazy comparing the two men. Her thoughts whispered they couldn't be compared since only one made her pulse pound.

As the doorbell pealed, the image of Graham dressed as an eager beaver flashed in her mind. She tried to wipe the picture away as her shoulders shook from laughter. With a quick pinch of her cheeks, she grabbed her purse and headed downstairs. The sound of hushed voices filtered up the stairs.

"We won't be late, Mrs. Stone." She looked over the banister to see Graham shuffle in place as he spoke.

"That's fine." Audrey finished her way down the stair, and her mom turned to smile at her. "Have a good time, Audrey." Her mother's soft voice calmed Audrey's remaining butterflies.

She gave Mama a quick kiss on the cheek and then accepted Graham's arm as they walked outside and to his car. When she sank onto the front seat, she tried to quell the voice in her head that compared it to Roger's Packard. She should be grateful he had a car and they weren't walking to dinner.

Graham ushered her into the King Fong Café with a flourish. After they sat and the waiter took their orders, the evening dragged as he talked about his job as a brakeman for the railroad. While every detail about the trains fascinated him, Audrey tried to hide her yawns behind her hand.

"Am I boring you, Audrey?"

"No, I'm sorry, I've had a long week." *And I wish I were curled up in bed, dreaming about tomorrow with Willard.* She owed it to Graham to speak up, but the thought of disappointing him after he'd tried so hard crippled her.

As she twirled her lo mein onto chopsticks, she told him about the Canteen and her students. Before long, Graham laughed as she regaled him with Petey Sedlacek's adventures. "He's got a good heart, but that boy can find trouble anywhere."

"Sounds like me when I was his age."

Audrey nodded at the similarities, remembering well the escapades that Graham had gotten into frequently in grade school.

Graham looked at his hands where they sat on top of the table. "Thanks for humoring me, Audrey. I wanted to know if there could be anything between us."

"Graham, we've been friends a long time, but I'm not interested in anything else right now."

"I understand." He placed a few bills on the table and stood. "Let's get you home before my coach turns into a pumpkin."

Ten minutes later Audrey offered her hand to him. "Thank you for a nice meal, Graham."

"You're welcome. I'm sorry we didn't work out."

As she watched him leave, Audrey hurt for him.

The night had confirmed that one man held her heart in his hands. She prayed Willard would hold it gently and that she'd made the right choice.

* * *

SATURDAY MORNING PASSED SLOWLY as she shook the evening with Graham aside and waited for Willard to pick her up. After hearing about Audrey's outing with Graham, Lainie had insisted Audrey adopt a grand scheme to remake herself. Lainie swore wearing a gown designed for a movie starlet would catch and hold Willard's attention. It might be a lunch date, but it was Valentine's Day, so every detail counted. Lainie hadn't relented until Audrey insisted she would be herself. As Audrey waited for Willard to arrive, she added her mama's pearls to the tailored A-line dress she wore. Its mint-green color had caught her eye the moment she saw it in the window of Rhode's Dress Shoppe. When Willard picked her up, his smile telegraphed how much he liked her look.

No matter how she teased or cajoled, Willard refused to tell her where they were going, insisting on a surprise.

Audrey squealed when he turned onto the lane that led to the country club on the outskirts of town. "If I didn't know better, I'd say you're a show-off."

"Why's that?"

"You keep taking me new places."

Willard parked the car and then got out and opened her car door. She placed her hand on his arm and followed him inside. A waiter led them to a table that overlooked the snow-covered course.

After admiring the view, Audrey turned to him. "Have you golfed here?"

"No, I don't have the time or patience for the game. Why chase a tiny ball for miles? I'll take a baseball diamond any day." He grabbed her hand and held it like it was his last chance. "Audrey, I have a couple of things I want to say before I somehow ruin our conversation."

"You don't do that ... often."

"Lately, I do it a lot. I've spent time trying to figure out my actions. I guess I get so mad when I see you around men in uniform, because I can't be one."

"Willard, there's no need to be jealous of them."

"I want you to respect me the way you respect them."

Her mind went blank at his words. Did he really think she didn't respect him? A waitress appeared before she could answer. After they placed their orders, Audrey pulled her hand free. "I don't see you any differently than the other boys. You're serving here, and that's important."

"It's not the same." His shoulders sagged as if he carried a large boulder.

She wanted to wipe the furrows from his brow. "I don't know how to help you, Willard. A uniform wouldn't change how I see you. I like the man you are." She paused until he looked into her eyes. "Just as you are. And a uniform of dungarees or olive green won't change that one bit."

"I believe you when I'm sitting next to you, hearing you speak. It's when I'm alone or see you at the Canteen that I doubt."

"You have to trust me, Willard. Why would I want a fling with someone who won't be around for more than twenty minutes, when I could build forever with you?"

A flash of emotion, possibly hope, appeared in his gaze. Maybe this time he'd truly understood her.

CHAPTER 20

*W*illard flexed his tired arms before grabbing another bale of hay and throwing it from the truck to the waiting cattle. A chill had settled deep in his bones, and he wanted the day finished. After heaving three more bales over the side of the truck, he knocked on the top. Father moved the truck over the hill to the next feeding site. The tires worked to find traction as the truck skidded along rough ruts worn into the hard ground. The sandhills didn't produce much for the cattle during the summer, but during winter it produced nothing. So they plowed across the hills, dropping hay to keep the cows alive through the cold.

As he rode, Willard hunkered down in the truck's bed among bales of hay. The wind had died, but the air penetrated his layers. He couldn't feel his toes any better than he could sense what his heart wanted. It seemed as barren as the hills that dipped into valleys around him.

Memories of time with Audrey slipped into his mind. The feel of her hand in his. The softness of her skin. He pulled each memory out and savored it. She was the best thing that had appeared in his life for a while. He needed to make his peace with the reality that he was stuck on the ranch and move on. She was right. Why throw away forever with her? It made sense. He just had to figure out how to live it.

Willard's head bumped into the back of the cab as his father slammed the brakes. He craned his neck and turned to see around the truck and spotted the cause of the stop. A young cow stood squarely across the ruts. Father honked the horn, and the cow turned and looked at him.

"Stubborn creature, isn't it?" Father hung out the window and looked back toward Willard.

"Dumb. Only a dumb animal would park in front of a truck."

"Oh, I don't know. I certainly won't go through him, and I can't go around him. Why don't you hop down and make him move."

Willard grumbled and jumped from the truck bed. His frozen feet vibrated with pain as he landed. "Stupid animal. Why couldn't you cooperate like a decent bovine? With a thousand acres to roam, you had to settle right here, didn't ya?" As he mumbled, Willard approached the animal slowly. It might be young, but a stomp of one of its hooves on his feet could shatter his toes. "Sounds like a young woman I know. Stubborn to the hilt and equally difficult to talk to. Actually, you aren't so bad. You don't talk back." Willard reached out and swatted it on the rump.

The cow mooed and kicked its heels.

Willard darted away and narrowly missed getting hit in the gut. "Now that wasn't nice. I see I'll have to be more forceful with you."

"What's taking so long, Willard? We've still got a lot of acres to cover before we head home."

"I know, I know." Willard pulled an apple from his pocket and eyed the cow. "This is supposed to be my snack. You can have it, if you can catch me." He held the apple under the cow's nose and slowly walked away. The cow considered him and then followed. Willard tossed the apple on the ground and rushed to the truck.

Father laughed as Willard climbed into the passenger seat to warm up. "I can't say I've seen a cow bribed with an apple before. Looks like a good trick."

Willard relished the sound of his father's pleasure. He missed the deep rumble of joy that had disappeared when he left to enlist. Now as they spent time together, a détente had settled. Three hours later they rumbled back home. Father pulled the truck into the barn, and Willard helped him close-up for the night.

"Next time let's pick a warmer day."

"Now, son, you know the cows have to eat regardless of the weather."

"I know. But my fingers and toes would appreciate some warmth."

They walked together in silence. As they climbed the porch steps, Father turned to him. "Are you all right? You've been all out of sorts for a while now."

"I'll be fine. Just have a few matters to sort through in my mind."

Mother pulled food from the warming oven for them as they washed their hands and faces in the backroom sink. Willard plopped onto a seat at the kitchen table and inhaled deeply.

"Smells great, Mother." Willard held his mug of coffee and sipped.

"Thank you. How'd your day go?"

Father shoved a forkful of green beans into his mouth and chewed quickly. "You should have seen him. Willard lured a cow with an apple. Worked like a charm."

"That's me, the cow charmer. I was so cold I'd have used anything to get him to move so we could come home."

After all they could eat and a slice of fresh apple pie each, they moved into the great room. Willard built a large fire and stood in its glow. He heard a familiar stride he could recognize without turning and smiled. Time for a game of checkers. "Hi, Roger."

"Howdy. Haven't you thawed out yet?"

"Nope, he turned into an icicle out there, if you listen to him." Father chuckled and settled in his chair with the paper.

Willard stood and brushed off his hands. "Ready to play some checkers?"

"Sure. Let me refill my coffee first." Soon Roger dropped into his usual spot in front of the fire. They spread out the checkerboard and launched a marathon round. After a while Father and Mother turned in, leaving them to their game.

"Someday we should take up chess. Up the challenge a bit." Willard jumped his piece across the board. "King me."

Roger groaned and handed him the last black piece he'd collected. "I'll stop playing since you beat me so much."

"But that wouldn't be much fun."

"Probably not. Look, Willard, I need to ask you something."

Willard stopped planning his next move, concerned by Roger's serious tone. He sat up and gave Roger his full attention. "Okay. Is something wrong?"

Roger stared into the fire for a minute. "There's something you need to know."

His tone told Willard he wouldn't like the words that followed. "Maybe we should turn in." Willard didn't want to hear whatever Roger wanted to say.

"No. If we wait, you'll hear it from someone else. I'll ship to Fort Riley in a couple weeks for basic training."

A rush pounding through Willard's head filled his ears. "I don't think I heard you. You're headed to Fort Riley?"

Roger nodded. "I report there March 2."

Willard didn't want to believe his ears. "You're serious?"

"Absolutely. My number got called, and I've passed the physical and other tests. I won't know where I'm posted until I report for duty. I'm on my two-week leave now."

"Have you told, Father?"

"No. I wanted you to know first. You're my best friend—have been since we were in grade school."

"Lucky guy, your life changes dramatically, and mine stays the same as always."

Roger held out his hand. "I'm headed back to the bunkhouse. Wish me luck?"

Willard clapped Roger on the back. "I'll pray for you, but let's enjoy the rest of our time here before we say good-bye."

"All right. Good night."

Willard stayed in the Great Room and watched the fire die down to embers. His mind raced.

Father, are You still with me? It seems You've abandoned me with everyone else. He shook his head as he wearily climbed the stairs.

CHAPTER 21

FEBRUARY 21, 1942

*A*udrey pulled coffee cups from the racks the Union Pacific had picked up in Hershey. Another Saturday spent at the Canteen. She'd arrived at 7:00 a.m. and would stay till the last troop train left the station if she could make it. If today were normal, up to twenty-three troop trains would stop in North Platte before the day ended. She scrubbed the dirty cups as quickly as she dared. The next train could arrive anytime, and if the cups weren't clean, the boys wouldn't get any coffee.

"Careful, Audrey. You'll scrub that one through if you keep at it." Mrs. Evans touched her shoulder lightly before joining the ladies from the Altar Society at the long sawhorse-and-plywood tables, where they made sandwiches.

Audrey straightened and examined the cup. It sparkled. Time to rinse it and move on to one of the hundreds of waiting cups. Twenty minutes later she picked up a dishtowel and started wiping the cups dry.

"I put the coffee on, ladies." Rae Wilson dragged into the kitchen behind her words.

The Altar Society ladies rubbed their hands on aprons and then stacked the sandwiches on platters as quickly as they could. Audrey watched Rae leave, concerned about the ragged way she moved. Audrey walked over to where Mrs. Edwards stood slicing a cake. "Is Rae all right?"

"Nothing a little rest won't cure. That girl works herself to the bone here." Mrs. Edwards examined Audrey carefully. "You're not far behind her if I'm right. Working at the school all day and here most nights. You need to slow down, or you'll become one of my husband's patients. You can't serve every serviceman, Audrey."

"Maybe not, but I want to serve as many as I can."

Mrs. Edwards patted her shoulder, and Audrey walked through the lunch-room with a tray of coffee cups. The train had already reached the station, and men piled off the train. They came faster now and without much coaxing. Word had spread that the best meal of the trip waited at the Canteen, so they detrained and ran inside. Audrey fought the sensation she could drown as the men flowed past her to the heavy-laden tables.

"Audrey, come on." Lainie looked frazzled as she set out pie as fast as the soldiers grabbed the plates.

"Coming." She scurried through the crowd to the coffee table, where she unloaded her tray and helped a hard-working kid named Daniel fill the cups as fast as they could.

"So where are you from, Daniel?"

"Arthur. We left at four this morning so we could get here in time to help."

"Thanks for doing that. I couldn't keep up on the coffee by myself." Audrey marveled at how many citizens from communities around North Platte volunteered. Groups signed up to work certain days and brought baskets and plates of food with them. The towns and groups competed among themselves. If Cozad helped this week, the fine citizens of Eustis would serve the next week. Sometimes she would enter the Canteen and find she knew very few of the volunteers. Instead of losing energy, the workers and donations expanded each day.

Audrey surveyed the crowd of soldiers and volunteers. She sensed security in the large room when it filled with its honored guests. The uniforms promised the Japs and Germans would lose. That Nebraska and the rest of the country wouldn't change. At least she prayed they wouldn't.

"You're not going to let me beat you, are you?" Daniel quirked an eyebrow as he worked.

With a grin, she started filling the cups again. "Not till the coffee or the soldiers run out." Inside she stifled the fear that the soldiers would run out before the war did.

Hours later she slumped against the white fence surrounding the platform. Even though snow threatened to fall again, she needed a few minutes to herself in between loads of visitors. She heard the clipping sound of high heels but didn't bother to turn.

"Audrey, are you okay?" Lainie joined her at the fence.

"A little weary. Every day is the same, and I'm worn."

"Could it possibly be all your work? Between school and the Canteen, you don't take time to stop. Are you sure you need to slave so hard? Haven't you noticed the new volunteers?"

"I have. It's wonderful." She couldn't force enthusiasm into her words. Lainie wouldn't buy it for a minute.

"So you'll save the world and yourself by killing yourself at the Canteen. Sounds reasonable to me." Lainie paused for a minute, but Audrey didn't interrupt her. "Roger and I are going to the movies tonight. Will you and Willard join us?"

"I don't think so."

"Why?"

"I haven't heard from or seen him all week. Maybe he's decided I'm not worth the trouble." Audrey fought the urge to cry. She'd vowed to do that in the privacy of her bedroom. Not here with Lainie, who'd tell Roger, who'd mention it to Willard.

"I think Willard's having a hard time with the war, Audrey."

"He's not the only one, but he's the only one he'll allow to feel anything."

"Roger enlisted the other day." Fear filled Lainie's eyes.

"Oh, Lainie. I'm so sorry. Are you okay?"

"It was a matter of time. We weren't too serious."

"Sure, you just spent every weekend together because he's your friend."

"He's mentioned getting married since he doesn't want to leave with us in limbo. Can you imagine my dad's reaction? One of us would get hurt, and knowing me, it'd be Roger."

Audrey threw an arm around Lainie and tried not to laugh. "You're probably right. You're the social butterfly of our duo."

"I can't imagine being married right now. Not with him in a war."

"Then wait. If you love him, you can marry him when he comes home. Don't rush." Audrey looked up as the faint sound of a train whistle pierced the darkening sky. "Guess it's time to get back to work."

"Before we go in, I have to ask you one question." Lainie studied her intently, concern replacing her fear. "What are you running from?"

Audrey stepped aside and turned toward the door. "What are you talking about? I've got work to do." As she scurried inside, she couldn't escape Lainie's parting shot.

"You're running right now, Audrey."

As soon as the train left with its passengers, Audrey hurried from the station. She wanted to dodge another encounter with Lainie. How had things evolved to the point she avoided her best friend? She wound her scarf around her neck and buttoned her coat to the very top. She kept walking, not caring where she went.

Snapshots from the last three months played through her mind. Dancing with Willard and feeling swept off her feet into a new world. Bombs dropping on Pearl Harbor and listing to FDR declare war as she sat in a cafeteria packed with school children. Sharing cookies with servicemen from Kansas. Seeing movies and laughing with Willard. Counting down to 1942 in the Crystal Ballroom with him. Spending every spare moment at the Canteen since it launched. Why did sorrow and exhaustion taint each memory?

There was no earthly reason Willard would pick her out of a crowd at a large dance. Certainly, she hadn't forced him to take her to movies and meet her for meals. They'd both enjoyed their time together, and if not, Willard had given a convincing performance. She believed he wanted to spend the rest of his life with her. He even said he loved her.

As a chill seeped through her coat, Audrey bought a movie ticket and entered the theater's lobby. The last time she'd watched a movie, Willard sat next to her and whispered comments to her throughout the movie. Warmth seeped inside her at the remembrance of Willard's fingers twined around hers.

She settled into a seat in the darkened theater, the seat next to her vacant. In front of her, a girl snuggled into the shoulder of her boyfriend, and he placed his arm around the back of her chair. Tears trickled down Audrey's cheeks before she could stop them. She grabbed a handkerchief from her bag and tried to staunch the flow.

"Is this seat taken?"

Audrey jumped at the sound of Willard's voice. "What are you doing here?" She hissed between clenched teeth. "How did you find me?" She swiped the handkerchief across her cheeks, and looked straight ahead. She refused to look at him even as he settled into the seat.

"Thanks for the invitation. Interesting movie selection." Willard pulled a bag of popcorn onto his lap and fixed his brown eyes on her.

Audrey didn't know how to respond other than jump up and leave, but the opening credits were scrolling across the screen. She decided to ignore Willard and enjoy the film, *Woman of the Year*. Kate Hepburn's comedic ways always made Audrey laugh, though she'd never seen a movie with Spencer Tracy. She reached over and took the bag of popcorn.

Willard laughed under his breath and patted her knee. "You can have the popcorn. You've earned it putting up with me lately." He tipped her chin until she was looking at him. "I'm sorry for how I've acted and not calling. It's been crazy on the ranch, but I've missed you."

Audrey stilled at his voice. She refused to read one solitary thing into his comments. Instead, she focused on the movie and giggled through the first hour of the movie while the reporters jockeyed for position. Then, as the relationship on-screen unraveled, Audrey wondered if she and Willard had found their way back to each other. She wanted to believe they had. Being with him felt right, the times apart all wrong. As his hand slipped over hers, she never wanted him to walk away again.

The lights came up in the theater, and Willard turned to her. "Can I buy you a banana split?"

His gaze pierced her heart, and Audrey wondered what he saw. Whatever it was, his smile told her he liked it. "I'd like to, Willard. But I need to know where we stand. I'm confused by roses and Valentine's Day, and then not hearing from you until you surprise me here."

"It was a long week at the ranch. I promise I'll do better. And I want to start with that split. Don't tell me you aren't already tasting the chocolate and strawberry syrups."

She studied his eyes and saw nothing but honesty and love reflected in them. The playful twinkle suggested some teasing, too. "All right. Just make sure they put an extra cherry on top."

"As many as you desire." Willard stood and then offered his hand.

Audrey smiled and took his hand. "I think two would be perfect."

CHAPTER 22

FEBRUARY 22, 1942

*S*unday morning, Willard sat in the backseat of the family car with his left shoulder squeezed against the door. He whistled as he remembered last night. Audrey hadn't jumped up to welcome him when he'd appeared next to her. But he'd sensed her emotion when he'd reached for her hand. She hadn't pulled it away. She also hadn't run from him when the movie ended. He'd wanted to throw his arm around her as they walked, but the wall he'd erected between them still stood from her side of the divide though the bricks started to tumble when he brought her the banana split with two cherries.

Since Roger had told him he'd been drafted, Willard had worked with him while avoiding thoughts about what came now. With Roger's departure the nights filled with checker games in front of the fireplace would end. He would miss their easy camaraderie as they did the simple chores that kept the ranch running. And when he was honest, he was a little jealous that his friend would get to play role in the war that he couldn't.

Willard faced a crossroads of his own making. As he examined his choices, he wanted to keep Roger and Audrey in his life. Somehow, he had to get rid of the weight hanging around his ankles since Andrew died.

He would do it. His other choice was self-imposed misery.

The car bounced to a stop in front of the church. Willard quickly wiggled out of the car and ran to open the door for Mother. When his sisters were out, he shut the door. Father pulled around to park the car, while Willard escorted the ladies to the church.

As he walked, he looked for Audrey, eager to see if her eyes would sparkle when she saw him.

* * *

Audrey hid in the fellowship hall until Dad found her.

"What on earth are you doing in here?"

"Helping with the fellowship-hour clean up." *Please don't let him see through that excuse.* She grabbed for a plate and cup to carry toward the kitchen area.

"Honey, you do too much cleaning and helping. It's time to get into the sanctuary. Pastor Evans is ready to start the service."

Audrey followed and prayed she'd wasted enough time to avoid talking to Willard. Her feelings were so jumbled after their time last night that she'd decided she was a fool. Only a fool would enjoy being with Willard so much. Only a fool refused to say no when he asked her to join him for a banana split after a movie he wasn't invited to attend. She was a sucker for Willard and the way he made her feel safe and protected when he wasn't confusing the Dickens out of her. Avoiding him was her only defense, but she didn't want to.

* * *

Willard watched Audrey follow her father into the sanctuary. She held her back perfectly straight and looked straight ahead. She eased next to her father and sat with stiff posture as if something prickly tickled her throat. She never twisted her head or looked around. While she refused to look for him, he couldn't take his eyes off her. Yesterday he'd been desperate to find her. Today he was distracted by the sight of her.

As Pastor Evans approached the rostrum, Willard pulled his attention from Audrey and forced himself to listen. The pastor rearranged his papers on the surface and then opened his Bible. A shuffle rippled across the sanctuary as people reached for their Bibles or those tucked in the backs of the pews.

"This morning our text is John 15:12-14." Pastor Evans paused while everyone found the passage. "There Jesus told those gathered, 'My command is this: love each other as I have loved you. Greater love has no one than this, that he lay down his life for his friends. You are My friends if you do what I command.'" Pastor Evans removed his glasses and tucked them on a shelf under the lectern. He gazed around the sanctuary and let the words linger before he continued.

"In Romans, Paul reminds us that Christ demonstrated God's love for us when He died for us while we still lived in sin. He didn't wait till we were clean and worthy to offer Himself in our place. He willingly laid down His life in exchange for ours. My friends, we live in a time when many are asked to consider this sacrifice. Many made that supreme sacrifice, some from our congregation. I wish I could tell you Andrew Johnson will be the sole local casualty, but I can't."

At his brother's name, Willard leaned forward on the pew and tried to digest what he heard. The Bible's words were clear. "Lay down your life." What else could it mean than be willing to die as Jesus had? Pastor Evans continued as if he'd heard Willard's question.

"Today I want to broaden our understanding. We make laying our lives down too narrow if we read it to mean the sole way to do it is to die for somebody else. God does not ask many to literally do that.

"Instead, I believe He meant we are to lay down our lives daily, in the many choices we make. And we are to make the decision to die to our own desires and wants out of our love for others. We are not to do it as martyrs, but out of hearts that love others more than we love ourselves. That we esteem them more highly than ourselves." Pastor Evans paused and pulled a big handkerchief from his back pocket. He swiped it across his brow and upper lip before sliding it back in its place.

Willard watched Audrey shift in her seat. During the sermon, she'd grown increasingly agitated, as if she couldn't sit a moment longer. Willard expected her to stand and leave at any second, and fought the same urge.

"Love. As usual, Jesus couches the hardest concept in a simple phrase. Love your brother enough to lay your life down for him. That's all there is to it. But life removes the simplicity.

"Let's look at the larger context, the larger passage. In John 15, Jesus gives us the illustration of the vine and branches. He is the vine, and we are the branches. We cannot expect to have the strength to lay down our lives, our rights, for others until we are firmly growing in a deep relationship with Christ. A superficial relationship is not sufficient. Without more, we will fail every time in our attempts to die, because we attempt to do it without the strength and love God gives."

Pastor Evans continued, but Willard heard a buzzing sound. The world stopped as he considered the pastor's words and what they meant. As he ruminated over the message, he didn't like the implication it had for his life.

* * *

AUDREY FOLLOWED her brothers home and tried to dodge the snowballs they pelted at each other and any hapless bystander. Usually, she would have joined them in the game, but she couldn't. The sermon weighed on her heart, so she focused on understanding why. *Father, this uneasy feeling must mean I'm doing something wrong. Show me what it is.*

After a snowball hit her squarely in the chest, she stooped and packed a snowball of her own. She threw it and watched it sail through the air and land on Robert's right shoulder. He yelped, and she danced in a circle. "Don't throw one at me unless you can handle it."

Mama joined her as Dad ran ahead and pelted the boys. Audrey hooked arms with her, and they strolled down the street. After taking a deep breath, Audrey broke the silence. "Mama, how does the sermon apply to me? It's not like I can go enlist or serve by laying down my life. Even though I would like to."

Mama walked for a minute. As the pause lengthened, Audrey wondered what Mama's answer would be and if she'd like what she heard.

"Audrey, are there opportunities here in North Platte where you can love others by serving them at your expense?"

"Yes. The Canteen is one. But why do I feel so much pressure not to spend time at the Canteen with the servicemen?"

"It's not bad in and of itself, honey. But the reason you do it can become

117

wrong if you feel you must do it. At the Canteen you get to serve soldiers and lift their morale. That's a wonderful thing. But if you do it and exclude everything else because of it, you need to ask yourself why. You have a wonderful heart, Audrey. I am proud of you and the woman you are becoming, but don't forget how to be still and rest."

They reached home and rushed inside to warm up for lunch. Audrey listened to her family banter around the table. But her heart kept asking God one thing. *Please don't make me give up the Canteen. It's the one worthwhile thing in my life right now, even if it may be for the wrong reasons.*

Surely God wouldn't ask her to give it up.

CHAPTER 23

FEBRUARY 26 1942

*S*unday's sermon dogged Willard's every step that week. By Wednesday, he wondered if he'd gone crazy without noticing.

On Thursday Father sent him out alone to check on the cattle.

"Don't come back until you're ready to join the family again."

He looked over his shoulder to make sure the door didn't hit him in the backside as he strode to the truck. He hadn't been that gruff, had he? As he bounced over the first hill, he turned the radio dial, looking for anything to fill the silence. When static crackled through the cab, he groaned and turned off the radio.

The truck jounced between the ruts and bounced Willard around the cab. The snow had melted in patches, leaving spots of barren soil to poke through. He dragged in a breath and watched it swirl in the air when he exhaled.

After a couple of miles, he stopped and checked the cows huddled together in a grove of poplars. Several bales of hay remained where he'd thrown them days earlier. "Hang in there, girls. Won't be long and spring'll be here again." He climbed back into the truck and drove to the next group of cattle.

As the minutes ticked by, the silence grated on his nerves.

"Okay, Lord. You have me out here by myself. What do You want?" Willard fought the feeling he was a fool. Growing up, he'd talked to God out loud while he roamed the ranch. Sometime during the last few months, he'd stopped. He waited with rusty ears to hear anything. Nothing.

In the emptiness Willard knew what he should do. But he didn't want to do it. The very idea made him want to rear back and fight. Wrestle with God like Jacob.

"Lord, You ask too much. How can staying here, doing this, be Your will for me? There must be more." But as the miles passed, the word echoing through Willard's heart was *stay*. "Stop. Stop!" Willard slammed on the brakes and threw the vehicle into Park. He jumped out of the vehicle and kicked a tire. "Lord, You can't make me stay."

Surrender. One simple command, but Willard warred against it. If surrender meant staying, he couldn't do it. He looked across the hills at the horizon and could almost taste freedom. Maybe he should get in the truck and drive till he reached Kansas or Colorado, where nobody knew him. That tasted like freedom.

He turned around and saw the ranch house nestled in a valley. Shame settled around his shoulders. He'd slipped into an attitude with Audrey, his family, and Roger that he didn't like, taking out on them the frustration he felt. Something had to change, and since his responsibilities on the ranch wouldn't disappear, it looked like he had to.

"Lord, I bring this to You. Reluctantly, but I bring it. Help me surrender to You. I can't do it myself. Show me how to make things right."

* * *

THURSDAY MORNING AUDREY fought for patience. Her classroom wobbled on the cusp, ready to spin out of control. The students refused to sit still and focus on the lessons. Audrey wanted to blame it on spring fever, but feared she simply couldn't control them. Audrey stifled a scream when Petey Sedlacek jumped out from behind his desk for the third time in thirty minutes.

"Okay, kids. We're having recess early today. Get in a line by the door. Petey, you're at the front." The little boy flashed a big, gap-toothed grin at her. Usually he got punished for acting rambunctious. Maybe the change would encourage his cooperation. Audrey desperately needed something to work before she lost her mind.

It took five minutes to get the twenty-one students into a semblance of a line. Audrey threw the door open and pointed toward the gymnasium. "March quietly, munchkins."

The kids high-stepped down the hall and ran into the gym as soon as the door opened. Audrey quickly organized the kids into games of dodge ball and Simon Says before slumping onto a bleacher.

Principal Vester looked in the gym as he walked by. Audrey waved, and he joined her.

"Rough morning?"

"I could use a bit of their energy today. Rather than let them destroy the classroom, I called an early recess."

The principal chuckled as he watched the kids. "Timmy, aim for their legs, not their heads." He turned toward Audrey. "I remember days like that. Days I knew the kids ran the classroom, and the best I could hope for was survival. Hang in there. You're a good teacher."

"Thank you, sir." She watched the children tire of Simon Says and start a game of Red Rover. She'd have to watch Joe Burns, or he'd knock several kids over when it was his turn to run. "I know tomorrow's another day. I need strength for today."

"Are you still spending a lot of time at the Canteen?"

"Three or four nights a week plus Saturdays." Audrey tried to hide the pride that attempted to sneak into her voice. "I guess you could call me a regular."

"I'm sure it keeps you busy, but it might be why you're dragging so much, too."

"Maybe, but I don't think so."

Principal Vester smiled at her and stood. "I need to get back to the office. Let me know if you need anything, Audrey."

"I will."

As he left, Audrey mulled his words. Everywhere she turned she heard the same message whether or not she asked. Was she really working too much at the Canteen? How could she when it was such a good thing to support?

Lord, give me wisdom.

* * *

WILLARD WALKED into the house and kissed Mother on the cheek.

"Well, hello. The smell of manure and hay. Must have been a fun day." She winked at him and then turned back to the table where she kneaded bread.

"Another day on the ranch, ma'am. Gotta keep the cattle fed and watered." He raked his cowboy hat off his head and threw it on its hook by the back door.

"What has gotten into you? I like this Willard very much."

"Not much. I'm glad to be back inside. Have you seen Roger today?"

His mother shook her head. "I think I heard his jalopy come back, but he hasn't come in the house."

Willard rebuttoned his coat. "I'm going to head down to the bunkhouse, then. See you at dinner."

As he walked the quarter-mile to the bunkhouse, he prayed trying to solidify what had occurred while he'd been driving. A dam had burst while he'd wandered the hills, and the prayers poured from his mouth like spring-fed creeks. When he reached the building, he bound up the steps and rapped the door firmly. After waiting a moment, he entered.

"Roger? You in here?" He looked through the gloom of the large rectangular room. The bunkhouse consisted of three rooms. A galley kitchen, a dormitory-style restroom, and the sleeping room which was where he stood. As he waited, the door to the restroom opened, and Roger walked out.

"Hey, stranger. What do you need?" Roger walked to his bunk and went back to packing an olive dufflebag.

Willard sat on the bunk by the door. "Roger, I wanted to wish you well as you start training. I'll be praying for you each day until you return."

Roger turned toward him and stared. "I welcome your prayers"

"You've been my best friend for years, Roger. I hate to see you leave, but I know you're doing what you need, and I'll do my part from here."

"I do like to eat you know. Keep those cattle happy, so my C rations are full."

"I can do that." Willard stood and took a halting step toward Roger. Roger met him halfway and gave him a bear hug.

"So are you up for a game of checkers tonight?"

"I'll come up in plenty of time for a few games. That is if you aren't headed to town to talk to someone." Roger stepped back and grinned at him.

Everything in Willard wanted to steal Roger's keys and head straight to town. Instead, he weighed his words. "Yes, but I'm praying about the best way to let her know how I feel."

"Don't wait too long, friend. She's good for you. I'd hate to see her slip through your fingers while you figure things out."

CHAPTER 24

MARCH 3, 1942

"*M*iss Stone, is it time yet?"

Audrey jerked as Janey Thorson yelled from the back row. A titter of giggles swept the room, making Audrey wonder how long she'd sat at her desk without acknowledging her students. She hurriedly looked at her watch and stifled a gasp. Two forty-five already? She had fifteen minutes left with the children and still had a quiz to administer.

"Okay, students, it's time for the math quiz. You'll have fifteen minutes to answer fifteen questions. When the bell rings, your time is up." She handed out the papers to each student and returned to the front of the room. "You may begin."

Across the classroom, children sat at their desks with heads bowed as they scribbled away. Audrey watched with pride as the students worked. Their parents entrusted these children to her in September. They'd worked hard and learned much in the school year. In three short months she'd return them to their parents and pray they were better children for their time with her. Three months. That didn't leave her much time with them. Audrey glanced at her watch and gave the students a warning. "Five more minutes."

Several students raised their heads to look at her with panicked expressions before diving back into the quiz.

Audrey couldn't hide her smile. This is what she loved about second graders. They didn't have the artifice to hide what they felt. The world would be so different if adults behaved like her kids. Why couldn't Willard act like them rather than play with her emotions? She stood up and moved around the classroom. Her thoughts were headed in a dangerous direction, and if she wasn't careful, she'd find herself back in a haze of what-ifs. Willard invaded her thoughts and dreams. She couldn't escape the fact she longed to see him. She needed to shake his hold on her, or she might lose her contract for the coming year.

The bell rang and she jerked.

"Okay, children, pass your papers to the front, and I'll collect them." She waited as the papers slipped through little hands and chubby fingers to the front. "Thank you."

The children fidgeted in their seats while they waited for her to release them.

Audrey smiled at her charges. "You did very well today. Even you, Petey. You are dismissed, and I'll see you in the morning." She accepted hugs from a few as they rushed to freedom. When all the children had left, she picked up an eraser and wiped the chalkboard until it was clean. *Lord, could You wipe away my mistakes that easily, please?*

She closed the door to her classroom and returned to her desk. The weight of all that might be but wasn't pushed her into her chair. She lowered her head to her crossed arms and fought the overwhelming urge to cry. *Where are You, Lord? I feel so utterly alone and exhausted. Like You've stripped everything from me that held hope. Help me, Lord. I'm sinking on my own. Show me what to do.*

The quiet of the empty classroom enveloped Audrey. She sat and soaked in peace. No students cried her name, and no soldiers vied for her attention. Willard and the confusion he brought were far away. As her heart stilled, tears flowed on her face. Each tear added to the rivulets running over the walls around her heart. *Lord, help me tear down my walls.*

Forgive him.

The words whispered across her heart so quietly Audrey wanted to pretend she hadn't felt them.

Forgive him.

Why, Lord? she silently asked.

She sat there and considered the pictures that developed in her mind. Scene after scene with Willard flowed. Then she saw the wall of protection she'd built around her heart rather than trusting her future to the One who loved her most.

Forgive him.

As the phrase vibrated through her heart, Audrey resisted.

Trust Me, child.

The tears fell faster. Audrey could sense peace, right outside her grasp. *I am weak, Lord. Give me strength.* Even as she whispered, a load tumbled from her. Wiping her tears, she smiled tentatively. "Lord, help me do what You ask. I can't do it on my own."

She looked at her watch and stood. Time to walk to the Canteen to help with the evening's trains. As she headed outside, peace touched her heart and filled her soul. Peace she hadn't known since Pearl Harbor. "I'm so glad You are in control, Lord."

Audrey walked east from the school until she reached Walnut. Today, she wanted to avoid downtown and anybody she knew, so she followed Walnut to Front Street and the Canteen. As she neared the Canteen her steps slowed. The thought of putting in more time with the servicemen exhausted her before she stepped into the building. "What is wrong with me?"

Trust Me.

The echo in her heart stopped her steps. *Help me trust You.* Audrey set her jaw and looked at a train slowing to a stop across the tracks from her. She opened the door and tore off her coat. God would show her the right balance as she served. "Where do you need me?"

* * *

WILLARD DROVE Roger's Packard into town and wished Roger were the one driving. His train had left early the previous morning. Before he boarded the train, he'd tossed Willard the keys and asked him to take care of the car until he returned. Willard pulled into the Sixth Street Grocery parking lot and stopped the car. He had loaded the car down with supplies to help the Canteen. Lainie had told him he'd find Audrey here, but that wasn't why Willard had come. If Audrey worked somewhere in the Canteen, he'd say hi. Either way, he wanted to do his part to support the effort.

It took three trips to unload everything Mother had sent with him. She'd boiled dozens of eggs and packed them carefully in two wicker baskets. His sisters had baked cupcakes last night and packed them in a couple of boxes. Mrs. Wheeling directed him to the kitchen with each load. Though he looked for Audrey with each pass, he didn't see her.

"Is there anything else I can do for you, ma'am, before I head back to the ranch?" Willard stood in a corner of the lunchroom and watched women buzz around the room, restocking the tables for the inevitable next train.

"Would you carry the bags of trash to the receptacle? Otherwise, we're fine. Please thank your mother for her donations."

"I'll be sure to do that. Now where's that trash?"

Willard followed Mrs. Wheeling through the lunchroom to the back of the kitchen. She pointed to three bags of trash that he hefted.

"Good night, ladies."

The eight or nine women gathered around the table, making chicken salad sandwiches, waved. He hefted the bags and left through the back door. After depositing the trash he walked toward the car and heard a familiar piercing whistle. *Lord, keep the troops safe. And thanks for changing me.* He whistled as he opened the car door. Even without seeing Audrey, coming had been the right thing to do.

* * *

AUDREY RELEASED her breath as Willard loaded down with trash walk out the back door. She turned to Mrs. Wheeling. "Are you sure he's gone?"

"Yes. I'm sure. But why does it matter? He's a very polite young man who brought some wonderful donations. The servicemen will love them."

"I know. That's what has me worried." Audrey didn't know what to make of the new Willard she'd seen. He didn't know she was there. He hadn't even sought her out. Enough people knew she was around that it wouldn't have been hard to find her even though she hid. "He's different today. I'm not sure what to think."

"Well, don't think too much without something for your hands to work on. There's still lots of work to do."

The rest of the night passed in a blur for Audrey. The next train turned into two as an eastbound train arrived five minutes after a westbound. She'd never seen the lunchroom so full. The soldiers spilled over into the station once they'd been through the food lines. Audrey ran till she thought she'd fall over from exhaustion. At nine thirty, Mrs. Wheeling sent her home. As she hiked the blocks, Audrey decided sleep sounded wonderful.

When the morning arrived, Audrey longed to block out the sunrays and curl up into a tight ball in the middle of her bed. Images of the times she'd spent with Willard had filled her dreams. She missed the fun they'd had together. No, when she was honest with herself, she missed the Willard of December 6. The one with chocolate eyes that melted her heart. The one who made her laugh and forget about herself. The one who said he loved her.

"Audrey?" Mama knocked softly on her door. "Are you all right?"

"I'm fine, Mama. Just tired." She watched her mama enter the room and tried to pretend everything was as it should be.

"Are you ready to talk about it?"

"No. Yes. I don't know. I'm so confused and exhausted right now."

"You've been working awfully hard."

Audrey scooted over as Mama sat beside her on the bed. "I know. Maybe it's time to step back from the Canteen and volunteer a one or two days a week. But what will I do then?"

"What you always did before. You had a fulfilling life before the Canteen."

"It's true." Audrey tugged her blanket over her head. "But we weren't at war."

"And you hadn't met Willard."

Audrey reluctantly nodded her head. "Yes, that is part of the problem."

"Oh, honey." Mama lowered the blanket and pulled Audrey close. "Do you love him?"

"I don't want to, but I do." Audrey pulled away and looked into her mother's eyes. "He came to the Canteen last night. I don't think he saw me, but he brought a load of donations. He seemed, I don't know, glad to do it and be there. So unlike the Willard I've seen the recently months. Do you think he's changed, Mama?"

"I don't know. But I know he can change. Willard is a good man, from a fine family, and he's earned a worthy reputation. It sounds like your heart wants to see if he's changed."

Audrey stared at her hands. "What time is it?"

"Time for you to carefully consider and pray about what you want. And time for you to run if you're going to reach work on time."

"Thanks, Mama." Audrey kissed her mother on the cheek. "Some days life gets so complicated I wish I could hide in bed. I love you."

"I love you, too. Now scoot before you're late."

Audrey looked at her clock and bolted to her feet. Right now she hoped her mama would pray that she got to school on time. God would have to handle her feelings for Willard.

CHAPTER 25

MARCH 6, 1942

*W*illard crossed his fingers. He'd prayed about how to approach his friendship with Audrey, and this was the only idea he had. He strode through the Franklin hallway toward Audrey's classroom. He had checked with the office so he could time his arrival for when her class played in recess. He hoped she would be in the gym with them, since he hadn't seen kids on the playground when he arrived. But maybe he'd missed them on their way to the gym or outside. Either way he just knew he wanted to surprise her in a good way for once.

He peeked through the small window on the door to the classroom. No one sat at any of the desks, so he slipped inside. He walked to Audrey's desk and placed a handful of pink carnations tied with a rosy ribbon on her desk. After finding a piece of paper, he scratched a note to her. With a deep breath, he tucked the note beside the flowers and left.

* * *

AUDREY LED her tired second graders back to the classroom after recess. Spring whispered an imminent return on a soft breeze. The kids had romped outside, thrilled to be outdoors instead of trapped in the gym on the days the temperature sank below freezing or the snow fell. The playground was saturated with melted snow, so they'd gone on an exploration, pretending all the while that Piglet and Pooh joined them.

She stilled when she saw a small bouquet of flowers placed on the corner of her desk. The delicately frilled edges of the carnations begged her to touch them.

"Who are these from, Miss Stone?" Emilene Wilcox gently touched the ribbon. "They're beautiful."

"I'm not sure, honey. It's what we call a mystery. Some unknown person left them for me. How could we figure out who they're from?"

Janey raised her hand. "Read the note. I bet that'll tell you."

"You're always thinking, aren't you?" Audrey smiled at her students. "All right. Everyone back to your desks. We'll solve the mystery if we have any time left after geography."

Audrey ignored their groans and pulled the large world map down over the chalkboard. As she walked them through the countries in Europe, her thoughts wandered back to the flowers and whether Willard doubled as the mystery bearer who left them for her.

When the bell finally rang at the end of the day, Audrey waved her students off and settled behind her desk. She reached for the note, but then sank back. She'd avoided reading it all afternoon and successfully distracted the kids from it. She'd enjoyed not knowing, and now lifted the carnations to her nose to inhale their clean, lightly sweet scent.

Audrey returned the bouquet to her desk and picked up the note. What could he say that would settle her emotions? She replaced it unread on the table, afraid its message would somehow confuse her more.

She reached past her fears for the note and unfolded it. A firm script wove across the page. *Dearest Audrey, Please join me at the Canteen tomorrow? I would like to spend time serving with you. Willard*

As the words sank in, Audrey grabbed the flowers and danced around the classroom. "I'll give you another chance, Willard. Please let us work this time, Lord."

She came to an embarrassed stop when she saw Coach Wellington looking through the window. With a sheepish smile, she darted to her desk and collected her items. Burying her face in the bouquet, she made her way out of the school and headed home, her mind whirling with possibilities.

Saturday morning Audrey stood in front of her wardrobe and considered her options. Usually what to wear for a day at the Canteen didn't require much thought. She would pick a clean blouse and skirt that were comfortable and made her look nice. If she had Lainie's choices, she knew she could hit the right balance of eye-catching and practical. But she'd run out of time and was limited by her smaller assortment. Finally, she settled on a dove-gray flannel skirt with a green long-sleeved blouse. The detail work on the collar caught people's attention, and the color highlighted her clear skin and hair. The outfit should turn Willard's head without looking like she'd made the attempt.

When she arrived at the Canteen at eight, Willard already held a place in the sandwich assembly line. She couldn't prevent her jaw from dropping as she watched him slap homemade mayonnaise on slice after slice of bread while keeping the conversation around the table running. His family joined him, with even little Norah helping get food ready for the soldiers.

"Cat got your tongue, Audrey?" Pastor Evans winked at her with a glint of glee in his eyes as he placed slices of beef on the bread Willard passed to her.

"I guess I didn't realize it was the church's day to serve. You've already accomplished a lot for so early."

"You're a bit late." Willard flashed his Clark Gable grin at her. Oh, how she'd missed that. "The first couple of trains have come and gone already."

"You should have seen them snatch all the donuts Mother made last night." Margaret scrunched her nose as if locusts had descended on her mother's precious offering.

Audrey laughed at her expression and looked at Willard. "Is there room at the table for me to help?" She stopped breathing at the look that softened his gaze. It held so much promise of not just today, but all of their tomorrows, too. As she moved to the spot beside him, she prayed he could live up to everything his eyes promised.

The time flew. Audrey hadn't laughed so much in a long time. Willard turned every mundane task they undertook into an adventure. She realized that, until then, their friendship had revolved around movies and food. As the hours melted away, she saw parts of Willard he'd never shown her. His depth of character drew her as he interacted with everybody in the kitchen equally.

Still, she wondered how he would react if asked to help serve the soldiers face to face. She needed an answer to that question.

* * *

As two o'clock approached, Willard wanted to run up Dewey and shout. It had worked! Audrey couldn't believe he was serving. She'd brightened progressively over the course of the morning, but he could see a question hiding in the shadows of her eyes. He needed to resolve her question, whatever it was.

He carefully considered everything he'd done. Had he missed anything? Had he overstepped in any area? He didn't think so, but couldn't afford to miss it. Nope. Everything seemed fine on those fronts. What could it be? Willard looked around the room and it hit him. He'd hidden in the kitchen all day without realizing it. The only time he'd entered the lunchroom was to help with trash after the soldiers had reboarded their trains.

The phone rang, and a woman answered and then yelled, "I have the coffee on." He took a deep breath and took Audrey's hand. "Let's find a job in the lunchroom for this train. I'm tired of the kitchen."

The smile she gave him blinded him. They worked side by side at the coffee table until five. At that time, Rae Wilson came by and shooed them out of the depot. "The reinforcements have arrived. You lovebirds go find somewhere else to shine your sappy smiles at each other."

Willard itched to get out of there and spend time with Audrey without the crowd of observers. He also knew he would return. "Let's get a bite to eat at Molly's."

"How could you want anything to eat after being around food all day?" She swung his hand as she teased him.

He looked down into her face and stopped. As he gazed at her, he understood something was missing. The lingering doubts were gone. He tipped her chin up and leaned down. He read her expression, looking for any sign of hesitation. Instead, all he saw was a gentle invitation. After his lips brushed hers, he said, "I love you, Audrey Stone, woman with a servant's heart."

A grin stretched his cheeks as he watched contentment flood her face with fresh beauty.

CHAPTER 26

MARCH 12, 1942

*A*udrey sat by the window in her room, Bible open in her lap. Since Willard had helped at the Canteen, she'd noticed fresh peace and purpose in him. Many of his doubts seemed to have disappeared, and their relationship had already improved.

The only problem was her schedule. He had more time to spend with her than she did with him. Snippets from Pastor Evans's sermons and her mama's words vied for her attention. Even as she dreaded the thought, she knew it was time to quit spending every free moment at the Canteen. It was time to obey the prompting in her heart and find balance in her life.

"Phone's for you, Audrey."

She jumped as Robert bellowed up the stairs.

Audrey flew from her room and downstairs. Reaching the hallway phone table, she snatched the receiver from Robert and took a deep breath. "Hello? This is Audrey." She waited, knowing Willard sat on the other end of the line. Since Saturday, he'd called her every night. Never for long, but always enough to make her feel cherished.

"Hey, darlin'. How was your day?" His voice reflected the long nights he'd spent calving.

"Ready for spring break next week."

"Will you be at the Canteen all week?"

Audrey considered her words. He needed to understand what she wanted to say, but she considered her words with care in case a neighbor who shared the party line eavesdropped on the call. "I'll go once or twice, I'm sure. So many groups help now, there are more volunteers than needed." She bit her lip as she thought. "Besides, I don't need to pass time there. I've found what I was looking for."

Audrey's heart raced as Willard stayed silent. "Say something." She fought the desperation that wanted to leak into her voice. "Please."

"I don't know what to say. I've wanted to hear those words for months."

Audrey giggled. "We've only known each other for months."

"I know." Willard's voice reflected a seriousness that made Audrey stifle other giggles. "But you're special, something I've known since we met." He sighed. "I have to get out to the barn. Father and I need to go make the rounds with the cows. I love you."

"I love you, too. Be careful."

"See you Saturday if the cows cooperate." Willard clicked off before she could say good-bye.

Audrey eased the telephone back to the table.

"He's so dreamy." Robert stood from the step where he had perched, hands tucked by his face and batted his eyes.

Audrey ignored him and danced up the stairs.

"Who was it, Audrey?" Father followed Audrey up the stairs and sat beside her on her bed.

"It was Willard, Dad."

"You should be careful, honey. You don't tell anybody you love them unless you mean it for the rest of your life."

"I do. Dad, I can't imagine my life without him."

"You haven't known him long."

"I know, but it feels like forever in some ways. So much has changed since we met. And we've been through a lot and had to grow." Audrey tucked her legs beneath her and leaned into her dad. "I don't know how to explain it."

"Have you prayed about it?"

"I have. I still am."

"Then your mama and I will pray, too. We want God's best for you, and if that's Willard, we won't stand in the way." He kissed her on the forehead and stood. "Try to get some sleep."

Audrey nodded. "I love you."

As she watched Dad leave the room, Audrey pondered his advice. While it was true she'd prayed about Willard, she needed to change her prayer. Time to to pray about whether God had a future for them. Together. Shivers slipped up her spine at the thought of a future with Willard.

* * *

TIME DRAGGED FOR WILLARD. He and Father drove the ranch's acres hunting for cows in labor. Calving season meant nights of boredom broken by moments of pure glory as another calf entered the world. Saturday night Willard found his aching backside plastered to the truck's bench again. Not the soft movie theater seat he wanted to sit in.

The hours passed quietly in the cab as they checked the cows. The silence wasn't comfortable like last year. Instead, it was burdened by unspoken thoughts.

Heavenly Father, give me the words to make things right with Father. I want to heal our relationship, but know only You can do that. Willard waited. Nothing came, but peace sank into the fiber of his soul.

After another thirty minutes of quiet, the truck hit a large dip. Willard was thrown into the cab's ceiling. "Ouch!" He rubbed his head and held his tongue.

"Sorry, son."

Willard stopped massaging his head and looked at his father. "What did you say?"

"I'm sorry you hit your head."

Thank You, Lord. Willard could count on one hand the number of times his father had apologized to him. "It's okay, Father. Could I say something?"

"It's not like I could stop you."

"I'm sorry I rebelled against you. I shouldn't have tried to enlist when I knew you didn't agree. Will you forgive me? If I'm going to be on the ranch, I'd really like your forgiveness."

Father rubbed the stubble on his chin. He glanced out the window and then turned to Willard. He opened his mouth, closed it, and then sighed. "Son, you're forgiven. I've been a bit stubborn, too. You've come back, and you've worked hard. I appreciate it. With Roger gone, I really need your help."

Relief rolled over Willard, lifting a burden from him.

"Thank you, sir. I won't let you down again."

"You might, but I'll still love you. You're my only son now, Willard. I'm not willing to waste any more time with my stubbornness."

Nothing else changed that night, but Willard felt a renewed kinship with his father that he had missed.

* * *

SUNDAY MORNING AUDREY wandered through the fellowship hall looking for Willard. Mrs. Johnson and his sisters munched on donuts, but Willard didn't make an appearance. Since Roger wasn't around for her to ask what had happened to him, she steeled herself and approached the table his mother sat at.

"Good morning, Mrs. Johnson."

"Hello, Audrey. How are you today?" A smile illuminated her round face and made her blue eyes shine.

"I'm fine. Is Willard okay?" Audrey twisted the handle of her handbag as Betty Gardner leaned in to listen. Why couldn't Betty leave her alone?

Mrs. Johnson wiped some sugar from Norah's face as she answered. "He and his dad were out all night with the cows again. They'll sleep most of the day, I imagine, until they get caught up on their rest. Calving season is usually like this. It's a good two weeks without much sleep."

"I'm glad to hear he's not sick." Audrey started to step away. "Have a wonderful Sunday."

"Wait a minute, child. When are you going to join us at the ranch for Sunday dinner?"

"I guess you'd have to ask Willard. He hasn't invited me yet."

"We'll have to rectify that soon."

Audrey turned and left before she panicked. Had his mother invited her to the ranch? Audrey supposed she would need to spend time there soon. Especially if what she dreamed turned into reality. A rancher's wife. What did she know about a ranch? Absolutely nothing, but she'd learn if Willard asked her to share his life.

Audrey turned back and caught Lettie Johnson watching her. Audrey waved and joined her family in the sanctuary. She'd be content with another phone conversation that evening. Soon she'd see him again. She had to, or she'd go crazy.

* * *

THE TUESDAY MORNING of spring break Audrey looked at the pair of dungarees on her bed and groaned. Today she would visit the ranch, but the thought of wearing the practical pants didn't appeal to her. How could she look feminine in them? She had imagined people staring at her when she purchased them at Montgomery Ward's Monday night. She would have walked out without them if Willard hadn't insisted she would enjoy the ranch more in pants. Audrey couldn't fathom how he was right, but chose to trust him.

She stepped into the navy pants and then put on an emerald-green shirt. Maybe if all he could see was her eyes, he wouldn't notice she'd actually worn pants. As she looked at her reflection in the mirror, she groaned. "I hope Willard's right."

Audrey turned from the mirror and hurried down the stairs to wait for Willard on the porch. As soon as he picked her up, she forgot all about the pants as she fell into his open arms.

"Where have you been hiding? A girl can feel abandoned you know."

"Tell that to the cows. Let's get out of here. I'm ready to introduce you to my world."

They ran to the Packard and laughed as they caught up. A mere week had passed since they'd seen each other, but it seemed an eternity to Audrey. The feel of Willard's hand holding hers stopped her heart. *Security* was the one word to describe the feeling.

They flew over hills, but as Willard crested a particular one, he slowed down. Audrey gasped when she saw a house, barn, and several other buildings tucked in the valley.

"It's beautiful." Audrey twisted in the seat to see the complete panorama.

Willard chucked her under the chin. "I think you mean it's breathtaking."

Audrey laughed. "Okay, it's breathtaking."

The day passed in a daze for Audrey. They drove for hours along the rutted paths and picnicked near a grove of trees, where cows stood with their young calves.

"I've never seen anything like this, Willard. I'll never forget it."

Willard smiled and pulled Audrey across the blanket into his arms. "I hope you'll never want to forget."

She snuggled in and smiled. Forgetting was the last thing she wanted to do.

CHAPTER 27

MARCH 25, 1942

*A*udrey sulked home after her students finally left. She had exactly six blocks left to work on her attitude before she arrived. At the rate she was going, she'd need a dozen more to change anything.

"So much for a happy birthday." She hated the whiny tinge to her voice, but couldn't help it. Maybe if she talked enough on her walk, she'd use up the whine before Mama heard it.

Things had been going so well with Willard. After the day on the ranch, he'd called several times and taken her out for lunch Sunday after church. She'd laughed until her sides ached as he told her story after story about growing up on the ranch. The afternoon had merely confirmed her growing certainty that she wanted to spend the rest of her life with this man. She couldn't imagine how empty she would feel if he stopped looking at her with such devotion. In his eyes, she saw the beautiful woman that she longed to be. And when he told her why he loved her, she believed him.

If he could see her now, he might change his mind. Still, she couldn't stifle her disappointment.

"He didn't even call last night. No note this morning. No present left at school. Now he'll probably babysit cows all night. Some birthday." From the sidewalk, she examined the flowerbeds in each yard she passed. "And no daffodils. Perfect. Happy twenty-first birthday to me."

She kicked a clod of dirt across the sidewalk and marched the rest of the way home. Might as well get the day over with and move on. Some days were best left as quickly as possible, and this had all the markings of one of them. She cut through the alley and walked up the steps to the back door.

"Mama, I'm home."

"In here, dear."

"Where's here?" Audrey mumbled.

"The living room. Put your things down and come join us."

Us? Who else could there be? Robert and John would be off with friends. Dad worked until five o'clock. Audrey hung up her coat, and then walked down the hall to the living room, curiosity quickening her steps.

"Hello, Audrey."

With those two words, Audrey's heart melted. Willard hadn't forgotten.

"These are for you." He handed her a simple vase overflowing with a dozen sunshine-yellow daffodils.

Tears threatened to slip past her lashes as she accepted the vase. She buried her head in the blossoms and tried to collect her thoughts. "I love daffodils, but they aren't blooming yet. Where did you find these?"

"It doesn't matter. I couldn't let your birthday pass without giving you a reminder that spring is around the corner."

Audrey set the vase on the lamp table and rushed into his arms. "Thank you. I thought you'd forgotten."

"How could I forget the most important day on the calendar?"

As she stepped back, Audrey saw another vase filled with roses on the coffee table. "Who are those for?" She looked at Mama and puzzled at her bright smile.

"Those are for your mother. I had to thank her for the gift of you."

The tears rushed back into Audrey's eyes as she heard those words.

"Willard, I think you'd better get Audrey out of here before she floods the house with her tears."

"My pleasure, ma'am. Will you join me for supper, Audrey?"

Audrey nodded and felt foolish for the fears she'd allowed to play through her mind on the way home.

In no time they were bundled in the Packard and headed downtown. Willard escorted her to Molly's and requested a table by the fireplace.

"I want to replace some bad memories I created with good ones, Audrey. You deserve only good ones."

Audrey had to look away from the love that shone in his eyes. "I'm overwhelmed, Willard. Where did you find the daffodils?"

"It's a secret."

"Please tell me." She batted her eyelashes and smiled.

"How can I resist that? I had Helen's Flower Shop find them for me."

Audrey blinked and sat up. "Oh. I guess that means spring isn't quite here."

Willard laughed and reached across the table for her hand. Grasping it lightly in his, he ran his thumb across her fingers. "Not quite. But spring is around the corner."

Her heart stirred at the look that promised more days with Willard.

The meal passed with banter. Audrey glowed, not sure whether it was from the fire behind her or from the attention Willard showered on her. After they split a piece of cake, he suggested they go for a walk. Audrey eagerly agreed. She'd walk to Siberia for the opportunity to extend the most perfect evening of her life.

They strolled down Dewey toward the railroad tracks. At Front they turned right and approached the station.

A train huffed on the tracks as the conductor yelled, "All aboard!" They watched as a flood of uniforms raced to the train, and laughed as the last soldier tried to stuff extra sandwiches in a pocket while he balanced a boxed birthday cake with the other hand.

"I wonder if it's really his birthday."

Audrey smiled. "It doesn't matter. He feels like a king carrying that box. It'll taste sweet either way." They reached the platform and stood against the railing looking at each other.

"Speaking of sweet." Willard leaned down and kissed Audrey, stealing her breath.

"Oh. You would know how to make this night absolutely perfect." Audrey leaned into Willard as she tried to find her breath. She was jostled away from him when he shifted. She watched in confusion as he stepped away and then dropped to one knee. Her hand flew to her heart and tears pooled in her eyes. She wanted to jump, run, and dance all at the same time. Instead, she stopped as if frozen by a north wind.

"Audrey, you have made my life so rich. Your father has given me his blessing to ask you the most important question of my life. Will you do me the honor of agreeing to marry me?"

Her hand fluttered from her heart to her throat, and she searched his eyes. Fear and anger were gone, replaced by a love so deep she could drown in it. She nodded her head and started to squeal. "Yes. Yes, Willard, I'll marry you."

As clapping floated to her ears, Audrey turned and saw her parents, brothers, Lainie, and a bunch of Canteen volunteers standing by the lunchroom door. Somehow, in that moment, Audrey knew everything was as it should be.

"Kiss me please, Willard." Everything faded except the love on his face as he leaned toward her.

EPILOGUE

JUNE 23, 1942

Dad stood next to her in the hallway off the side of the sanctuary. Audrey wished the butterflies dancing in her stomach would choreograph their movements. The excitement of the moment made it hard to stand still. The questions of what the future held made her want to run. Was this too fast?

The three months since Willard proposed had flown. Between completing the school year, serving at the Canteen, and preparing for the wedding, she'd met herself coming and going.

Somehow everything had gotten done, but even now she wondered how.

Audrey fidgeted with the fabric of her skirt. The war had made silk impossible to find, since the government took it all for parachutes. Instead of silk, her dress was a soft white satin. She and Mama had found it at Rhode's Dress Shop and its elegant cut matched the dress of her dreams. The cap sleeves sat off her shoulders and flowed into a heart-shaped neckline. The bodice fit her perfectly with simple lines that flowed in one piece of fabric through the skirt and ended in a tea length. She felt almost as elegant as Ginger Rogers in this dress.

She reached up and touched the crown of baby's breath woven in her hair.

"You look lovely, sweetheart." Her dad's voice cracked as he stroked her cheek.

Joy threatened to overflow as she took a deep breath. "Do you think so, Dad?"

"He's a lucky man, Audrey. And he's worthy of you. I wouldn't have given him my blessing if I didn't believe that with all my heart."

"Thank you ." She cherished his words and the peace they gave her. He wouldn't let her do anything that wasn't for her best.

The sanctuary doors opened, and the organ music poured through the opening. The sound of *Pachelbel's Canon in D* reached Audrey's ears.

"It's time, Dad."

He patted her hand and looked deep in her eyes. "I will always love you, Audrey. You are my only daughter, but today you become Willard's wife. I pray you will be as happy as your mother and I have been." He kissed her gently on the cheek and then offered her his arm.

Audrey dabbed at a tear that wanted to escape. She straightened her back and took her dad's arm. As she did, the few remaining questions that shadowed her heart disappeared.

It was time.

As she walked through the open doors and floated down the aisle, everything but Willard faded from her vision. Audrey focused on the future that waited for them. Together.

She mouthed *I love you*.

Her heart stilled as he repeated them.

Truly, her dreams had come true.

SANDHILL DREAMS SNEAK PEEK

MAY 7, 1943

As a child, the rocking of the train, the clunk of the wheels on the tracks, had promised adventure, excitement, but not this time. Sitting on a train headed to the farthest corner of Nebraska was the last thing Lainie Gardner had imagined for her life. Her dreams shimmered in the distance like a hallucination. She should have crossed the Atlantic Ocean with her friends, and fellow nurses, from the 95th Evacuation Company, bound for the European front. Instead, she waited for the train to stop long enough for her to disembark in Crawford.

She tugged a lace-trimmed handkerchief from her jacket pocket and wiped a small circle on the train window. Dust blew in waves across the desert landscape of the sandhills. The few trees squatted against the horizon. The emptiness mocked her, mirroring the barrenness inside.

The conductor swayed between the seats of the car to the rhythm of the clacking wheels. "Next stop. Crawford." Even his words were as lifeless as the tumbleweed that paced the train.

The car jerked from side to side as it slowed. People jumped from their seats and collected their items. A dark-haired toddler jostled against his mother. He bounced on the seat and his sandaled foot slipped. Lainie sucked in a breath. With a thud, his head collided with the hard bench seat, and he wailed. He lifted his head, and Lainie noticed a gash on his forehead and a trickle of blood.

Lainie attempted to leap from her seat to help him, but stopped short as her book tumbled from her lap. Her joints refused to unlock. Not too long ago she'd been active and healthy, but not any more. Rheumatic fever had struck quickly and left her weakened and vulnerable.

The commanding officer's words raced through her mind. *Young lady, being a nurse requires strength and stamina, of which you have neither.* Oh, she'd fought that pronouncement, but in the end she lost.

The boy's mother pressed a handkerchief against the wound. Lainie sighed and collapsed back on her seat. There was little more she could do to help this young boy. But she could have done much for the soldiers.

"Next stop. Crawford." The conductor continued his travels through the car.

Lainie shuddered and then swiped the handkerchief across her forehead. Her stomach knotted and doubts raced. She'd skipped the planning that would make this trip a success. "I must be crazy."

The matron across the row quirked an eyebrow as she glanced at Lainie and then returned to her book.

Lainie blushed. The words weren't supposed to trip from her mouth like the tumbleweeds blowing across the hills. She fingered the veil of her hat and turned back toward the window, ignoring the questions reflected in the woman's eyes. She'd answered too many queries already. No need to entertain a stranger's.

The click of the train's wheels against the track slowed its tempo. She tucked her paperback and handkerchief inside her handbag. The knots tightened their hold as she wondered what she'd find at Fort Robinson, a couple miles down U.S. Route 20 from Crawford.

Compared to North Platte, Crawford would seem like a hamlet. She shuddered. North Platte had never seemed like much of a town to her. Not that it mattered now. She couldn't go back to what her life had consisted of before she left for nurse's training. A cycle of endless parties and flirtation held no appeal after she tasted the opportunity to make a difference.

Lainie pitched forward when the train lurched to a stop. She leaned down to look out the window, and her heart sank as she fell back into her seat. "There isn't much to Crawford."

"No. It's a small extension of the fort and a few ranches. But those of us who call it home love it." The matron's steady voice soothed the fear that gripped Lainie. She searched Lainie's eyes a moment before she continued. "This your first time here?"

"Yes, ma'am. I'm hoping to get a job. You know, free a man to fight and all that."

The woman pursed her thin lips, a pinched expression settling on her sharp features, almost like she'd heard that story many times and watched others' hopes crumble. "Yes. Well, good luck." The woman's ample form side-stepped into the aisle, releasing Lainie to stand.

Lainie almost ducked to look under her seat for her courage. It had been in full force when she convinced her family moving to Fort Robinson was the right step. With the girls from the 95th Evacuation Company shipped out, she'd thrown caution to the wind, packed her bag, and bought a train ticket in the opposite direction and a thousand miles closer to home.

She sidled down the aisle toward the door, a tightness and deep ache pulsing from her muscles. She swallowed against the pain. The effects of rheumatic fever lingered, and the train ride had been harder than she'd anticipated.

Loud, almost frantic barks ricocheted off the train as she stepped off the train. She shielded her eyes and scanned the platform. She walked toward the wooden crates stacked two high and at least six wide. Snouts and paws pushed against the chicken wire fronts. The barking escalated as two men placed an additional crate on the pile.

The dungarees and cowboy boots they wore with their khaki standard issue shirts were a far cry from the uniforms the servicemen wore as they rushed through the Canteen back in North Platte. Did they have a unique outfit for Fort Robinson? One slipped back into the car while the other adjusted a crate.

"What is all this?" She raised her voice over the din.

The soldier reached into the gap in the train's side to accept one end of another crate.

Lainie pulled herself to her full height, all five feet and a couple of inches of it, and edged toward the soldier. "Excuse me."

The soldier dropped the crate he'd picked up and then spun on his heel rubbing his ear. His gaze took her in and swept over her again. "You didn't need to shout."

Lainie thought she'd never seen eyes as clear blue as his, without a hint of iciness. He ran a finger over a scar on his hand, almost like a forgotten habit. "Had to make sure you heard over the barking."

The soldier closed his eyes and rubbed a hand over his face. She couldn't tell if he was frustrated with her or trying to hide a smile. "Ma'am, you've made me drop valuable Department of War resources. If that animal's injured, my officer will have my hide."

"Why don't you check and see?"

He leaned down, careful to keep his face a good three feet from the wire. "It's a quiet one. I hope that means it's fine. If you'll excuse me, I have a job to do."

His words ricocheted through her mind. Yes, he might have a job, but he didn't have to rub her nose in it. But how could unloading dogs in Nowhere, western Nebraska be important to the war effort?

Balling her fingers into fists, she stomped toward her suitcase. The dogs' continued barks pierced her head and made her long for a quiet room. She scanned the platform and her heart sank as she realized no one remained who could help her. She plopped on top of her suitcase, shoulders slumped.

Well, there was one man who could help, but she wasn't about to ask him.

Click to buy now

143

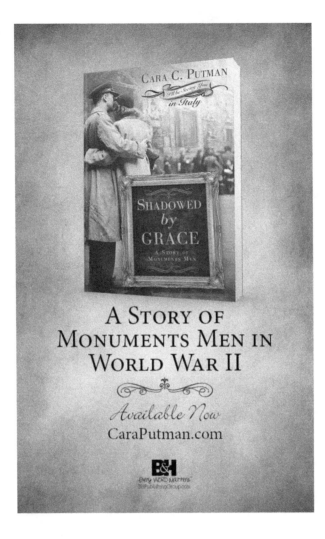

DEAR READER

Thank you for reading CANTEEN DREAMS. This was a story of my heart because it allowed me to marry my love for WWII with a pretty incredible real event from my home town with the details of my grandparents' story. The story wrote itself, and it was a thrill when it one the ACFW Book of the Year for short historical in 2008. What's even more exciting is knowing you've taken Audrey and Willard's journey.

Haven't we all had a time when we wondered if we were doing enough, being enough? That's really Willard's story as he watches men go to war and he's sent home time and again. It's also Audrey's story as she tries to find a way to make her own contribution to the war effort. Her challenge becomes balance… something I struggle with each month and season. I've had to learn to accept that my balance isn't going to be my neighbor's or yours, but as long as I'm asking God to help me find the right balance, He is pleased with my efforts.

If you enjoyed Audrey's story, I hope you'll continue with SANDHILL DREAMS. In SANDHILL DREAMS you'll learn what happens to Lainie. Her story was a fun one to write and I hope you enjoy it, too!

Blessings,

CARA PUTMAN

p.s. New reader friends, let's stay in touch! I'd love to connect with you on Facebook, Twitter, Pinterest, Goodreads, or Instagram. And I send out a fun, never-spammy e-newsletter every now and then. Sign up to receive it here.

p.p.s. Also, please know how much it means to me anytime you leave a review of one of my books! Reviews are incredibly helpful . . . and I'm incredibly grateful.

SANDHILL DREAMS

ACKNOWLEDGMENTS

No book is a solo endeavor. Thanks so much to my first readers Sabrina Butcher, Sue Lyzenga, and Janna Ryan, and to Tricia Goyer for sharing her time and experience. Thanks also to Emilie Eros and Virgene Putman for investing in my children while I raced toward a deadline. And last but certainly not least, many thanks to Tom Buecker, curator of the Fort Robinson Museum, who freely gave of his time, knowledge and extensive files during my visit. You made the war at the fort come alive. Tom's book, *Fort Robinson and the American Century*, is fantastic.

Special thanks to my editor JoAnne Simmons, who believed in this series of World War Two stories when I wrote them for Heartsong Presents. It has been an honor and privilege to work with you. And thank you to Andrea Cox for helping me proof this book as it gets ready for a second life. Her attention to detail and love for the stories makes them sing.

To Eric, for always believing I would be more than a one-book wonder and cheering me from those first words ... "so did she tell you she wants to be a writer?" I'll be forever grateful that you said what I couldn't. And even more, that God put us in that same corner of Colorado in 1990. The rest, as they say, is history. Looking forward to seeing what the next fifty years hold!
And to Mason, truly one of man's best friends. We all miss you.

VERSE

"But now, thus says the Lord, your Creator, O Jacob, And He who formed you, O Israel, "Do not fear, for I have redeemed you; I have called you by name; you are Mine! When you pass through the waters, I will be with you; And through the rivers, they will not overflow you. When you walk through the fire, you will not be scorched, Nor will the flame burn you. ... Do not fear, for I am with you."
   Isaiah 43:1-5 (NAS)

CHAPTER 1

MAY 7, 1943

*A*s a child, the rocking of the train, the clunk of the wheels on the tracks, had promised adventure, excitement, but not this time. Sitting on a train headed to the farthest corner of Nebraska was the last thing Lainie Gardner had imagined for her life. Her dreams shimmered in the distance like a hallucination. She should have crossed the Atlantic Ocean with her friends, and fellow nurses, from the 95th Evacuation Company, bound for the European front. Instead, she waited for the train to stop long enough for her to disembark in Crawford.

She tugged a lace-trimmed handkerchief from her jacket pocket and wiped a small circle on the train window. Dust blew in waves across the desert landscape of the sandhills. The few trees squatted against the horizon. The emptiness mocked her, mirroring the barrenness inside.

The conductor swayed between the seats of the car to the rhythm of the clacking wheels. "Next stop. Crawford." Even his words were as lifeless as the tumbleweed that paced the train.

The car jerked from side to side as it slowed. People jumped from their seats and collected their items. A dark-haired toddler jostled against his mother. He bounced on the seat and his sandaled foot slipped. Lainie sucked in a breath. With a thud, his head collided with the hard bench seat, and he wailed. He lifted his head, and Lainie noticed a gash on his forehead and a trickle of blood.

Lainie attempted to leap from her seat to help him, but stopped short as her book tumbled from her lap. Her joints refused to unlock. Not too long ago she'd been active and healthy, but not any more. Rheumatic fever had struck quickly and left her weakened and vulnerable.

The commanding officer's words raced through her mind. *Young lady, being a nurse requires strength and stamina, of which you have neither.* Oh, she'd fought that pronouncement, but in the end she lost.

The boy's mother pressed a handkerchief against the wound. Lainie sighed and collapsed back on her seat. There was little more she could do to help this young boy. But she could have done much for the soldiers.

"Next stop. Crawford." The conductor continued his travels through the car.

Lainie shuddered and then swiped the handkerchief across her forehead. Her stomach knotted and doubts raced. She'd skipped the planning that would make this trip a success. "I must be crazy."

The matron across the row quirked an eyebrow as she glanced at Lainie and then returned to her book.

Lainie blushed. The words weren't supposed to trip from her mouth like the tumbleweeds blowing across the hills. She fingered the veil of her hat and turned back toward the window, ignoring the questions reflected in the woman's eyes. She'd answered too many queries already. No need to entertain a stranger's.

The click of the train's wheels against the track slowed its tempo. She tucked her paperback and handkerchief inside her handbag. The knots tightened their hold as she wondered what she'd find at Fort Robinson, a couple miles down U.S. Route 20 from Crawford.

Compared to North Platte, Crawford would seem like a hamlet. She shuddered. North Platte had never seemed like much of a town to her. Not that it mattered now. She couldn't go back to what her life had consisted of before she left for nurse's training. A cycle of endless parties and flirtation held no appeal after she tasted the opportunity to make a difference.

Lainie pitched forward when the train lurched to a stop. She leaned down to look out the window, and her heart sank as she fell back into her seat. "There isn't much to Crawford."

"No. It's a small extension of the fort and a few ranches. But those of us who call it home love it." The matron's steady voice soothed the fear that gripped Lainie. She searched Lainie's eyes a moment before she continued. "This your first time here?"

"Yes, ma'am. I'm hoping to get a job. You know, free a man to fight and all that."

The woman pursed her thin lips, a pinched expression settling on her sharp features, almost like she'd heard that story many times and watched others' hopes crumble. "Yes. Well, good luck." The woman's ample form side-stepped into the aisle, releasing Lainie to stand.

Lainie almost ducked to look under her seat for her courage. It had been in full force when she convinced her family moving to Fort Robinson was the right step. With the girls from the 95th Evacuation Company shipped out, she'd thrown caution to the wind, packed her bag, and bought a train ticket in the opposite direction and a thousand miles closer to home.

She sidled down the aisle toward the door, a tightness and deep ache pulsing from her muscles. She swallowed against the pain. The effects of rheumatic fever lingered, and the train ride had been harder than she'd anticipated.

Loud, almost frantic barks ricocheted off the train as she stepped off the train. She shielded her eyes and scanned the platform. She walked toward the wooden crates stacked two high and at least six wide. Snouts and paws pushed against the chicken wire fronts. The barking escalated as two men placed an additional crate on the pile.

The dungarees and cowboy boots they wore with their khaki standard issue shirts were a far cry from the uniforms the servicemen wore as they rushed through the Canteen back in North Platte. Did they have a unique outfit for Fort Robinson? One slipped back into the car while the other adjusted a crate.

"What is all this?" She raised her voice over the din.

The soldier reached into the gap in the train's side to accept one end of another crate.

Lainie pulled herself to her full height, all five feet and a couple of inches of it, and edged toward the soldier. "Excuse me."

The soldier dropped the crate he'd picked up and then spun on his heel rubbing his ear. His gaze took her in and swept over her again. "You didn't need to shout."

Lainie thought she'd never seen eyes as clear blue as his, without a hint of iciness. He ran a finger over a scar on his hand, almost like a forgotten habit. "Had to make sure you heard over the barking."

The soldier closed his eyes and rubbed a hand over his face. She couldn't tell if he was frustrated with her or trying to hide a smile. "Ma'am, you've made me drop valuable Department of War resources. If that animal's injured, my officer will have my hide."

"Why don't you check and see?"

He leaned down, careful to keep his face a good three feet from the wire. "It's a quiet one. I hope that means it's fine. If you'll excuse me, I have a job to do."

His words ricocheted through her mind. Yes, he might have a job, but he didn't have to rub her nose in it. But how could unloading dogs in Nowhere, western Nebraska be important to the war effort?

Balling her fingers into fists, she stomped toward her suitcase. The dogs' continued barks pierced her head and made her long for a quiet room. She scanned the platform and her heart sank as she realized no one remained who could help her. She plopped on top of her suitcase, shoulders slumped.

Well, there was one man who could help, but she wasn't about to ask him.

* * *

THOMAS HAMILTON CHOMPED down on his lower lip as he tried to ignore the dogs stacked around him and the young woman stalking away. He'd almost told her she had a swipe of soot across her forehead, but then the crate had dropped. The mark added a hint of frailty to her appearance, but he figured she'd be horrified to know it existed, even if it didn't mar her dark beauty one bit.

"How many more are in there?" he mumbled to his partner. "The conductor looks anxious to move on."

"Just a minute." John Tyler disappeared into the dusk of the car. A skinny string bean of a man, he fit easily inside the cramped area. Tom had tried it once and decided he'd rather be trapped in an underground cave for hours than surrounded on all sides by nervous dogs in a space with little to no room to turn around. John's feet stomped against the wood floor. "It looks like we've got six more crates. How are we supposed to get all these mutts back to the fort?"

Tom eyed the crates and shrugged. "We'll fit as many as we can. Worst case, I make two trips. You wait here with what we can't load."

"Yeah, well, you cool your heels while I drive back and forth." John crossed his arms and stared at Tom.

He held his position. It wasn't his fault the Army decided he could best serve by working with animals. Dogs of all things. Who in their right mind joined the military and expected to spend day after day surrounded by yipping, yapping, barking, four-legged nuisances? Certainly not him. No, he came to work with the herd of horses. And with thousands at the fort, that seemed like a safe assumption. But this was the Army and plans changed. So John could stare all he wanted. Tom would not babysit crated dogs. Maybe he'd get orders to ship out soon. Others had and now saw action in Africa or the Far East. A guy could hope.

"Fine." John took off his work gloves and threw them on the ground. He jumped off and walked toward the stack of crates. "Let's get the last crates out of here."

With a grin, Tom slapped John on the back. "Now there's a reasonable plan." In no time, they'd stacked the last of the crates on the platform. "I'll back up the truck. Don't worry, it won't take long. In no time I'll collect you and the rest of the dogs."

John grumbled under his breath as he followed Tom.

They worked quickly, loading the crates and tying them down in record time. All the while, Tom watched the young spitfire paced the platform before sinking onto her suitcase. Now that she'd left him alone, she looked lost and uncertain. Like she hadn't a clue what to do next.

Her fingers twisted the handle of her bag as her gaze flitted around the platform. She glanced at him and her back straightened. He smiled as he watched her force her shoulders behind and tilt her chin. She was a petite thing, not even hitting his shoulders, and her black hair and porcelain skin reminded him of movie stars like Linda Darnell. The beauty had spunk. He'd give her that. Even if she looked out of place on the wooden platform. Surely, she'd gotten off at the wrong place, misunderstood the conductor. She looked like she was better suited to a city like Denver than to the wide-open expanse around Crawford.

"Are you done lollygagging and ready to finish this job?" John eyed him with the hint of a smile tipping his lips. "I think I'll spend the time I'm waiting to ask that nice-looking dame to Mrs. Babcock's for pie. Sounds like a good way to while away the time to me."

"And what would Naomi say about that?" John's cute wife had a steel backbone anytime John stepped out of line.

John rolled his eyes and did a jig along the platform. "She'd say I made a good addition to the welcome committee. Let's get you off to the fort."

Tom glanced back at the woman and noticed her watching them. He stilled as she stepped toward him, picking up speed as she walked.

"Excuse me. Did I hear you say you're headed to the fort?"

Tom nodded his head until he could find his voice. "Yes, ma'am. I'll leave in a minute."

"Wonderful. Could I catch a ride with you? It's important I reach the fort today."

Tom turned to block John's glare. "Ma'am, do you have an appointment or other reason to travel to Robinson? I can't give everybody who wants space a ride. One of the shuttles can take you later."

She chewed on her lower lip and glanced away. "I don't have an appointment. Surely that doesn't matter if you have a space."

John harrumphed behind him. Tom rubbed the back of his neck and considered his options. There wasn't a clear rule, but civilians didn't get rides. "I'm sorry."

"Fine." She looked back at Tom, and fire flashed from her eyes. She squared her shoulders and turned on her heel. He watched her stride across the platform. "If you won't help, at least point me in the right direction."

"Don't tell me you intend to walk."

"You've left me with no other option." She looked from him to John. "Maybe you'll be so kind as to point me toward this shuttle."

John rubbed his hands together. "How about a slice of Mrs. Babcock's pie first?"

"You're as impossible as he is. I'll find someone who'll help." She grabbed her suitcase and stalked toward the small station. If she was lucky, she might find someone in there. Likely, Ed had closed up and headed for lunch now that the train had moved on. She rattled the door and drooped when she couldn't get in.

"For crying out loud." He couldn't leave her there like that. Tom hopped in the cab of the truck. "John, I'll be back soon as I can."

He eased the truck to a stop next to her. She remained focused on the road in front of her. "Hop in." He jumped out and opened the passenger side door for the woman. "Please. My mama raised me better than to let you walk."

Pallor had settled on her face, highlighting bright spots on her cheeks. "Are you okay?"

She stopped. "I will be." She turned to him and a thin smile graced her lips. "Thank you." She accepted his hand and climbed onto the seat.

"John, come grab her suitcase, okay." Tom settled behind the wheel of the truck and looked at the woman. "We'll get your suitcase later; the back's too full right now to squeeze it in. Where do you need to be dropped off?"

She glanced at him, then back out the windshield. "I'm not really sure. I'm here to apply for a job, so the administration building I guess."

Tom scratched his head and swerved to miss a wheel-sized hole in the road. The highways around here weren't used to all the traffic the war had brought to this small fort tucked in northwestern Nebraska. One he'd never heard of before enlisting a year ago. "By the way, I'm Specialist Thomas Hamilton. All my friends call me Tom."

"Lainie Gardner. I appreciate the ride." She eased against the seat and closed her eyes.

Concern flooded him. "Are you sure you know what you're doing?"

Her eyes flew open. "Of course I do. Why would you think differently?"

"Well, you don't seem to have a plan, Miss Gardner. Don't you think it would have been a good idea to have a job before making the trip?"

"Certainly not." Her lips firmed into a hard line.

CHAPTER 2

$\mathcal{L}$ainie fumed and stared straight ahead, expecting the man's laughter at her plight. If she wasn't so angry, she'd laugh herself. She'd done it this time. She was stranded in the middle of nowhere, without a job or a place to sleep. Now she bounced around the cab of a military truck with a strange soldier. Her mother would be horrified.

Tall outcroppings of white rock pushed through the sandhills to the north of the highway. Their ragged edges showed the centuries of rain that had molded and formed them. The formations were unlike anything she'd seen.

"What do you think of the buttes?"

"Is that what you call them? Lovely." She turned and stared at the man. "That it? Your best attempt at conversation? Asking what I think of the scenery?"

"Other than continuing to mention you're a fool to come without a plan? I thought the view was safer."

Lainie snorted. "You don't understand women, do you?"

Color crept up his neck in a way that would have been endearing if she wasn't so annoyed. "Women overrun the fort. Wait until you see the hordes."

"All the more reason for me to come."

"Sure. And in two weeks you'll be married and unwilling to work."

"You are insufferable." She jostled against the door, her backside connecting with the firm bench. "Ouch." She resisted the urge to rub the ache away.

The landscape flattened as they barreled down the road. A row of buttes pushed up the earth at an angle from U.S. Route 20, which laced the plain. Prairie grasses grew with trees scattered along the ridges, but the majority of the landscape was wide open. Barren. Like her heart. Shattered like her dreams of joining the war effort. Lainie clenched her teeth and vowed she would talk her way into a job at the fort.

"Look, I'm sorry we got off on the wrong foot." The private whipped his cap off with one hand and rubbed his forehead. "You have every right to be here. So why did you come? You don't seem like the type to run up here without the semblance of a reason."

"Thanks, I think." Lainie smoothed her skirt, and her fingers played with the navy worsted wool fabric, twisting and untwisting it. She eyed him. Was his apology honest? She sucked in a breath and decided to treat it as such. "My mother read an article in the *North Platte Bulletin* about the push for civilians to free enlisted men to ship overseas. I can help."

"Why not stay in North Platte or wherever you're from?"

"I had other plans that didn't work out. And this is far enough away from home to keep my folks from hovering."

"What can you do?"

"I'm trained as a nurse, but need something less strenuous. I'll take clerical work." South of the highway, row after row of narrow, wooden buildings lined a road. It looked like a hastily constructed camp or barracks. "Is that part of the fort?"

"That? No, it's a prisoner of war camp. Construction's well under way, and the first prisoners should arrive in this fall."

Lainie hadn't expected to see such evidence of the war this close to home. Soldiers—at least she assumed they were soldiers in their jeans—walked between the buildings, but none looked at the truck. What were they doing if they didn't have prisoners to guard? She pushed a piece of hair behind her ear as she turned her attention back toward the highway.

"How long have you been stationed here?"

Private Hamilton shrugged. "Since I enlisted. I thought I could help with the horses, and signed up here twelve months ago. However, the Army, in its wisdom, decided I'd work with war dogs. So here I am, a private specialist who works with canines all day." His fingers tapped against the large steering wheel. "I'm hoping to ship overseas soon."

"Were are you from, soldier? You don't sound like a native Nebraskan." Lainie smiled as the routine questions she'd used at the North Platte Canteen flowed.

"A little bit of here and there, but mostly Wyoming." The truck crested a slight hill. "Here we are."

Lainie gaped as the fort spread before her, filling both sides of the road with activity.

"That bus coming toward us is what you'll take to get to the fort in the morning. It shuttles folks back and forth from Crawford."

"Okay. Wat should I expect to see?"

"Scattered around here is a herd of around four thousand horses in various stages of enlisting in out of the Army, and a herd of mules mustering in and training. The British Army appreciates our well-trained mules." He looked at her and quirked an eyebrow.

A pleasant shiver chased down her spine at the look, and she smiled. "Where are the dogs housed?"

"Off that way." He pointed over the hills. "We house and train them at the War Dog Training Center to the south of the highway. There's plenty to keep us busy out here."

She pulled her attention back to his words and wrinkled her nose as she tried to decipher them. "War dogs?"

"Dogs. Mutts. Heinz 57s. Whatever you want to call my cargo. They get shipped here from all over the country, courtesy of Dogs for Defense."

"What do you do with them?"

"We train most as sentries. A few get shipped back to their owners if they don't have what it takes. Then those who make it through the basics proceed to advanced training." He turned right into the compound and stopped the truck in front of a two-story brick building. "Here you go. The private inside can direct you to whoever you need to see."

Lainie stared at the building. Every certainty she'd had that this was the right step washed from her as she considered what she had to do next. She urged her limbs to cooperate, to propel her out of the truck and up the stairs, but couldn't move. As she sat there, Private Hamilton bounded from the truck and opened her door.

"Look, we got off on the wrong foot. My momma always told me to treat a lady well. A lady waits for her door to be opened." He swiped his hat off his head, wiped his forehead, and then replaced the hat with a slight bow. "It's been a pleasure."

She looked into his kind eyes and saw the friendship he offered. "Thank you for the ride, soldier." She accepted his proffered arm and climbed out of the truck. Jutting her chin out, she gripped her handbag and walked up the wooden steps to the building. She hesitated a moment, then pushed open the door.

As soon as she opened the door, stale air thick with cigarette smoke threatened to choke her. A thin man behind a metal desk nailed her with a glare. "Can I help you, miss?" Derision dripped from each word.

Had any of these soldiers received training on how to welcome people to base? Built on her early interactions, it sure didn't seem that way. By the stripes on this one's shoulder, it was plain to see he wasn't who she needed to talk to. "I'd like to speak with the commanding officer, please. I'm here for a job."

"Do you have an appointment?" The man looked at her like he knew she didn't.

Lainie stood straighter and looked down at him. "No. However, he'll want to see me anyway."

"Miss, I don't know where you came from, but you don't belong here. We are not a temporary agency, nor do we invite random citizens to park themselves here. I suggest you move yourself out of this building and off this base. We do not have time to entertain young ladies."

With each word he spoke, heat slipped up her cheeks. She clenched her fists and tensed. Lainie knew she should hold her tongue, take whatever he had to say, and hold her ground. But before she could stop herself, she erupted. "Excuse me, but you have no idea what's brought me here. I have volunteered with the North Platte Canteen, serving soldiers like yourself when their trains stopped for a quick break. I received nurse's training and enlisted with the Army Nurse Corp. My unit is currently headed overseas."

"But you aren't with them, are you?" He sneered. "I would think that if you aren't good enough for them, you certainly wouldn't be for us."

"I am here, because I can no longer serve as a nurse. However, I can still free a man to serve, and you have civilian openings. I would like to speak to your commanding officer." *Even if a job means I have to work with an arrogant man like you.* She forced a tight smile on her face.

"If you hurry, you might catch the next shuttle to Crawford. If you're really lucky, you might even get to town in time to catch the final train." The impossible man had crossed his arms and leaned away from her. He couldn't be less interested if he tried.

The fight left Lainie and the pressure of failure built. She'd deluded herself into thinking she could accomplish something here. Without another word she turned and left the building, letting the screen door slam. She looked around the parade grounds for the shuttle, and finally found it as it headed toward Crawford. She slumped against the outside wall. Maybe Daddy had been right. She should go back to North Platte and give up any thought of doing something important. She could dance the war away at the Canteen, while she waited for the end of the war and her life to begin again.

Where are You, God? Haven't You taken enough from me? She closed her eyes, relieved to feel the pressure ease.

A plan formed in the shadows of her mind.

She'd walk to town, but not to catch a train. She pushed her exhaustion to the side and trudged down the stairs. Surely someone had a room she could rent. One foot in front of another, Lainie reached the highway. Her breath came in gasps as shards of pain pulsed in her joints. She looked back and groaned. The administration building was only a couple of blocks behind her.

So there wasn't a job waiting for her. There had to be a way. And if there was, she was the woman to find it. If only she could make it back to Crawford.

CHAPTER 3

*T*he din from almost fourteen hundred dogs pounded his ears. Row after row of waist-high wooden boxes stretched across the field in front of Tom. He grimaced and pulled his hat lower to muffle the noise. The cacophony echoed day and night across the compound past the barracks, almost back to Crawford. Some days he'd give a month's salary for ten minutes of quiet.

He pulled in front of the War Dog Reception and Training Center. It sat low and squat against the horizon, looking as if it had grown out of the earth from its concrete foundation. Inside that building the dogs he transported would get a cursory inspection and be released to the quarantined kennels to recover from their journey. Then they'd be inspected, weighed, groomed, inoculated, and remain in quarantine for a week. These animals would receive a trainer, start basic, and run through their paces until they understood key commands.

Several men ran up to the truck as soon as Tom popped it out of gear.

"What did you bring us today, Hamilton?" Sergeant Lewis strutted to the truck and slapped the top with his beefy hand.

Tom jumped at the noise and opened the door into Sarge's stomach. "Just the routine load of German Shepherds, Collies, and a Great Dane or two. I think I saw a Lab as well."

"Watch it." Sarge backed away and grimaced as he rubbed his pouch, where the door had connected. "Someday they'll quit sending us hunting dogs that chase every scent they pick up."

"It'll take a bigwig or two on sentry duty with a Lab who gets a whiff of some animal. By the time the dogs drag them back to base, they'll listen."

"Let's get these off-loaded." Sarge looked around. "Where's Private Tyler?"

"Waiting with several we couldn't fit on."

"What kind of pie does Mrs. Babcock have today?" Sarge smacked his lips.

"She was getting off the train, so I doubt she whipped any up yet."

"That woman's amazing. I bet she had one in the oven the moment she arrived."

Tom smiled at the thought. She enjoyed taking care of the soldiers. Did more than her part to keep morale high, far as he was concerned. Soldiers often fought to slip into Crawford and wander by her boarding house. Inevitably, they left with their bellies stuffed with thick slices of pie and a glass of fresh, creamy milk.

Several men hustled about and emptied the truck of its crates. Others hauled the enclosures inside where soldiers would release the dogs. Days like this Tom was particularly glad he wasn't a vet tech. Little sounded worse than examining a bunch of scared dogs minutes after they'd arrived. A sure recipe for attacks. Maybe if he slowed down the trip back to Crawford, he could avoid processing, too. Then all that would be left when he returned would be introducing a couple of the dogs to the wide-open prairie. That he could handle.

Private Donahue yanked on the last crate, and Tom hurried to help him ease it to the ground.

"I'll go get the rest." Tom climbed back into the cab.

"Hurry back, Private. We need to talk about your dogs."

Tom stifled a groan as his gut clenched. He swiped the sweat drenching his palms onto his pant legs. "I'll rush back, sir."

"Be sure you do. Would hate to have to send a team out to find you." Sarge stalked into the building behind the last dog.

"Sure thing," Tom snapped.

Several soldiers snickered, and Tom rolled his eyes. They didn't understand his fear a dog would attack him or his hope that, with each set of dogs that shipped out with their new handlers, he'd get reassigned. Foolish, but he maintained hope nonetheless. Anything to get a change in task. Dad promised his fear would disappear at some point. Tom doubted it, especially after a year of close encounters with his four-legged friends. He snorted. Dogs might be man's best friends, but they'd never been his. Still fuming, he turned the vehicle around and headed out.

He hit the open stretch of highway between the fort and town, and his thoughts turned back to the spitfire he'd given a ride. There was something captivating about her—even if she had been all sparks during the trek. He slowed when he saw someone on the side of the road. The woman stumbled along, holding her shoes in her hand. If it weren't still early afternoon, he'd wonder if she'd been drinking as she staggered around with stiff motions. He pulled to the side and slammed the brakes. That gal, Miss Gardner, didn't even turn.

"Lainie? Miss Gardner?" Tom ran the few steps to her side. She turned glazed eyes on him. "Can I give you a lift to town?"

Fatigue pulled her features down, even as her eyes darted as if looking for options. He settled back against the car seat. If she thought she had a better way, fine. But he was her only possibility, whether she wanted to believe it or not, and he wanted to help her.

Finally, her gaze shifted to him, and she smiled. "I don't want to be a bother."

"The bus won't be back for a couple of hours. It's not out of my way to drop you off."

Color flashed up her cheeks. "Thank you. You seem to be the only one with time to help. And then my heel broke."

"It might be your air." He shrugged his shoulders to soften the words.

"My air?"

"Well, we're not used to people acting like they own the place."

"I don't." She sputtered to a stop. "Okay, so maybe I have. I tend to do that when I'm unsure. I don't belong here anymore than I do on some battlefield."

"Then let me help. Hop in." He offered her his arm. She looked at him, hesitated, and then accepted it. With her light touch on his arm, he felt a shock wave of electricity shoot straight to his heart. *Steady, boy.* It hadn't been that long since a beautiful woman had accepted his help. There was something different about this gal, though. When he searched her eyes, he saw a woman whose dreams had been replaced with emptiness. It made him want to overlook the ways she lashed out, because, like one of the injured dogs he helped, the growl meant she was hurt.

"Anything I can help you with other than the ride?"

"Know of a job for me?" The corner of her lips quivered.

"Wish I did. You'd think they'd be looking for people. It's a bit isolated for some."

"I can see that. The sky stretches forever here. Do you like it?"

"I grew up in Wyoming and followed my father from ranch to ranch. He was a vet and got called at all hours to help with sick or injured livestock. That part of the country isn't much more populated than this." Tom paused and looked around, trying to see the place through the eyes of a newcomer. "It may seem desolate, but I see God's creativity. He could have decided fertile valleys or the ocean were the perfect landscape. Instead, He created this area between the Rockies and the farmland to remind us of his bigness. It might be rough, but it's got an innate beauty. You just have to look for it."

Lainie's lips curved upward. "I do believe you have the soul of a poet hidden underneath that uniform. The land has captured you."

"I hope its Creator has, ma'am."

"Maybe it's the heart of a preacher buried in your soul."

Tom wrenched away from her intense gaze. That was the first time anyone had called him a preacher, and he couldn't quite label how that made him feel. Was he too transparent with a stranger? Or too reserved around his friends? He chuckled wryly. Rubbing his forehead, he slowed the truck. "I don't know about that. But I do know there's something about this place that grabs me. Now, where can I take you?"

"I don't know. I'll need my suitcase, but have no idea where to stay tonight."

Tom smiled. This was an easy problem to fix. "Mrs. Babcock's it is."

"Mrs. Babcock?"

"She has a small boarding house for young women and a restaurant. If she doesn't have room, she'll know who does."

Lainie pulled in a shuddering breath. "Okay."

He stopped the truck in front of the station. Hopping out, he said, "Wait while I get your bag."

Tom looked up to see John Tyler watching him with his arms crossed over his chest.

"About time you got here. What's she doing with you?"

"Things didn't go as hoped. I'm running her to Mrs. Babcock's and will be right back."

Metal clanged and loud barks filled the air.

John slouched against the stack of crates. "Thanks for waking them up, Tom."

Tom shook his head and walked back to the truck. "See you in a few."

"Yeah, yeah."

It took approximately two minutes to cross Crawford and pull the truck near the white picket fence that surrounded Mrs. Babcock's three-story Victorian. The house looked oddly oversized to Tom each time he pulled up. He supposed for her line of work, running a boarding house with a small restaurant on the first floor, it was perfect.

The sun's rays reflected off the fresh coat of paint a group of soldiers had applied three weeks before. Clumps of plants struggled to grab a foothold in the rocky soil around the front porch. Even a load of manure hadn't helped.

"Here it is." Tom turned the ignition off and tapped the wheel with his hands.

Silence greeted him. He looked at Lainie, saw her swallow. He fought panic at the thought she looked near tears. What would he do if she broke down and cried?

She swallowed again. "There isn't much to Crawford is there?"

"You should have seen it before the war. And the people are friendly. I think you'll like it here. If things don't work out, I'm sure you can always go back to wherever you came from."

She turned from him and swiped at her eyes. "You're right. It will be great. I'll feel better when I know I have a place to stay."

"Mrs. Babcock has a heart of gold. You'll see." As Tom helped the young woman up the stairs, he prayed he was right, because suddenly, he didn't want to see Lainie leave.

CHAPTER 4

MAY 8, 1943

The sun's warm rays tickled Lainie's cheek. She peeked at the light and groaned. She hadn't slipped into a nightmare. She truly lay in a strange bed, in a strange room, in a strange town.

The room felt tiny, with barely enough room for the narrow bed, an oak vanity, and a heavy wardrobe. Floral wallpaper decorated the walls, and a rag rug covered the floor next to the bed. Its rose and blue colors brightened the room. She only wished her spirit was as bright.

She curled up in a ball and pulled the quilt over her head. She should have listened to everyone who told her to stay home.

No. When she'd boarded the train to Kentucky for nurses training, determined to make a difference for whichever soldiers she nursed, she'd set her course. To go back would prove to everyone she was still a child in need of care.

She pinched her eyes shut and scrunched her nose. Maybe if she wished hard enough, the world would miraculously right itself. The war would end. The boys would return home. And she would regain a life of ease. Was that what she wanted? Did it fit her anymore?

Someone stomped down the wood floors of the hallway. Lainie pulled the covers down and opened her eyes. A knock shook the door in its frame.

"Still in bed, Lainie? Get up or you'll miss breakfast." Mrs. Babcock's alto voice filtered through the door. The woman welcomed her last night and led her to this room as if she'd expected Lainie to occupy it.

Lainie tried to relax from her tight ball, but her joints fought her. The train ride had pushed her weary body too far. Pain seared her arms and legs. She gritted her teeth and breathed deeply. One. Two. Three. She exhaled and relaxed her muscles.

"You okay?"

Lainie grimaced. "I'm fine. I'll be down in a minute."

"All right." The words sounded doubtful, as if Mrs. Babcock thought she'd turn over and ignore the day.

Lainie sat and pushed off the bed. After a moment, her limbs unlocked, and she lurched to the wardrobe. She opened the door and stared at the clothes. What would she do in a day that stretched in front of her with nothing to fill it? She didn't have anyone to impress. She reached for a serviceable navy skirt and white blouse, then stilled when she spotted her red sweetheart blouse. The town would surely flood with soldiers for the weekend. Yes, red was perfect.

Moments later she tugged a brush through her curly hair and straightened her skirt. She slipped down the stairs and headed to the dining room. Dirty dishes loaded one table. A few scrambled eggs and a slice of toast were all that remained at the buffet.

Mrs. Babcock bustled through a door, a stained apron tied tight around her ample middle, arms filled with plates of bacon and pancakes. "Here's some fresh food, missy. Please make it down with everyone else in the future. Breakfast is at seven o'clock sharp."

Lainie's mouth watered at the crisp aroma of bacon. "Yes, ma'am. Smells wonderful."

A smile tipped the corner of Mrs. Babcock's mouth. "I serve nothing but the best here. I serve two meals a day: breakfast for boarders and supper for anyone who comes with a dollar and an appetite. This particular slab of bacon came from Elmer Jackson. He does something that makes it extra smoky. Enjoy."

"Since I'm the only one here, why don't you join me? I can help clean later."

"It would feel good to sit a bit. It's been a long morning."

Lainie glanced at the clock on the buffet. She hated to think how early Mrs. Babcock had gotten up if she thought eight a.m. constituted a long morning. After Mrs. Babcock shoveled three pancakes and four slices of bacon onto her plate, she bowed her head. Lainie stared.

"Don't mind me. I hate to miss an opportunity to tell my Lord thank you."

Lainie nodded, then stabbed a piece of pancake and ran it through the maple syrup pooled on her plate. She savored the sweet bite and dove in for more.

"What are your plans for the day?" Mrs. Babcock dabbed her lips with a napkin.

"I need to find a job at the fort. The gentleman I spoke with yesterday was less than encouraging. Apparently, he hadn't heard the fort needs civilian workers."

Mrs. Babcock scooped applesauce on top of her pancakes and smeared it around. "Availability of jobs depends on who you know. What do you want?"

"To be on a boat crossing the Atlantic. But I'll settle for anything."

"You've got ideas. Otherwise, you'd be at Kearney's Air Base, working a factory job, or at a base in Lincoln or Omaha. Folks don't come to Robinson without a specific reason."

Lainie studied her plate. She didn't know this woman or if she could trust her with her hidden hope.

Mrs. Babcock waited.

"I've never done anything that mattered before. Somehow I have to contribute to the war. My best friend, Audrey, works at the North Platte Canteen."

"I've heard of it. Boys rave about it. Did you volunteer?"

"From the first day. But I have to do more than give cookies and fruit to soldiers. I planned to nurse." Lainie swallowed against the pain. "But that died when I got sick. I have all the training but can't use it. I guess I'm typing pool bound."

"So you type?"

"Never tried, but I can learn."

Mrs. Babcock smiled and pushed back from the table. "I know what we'll do after the dishes, then."

Before Lainie knew what had happened, she found herself standing beside Mrs. Babcock in the kitchen, drying dishes. After what felt like hours, the last teaspoon and glass were tucked into their spots in the cupboards and drawers.

"Follow me." Mrs. Babcock bounced down the hallway, quite a feat considering her girth. Lainie giggled as she followed behind. "I have the ticket to get you ready for the typing pool." Mrs. Babcock pushed open a door with her hip and waved Lainie in.

"Welcome to my office. You'll care about the typewriter sitting on that small table over there. You'll type fifty words a minute in no time."

Three hours later, Lainie decided her idea of practice and Mrs. Babcock's didn't match. At all. Everything from her fingers to her shoulders and back ached from huddling over the typewriter for so long. And her ears hurt from Mrs. Babcock's constant instructions. *No, not that finger. Raise your wrists. Feet flat on the floor.* She was worse than a drill instructor in the Army. Lainie had proven to be all thumbs as she fumbled to copy a newspaper article. She'd had no idea typing had rules.

When she'd decided she couldn't take one more minute, Mrs. Babcock stood. She grabbed her hat from the desk. "Enough of that."

Amen. Lainie launched from her chair, then stretched her arms to work out the kinks.

"Now we head downtown for lunch, and I'll introduce you to folks who can help."

"Maybe the typing pool isn't a good idea."

"Nonsense. You'll get better, give yourself some time."

Lainie groaned at the thought. Kindhearted as Mrs. Babcock was, she had no idea what sort of project Lainie could be. "Did I mention I dropped typing in high school?"

"No, but you have enough training to be inefficient. And quit calling me Mrs. Babcock. You've got me looking over my shoulder for my spinster aunt, God bless her soul. Esther will do just fine, especially seeing as you're a boarder."

Lainie smiled. She'd accept any offer of friendship. She followed Esther down the hall and watched as she pinned a floppy hat to her bun. The woman certainly had her own sense of style. "I'll grab my handbag and be right back." Lainie hiked up the steps and slipped into her room. She grabbed a navy pillbox hat from the wardrobe and pinned it to her upsweep. She lined red lipstick across her lips, and then studied her reflection. Yes, she would make the right kind of impression. A confident woman who knew what she wanted. She straightened her skirt and eased down the stairs.

After walking a block past small houses dotting Third Street, Lainie followed her hostess to Second. Silence hung between them until Lainie wondered what had happened to her order-barking hostess. They strolled up Second toward what Lainie assumed was Main Street. With each block, the houses thinned out, replaced by businesses. In the business district, none of the buildings stood taller than two stories and all were constructed of brick or wood.

Cars and trucks lined the streets in front of the storefronts.

Mrs. Babcock leaned toward her. "The ranchers have hit town for supplies."

Lainie looked around and noticed that something was absent from the scene. "Where are the soldiers?"

Mrs. Babcock sniffed and crinkled her nose as if she'd caught a whiff of a boarder's soiled laundry. "Look here, missy, if you want to find a beau, you'd better get back on the next train south and return to your Canteen."

Lainie stopped and stared at her. "Excuse me?"

"Look at you. All dressed in red, with flaming lips to boot. You are a walking advertisement for a date."

"There is nothing wrong with wanting to look one's best."

"Honey, this ain't no excursion. In fact, if that's what you're looking for, maybe you need to head up to Rapid City and gawk at Mount Rushmore. If you stay around here, the only thing folks'll gawk at is you."

"While I would like to see Mount Rushmore, I highly doubt I'll draw the same attention. Of all the suggestions. I am no floozy."

"I doubt we'll see many privates down here today. Those with Class A passes usually seek greener pastures in other towns." A sly sparkle danced in Esther's eyes. "Instead, I want to introduce you to some of the ladies in the civilian pool. If they like you, you're halfway to a job."

Lainie's shoulders slumped. This was not what she'd anticipated when they left the boarding house. All that hiking and pretending she felt fine, but no job. "Lead on."

They strolled into Mae's Diner. Green-checked oilcloth covered the tables, and mason jars stuffed with silverware and napkins graced each one. Four women huddled around a center table, talking with gestures flying. It was a wonder no one got slapped. Esther waved Lainie forward. "These are some of the gals who work over at Robinson. Barbara Scott is in the post headquarters along with Naomi Tyler."

Lainie nodded at the two.

"Mary Nelson works with the war dogs, and Liz Czaplewski floats."

In minutes, Lainie hovered over a slice of apple pie and cup of steaming coffee. The women rushed over each other's stories about working at the fort. Lainie's mind spun with the mass of information. Not even the coffee could keep her mind focused on the forest of details.

It was a relief when the redhead, Naomi, jumped up.

"Sorry, gals, but I've got to scoot. John'll be looking for me."

Liz sighed. "Ah, the life of newlyweds."

"That's right, sister. Can't keep him lonely at home." Naomi grabbed her hat and bag, then wiggled her fingers in a salute. "Until next week."

One by one the girls finished their drinks and slipped away. Esther and Lainie followed Liz out, then walked home. Once she returned to her room, Lainie pulled out her hatpins and plopped the hat and pins on her vanity. She eased onto the bed and relaxed against the pillows. After a full day, she'd come no closer to a job. What should she do?

The next morning, Lainie walked the couple of blocks to the First Christian Church she'd noticed during Saturday's walk. She entered the wooden chapel and found a spot on a bench several rows from the door. Families and an occasional soldier sat in the pews. Lainie sat there waiting … for something. Instead, she felt nothing. Emptiness had dogged her steps. Ever since she'd gotten sick, it seemed God had turned His back on her. She'd prayed to no avail. He surely knew her dreams of becoming a nurse, yet here she sat in a strange place with the body of a ninety-year-old woman. Crawford might be a new town, but she was dealing with the same God. One who didn't seem interested in her any more.

CHAPTER 5

MAY 9, 1943

The German Shepherd pulled hard against the lead, and Tom hung on. He would not allow this animal to best him. Warrior—the name fit the beast.

Tom hated working Sundays, but had to get this dog, and others like it, introduced to the prairie. Tomorrow a fresh unit of men arrived, eager to dive into their training. So after the chapel service, that thought propelled Tom across the prairie with this dog.

A handful of dogs needed an assessment before being assigned. Tom and the cadre stationed permanently at the fort had to guess which dogs were suited to which man as quickly as possible after additional men and dogs arrived. The process went smoother if he walked the dogs around. If only the dogs didn't sense his reservations so readily.

Warrior took off to the right, chasing the shadow of a prairie dog scent no doubt. Tom yanked hard on the lead. The dog didn't break stride, and Tom found himself flying down the hill toward the obstacle course. Crazy dog would get them hurt if he didn't slow down.

"Need help, Hamilton?"

Tom couldn't stop to locate Sid Chance's voice. His ankle twisted in a dip, and he grunted around the rush of pain. Warrior collapsed on his haunches, and Tom flew by him. Finally, he flopped down in a tangle of lead, dog, and feet.

"We'll change your name to Brer Rabbit. Sure you aren't part Lab?" Tom glared at Warrior, who grinned at him, tongue hanging. "So you like a good run to start your day. I'll make a note of that." Tom whipped his cap off and ran a hand across his sweaty forehead. He shook his head and then slapped the cap back in place. "You'll be a handful for your trainer. Show me some of that intelligence Shepherds are famous for." He'd assign Warrior to a military policeman and see how the two weeks of basic training went. If Warrior survived that, there'd be advanced training for six to ten weeks. If he had to guess, Warrior was headed to sentry duty.

Footsteps sounded behind Tom, and he turned to see Sid and a Dalmatian headed his way.

"Haven't painted her yet?"

"No. Sarge decided to wait until right before the Dalmatians ship out to paint them. I guess that'll signal they're really in the Army." Sid plopped beside him. He rubbed his hands along the dog's sides in a relaxed manner Tom envied. "Ready to train the new group?"

"Sure. Then they get to handle the dogs."

Sid rolled his eyes and flopped against the dog, using her like a pillow. "You've got to relax, Tom."

"Don't you think I know that? Some things run too deep."

"Where's your faith in God when you really need it?"

Tom grimaced at the challenge. He wanted the guys around him to see God was a real, vibrant force in his life. He couldn't change he'd been afraid of dogs since one attacked him as a kid. If working with dogs nonstop for a year hadn't cured his fear, Tom didn't know what could. "I know God could take care of this fear, but He hasn't chosen to."

"Have you asked Him?"

Tom rubbed his neck. Sid wasn't letting him off easy. To be fair, Tom couldn't think of the last time he'd asked God to remove his fear. He knew what to expect from fear. Dogs, on the other hand, were unpredictable beasts. But then a parade of the friendly ones he'd worked with marched through his mind. He shrugged away the image. "Didn't you have a Class A pass this weekend?"

Sid looked across the obstacle course to the highway and buttes beyond. "Yeah, but my girl told me she's not mine anymore, so I stayed here. No sense wasting a good weekend moping."

Silence fell between them. After a bit Tom struggled to his feet. "Time to get these dogs back to their homes."

"Yep. Only another twenty to check."

Tom hiked up the hill, Warrior walking at his side as sedate as a newborn calf. "Now heel, you fraud."

* * *

MONDAY MORNING LAINIE eased down to breakfast bright and early, ready for a cup of coffee and piece of toast. Today she'd find a job at the fort if for no other reason than necessity. Esther hadn't heard anyone in town needed help, but Laine'd make those rounds, too. Gingerly she touched her fingertips together. She could feel each hour she'd spent Saturday and Sunday pounding the typewriter. She hoped a typing test wasn't required. She still missed more letters than she nailed, but had developed more speed in her inaccuracy. Maybe they'd take her word that she was a quick learner. She sipped her coffee as she contemplated the best plan of action.

"Hurry or you'll miss the bus." Mrs. Babcock's words grated in the morning quiet.

Tanya Johnson, the remaining boarder at the table, shoveled food into her mouth even though she didn't take the bus. A quiet gal, she worked downtown at the library rather than at the fort. The job suited her bookish looks and personality.

Lainie shoved the last bite in her mouth. "I'll see you tonight, ladies."

She'd have to fly to make it to the pick-up before the shuttle left. It felt like it would be a good day. She didn't ache intensely and could move with relative freedom. Maybe the reminders of the fever would lift with time. The doctors in Kentucky had warned her the possibility existed she'd feel the effects for life, but this morning her body ignored the prognosis.

The bus driver eased to a halt when he saw her. "Need a lift, ma'am?"

"Yes, sir. Can you take me to the post headquarters?"

"That's a stop. Hop on board."

Lainie settled against an empty seat and prayed this search would be different from her last attempt. Hope chased her. She smiled and enjoyed the sensation.

One hour later Lainie struggled to remember the hope she'd sensed. The same surly private refused to give her access to anyone who could help her.

"Go home, miss. There's nothing for you here. If you're set on working, go somewhere else. The Women's Army Auxiliary Corp is here, and that's all the single women this outpost needs." He turned as if to dismiss her.

Lainie bristled at his condescending tone and treatment. Sure, there might not be a job here—though she doubted that. However, he should treat her with the common decency all people deserved. She stood rooted to the floor and stared at him. She'd wait to get his attention.

Color crept up his neck, but he focused on the report in front of him.

"I'm a quick study. I know how to type and am practicing to get faster. I can file. I have nursing skills."

"Then join the Red Cross. Look, we don't need you."

Lainie sputtered.

The door behind the private's desk opened, and a man stepped out. His uniform bore sharp creases and the silver leaves of a lieutenant colonel. His nose was sharp, but wrinkles softened his eyes like he enjoyed a good laugh. This had to be the post commander.

"What's the issue, Jamison?"

"This woman insists she needs a job. Here. Hasn't followed procedure."

The colonel turned toward her. "Ma'am?"

"He won't even give me an application. I traveled here Friday, because I heard you needed civilians to free men for other jobs. I traveled all the way to Crawford, and I want a chance."

The colonel examined her, and heat climbed her cheeks. He gave a slight nod. "Private, make sure you take her name and information. Ma'am, I don't know that we have the right posting at this time. However, if you can make the effort to come, we can take time to explore options. Good day."

"Thank you, sir." Lainie watched the colonel leave, then turned to Private

Jamison. "Looks like we need to talk." She wore her sweetest smile and leaned against his desk. "What would you like to know?"

Her momentary victory evaporated as the insufferable man sent her out without a job or a typing test. She left the building and stood on its broad porch, an uncomfortable repeat of Friday. She was stranded on base for two hours waiting for the shuttle.

Lainie eased down the steps and followed the road to the right. Officers' quarters and soldiers barracks ringed the side of the parade grounds in front of the headquarters. Brick buildings stood next to simple white-washed wood structures. Soldiers hurried past her along the road and sidewalk. Most tipped their hats as they rushed past, but none stopped to talk. If only she had something to rush to. She'd rarely felt this useless and alone. The flow of soldiers eased. Lainie smiled as these soldiers eagerly stopped. In no time she felt like Scarlett O'Hara at a picnic, surrounded by a crush of admiring men.

When the bus lumbered to a stop in front of headquarters, Lainie was sorry to see it. In twenty minutes she sat at the kitchen table, peeling potatoes for supper and spilling her woes to Mrs. Babcock.

"I can stay here for a few days without a job, but not much longer before Daddy'll have to send money." Her face twisted at the thought. She could imagine his response to the request. Something along the lines of "come on home where I can take care of you."

Lainie squared her shoulders and set her chin. She'd stand on her own. But without a job ...

"I could use some help around here. There are several items on my spring cleaning list I haven't checked off yet." Esther looked up from the pies she was crimping. "The gal who usually helps decided to marry a GI. Doesn't need this job anymore. I'll give you room and board in exchange for your help."

"And a dollar a day on the days I work more than a morning."

Esther smiled. "All right, then. We have a deal."

The days passed, and Lainie believed Esther had received the better end of the bargain. Lainie's hands had never been so chapped from dishwater. And her body ached from the physical activity followed by an hour or two practicing her typing. Each afternoon, after she'd finished the day's tasks, she'd change and head downtown.

She walked from storefront to bank to restaurant. No matter how often she asked or how big she smiled, each owner denied needing workers. With each no, she wondered if she'd ever hear a yes. There had to be more than cleaning rooms and washing dishes.

If there wasn't, she didn't know how much longer she'd last.

One afternoon, when she couldn't take another no, she traveled to the fort. She considered going to the administration building, but couldn't muster the energy to deal with the arrogant private.

Instead she turned toward the parade grounds. Maybe she'd walk and try to clear her head. She stilled as she reached the flagpole and spotted at least fifty men and dogs in the center of the field.

The men barked commands, and the dogs obeyed. Instantly. Heel, and each dog nailed his shoulder to his man's knee. Sit, and the dogs promptly sat on their haunches. Stay, and the dogs waited while the men proceeded past them. Each dog had eyes only for its soldier.

Lainie studied the soldiers, smiling when she saw Tom. He stood at the front of the group, his profile toward her, watching and making notes on a clipboard.

The men switched to hand commands, then dropped the leashes, and the dogs continued to obey. It was an amazing sight.

"All right, men. Ten minutes to report to the obstacle course." Tom turned toward her and grinned. "Hey, Lainie. Didn't expect to see you here."

"That was fascinating. How long did it take to train the dogs to do that?"

"A couple of weeks of basic training." His eyes crinkled around the corners. "You want to watch them on the obstacle course? We're going to the one across the highway today."

Excitement pumped through Lainie at the thought. "I'd love to."

"Walk with me." Tom cocked his arm, and Lainie slid her hand onto it.

They strode across the highway and another couple of blocks, through the gate into the war dog compound, and up a hill. Tom settled her on a rock.

"You should see everything from here. Notice that ridge along the dip there? That's where the dogs work. To them, this is a reward for a job well done." Tom watched the gathering group of men at the obstacle course below. "Will you be okay here while I run them through their paces?"

"Yes."

In minutes, Tom had the men organized into groups. He timed the teams as they raced through the course. The dogs scrambled over bridges and into ravines, scaled rocks, and tore along the flat spots, pulling their trainers with them. Many seemed to know exactly where the finish line was, as they'd brake to a stop and grin with tongues lolling.

Lainie watched them and knew. This was it. She'd serve with these dogs.

CHAPTER 6

MAY 18, 1943

$\mathcal{T}$om couldn't decide which was worse, handling the dogs himself or watching the current group of trainees man-handle the animals. For men screened for war dog training prior to shipping to Robinson, they sorely lacked an understanding of how to care for dogs.

The simple concept that you worked with a dog until he finally accomplished a task and you could reward him eluded their grasp. The poor animals were so confused Tom didn't think they'd ever understand how to heel, let alone be successful on difficult skills like an obstacle course.

At this rate, eight weeks would be insufficient to get the pairs ready to ship out.

One kid from New Jersey acted like he'd never seen a dog other than in a newsreel. Another from Alabama may have had dogs but not as a working animal. He constantly slipped human food to his dog—a bad habit if they landed in a jungle with limited food available.

The day's exercises finally ended, and Tom marched back to barracks. He collapsed on his bed and blotted out the day. At a rap over his head, he looked up. Sid stood next to his bed.

"I'm not hungry for mess here tonight. Want to ride into Crawford and catch a bite at Mrs. Babcock's?"

Tom's mouth watered at the thought of her home cooking. Her coffee didn't taste like old socks, and the pie melted in your mouth. "Say when."

"Let me gather the rest of the guys."

Tom stood and ran a hand across his hair. It probably stood up in all directions, but he couldn't wear a hat in Mrs. Babcock's restaurant. She had strict rules about etiquette.

He pulled out a fresh shirt. His dungarees didn't look too bad, and he needed his other pairs for the balance of the week. Then he thought of Lainie. Was she still in town and at Mrs. Babcock's? He pulled on clean pants in case he saw her. A whistle pierced the long room.

"My, don't you look dandy." Sid grinned at him, with Bill Byers and Dan Case looking over his shoulder. "Let's boogie while the food's still hot."

In no time they tramped up the stairs to Mrs. Babcock's and hung their hats on the hooks waiting on the porch.

As Tom walked in, he searched the large dining room for Lainie. Her face popped into his thoughts periodically, and each time, he'd prayed for her. Had she found a job? Or had she returned home with her tail between her legs? He couldn't imagine her doing that willingly. No, she'd fight until forced to admit defeat.

He didn't want that to happen.

The door at the back of the room swung open, and Lainie stepped through. She'd tied an apron over her dress and scurried from table to table refilling empty glasses with fresh milk or water. Nothing but the best for Mrs. Babcock's guests.

Guess he had the answer to his question. It looked like she'd do anything to stay.

She stopped and milk sloshed out of its container when her gaze landed on him. She forced a smile on her lips. "Have a seat anywhere you like, soldiers. Mrs. Babcock will be out in a moment to help you."

"What if we'd like you?" Bill Byers leaned closer to her, clearly captured by her.

"You can always make a request, boys, but tonight my job doesn't include helping you. Better luck next time."

Despite Bill's efforts, Lainie stayed far away as Tom and the guys ate their meals. The shepherd's pie tasted as wonderful as he'd hoped, a welcome break from the fare at the mess hall. It was a good thing it was a straight shot from his plate to his mouth, because he couldn't take his eyes off her. Tonight she looked like Linda Darnell, with her dark hair falling in curls around her face. It made her look soft while enhancing her natural beauty. He wondered what it would be like if she took that extra care for a guy like him.

"Ask her to the USO dance Friday." Sid grinned as he poked Tom in the ribs.

"Quit mooning." Dan winked at Bill. "If you won't ask, Bill will. You know how he's always looking for a new gal to entertain."

"Yep. She's a pretty thing. I could show her a good time."

Tom grimaced at the thought of what Bill would include in that endeavor. His exploits were well known, but maybe not for a gal new to town. He had to protect Lainie from that.

He looked up to find her standing next to him.

"More milk?"

"I'm fine." She turned to leave, but he grabbed her elbow. "Do you have any plans for Friday night?" He rushed on when she opened her mouth. Maybe he could cut off her no. "The USO's hosting a dance, and I'd be honored to escort you."

Lainie turned away from him. When he kept his hand on her elbow, she sighed and looked at him. "I appreciate all your help the other day, but I can't go with you. Someone else already asked."

He released her and forced a smile. "Maybe another time."

"Maybe." She slipped away toward the kitchen.

The guys watched him intently.

"Better luck next time, bud." Jonesie chortled.

"Yeah." Same leaned back. "Can't say I'm surprised someone already invited her."

Tom nodded. "Some guys have all the good fortune. Then there are guys like me."

His voice must have carried further than he thought, because she turned back to their table with a glint in her amber eyes. "The only reason I can't go is another soldier already asked. We danced once at the North Platte Canteen, so I said yes. He said that was the best day of his enlistment. Who am I not to help? If you're there, Tom Hamilton, I'll save a dance for you." She waited until he nodded, then her shoulders eased. "I'm not so sure about the rest of you, though. You'll have to be really nice to get a dance." She winked and walked away.

Sid's pleas followed her across the room.

"Fess up, Tom. What did you do to be so favored?" Bill leaned across the table.

"Gave her a ride last Friday. Seems she wants a job at Robinson."

"Remind me to volunteer to get the next shipment of dogs in Crawford." Sid knocked Tom in the shoulder.

Bill chuckled and shook his head. "All I ever get are dogs. You find a beautiful dame on your trip."

"It's not like she's overly fond of me. And we'll probably never have someone like her come to Crawford again." Tom leaned back in his chair, ears still burning from her rebuke. "Trust me, you're better off focused on one of the gals with the Women's Auxiliary Corp or gals in Lusk."

"But those gals like Wyoming. And you know the WACs are off-limits." A wicked gleam filled Dan's eyes. "That's only officially."

Tom leaned back in his chair as the men turned their attention from him and to stories of their escapades.

* * *

LAINIE LEANED against the table and searched the room for any excuse to remain in the kitchen. Her hands still shook from the humiliation of those men talking about her like she was a prize to win. Tom hadn't entered in, but he hadn't exactly protected her either.

And why couldn't he ask her earlier to the dance? She would have said yes, if only to avoid other offers. The men here were a little too eager to be around a pretty woman. She should have anticipated that at a fort in the middle of nowhere. Tom was different with a noble thread she trusted.

Shame flooded her at the thought he'd caught her at this job. She hadn't wanted him to see her like this. Ever since he'd driven her to Robinson and back, her thoughts had trailed toward him. Why? He was practically a stranger. She couldn't explain it, but she cared deeply about him which made no sense.

"Quit gathering wool, and scrub these plates. I've got to use them to serve that new table of folks." Esther swiped her arm across her forehead, smearing the sweat around. "I don't know why everyone decided tonight was the night to grace us with their presence. I've only got one shepherd's pie left. Hope it's enough. I've never run out of food." She threw plates on a tray and hurried back toward the dining room.

Lainie glared at the sink full of suds and dishes. Her hands would never be soft again after all the time she spent with her hands dunked in the burning water. Mama would be horrified, but she couldn't stop Lainie. And Lainie had come to like her little room. She wouldn't leave until she had a job here and made her way. If that meant washing dishes by the sink load, she'd do it. She dove into the pile of dishes with a rag.

She hummed a hymn as she worked. *It is well with my soul.* The words filled her mind with peace and replaced the tightness around her heart. She continued to hum and pondered the words.

Could it be well with her soul when everything around her had fallen apart? Her dream of serving in Europe lay in ashes around her feet. Her health still hadn't recovered, but she had more good days now. She didn't have the job she needed ... yet. But peace flooded her heart.

She longed for a way to bottle the feeling, seal it inside for those moments when the fear and disappointment overwhelmed her. Elbow deep in the water, she sang the words until they saturated her soul. "It is well with my soul. It is well, it is well with my soul."

CHAPTER 7

MAY 21, 1943

Strains of a Benny Goodman number ricocheted around the recreation building. Tom grimaced as the clarinetist with the post orchestra hit a sour note. Though the group got better with each performance, rough spots remained in the music. The tones didn't appear to bother anyone already dancing.

He glanced around the room and watched the soldiers lining the walls. A group of pretty ladies and their chaperones congregated near the punch bowl. He could walk over and ask one of them to swing. Instead, he joined John and Naomi Tyler in a corner.

"Why aren't you two dancing?"

Naomi giggled and looked at John with eyes filled with adoration. "We've already danced until I was breathless."

"You missed the Charleston, Tom. We really cut up the floor."

The image of gangly John swinging his arms and legs in the Charleston filled Tom's mind. "Now that's a scene I'm not sorry to miss."

"I'm not that bad." John looked Tom over. "We can have a contest sometime if you like. See who Charlestons better."

"No thanks. Those arms and legs of yours are long enough to hurt someone. You need some kind of warning system."

"Har, har, Hamilton." John looked across the hall. "Isn't that the dame you gave a ride?"

"Yes, that's her." Lainie breezed by in the arms of some private with the Remount Service.

"Mrs. Babcock introduced us on Saturday. I hear she's looking for a job." Naomi's words gushed out. "She seems nice enough."

"She is, with a sharp wit. She'll tell you exactly what she thinks."

"Nothing wrong with that." Naomi frowned at him and crossed her arms "Don't you need more help in the war dogs' office?"

"Not in my area, right, John?"

John shook his head and grinned. "Don't look to me for help, Hamilton. You know how Naomi gets when she has an idea. Might as well agree to help and save yourself a lot of misery."

What would it be like to enjoy Miss Gardner's sparks on a daily basis? The question intrigued him. She got even more adorable when her eyes lit up in a challenge. And he loved a good challenge. First, he had to get her to look at him. Without rolling her eyes or spouting off.

"Well, I'll collect that dance she promised me."

John grabbed Naomi and spun her around. "Sounds like a good idea. Let's swing, honey."

Naomi giggled in delight. Two bright spots of color bloomed on her cheeks. Watching the two of them, Tom longed for the same type of relationship with a woman. One tailor-made for him.

Lainie whizzed by in the arms of another soldier. This time it looked liked panic caused the color on her cheeks. She kept pushing space between her and the soldier, only to have him yank her closer again. Tom watched another moment, then stepped onto the floor. In a few steps, he caught up with the pair.

"Excuse me, but I believe you owe me a dance, Miss Gardner."

Lainie looked at him with a tight smile. "You are correct. Soldier, I'm afraid our dance will have to be cut short." She tried again to pull away from her partner.

"You heard her."

The private grimaced at Tom. "You can dance after the song ends."

"You can't force her to continue." As Tom tried to decide how to handle the situation without it exploding into a brawl, Lainie raised her foot and brought her heel down on the man's shoe. He howled and hopped on the other foot.

"Thank you for the dance. Please lead on, Tom."

"It would be an honor." He pulled her slight body into the circle of his arms and began to sway to the music. As he held her, his senses went on high alert. He could smell her flowery perfume. The conversations around them faded away until all he saw was Lainie.

* * *

LAINIE TOOK A DEEP BREATH. When that didn't calm her racing pulse, she took another. That last soldier had rattled her with his insistence that she dance close to him. Now, as she whirled with Tom, she felt sheltered, protected even. There was nothing pushy about the way he guided her around the floor. Far from a clod with two left feet, he led her through the dance with grace.

"Thank you." Her words whispered into his collar.

"For what?"

"Rescuing me from that bore." She tipped her chin up so she could see his eyes. Tonight they looked like they could be green or blue. A mystery mix of color and emotion. "So where's your date, Tom? I'm sure she's not happy you're with me right now."

"Why would you say that?"

"I seem to have that effect on women. They see me as competition rather than as friend material. Something of a Scarlett O'Hara, I'm afraid."

"You're blunt aren't you?"

"And you ask lots of questions."

Tom laughed at that statement, and Lainie decided she liked the sound. "You don't laugh much do you?"

"Turning the tables on me?" Tom nudged her.

"As often as I can. It's part of my charm."

"You seem to have an abundance of that."

"My Mama taught me well." Lainie waited for his reaction.

Tom guffawed, and Lainie smiled in delight.

"To answer your question, I came alone." Tom smiled down at her, and she determined his eyes were definitely a soft blue, like the sky on a clear summer day. She could search their depths for a long time and see only a small fraction of his soul.

"You are not a simple man, Specialist Hamilton."

"Nope. My dad didn't raise a fool. He thought I should be a Renaissance man."

"All while living in Wyoming." Lainie followed his steady lead as the band continued to play.

"Not everyone can be fortunate enough to live in that great state. The land is filled with big sky there."

"From what I've heard, there's not much else. Frankly, it doesn't sound much different from here."

"Maybe that's why I like Fort Robinson. There's the same sense of wide-open space. A man isn't crowded. There's plenty of air to breathe and acres to roam on the back of a horse."

"So you have the heart of a cowboy?"

"First, you tell me I'm a preacher, now a cowboy." Tom shook his head.

His dance steps slowed as the clarinet wailed the last notes of the song. Lainie quirked an eyebrow at him when he stepped back.

"Thanks for the dance, Lainie. I won't monopolize your time tonight."

The ember of temper ignited in response to his words. Had she missed something? They'd been in the middle of an amusing conversation, but in this moment he backed away? She turned and flounced the other direction. Two could play that game. She didn't look over her shoulder even when she felt his gaze.

A corporal jostled against Lainie. She stepped back and landed against the wall.

"Excuse me, miss." He let the last syllable expand, as if waiting for her to fill in a blank.

Instead, she nodded to him, then swiveled toward the refreshment table. She'd had her fill of uniforms for one night. Tom's abrupt dismissal ended the evening on a sour note. She should shake it off and let the corporal dance with her. Fatigue weighed her down, and she didn't have the energy to pretend she cared about another dance.

Out of all the soldiers she'd danced with, only one had proven worthy of her sparring. And he'd abandoned her after one wonderful dance.

The room closed in on her, so she left. Once she reached the outside of the building, the sounds of the orchestra faded. In the growing stillness of the night, she looked at the sky and gaped at the infinite number of stars glowing against the inky backdrop.

"It's breathtaking, isn't it?"

Lainie jumped and turned to see Tom standing to her side. "Don't you ever announce yourself?"

"Didn't want to ruin the moment."

"Like scaring the life out of a girl doesn't accomplish that." She took a deep breath and peered into the darkness. "It is amazing."

"God must delight in creating. Think about each of those stars, and there must be more that we can't see."

"You're in preacher mode?"

His white teeth shone in the darkness as he smiled. "I guess I am. There's something about the vastness of creation that points my thoughts to God the Creator. Evenings like tonight make it easy." He looked at her a long moment, and Lainie couldn't break from his gaze. "Do you have a ride back to Mrs. Babcock's?"

"No, I didn't think about when the shuttle would run into Crawford."

"You don't plan much, do you?"

She swiveled toward him, spine stiff and chin raised high. "I thought I'd ask someone else who had to go back to Crawford for a ride."

"Does this someone have a name?"

"No. But that doesn't mean I'm stranded."

"Maybe, but walking isn't a great idea in the dark."

"Thanks for the words of wisdom. I'll be sure to keep them in mind." She shrugged. "Besides, my shoes'll never recover from my last attempt."

Tom exhaled a breath like he blew out a candle.

Lainie waited, foot tapping, for the next barrage of words. "Come on, spit it out."

"What?"

"That you think I'm a sucker and should have never come. That the town and fort would be better off with me at home being spoiled by a daddy who's over-protective. That I shouldn't expect to do anything more than be coddled the rest of my days. And that I'll die of boredom, but that's my lot in life..." Lainie ran out of air and sputtered to a stop.

Tom shook his head. "You misunderstood. While I like to have a plan, that doesn't mean you should go home. Let me give you a ride. I'll rest better knowing you're safely home."

"Okay." Lainie relaxed her shoulders and smiled. "Maybe we can last the few minutes without annoying each other."

"I sincerely doubt that. My car's over here." Tom settled her in his black Chevy coupe, climbed in, then pointed the car down the highway.

Lainie gazed out the window at the stars illuminating the sky like a million twinkling nightlights. In no time, Tom pulled the car to a stop in front of Mrs. Babcock's. He hopped out and opened her door.

"Here you go." He offered her his hand and helped her from the car.

She found herself next to him again, could feel the warmth he radiated surround her. She drew a steadying breath, but couldn't move. He stroked her cheek with his finger. The action sent a jolt through her, making her aware of every detail. The fragrance of lilacs hung in the air, and a slight breeze chilled her skin. His gaze slipped from her eyes to her lips, and she couldn't breathe.

The screen door slammed, and Lainie jumped. "I should go in."

"Join me for a walk after church? I'll give you a tour of the fort."

"Okay. See you Sunday." Lainie floated to her room, wondering what his kiss would have felt like. She could only imagine.

CHAPTER 8

MAY 23, 1943

*L*ainie slid into the pew at First Christian Church next to Esther. She wondered if Tom would attend services here or if he'd come for her later. She'd spent yesterday wondering how he'd find her, then decided she'd have a hard time hiding in a town this size.

The organist played the opening notes to "Amazing Grace," and Lainie tried to settle her thoughts. She couldn't help that they continually wandered to a man who raised her blood pressure faster than anyone else. But his innate kindness also set him apart from other men.

The service passed in a blur as Pastor Stevenson focused on Isaiah 43. "Read with me. 'But now, thus says the LORD, your Creator, O Jacob, And He who formed you, O Israel, "Do not fear, for I have redeemed you; I have called you by name; you are Mine! When you pass through the waters, I will be with you; And through the rivers, they will not overflow you."'"

If that was true, then where was God when she'd been so sick? She'd cried out, but had been so incredibly alone in Kentucky with no one to care what happened to her. Her mom had planned to make a quick trip until her father decided her illness wasn't life-threatening. The memory of her isolation overwhelmed her, and she shivered. She would do everything she could to avoid that feeling again.

Pastor Stevenson's voice rose and pulled her attention back to his words. "'Since you are precious in My sight, Since you are honored and I love you, I will give other men in your place and other peoples in exchange for your life. Do not fear, for I am with you.'" If He'd truly been with her, why had her dreams of serving as a nurse been crushed? Hadn't that been a good thing for her to do? If it wasn't going to happen, why didn't God prevent her from wasting so much time in training?

People around her stood, and Lainie looked up to find them holding hymn-books. Somehow she'd missed the prior twenty minutes, trapped by the doubts swirling in her mind. Esther poked her in the side and frowned at her, her hat feather bobbing and dipping. Lainie stood and glanced around the sanctuary for Tom. Her heart sank when she didn't see him. She opened a hymnal and sang with the congregation.

After the benediction and dismissal, Lainie slipped from the pew and dashed to the entrance. Her mind spun. The phrases from Isaiah couldn't apply to her. She certainly didn't feel precious in God's sight. No, ignored or forgotten fit better.

She gasped for air as she hit the sidewalk.

"Are you okay?"

She looked up to find Tom leaning against his Chevy in front of the church. She pasted on a smile. "I see you found me."

"Not a difficult task. Everyone knows which church Mrs. Babcock attends. I figured you'd join her."

"Good guesswork, soldier." Feeling less wobbly, she forced the concerns from her thoughts and approached him. She tilted her head to catch his gaze. "I believe you owe me a tour."

He opened the passenger door for her. "My chariot awaits."

He handed her into the car, then hustled around the car. In moments, they headed toward the highway and then the fort. Lainie watched the landscape fly past. She pivoted toward Tom and considered him. His strong profile hinted at his steadiness. Nothing rattled him, and if anything did, he'd approach it with steady steps and a clear head.

He glanced her way and arched an eyebrow. "What?"

She ducked and felt heat climb her cheeks. She tried to cover the grin that pushed up her cheeks.

"It can't be that bad."

"You look like an unshakable rock." Lainie peeked up at him.

His shoulders shook and he pulled his hat low over his eyes.

"Hey. You're the one who asked."

"I suppose I did. I'm a touch scared to hear the next label you'll slap on me. Cowboy. Heartthrob."

She playfully nudged his shoulder. "Stop it. And don't think for a minute that I'll answer your interrogation the next time you ask."

"Duly noted." He slowed his car and pulled to a stop in front of a white concrete pad with posts.

"What's this?"

"The area in front of the post swimming pool. But we're headed to the war dog area. Those buildings on either side of the pool are barracks. And there are a few barns to the right. But over here to the left is my world."

Lainie hurried to follow him from the car and match his stride. She had to two-step to keep up. She stopped after a few minutes. "Tom, if you really want to show me, you either need to slow down or carry me."

He sized her up like he thought she seriously wanted him to haul her around.

She waved her arms and backed up. "That's a figure of speech. I'm shorter than you, and this isn't a race."

A sheepish grin covered his face, and he rubbed his neck. "Right. Sorry about that, Lainie."

She lingered on the way her name rolled off his tongue. She could get used to hearing that. He gazed at her so long she realized her look must appear rude. "You must love your dogs."

He frowned at her. "Why would you say that?"

"You're so eager to show them to me."

"I'd rather work with one hundred stubborn mules than ten dogs." He rubbed a scar that ran the length of his hand.

"Maybe, but you're sprinting toward the dogs."

"True." He cocked his elbow and, once she accepted it, stepped forward in mincing steps. "This better?"

"Much." His arm felt solid beneath her fingers. She inhaled the clean air. "You know what I miss? The flowers and trees that scent the area with spring. Out here, you can't smell any of that."

"Watering plants isn't a high government priority. You'll grow fond of the prairie grass." They crested a shallow hill, and Lainie stopped walking. A small compound of buildings stretched before them. "To the left stand the administrative buildings. Farther up the hill, do you see that small brick building?"

Lainie nodded. It looked more like a shed than a usable space.

"We store fireworks and arms there."

She looked from the building to him. "Why would you have that here with the dogs?"

"We use the fireworks to prepare them for what they'll hear if they're sent to the front."

She trembled at the thought of a dog like her family's undergoing that stress. Poor Mason spent each thunderstorm dashing from window to window in an effort to protect the house. She calmed only when the thunder ended.

"Over to the right is the main receiving building and the hospital. We can handle about eighty dogs at a time there." Tom led her up a winding road to the top of another hill. The arms shed now stood immediately to their left, and in front of them spread a plain with a track running in a loose oval around the perimeter, and the highway beyond that. A large pond stood to the right with a fence around it.

"What's the fence for?"

"The colonel ordered it up after Pearl Harbor. Somebody decided the only thing saboteurs would want to attack is our water source." He spoke louder to be heard over the growing din. Lainie turned to search for the source of the sound. "Look over to your right."

She followed his arm and her eyes widened. Row after row of wooden six-by-six boxes lined an open field. A line of trees separated another field from the first. "How many dogs are out there?"

"Somewhere around eighteen hundred. They come and go in waves. Most will have eight to twelve weeks for training. After that they may stay a few additional weeks before we match them with a trainer."

As she listened to Tom, Lainie wandered down the hill closer to the first row of dogs. A beautiful Collie sat in the shadow of the first hut. She knelt in front of it and reached out to stroke its coat.

"What are you doing?" Panic laced Tom's voice. He yanked her away from the animal before she could answer.

She pushed his grasp away. "What? I only wanted to pet the dog. She's gorgeous."

"Lainie, you can't do that. We train these animals to be war dogs. Not pets. You don't know if that dog has had aggression training. It could attack simply because it's trained to." He looked at her with eyes darkened by emotion. "You must treat each dog like it's dangerous." He hustled her back to the coupe.

The air between them crackled. If he was so afraid, why work with dogs? She wanted to ask, but he wouldn't stop talking long enough. The tour turned into a preemptory one of the fort's main compound. She sighed in relief when he finally dropped her back at Esther's.

Monday morning Lainie helped with the chores before settling into a rocker on the wide front porch. She watched the world ease by and wondered what she should do. She needed a strategy beyond washing dishes and typing nonsense. Something had to happen soon.

The screen door opened, and Esther stepped out with her hat on and bag in one hand and Lainie's bag and hat in the other. "What are you sitting there for? It's time to find you a job."

Lainie jumped from the chair and grabbed the hat and bag Esther handed her. She had to smile at the way Esther hurried down the stairs and down the sidewalk without a glance back to see whether she followed. "What do you have in mind?"

"There are a few more folks for you to meet. And Mary Nelson told me yesterday there might be an opening with the war dogs. You were too busy talking to Tom to hear."

Lainie considered protesting, but decided it wasn't worth the effort. Esther had her mind made up. In one short week, Lainie had learned there was no point in trying to change the woman's opinions. They strolled downtown, and soon Esther had reintroduced Lainie to half of the business owners. Even with Esther's endorsement, the shops didn't need help.

"Mary said she'd meet us at Mae's for lunch." Esther waited for a passing soldier to open the door, and then entered.

Lainie smiled at the sergeant and tilted her head before following. She glanced around the diner for Mary, taking in the specifics she'd missed last time. The inside was small with a handful of tables scattered across a worn linoleum floor. Faded Coca-Cola wallpaper lined the walls. The scent of old grease hung in the air, mixing with the sweetness of ice cream and candy. Lainie closed her eyes and imagined she'd been transported back to Wahl's Drugstore in North Platte to share a cherry Coke with Audrey.

"Are you going to sit down?"

Lainie opened her eyes and frowned. She was very much in Mae's and not Wahl's. Esther smiled at her from the corner table.

"Have a seat. I'm sure Mary will be here momentarily." Esther peeled off her gloves and then placed them on the table.

Lainie pulled back a chair and sat. "Do you think I should stay?"

"I think you need to wait until you've given this a fair chance. Did I ever tell you why I run a restaurant? I don't need to, you know." A faraway look settled in her eyes. "My father paid off the mortgage and left the house to me, free and clear. I thought about selling and going to a new town. Start a life somewhere and do something important. Something that really mattered. Well, twenty years later, I'm still here, and it's exactly where I'm supposed to be."

"How can you know?" Lainie yearned for that assurance.

Esther looked at her and smiled. "Each of those boys who walks through my door longs for a friendly face and a slice of homemade pie brings an opportunity to minister and serve. I can't think of many other places where I could mother so many boys at one time. They're good men, but many of them are on their own for the first time. Few imagined they'd spend months in a little place like Crawford. With each slice of pie, I pray for the man receiving it. And that's enough."

"But why help me?"

"Because it's been placed on my heart to assist you." She leaned across the table and touched Lainie's hand. Comfort flowed from her . "You're like a little bird that's lost its way. I'm here to assist you as you find it."

The door burst open, and Mary rushed in. "Oh, I hope you didn't wait long." The words babbled from her mouth in a rush. "But, Mrs. Babcock, I think you'll be pleased. Oh, I hope you will be."

CHAPTER 9

MAY 24, 1943

*M*onday flew by in the routine of tending the dogs. Tom rubbed his scar and cringed at the memory of his reaction when Lainie reached out to the Collie. She'd have been fine with that animal, but other dogs were a different story. He'd overreacted but wouldn't change it. She had to understand the kind of animals that were out here before she got hurt.

He wished the air hadn't changed between them. One moment it had been the best afternoon of his life, as he showed her pieces of his world. The next she looked at him like he'd gone insane.

It wasn't insanity. Not really. And someday he'd find a way to make her understand what it was like to confront your fear on a daily basis and pray God would remove the fear or the job.

Well, today that prayer was partly answered. He'd only work with the dogs half days for the next six weeks. Basic training had arrived at Fort Robinson, and it was his turn to experience the joys.

John Tyler stomped through the door of the war dog training building. "Can you believe we get to play soldier today?"

Tom grinned. "If you haven't noticed, we are soldiers."

"Yeah, but we've never been that kind of soldier. Why do I need hand-to-hand combat training when I'm stationed here? I mean, what's the Army going to do? Ship me overseas?" His eyes bugged, and he shook his head. "You don't think they'd send me out?"

"You are a member of the Quartermaster Corps. I suppose anything's possible."

"Don't tell Naomi. She'd pass out on me."

Tom got up from the desk and jostled John. "I'm afraid you should have thought about this before you enlisted."

"But that's exactly why I enlisted here. You come here when you want to work with animals and stay here in the boondocks." John swallowed and his Adam's apple bobbed up and down his throat. He wiped beads of sweat from his forehead and took half a step toward the door.

Tom grabbed him before he could bolt. "Don't do anything crazy. Let's just get through this and then worry about what's next. At least they aren't shipping us out for the training. And I don't mind the break from our regular duty. We might even learn something interesting."

John nodded slowly. "Anything's possible."

Tom reached for his Daisy Mae hat and shoved it on his head. Time to get John moving before he thought about it anymore. "Come on, they'll be looking for us if we don't head out."

Together they hiked across the highway and over to the field that had been designated for the basic training. Tom had talked to some of the guys who'd gone through the first round of training. It didn't sound like it would be too rigorous. Some shooting, some marching, some hand-to-hand combat. Maybe a little book learning, but not much.

At the first words from Master Sergeant Maxwell, Tom wondered if the men he'd talked to had actually experienced basic training. If so, they must have had a different instructor. Sergeant Maxwell seemed determined to beat them into soldiers in an afternoon. Push-ups, running miles in boots, and endless lectures weren't enough. After Tom couldn't wait to collapse in the barracks, Sergeant made them march in formation around and around the post parade grounds until Tom was dizzy. Finally, Sergeant released them.

Tom plopped on the ground. "Day one down. Do you think the others will be like this?"

"Probably." A hang-dog look dragged John's face down. "Guess I'll head to town."

"We still have our regular late afternoon duties with the dogs." Sid panted as he collapsed alongside Tom on the ground.

John and Tom looked at each other and groaned.

"You're kidding, right?" Tom waited for Sid to give any indication it had been a joke. "No one mentioned that to us."

"Welcome to the real Army, Hamilton."

Fatigue washed over Tom in a wave at the thought of hours of work caring for the animals. Slowly, he stood. "Maybe today was designed to test our mettle. Let's go, John."

* * *

The week slogged by in a rushed routine. The days developed a cadence that led him through each activity. He spent the mornings instructing the new handlers in the care of their dogs. Even the most mundane activities, like checking for ticks, seemed strange to some of the city boys. Once they started exercises in the field, the importance of those grooming habits would become clear.

In the afternoons he struggled through the basic training exercises. He'd always expected to receive orders to ship out. Some of his friends got those exact orders; a few headed east to Europe, others west. Now that he knew the skills the Army deemed key in its soldiers, his duties at the fort took on a whole new light.

He'd heard stories from the initial group of soldiers who'd shipped out with dogs had told about combat in the Far East. He could imagine the brutality of war from the headlines and from the tales he'd heard from his uncles about the Great War.

But now ... now he wondered how he would behave in combat. Sometimes he dreamed about being the hero, but here he knew what was expected of him and that he could perform his tasks well, even if reluctantly. He wanted to think his fear had abandoned him. Then he considered donning the pads required for aggression training and wanted to abandon post quicker than a pheasant running across the road.

Ready or not, each day of basic training got him closer to shipping out.

"Hey there, soldier."

A perky voice pulled him from his thoughts. He looked up to see Lainie Gardner walking across the war dog area toward him. "What brings you to my neck of the woods?"

"A job." Her smile reached her eyes, a sight he hadn't seen before. The joy in her eyes knocked the breath from him, and he had to remind his lungs to inhale.

"That's great news. Where are you stationed?"

"Right here." She shrugged and nodded toward the office building. "I get to type responses to the letters families send. I'll probably draft honorable discharge papers soon. Who would have thought dogs could receive that honor?"

"It seemed fitting when we sent the initial dogs home."

"Clever. I'm sure the families appreciate it." She cocked her head and looked up at him. "Walk with me?"

He nodded and matched his stride to hers.

"I thought I'd see you more." Lainie pouted and then stumbled. He offered his arm to steady her.

"Basic training's in full swing. I'm running every direction right now." Tom looked at her hand resting on his arm, her fingers delicate against his rough uniform.

"Seems a little backward to me, taking basic training a year after you enlisted."

Tom shrugged. Lainie didn't seem to be headed anywhere in particular. "Can I escort you somewhere? I need to get back to my duties before Sarge looks for me."

"Will you come to Mrs. Babcock's for dessert tonight? She planned to bake pear pies."

"I can't say I've ever had that kind of pie, but I'll try to come."

"Good." She bobbed her head, and her straw hat tipped with the action. She reached up and tugged it back in place. "I'll see you then."

Lainie stepped away and headed toward the office. She looked back over her shoulder at him, and he grinned. She was something else. As he watched, another soldier approached her, and she smiled up at him. Whatever she said to him caused him to laugh, and Tom frowned. She flirted with all the boys. He shouldn't feel flattered by her attention. Instead, he wouldn't be surprised if he found Mrs. Babcock's filled with a dozen soldiers surrounding Lainie.

He'd kept both of his sisters out of trouble with their beaus. He could do the same for her. It looked like she'd need it.

He managed to slip away after mess, and took Sid with him. Tom was surprised to find the street empty of extra cars when they pulled up to Mrs. Babcock's. Maybe his assumption had missed the mark.

Sid and Tom clomped up the stairs, hung their hats on the hooks, and knocked on the front door before opening it and going inside.

"Good evening, boys." Mrs. Babcock waved them in with her motherly way and ushered them to the dining room. "Sit down over here. I'll be out in a minute with some pie and fresh coffee. How's that training going?"

"Just fine, ma'am. Thank you." Tom settled onto a chair at the table she'd pointed to. The radio played swing music in the background. Sounded like WLW out of Chicago playing the latest from Duke Ellington.

Sid sank onto another chair. "I thought others would be here."

"Guess not."

Someone clacked down the wood floors, and Tom looked up, expecting to see Mrs. Babcock with her tray of goodies. Lainie stepped into view. She was wearing a fresh green dress that brought sparks to her eyes. She'd swept her hair off her shoulders.

She grinned at him, then included Sid in the expression. "Glad you boys could join us. I knew I'd need help eating all this pie."

She sat down, and in a moment, Mrs. Babcock joined them. Another boarder or two filtered down, probably attracted by the sound of their laughter. Mrs. Babcock grabbed a deck of cards from the stack of games in the corner, and they played a round of canasta. Tom relaxed the longer they played. Lainie seemed to have lost her airs and developed into an evening of pure fun. He could get used to nights like this. No pressure, just entertainment.

CHAPTER 10

MAY 27, 1943

On Thursday Lainie breezed into the K-9 office. She'd worn her link-button worsted suit and felt smart in it. The gray offset her dark curls, which she'd worn loose. She was prepared to tackle the day.

"Good morning, Mary."

Mary Nelson sat behind a battered wooden desk that looked like it had first seen service during the late 1800s. Five more desks filled the center of the office space. The walls were lined with equally beat up metal file cabinets. Lainie glanced around but didn't see the other staff in the office.

"Are we it?"

"Today. The rest are in Chadron for training. Don't worry, they'll liven things up when they return."

Lainie plopped her veiled beret on the coat tree tucked behind the door. Then she settled into her desk and looked at the stack of waiting papers. Her first assignment was creating a file for each dog that pranced through the gate of the War Dog Training Center.

She noticed how quiet Mary was and turned to her. "Are you okay?"

Mary shrank behind her desk and shook her head. A tear trickled down her cheek.

Lainie hurried over and crouched beside her. "Tell me what's wrong. Please."

Mary shrugged and then edged away while swiping a handkerchief across her cheeks. "I'll be okay."

"You don't look it."

A moan leaked between Mary's lips. Lainie's gaze fell to the desk, and she stilled. A shredded Western Union envelope and crumpled telegram sat on the desktop. She'd heard about so many of those telegrams that she didn't think her heart could hurt for the families and loved ones who received them. She'd been wrong.

She hugged Mary and rocked her. After a moment, Mary straightened and inhaled around a shuddering sob.

"Who was he?"

"Philip Tucker." Mary twisted a ring on her left hand. "We were supposed to marry during his last furlough, but he decided to wait until he returned from the war. He didn't want me to be a widow." Fresh sobs cut off her words.

Lainie hugged her and prayed the right phrases would come from her mouth. Nothing came to her that didn't seem trite, so she stayed quiet. *Why do so many have to suffer like this, Lord?*

Mary tried to sit up, a watery smile pasted on her face. She picked up the telegram and smoothed out the wrinkles.

Lainie looked at her and renewed her vow to not fall for a man in uniform. She'd spend time with them and enjoy their company. But she couldn't invite the pain Mary and so many others had experienced since the war started. "Can you take today off?"

Mary nodded.

Lainie helped her stand and watched helplessly as Mary retrieved her jacket and headed out the door. "Please let me know if you need anything."

After Mary left, Lainie wandered around the small office, considering the stacks of papers waiting to be filed. Suddenly, it didn't seem so important that she had a job at a military post. The longing to be on her way to the fight overwhelmed her. She sank onto a chair and covered her face with her hands. *I'll never understand, God. Why did You have to kill that dream?*

She heard the door squeak in its hinges and squared her shoulders. Corporal Hutchinson stalked into the room.

"Where's Miss Nelson?"

"She just received word her fiancé died. Can I help you?"

He slapped a stack of papers on the corner of Lainie's desk. "Here's the next round of discharges to be processed."

She fought a groan at the paperwork that multiplied in all directions. If she didn't get to work, she'd be buried under the mess, and it would take weeks for them to find her body.

"Yes, sir." She picked up the first sheet from the pile.

The morning passed with Lainie's thoughts returning to Mary and her grief. War wounded so many more than those who served. One stack of paperwork filed, she grabbed the discharges and sat at her desk. She stared at the typewriter and prayed all those hours of practice paid off. Otherwise, she'd be out of a job before she saw her first paycheck.

"Here goes." She slipped a form into the back of the typewriter and rolled it until it curved toward her. She played with the levers until the page lined up properly. Looking at the order, her gaze darted back and forth as she hunted out each letter in the dog's name. "Sebastian. What happened to short names like Mutt?"

She mumbled her way through two crumpled attempts.

"Do you always talk to yourself?"

Lainie jumped and looked up to see a soldier standing in the doorway with easy Clark Gable elegance. She released a breath and fisted her hands on her hips. "You should announce yourself."

"Second Lieutenant Brian Daniels, at your service."

"Then hop behind that typewriter and get to work. I'm sure you can tell I need all the help I can get."

"Let me take you to lunch."

"Why would I do that when I'm so successful here? The work's simply evaporating."

"Maybe the break would make you more accurate. Your fingers must be starved for nourishment. That I can help with."

She scrutinized the soldier from his hat that looked freshly brushed down to tips of his polished boots. "You're visiting."

"How could you tell?"

"Few soldiers look that spit and polished after a few hours' work. If you haven't noticed, it's dry and dusty."

"I'm here to inspect the war dog center. And I'm sure in my orders I'll find one about taking the starving clerical pool to lunch."

Lainie threw her arms in the air. "You win."

She stood and accepted the lieutenant's proffered arm. A look of satisfaction settled on his face, and he steered her out of the cramped office. As a female civilian, Lainie could join the WACs for their meals or bring her own. The lieutenant took her to the officer's mess instead.

The aroma of Italian spices permeated the air. She took a bite of the lasagna that tasted almost like Mama's filled Lainie's plate, and she inhaled it. After she finished she asked Brian questions about his life back home. He regaled her with tales of growing up in Maine and the culture shock he'd received upon enlisting.

"You can just imagine this small-town boy from Nowhere, Maine, being berated by a drill sergeant from the Bronx. I could hardly understand a word he said. And no matter what he asked, my answer was the wrong one."

Lainie smiled at the familiar story. The war had a way of mixing men who'd never meet under normal circumstances.

Their dinner was interrupted several times by other officers stopping long enough to introduce themselves. Her mind swam with names and ranks before the rich cheesecake arrived.

She glanced at her watch and gasped. "Thank you for lunch, but I have to get back."

"Can I see you again while I'm here?" Brian stared intently at her as if memorizing every detail of her face.

Heat climbed her cheeks, but she refused to look away. "I suppose. Though I won't have time for two-hour lunches every day." He stood to escort her back, but she waved him down. "I'm sure you have other things to do. I'll walk alone the block or two back to my post. Thanks for a delightful lunch."

She strolled back to the office, searching each soldier's face that she passed and smiling at them. It wasn't until she reached her building that she realized she'd looked for Tom the whole time. He'd looked worn last night, but had relaxed and shown a competitive streak as tall as the buttes once the bridge game got underway. She hadn't laughed that hard in a long time, and it felt good, even as her sides ached.

She entered the office glad to see another warm body. "Liz, right?"

"Yes, ma'am. Liz Czaplewski. Don't worry, my last name is not required to get my attention."

"That's good since it's a tongue-twister. Glad to have company."

In minutes they developed a routine that had Lainie far from the typewriter and her aborted attempts to complete the paperwork. By the end of the day, the office looked transformed.

"This is why I love to float. I get to come into the middle of chaos and organize it."

Lainie had to agree. The to-be-filed piles had shrunk to fill the top of only one desk. Liz had dealt with the stack of discharge papers effortlessly. Not one had been crumpled and thrown to the ground. Lainie shook her head at the thought of all the practice she'd need before she mirrored that competency.

Waiting for the shuttle, Lainie realized she'd made an important advancement that day. She felt connected to a couple of the women in town in a way that held the promise of friendship. Add Esther to the mix, and Crawford just might come to feel like home someday. Hope sparked in her at the thought.

A wolf whistle brought her back to the ground. She turned to find the soldier and shook her finger at him with a playful grin. The soldier placed his hands over his heart and swooned. Boys. It didn't matter which corner of the country they were in; they all acted the same around pretty girls. Lainie's smile widened. She was definitely in the right place.

Other soldiers took up the call, and she refused to look around to find the sources. If the bus didn't arrive soon, she might strike out on her own. Slowly the voices died down, and she looked back toward the soldiers. The lieutenant from lunch approached Lainie with a steady stride.

"Looks like you could use some protection while you wait." He extended a hand.

Lainie nodded and accepted his help. "They're good boys."

"Not used to a beautiful woman like you standing unescorted." He squeezed her hand where it rested on his arm. "Don't worry. I'll take good care of you."

Lainie considered him carefully and wondered what he really meant. Part of her felt relief at his assurances. The other part detected an undercurrent she didn't understand.

CHAPTER 11

MAY 29, 1943

"*Y*ou're dismissed."

With those words Tom spun toward the barracks. He had an A pass in his back pocket and could taste the freedom of a couple of days without demands. After this week, he needed the break.

"Heading to Lusk this weekend, Hamilton?" Sergeant Lewis joined Tom.

"No, think I'll stick closer to base."

Sarge nodded. "Good work this week. You'll complete basic in seven, and life'll return to normal. At least for the quartermasters."

"Yes, sir."

"Keep it up." Sarge ambled off, and Tom shook his head. The exchange had a surreal feel to it. Where was the bark and bite Sarge prided himself on?

Tom took a quick shower, then felt like a new man. Sid and Bill entered the barracks, both looking a little wet around the ears. Lucky Bill had endured basic training before Robinson, so he'd spent the week filling gaps left by the men in training. Sid appeared as wrung out as Tom felt. Yep, the three would light Crawford up tonight. They'd settled on the pavilion dance in the park rather than travel to Chadron, Alliance, or Lusk.

Sid plopped beside Tom on his cot. "Time's wasting if we want a real meal before the dance."

They hurried out to Tom's '41 Chevy and hopped in. He revved the engine through the bends in the highway, and slowed only when they hit the gas station that signaled the beginning of Crawford. "Where to, fellows?"

"Well, there's Babcock's." Bill licked his lips as he rapped his hand against the window frame in time to the strains of "Don't Get Around Much Anymore."

Sid shook his head. "Already had pie there this week."

"That doesn't leave many options. We can always head back and inhale the wonderful grub at the mess hall." Tom looked away from the road long enough to grin at the other two guys.

"Yep. I mean, nope." Bill shrugged. "Mrs. Babcock's it is."

Sid nodded enthusiastically. "Maybe some of the gals would like a ride to the dance."

"Looking for the positive, aren't you?" Tom stopped in front of Mrs. Babcock's and hopped out. He looked for a short gal with dark hair and sparkling eyes. He stopped abruptly. He had no right or reason to look for Lainie Gardner. He jerked forward as Bill plowed into him.

"Come on, I hope we aren't too late for her stew." Bill bolted to a table and plopped onto the closest chair. The tablecloth slid across the table into his lap, a candle wobbling precariously. Bill steadied it.

"Slow down. You know she'll have something for us." Sid looked around the room. "It's a hopping place tonight."

A buzz rose from the tables surrounding them and formed a backdrop as Tom settled in. At most tables, couples stared deep into each other's eyes, but a few spots were filled with soldiers he recognized from the post.

Ellen, Mrs. Babcock's regular waitress, waltzed to Tom's table with her order pad in hand.

"What can I get you fellas tonight? The special is country fried steak with all the fixings." She disappeared into the kitchen with three orders for the special. In a moment, she returned with mugs of iced tea. She winked at Tom as she slapped them on the table. "Courtesy of Esther."

Sid groaned and picked up his mug. "This isn't exactly what I had in mind when I imagined holding a cold mug."

"Yeah, but you'll enjoy the night a whole lot more."

"Might even remember it." Bill snickered.

The meal tasted better than Tom had hoped, with Sid and Bill joking back and forth with a neighboring table. The gals boarded with Mrs. Babcock and seemed to enjoy the banter. Tom couldn't help noticing who wasn't at that table. "Hey, Ellen." He stopped her as she moved by. "Is Lainie Gardner here tonight?"

"No. Some lieutenant picked her up earlier. Think they're headed to the dance later."

For some reason, his stomach twisted at the thought. "Thanks."

"Trouble in paradise?" Sid grinned across the table at him.

Tom rolled his eyes. "You know better than that. Found someone to take to the dance?"

"Absolutely. These two beautiful women were waiting for us to accompany them."

Tom nodded to Dorothy Banks and Ginny Speares. "It'll be great to have you join us."

"Are you sure you'll have enough room?" The gal named Ginny leaned closer. Bill hadn't taken his gaze from her bright-blue eyes and mirrored her every move. It was almost comical to watch.

"No problem." Feeling like the odd man, he led them to his car. It was a five-seater with plenty of room, but he felt like a chauffeur. It wasn't the first time and wouldn't be the last. They crossed the train tracks and pulled into the city park. Tom wove the car along the road until he reached the end of a line of parked cars. Everyone piled out to walk to the pavilion. The sound of a band warming up accompanied the cadence of crickets and cicadas.

Clusters of people congregated around the edges of the open-air pavilion. A few shuffled dance steps along with the music. Tom scanned the crowd, looking for Lainie and her escort. He couldn't shake the bad feeling he had, and couldn't understand its source.

* * *

LAINIE TRIED to put a little space between her and Lieutenant Daniels. She'd been surprised when he showed up for dinner and insisted she join him. He'd kept their conversation freewheeling and light. He'd been attentive and made her feel like the center of his world during the meal. When he'd asked her to accompany him to the dance earlier in the day, she'd gladly tossed aside the current issue of the *Saturday Evening Post* with Norman Rockwell's cover art of Rosie the Riveter exchanging it for a fun night.

Now she wondered if she'd been smart to join him.

The band swung into a jive, and Brian kept her on the dance floor. She caught her breath and tried to smile. Maybe she should call a hiatus from dances. A cool breeze tickled the hair away from her neck as they jitterbugged. One dance turned into four without a pause. Lainie could feel the heat in her cheeks.

"I need a break, Lieutenant."

He eyed her and shook his head. His grip on her tightened, and she fought the urge to squirm. She glanced around, but everyone seemed absorbed in their companions.

She pushed back on his chest. "Let go of me."

"Sir, she's asked you to step back."

Lainie felt a flutter of hope at the sound of that deep, steady voice. A smile touched her lips when Tom Hamilton winked at her over Brian's shoulder.

Brian stiffened and turned. "Soldier, this is no concern of yours."

"She's a friend whose request you've ignored. It is my concern."

Brian pushed Lainie away and whirled on Tom. He sucker punched Tom in the stomach. Lainie stumbled backward and screamed. The music wailed to a halt, and everyone's attention descended on the two soldiers. When the lieutenant noticed, he took a step back and straightened his coat. "Your superior officer will hear about this."

Sid and Bill hurried up and helped Tom to his feet as Brian stalked away.

Lainie scurried up to Tom and clutched his hands. "Are you okay?"

Tom rubbed his stomach and nodded. "Don't think I'll dance much tonight, though."

"We have to quit meeting like this, or I'll add hero to your list of titles."

Tom laughed and then winced. "I'm far from a hero."

"I hope you don't get in trouble."

They walked away from the crowd and wandered through the park.

"If I do, it's all right. I have a low tolerance for men who don't listen to their dates."

Heat climbed Lainie's cheeks. "He asked me to join him tonight, and it sounded like fun. Maybe I'll avoid future dances."

"And spend all your nights holed up at Mrs. Babcock's? I doubt that."

"Okay, so that's not a great option. Especially considering me."

"Hmm?"

She stopped and waited until he turned to look at her with a quirked eyebrow. "You really care about the answer, don't you?"

"Yes." He shrugged as if that covered everything.

"You are one of a kind, Tom."

He grinned. "What's that make? Five labels? I'm waiting for Superman to join the mix."

"Keep this up, and it might."

Soft conversation filled the space between them as they walked. They crossed the tracks and headed back into the heart of Crawford.

Tom pointed to his right. "See that road? The fort extends all the way to this street. I doubt I'll ever explore all of it."

"It seems so contained when you're there."

"You haven't looked for the horses or seen the pack mules." Tom spread his hands wide. "The sheer size of Robinson is why many of us have jobs. Few places could handle thousands of horses and mules at a time. It even makes it the perfect place for dogs, with a ready food supply and room for maneuvers."

Lainie crinkled her nose at the thought. "You don't mean horse meat ..."

He nodded. "The dogs have to be fed something, and Army surplus works fine."

She shuddered at the thought.

* * *

THE SHOPS along Main Street had closed, and he steered her around the bars that had popped up with the influx of servicemen. Tom listened to Lainie talk about her family and friends in North Platte. She quieted, and he realized he'd enjoyed her stories. The people had come to life as she mimicked voices and mannerisms.

"You have a flair for storytelling."

"Is that your way of saying I'm dramatic?" She made a funny face and then wrapped her arms around her middle. "Too bad I can't parlay that into something useful."

"How about visiting soldiers at the hospital? I'm sure they'd love the break."

"Maybe someday. Right now it hurts too much. Reminds me of my dream. Besides, the doctors said I need to be careful for a while."

"Careful about what?"

"I contracted rheumatic fever while in Kentucky. That's why I got sent home." Her shoulders drooped, and Lainie kicked a pebble.

Tom stopped in the well of light from a home's front porch. Shadows had doused the usual sparks in her eyes. "You'll get through this, Lainie."

"Maybe. Not everybody does." She shrugged and walked ahead. "It's my road. Fortunately, most days are good. Unless I overdo it." She looked back at him and smiled. "I'd never do that."

He chuckled. He could see her doing just that.

CHAPTER 12

MAY 31, 1943

"So you'll help tonight, Lainie?" Esther looked at her, palms up in a pleading gesture.

It was only Monday morning, and Lainie already felt overwhelmed. But it wasn't Esther's fault she needed the help enough to beg. "I'll come straight back from work."

Mary sat behind her desk when Lainie arrived at the office. Mary looked wan but determined to get back to work. "Sitting at home alone doesn't ease the pain."

"I'm glad you're here. You'll never believe what happened while you were gone." Lainie soon had Mary doubled over with laughter as she told stories about Lieutenant Daniels. "So if you run into him, be careful. You now know the story behind the handsome face."

"No need to worry about me." The smile evaporated from Mary. "It'll be a while before I'm ready to enter that world. I'll live vicariously for now."

The day flew in the rough routine Lainie'd developed last week, but more smoothly with Mary and the other girls back.

That evening Lainie rushed to her room to change out of her work outfit, and slipped into a playsuit and skirt. She looked in the mirror and nodded. She could move freely like she needed to serve the guests downstairs for dinner.

Lainie entered the kitchen and slipped on an apron. The scent of chicken and dumplings flavored the room. "Where do you need me?"

Esther looked up from the stove, strands of gray hair pulling out of her bun. "Fill those glasses with water and give one to whoever needs one. Tanya should know who needs to place an order."

Lainie complied and slipped from table to table, depositing glasses on the tables. Tanya focused on the table in front of her as she took an order. Esther only served a couple of options a night. That kept the menu changing but serving simple. Lainie hadn't heard any complaints about the lack of choices. Instead, the delicious food disappeared, often chased by a slice of pie topped with fresh whipped cream. It smelled like peach pie tonight.

Many of the people in the room looked familiar to Lainie as she worked her way back and forth with food and drinks. That thought pleased her more than she'd expected.

"Hey, sweetheart." A soldier grabbed Lainie's arm as she walked by. "Can you join us a moment?"

The dining room had emptied as folks finished their meals. Right now Tanya could handle any new people that came in, likely only for dessert. She smiled at the eager private and his companions. "Sure."

One soldier pulled a deck of cards from the stack of games in the corner, and soon they were engaged in a hot game of euchre. Tanya wandered by, wiping tables in the empty room, and Lainie realized she'd never seen the girl interact with anyone beyond the required basics.

"Tanya, come join us. That fella needs someone to make sure he isn't cheating."

"I'd never do that," the private protested.

"Then you count cards."

"Nothing wrong with that." But he sidled his chair over to make room for Tanya. Another guy, this one a sailor, hopped up to pull a chair over.

"So what brings a sailor to an Army post?"

"Here to train with dogs. I'm working with four right now, but one isn't working out."

Carefully, Lainie pulled Tanya out of her shell and grinned as the girl began to enjoy the game. After they finally kicked the group out, Tanya headed up the stairs, but stopped and looked at Lainie. "Thanks."

"The group and game were more fun after you joined us."

Tanya nodded and ran her hand along the banister. "Still, I'm grateful. Good night."

"Night." Lainie watched Tanya disappear, then swept the room with one more gaze. Everything seemed in place for breakfast. She turned out the lights and headed down the hallway toward the small sitting room. A floor-to-ceiling bookshelf lined one wall. Books were stacked and shoved on it with reckless abandon. Her finger ran along the spines as she looked for something interesting. She itched to pull all the books off the shelf and instill some order to the chaos.

Many of the books were classics ... Dickens, Twain, Austen, Hardy, and more lined several shelves. Then she hit the row of Nebraska authors. Willa Cather, John Neihardt, Bess Streeter Aldrich. She stilled when she reached *A Lantern in Her Hand*. It had been years since she'd read the novel. Was it as good as she remembered? She pulled the book from the shelf and moved across the room to the small settee. Its upholstery had softened with age, and Lainie curled up in the corner.

In no time she was swept into Abbie Deal's story. Lainie's difficulties faded in importance against the backdrop of survival.

The light flicked off, and Lainie looked up. "Hello?"

"You still up, child?" The light came back on, and Esther appeared in the doorway. "I thought you'd turned in."

Lainie lifted the book. "I'm reacquainting myself with an old friend. I hadn't thought of this book since high school."

"It's a good one. Well, I'm off to bed. Morning comes too soon."

Lainie uncurled and stood. "I'll follow you."

"Thanks for helping tonight."

"I didn't do much."

"So you say. I watched you pull Tanya into your group. That was a kind thing. Well, I'll see you in the morning."

* * *

TUESDAY MELTED INTO WEDNESDAY, and Lainie decided to stroll around the parade grounds over lunch. The sun kissed her face, and its warmth felt wonderful. She sat on one of the benches and pulled the book from her bag. She'd just gotten engrossed in the story when she heard her name. She hesitated, hoping it wasn't Lieutenant Daniels, before scanning to see who called. A sailor ran across the parade grounds toward her.

"Hello, Lainie."

She studied him closer, trying to place him. "Oh, you ate at Mrs. Babcock's earlier this week, didn't you?"

His grin just about split his face in two. "I knew you'd remember, though the guys ribbed me about it."

"Of course, I do, but you'll have to help me with your name."

"Seaman Mike Harris, ma'am." He stood taller, and Lainie waited for him to snap a salute.

"At ease." She asked him about his week, and soon he sat next to her, hands flying, as he told her all about his home in New Jersey and what he missed about it. She glanced at her watch and startled. "Sorry, Mike, but I have to get back to work."

He jumped to his feet. "I'll be late, too. It's great to talk to someone." He took a step away before stopping. "Lainie, would you join me at the USO this week? It's a lot to ask ..."

"I'd decided to take a break from that for a while." His face fell, and Lainie wondered what harm would really come of it. Surely the incident with the lieutenant was an anomaly. Most men prior to him had treated her with respect. Then the image of Tom in a red Superman cape came to mind, and she fought a giggle. Maybe Tom would wait on standby. "I can make an exception since you're only in town a few more weeks."

"Wonderful! I'll come by the office tomorrow or Friday." He hurried off.

As she watched him go, she realized she wasn't in North Platte anymore. These boys weren't stopping for a twenty-minute break while their trains refueled. She'd need to be more careful. Fortunately, Mike seemed like a nice boy, but she'd thought the same of Brian Daniels.

* * *

BILL FLIPPED over the shoulder of the martial arts instructor, who'd arrived from Denver. Tom watched the action from the intermittent shade of a ponderosa pine. He'd slid as far from the focal point as he could without calling attention to himself. The moves the instructor demonstrated looked painful to him. He'd be grateful for learning them if he ever saw combat. Knowing his luck, he'd look more the fool than Bill had. The instructor called for his next victim, and John clambered to his feet.

"Now, private, I want you to rush at me." The instructor turned toward the assembled men. "Notice my feet are spread shoulder width apart, knees slightly bent. This puts me in a better position to redirect his energy as he comes at me." The man beckoned, like coaxing a reluctant dog toward him.

John cocked his head and eyed the ground behind the man. It was clear of rocks and other obstacles, but Tom thought it looked like a mighty hard landing spot. John rolled his shoulders, then lowered his center of gravity by crouching forward. With a war whoop, he charged the instructor, who casually side-stepped and let John fly by him.

"Much of hand-to-hand combat is keeping your opponent off balance and using your body as a lever with which you'll toss theirs where you will."

John rolled to a sitting position with a wild look in his eye. "Can I try again?"

"Ready when you are." The instructor resumed his odd bent-leg stance.

John rushed the instructor, but this time used his leg to sweep the instructor's legs out from under him. He looked down at the instructor where he sprawled in the prairie grass. "Another rule is to make your opponent underestimate you."

The instructor chuckled and reached up a hand. John hauled him to his feet, and he brushed off his seat. "Duly noted, private, but that would only work if you got a second chance. Unlikely in combat. Next victim, please."

After watching several more, Tom moved forward for his turn. He eyed the instructor and tried to think of some strategy that didn't land him on his back. Most of the others had stared at the sky and shook their heads as they struggled to their feet. The trick seemed to be feinting to one side or the other to knock the instructor over. Pulling in a lungful of air, Tom zigzagged toward the man. Just as he thought it might work, he felt a hand or foot connect with his hips, and he cartwheeled through the air. He landed with an *ohf* and screwed his eyes shut against the sun's glare. Something tickled his neck, and he slapped it away.

"Want another shot?" A shadow fell on his face and Tom opened his eyes to see the instructor standing over him offering a hand up.

Tom accepted the help and then shook each arm and leg, relieved they seemed intact.

"Charge me from behind." The instructor looked at the group. "When someone is coming from behind, you'll need to lean forward, almost roll, as they connect with you. That will propel them over the top."

Tom waited as the instructor turned to face the others. Tom rushed forward and tried to wrap the instructor in a bear hug. They tumbled to the ground, and the instructor sprang up with a grin. "That's how it's done, men. In war you only have one shot to get this right."

Those words rang in Tom's head as he walked back to the barracks. So much of life was about getting things right the first time. He hoped he wouldn't fail if his chance came.

CHAPTER 13

*L*ainie looked in the mirror and dabbed some red lipstick on. She pulled her strand of pearls out of their box and put them on. The drape of her dress's neckline was the perfect foil for the pearls. And the full, pleated skirt would whirl nicely as she danced at the USO.

Esther stuck her head in the room. "Better stop primping and get downstairs. Your serviceman waiting and nervous as a calf during branding season."

With a last glance in the mirror, Lainie grabbed her pumps. The stocking lotion had done the trick in giving her legs the look of nylons. She twirled and curtsied in front of Esther.

"You're lovely as a model in that dress. That blue highlights your eyes. Go on now."

Lainie smiled and hurried downstairs. Mike stood at the bottom of the stairs, shifting from foot to foot. He clutched a bouquet of wildflowers so hard his knuckles were white. The wild indigo and ground plum formed the perfect backdrop for the delicate white lady's slippers.

"Those flowers are beautiful."

"Not as lovely as you." His voice squeaked, and he cleared his throat. "Here."

She accepted the bouquet and buried her nose in them. She fingered the pouch-like slipper on one flower and marveled at the smooth petal. "These are wonderful. Let me put them in some water."

"Yes, ma'am."

Lainie hurried to the kitchen and filled a glass with water. She shoved the cluster in the glass and returned to the hallway. "I'll leave these here for now." She set them down and then picked up her purse. "Let's go."

Mike settled her into his car and then walked around to the driver's side. He slid in and sat ramrod straight for a minute.

"Are you all right, seaman?"

He swallowed and stared straight ahead. "Missing my girl, ma'am."

"First, quit calling me *ma'am*. I doubt I'm much older than you, so *Lainie* will do fine. Second, why don't you tell me about her while we drive."

Once he started talking, Lainie wondered if he'd stop. She soon felt like she'd met this Rebecca Miniver and would know her on sight. "I can tell she means a lot to you."

"I'm sorry to carry on."

"Don't worry. We'll walk into the USO, and you'll have a good time. One that you can tell her all about, too. Frankly, I'm relieved you have a girl back home. It'll make it easier when you leave if we're only friends."

He turned and studied her a moment in the pale streetlight that filtered through the windshield. "Thank you."

"Let's dance, sailor."

* * *

THE WAIL of a trumpet pierced the room and brought the USO to life. Couples jumped up from their seats and dashed to the floor. The wail turned into an instrumental version of "Boogie Woogie Bugle Boy." Tom stayed in his chair and watched the couples swing into the jitterbug. He rubbed his shoulder and then rotated his arm. A nice, deep bruise had shown up over the last twenty-four hours, probably a result of one too many flying leaps over shoulders.

The fort's orchestra slowed down its tempo and switched to a decent rendition of Glenn Miller's "In the Mood." Time for some refreshments.

He stood and bumped his way around the floor to a table loaded down with cake and cookies and a bowl of punch. Other beverages were available at the bar in the next room. He smiled at the two young ladies behind the table. The chaperones had brought a busload of women to the dance from Alliance.

A striking redhead handed him a glass of punch. "Enjoy."

He nodded. "Thank you." He turned and edged into a woman with hair as dark as the night sky.

"Fancy meeting you here." Lainie's eyes sparkled and matched her smile.

"Doesn't look like you need a hero tonight."

She shook her head. "No, the seaman I'm with is over the moon for a girl back home. Exactly the kind I like to spend time with. Though I wouldn't mind talking about something else. At least he can dance."

"Save one or two for me."

She quirked an eyebrow and studied him. He wondered what she saw. "Make sure you find me."

A broad-shouldered sailor walked up beside her. He placed his hand on the small of Lainie's back as he sized Tom up. "You all right, Lainie?"

"Sure am. Mike, meet my friend Tom Hamilton. Tom, this is Mike Harris."

Tom shook hands with the seaman. "Nice to meet you. I'll be by for that dance, Lainie."

The pair strolled off, and Tom settled back to wait for an appropriate time to collect his dance and leave. Then again, with her track record, maybe he'd stick around. This sailor seemed protective, a marked improvement over that last guy.

Tom couldn't figure out Lainie Gardner. She enjoyed his company, but from the looks of things, he was far from the only one. The shuffling of a couple of hundred feet against the floor stilled as the bandleader announced a break. Lainie whispered something in the seaman's ear and then walked toward Tom. She fanned her face as she came.

"Take me out for fresh air?"

Tom nodded and offered her his arm. Lainie looped her arm through his, and they worked their way outside.

"Lainie, do you have plans tomorrow?"

"No. There aren't an abundance of distractions in Crawford."

"Then join me. I'm going riding. It'll be a beautiful day, one made to spend outside."

She looked at him, concern on her face. "A horse? I've never ridden before."

"No problem. There are some gentle animals in the barns. We can commandeer one for you. Explore the hills around us."

"I'm game." A smile replaced her frown.

"I'll pick you up at ten o'clock."

"Should I pack a picnic?"

Tom nodded, the vision of a day spent out in God's wonderful creation filling him with excitement. "That would be great. We can take it with us. Don't forget some apples or carrots to share with the horses."

"All right."

"Have a great night, Lainie." He'd returned to the barracks before he realized he'd never collected on his dance.

* * *

THE NEXT MORNING Lainie stood in the kitchen, watching Esther put together a picnic for her. Esther added a container of homemade coleslaw, so the basket overflowed with cold fried chicken, cookies, apples, and a bottle of milk.

"That should do it."

Lainie eyed it and nodded. "I think that's plenty. We'll only be gone a few hours."

"All that fresh air could make you extra hungry."

"You're assuming we'll find a horse that likes me." Lainie grabbed the basket before Esther could stuff anything else in it. "Thank you."

She carried the basket to the front porch, where she sank onto the top step to wait. Several cars moved up and down the street. The sun warmed her face, and the scent of roses filled the air. Tom had been right; this would be the perfect day to spend outside.

Thirty minutes later, as she stared at horses that towered over her in the barn, she wanted to retract her agreement. "You seriously want me to climb on the back of one of these beasts?"

"Yes. We'll find a gentle one for you. The WACs love to ride, so Private Thorson here is used to matching women with horses."

Lainie eyed the skinny soldier and wondered what qualified him. "Aren't you a little small for a soldier?"

"I'm a world-class jockey on loan to the Army. Edgar Thorson, at your service."

"I can see your ego more than makes up for your stature."

"Yes, ma'am, and this horse is perfect for you."

He led a gray dappled horse toward her. Lainie stepped backward to avoid getting stepped on. The horse's back easily met her head.

Tom gripped her hands and forced her to look at him. "Lainie, you can do this. And you'll love it. You love your freedom, and nothing is better than racing across a field on horseback."

Spots floated in her vision, and her breath caught in her chest.

Concern flashed across Tom's face. "Don't worry. We won't race today. We'll let the horses walk, maybe canter, but only if you want to."

The horse snorted and lowered its head to nuzzle her shoulder. Lainie took another step away and shook her head. She considered the horse. Would it feel like freedom to soar across the plains on it? "What's this thing's name?"

Private Thorson grinned at her. "Daisy."

"Exactly the name I would have chosen." The horse pawed the ground and then stepped toward her. "Persistent thing, isn't she?" Lainie reached up and ran her fingers along the velvety muzzle. She inhaled and smelled the mixed scent of hay, horse, and sunshine. "You'd better get me on her before I change my mind."

Private Thorson led Daisy toward a block of wood standing next to the barn. "All you need to do is hop up on this block. Once you do, hold on to the saddle horn with both hands. I'll hold her steady while you put your left foot in the stirrup and throw your right leg across her."

"I'm sure it's that simple." Lainie rolled her eyes and pulled Tom with her as she stalked to the block. "You'd better catch me when she bucks me off."

"Daisy hasn't bucked in a long time, miss." Private Thorson continued. "Talk to her softly and let her know you're ready to climb on."

Tom helped her onto the block and then over the horse. Once perched on its back, she tried to still her shaking hands. Sure, she'd loved *Black Beauty* as a child, but this was a first. It should be easier than this, but her hands refused to clutch the horn.

CHAPTER 14

JUNE 5, 1943

*D*aisy flicked an ear at a fly, and a barn cat strutted out of the shadows to watch. Tom rubbed a hand over his chin to wipe away the smile that wanted to sneak out. If Lainie caught him laughing at her, he could imagine her reaction. Lots of sparks.

"Come on, Lainie. Daisy's a patient lady, but every horse has her limits." Daisy snorted and pawed the ground at Tom's words.

Private Thorson turned on the charm. "Both hands on the saddle horn. There. Now stick your left foot in the stirrup. Not that left foot. There you go. Now up and over. Good." He winked at Tom. "Hold Daisy while I grab Tornado."

Lainie perched on top of the saddle, back stiff and head high. Tom shielded his eyes from the sun to get a better look. Yep, a blank expression tightened the muscles around her eyes, and she looked ready to swoon. "We can do something else if you'd rather."

"No." Her voice sliced the air. "We'll do this, but if I get hurt, so help me, Tom."

"I won't let anything happen to you." He would do everything in his power to protect her from harm. Maybe someday she'd understand how serious he was.

Thorson brought out a gelding that stamped his feet in impatience. The horse tossed his head, mane flying.

"Hey, boy. Good to see you, too." Tom stroked the horse's neck.

"You act like good friends." Lainie's voice remained tight.

"I try to ride him as often as I can. Tornado and I enjoy a good run, don't we?" The horse pawed the ground with his right foreleg. "Thanks, Thorson. We'll be back in a few hours."

"Don't forget this." Thorson tossed the repacked picnic to him, and Tom pulled the more practical knapsack over his shoulders. There had been no way to carry the basket. "Have a good time. And relax, miss, Daisy'll take care of you."

Lainie pulled her straw hat lower over her eyes and nodded. "Thank you." She turned her head with a stiff jerk toward Tom. "How do I get her to move?"

"Squeeze her lightly with your knees. She'll get the idea." Tom, on Tornado, led Lainie and Daisy up the road and away from the highway. They clopped past the parade grounds and soon struck out from the post buildings. Within minutes, the barracks and officers' quarters were behind them with the sandy hills and buttes in front of them. Peace descended on him as it so often did when he snuck away for some time in God's creation. Some might call it rugged, but he thought the area showcased God's diversity and creativity.

"How ya doing, Lainie?"

Her body swayed in time with Daisy's gait. She remained perfectly balanced even as she gripped the reins so tightly her circulation almost cut off.

"I'm okay, though I'm not sure I can climb off her."

"I'll help." A funny feeling flooded his stomach at the thought of lifting her from the horse. She'd been light in his arms when dancing. And he could only guess how she'd feel as he handed her down. He swallowed and forced the sensation away. They had friendship only, and that was as it should be.

They traveled in silence. When she'd been quiet a while, he glanced over to see if she'd fallen asleep. He'd seen it happen to others, lulled by the gentle pacing of a horse's walk.

She caught his glance and gamely tried to smile. "I think I'm getting the hang of this."

"You look like a natural."

"Sure I do." Her shoulders dropped a bit, and the reins came to rest easily in her hands and across the saddle. "Thank you for talking me into this."

"My pleasure." A copse of chokecherry shrubs appeared over a hill a hundred yards in front of them. They were covered in yellow blossoms and would provide some shade. A thin rivulet ran behind the grove. "Let's head there for lunch. The horses can drink and forage while we eat."

He ground tied the horses and reached up to help Lainie off Daisy. She grasped his hands tightly and swung her right leg over the horse. She groaned and slid into his arms. His heart raced as his breath stilled. Her head fit perfectly under his chin, and she sagged into him.

"I'm not sure my legs will support me. It feels like I'm still moving." She murmured against his chest.

"Give yourself a moment." He should step back, put some space between them, but she leaned on him. How could he do it without dropping her on the ground? She looked up, a grimace marring her delicate features.

"Remind me to think twice next time. Parts of my legs ache that I didn't know could hurt."

"It'll get better." He stepped back and pulled her toward the shade. "Let's enjoy that lunch you brought."

Lainie uncurled as they ate. Her sharp wit kept him on his toes, and he liked it. He didn't have to wonder what she thought. She'd tell him without hesitation. They cleaned up the traces of the picnic, and he boosted her onto Daisy. A crease furrowed Lainie's brow, and she looked from him to the countryside.

"Even if I'm sore, thanks for encouraging me to come. It's amazing out here." Daisy flicked an ear toward her. Lainie smiled and leaned forward to rub Daisy's neck. "And you have lived up to your billing. Not bad for a first ride."

"I knew you'd like this." Tom hopped on Tornado and pulled the horse's head toward the fort. "Any time you want to go out again, let me know. I'd enjoy the excuse to break away and experience the peace out here."

* * *

ESTHER POUNDED on the door Sunday morning.

"Time to get moving or you'll miss church."

Lainie cracked open her eyes and squinted against the glare of sunshine streaming into the room. She shifted her legs to the side of the bed and bit off a squeal. Shards of heat skittered through her thighs, and her shoulders balled tight. She groaned and focused on releasing each group of muscles.

"Are you awake in there?" An echo of concern filled Esther's voice.

"I'll be down in a minute." Lainie gritted her teeth and pushed up. This was the pain of muscles used, not of muscles abused by fever. She should feel grateful. Instead, she wanted to question her sanity. Then she thought of the freedom she'd felt abandoning the fort and roaming the hills with Tom. Everything from the delicate chokecherry flowers to the scraggly branches of the pines stretching toward heaven had hinted at the handiwork of God. Only He could make everything so unique and detailed. If He cared so much about the details, why couldn't He care as intimately about her?

It must be Sunday if such thoughts rolled through her mind. The answers danced beyond her reach, so she forced the questions away. Maybe someday she'd find a response that made sense when compared to the reality of her life.

"If I don't hear some movement, I'm coming in." The door handle rattled in its catch.

"All right." Lainie stood up with a thump. "Did you hear that, Esther? I'm moving."

"Good thing. We've got to hustle, missy." The sound of Esther shuffling down the hallway, muttering to herself, filtered through the door.

Lainie shook her head and wondered if she'd have to hobble to get to church. "You'd think the horses would be the sore ones."

* * *

ALL WEEK LAINIE looked for Tom, but never saw him closer than across a field. If she didn't know better, she'd think he purposefully avoided her. He almost turned on his heel if they came within one hundred feet of each other.

He'd seemed to enjoy Saturday, and the conversation had flowed back and forth with plenty of barbs. As she sat at her desk Wednesday, she could almost sense the heat of the sun warming her face. Surely he'd enjoyed it as much as she. But the more she analyzed their time, the more she worried that she'd done or said something wrong. She couldn't figure out what that was, but he'd swerved inward the nearer they came to the fort.

Unfortunately, she kept running into Lieutenant Daniels. The fire in his eyes made it clear he continued to fume. She was just glad he didn't say anything, choosing to glower at her instead.

Wednesday afternoon Mary walked across the office and stopped in front of Lainie's desk. "You're a million miles away today. Something wrong?"

Lainie shook her head and shifted the intake papers piled on her desk. "Gathering wool, I guess."

"Are there many Gardners in North Platte?"

"No, all of Father's family is from Kansas. His job at the bank brought our family to town. Why?"

"I wondered, because Private Donahue brought in the newest stack of forms. This top one says the dog belonged to James Gardner of North Platte."

Lainie bolted out of the chair and rushed around the table. "Let me see that." She scanned the sheet once, then again, unwilling to believe the information typed on the page. "No, no, no. Why would they do that?" She spun and grabbed her hat from the coat tree before rushing from the building.

She stepped into the sunlight and stopped. Where could she go? She couldn't let the Army have Mason. The dog had been her confidant on too many occasions to count. The black Lab would settle back on her haunches and listen as Lainie poured out her woes. Mason didn't have an aggressive bone in her body nor did she chase every squirrel and bird like so many of her breed. "What were they thinking?" Mason would flop as a war dog, although part of Lainie feared the dog would excel with her intelligence. Lainie had to find Mason and get her discharged before the training harmed her.

But what could she do? Her thoughts froze in a jumbled mess, and she felt rooted to the ground. Lainie forced herself forward. Maybe Mason was still in processing. If so, she'd be at the War Dog Reception and Training Center. Lainie hurried across the street to the center.

She pushed open the doors and waited for her eyes to adjust to the dimness. The smell of antiseptic and bleach mixed with a doggy odor choked her. She covered her mouth and nose and looked for anyone who might be in charge. Her gaze fixed on Sergeant Lewis. He could help her, he had to.

"Sergeant." She hurried toward him when he didn't move. "Sergeant, please, I need to talk to you a moment."

He shifted from the dog he'd examined and looked at her. "Yes, Miss Gardner? What can I do for you?"

"Please, there's been a mistake." She thrust the papers at him. "This dog, she shouldn't be here."

"And how do you know that?"

"She's my family pet."

"Not anymore. Says right there she's property of the War Department for the duration."

Lainie's knees weakened, and she closed her eyes. She felt someone grab her arm. Clenching her teeth, she yanked her arm free. "I want her back. If my family's decided they no longer want her, I'll take her."

"Can't do that."

She opened her eyes and blinked to clear the tears clouding her vision. "She doesn't have the personality to be a war dog."

"If that's true, we'll find out during the training exercises." He shrugged. "The dog's in the Army now. I suggest you accept that."

Lainie spun to leave before the tears fell down her cheeks. The sergeant might think there was nothing she could do about Mason. Lainie refused to believe that. She'd find a way. She had to.

CHAPTER 15

JUNE 10, 1943

*L*ainie waltzed into the K-9 office, a smile plastered on her lips. In her hands she carried a still-warm strawberry rhubarb pie. Sarge had been at Mrs. Babcock's earlier that week enjoying a slice. She hoped he'd enjoy it enough now to start to see things her way.

She had to do something. She couldn't wait around until the military figured out they'd made a terrible mistake accepting Mason.

"Good morning, Sarge."

"Miss Gardner." The man swallowed hard as he eyed her package. Lainie perked up. Maybe this would work. Every woman she knew swore the stomach was the way to a man's heart. She didn't care about Sarge's heart unless it meant he'd help her get Mason back. "That smells mighty good."

"One of Mrs. Babcock's special pies."

"Now why would you bring that to me? It wouldn't have anything to do with that dog of yours?"

Lainie bit her lower lip. She must proceed carefully, get him to at least listen to her. "Does a girl need to have a reason to bring a gift?"

"Usually, yes. Why don't you tell me what it is you want."

"Mason." The word exploded from her mouth. She pasted her mouth together and took a breath. "Did you have a dog growing up?"

"Sure. Most kids do."

"Mason is that dog for me. I may have been a senior in high school, but she's been a special friend. I won't allow her to serve in the Army. She's a pet not a warrior." Lainie placed the box on top of Sarge's battered desk.

He pulled the box to him and lifted the lid. "Smells like strawberry rhubarb. Nobody makes it like Mrs. Babcock."

"I know." Her shoulders slumped as she read the set of his shoulders. "You won't help me, will you?"

"Look, Miss Gardner. Much as I like you and appreciate the pie, the Army has regulations that cannot be violated. Not for anybody. And not as a result of any bribe. You may not believe this, but I do understand." He pushed the pie back to her. "Bribe or no, Mason stays unless she shows she's unfit for duty."

A tear trickled down Lainie's cheek, and she brushed it away. Spinning on her heel, she hurried toward the door. "Keep the pie."

As she headed to her office, Lainie wanted to cover her ears to hide the sound of the dogs. Their barking seemed especially loud this morning. The noise hammered home how much she had failed Mason.

* * *

LAINIE STALKED across the grass leading toward the dog pens. Her dark curls bounced against her shoulders, and fire sparked from her eyes. Tom stilled and considered ducking behind the truck in front of him. What crazy idea did she harbor this time? Since Mason arrived at the center a week earlier, she'd gone crazy and he'd heard each and every story of her efforts to get her family pet released. Every day she had a new scheme to free her dog from the Army. She refused to accept the Army didn't work that way.

Last night, she'd cornered him.

"Tom, you have to help me." She'd batted her amber eyes and turned her face into a pleading mask. "No one else will listen."

When he told her he couldn't help, her spine had stiffened, and she'd sputtered. The Army had rules, and he lived within those. He'd expected the flames to scorch his back as she left.

Tom didn't want to experience a fresh wave of her anger now.

She hesitated when her gaze landed on him. Then she stiffened her spine and glared past him as if he'd disappeared. Nope, she hadn't forgotten.

There was a tilt to her chin that raised a red flag in his gut. He didn't know what she'd decided, but she'd made some decision. Tom followed her from a safe distance. Whatever she was up to, she might need help. Or someone to prevent her from doing something careless.

She stomped over the hill. He'd hoped she'd turn left toward the obstacle course or the water source. Instead, she veered to the right, aiming straight for the kennels. His heart started to pound to the beat of reveille. Hadn't she learned anything while she worked here? Just last week another soldier landed in the infirmary with serious bites to his arm and shoulder. How did she think she'd fare if an animal responded to her presence with aggression? If a large, square soldier had lost the fight, a slip of a girl would experience worse.

Her steps didn't falter until she passed the first row of waist-high trees. Someday, they'd shade the dogs. Today, they marked the beginning of a new section of kennels. Six rows down, she turned to walk the aisle.

"Lainie, stop." He tried to infuse his voice with a command, but she continued on. "Lord, why is she so stubborn?"

He held his breath. She'd miscalculated as she counted. Mason's crate stood one section over in a section reserved for quarantine. Tom didn't know these new animals well, and he examined their reactions to the invader. Some merely laid beside their kennels inside their pocket-sized fenced areas and watched. Others stood at attention and barked aggressively. A couple, though, had a look in their eyes that pushed Tom to close the gap between Lainie and himself.

"Lainie, stop now." He bellowed the words, a vise gripping his chest.

She shuddered to a stop and turned on him. "Who do you think you are? Yesterday you wouldn't help. And now you'll tell me what to do? Who gave you the right?"

"Look at the dogs."

She jerked her head from side to side. "What? There are a thousand dogs here, but I only care about one."

"But you should care about all of them. These dogs are training to become attack dogs. Didn't you read *Hoofbeats and Barks*? See the article about the attack? That could be you." He stared at her and tried to slow the rush of words, fight the tightening in his upper body. "Come to me this instant. Let's get you out of here and then discuss this."

She snorted and rolled her eyes. "These are dogs, Tom. They aren't going to hurt me."

"No, these are war machines, most trained to attack intruders. Take a look around. You're invading their territory."

A movement to the left caught Tom's attention. He turned and saw a German Shepherd pulling against its chain.

"Lainie, now."

She followed his gaze and finally moved toward him. The dog lunged as she darted past it. She screamed and leapt to the side. "Tom, help me."

He gulped against the fear and raced toward her, placing his body between her and the German Shepherd. "Run." He watched her slip back to safety and tried to keep an eye fixed on the dog. The dog lunged, and hot breath and snapping teeth dug at his arm. He shook his arm from the dog's reach, and raced away. When he reached Lainie, he doubled over and gulped.

"That is why you cannot come here. Lainie, you'll lose. Every time."

She grabbed at his sleeve, turning it over and twisting the fabric, probing for tears.

"Are you all right? I am so sorry." The words gushed past her lips, her voice higher than usual, eyes wide and dilated. "I could have been attacked. And you're hurt."

He placed his hands on either side of her face and forced her gaze from his arm to him. "I'm okay. It's a scratch. See, hardly any blood."

She focused on him. "Are you sure?"

"Yes. Promise you'll never do anything that stupid again."

Lainie nodded and a tear slipped from one eye. He lightly brushed it away and traced its trail. Her breath hitched, and she shuddered. His stomach tightened at the smoothness of her skin. He backed away, dropping his arms to his side. "These aren't family pets. You have to remember that."

"That's why I have to get Mason back. She'll be destroyed in this process.

She's not an aggressive dog." She wrapped her arms around her middle. "I can't let that happen."

The urge to shelter her in an embrace, protect her from her fear, overwhelmed him. As he debated what to do, Lainie walked away and slipped over the hill.

* * *

ON FRIDAY TOM still stewed about Lainie's actions and abrupt departure. Thoughts of her generated a war. Part of him wanted to find and comfort her. The other part, to shake her until she understood how dangerous and foolish her actions were. And every time he hoped they might form a friendship that went beyond saving Lainie from herself, she acted without thinking.

Tom tugged his thoughts from the raven beauty with bad decision-making skills, to the obstacle course in front of him.

Sergeant Lewis stood in front of the basic trainees, hands on his hips, feet spread apart in a balanced stance. "This afternoon your task is to complete this course."

Groans rose from somewhere behind Tom, but he refused to turn. The pack sat heavy on his shoulders. It shifted from side to side with each step regardless of how he secured it. And his boots chafed his feet, reopening blisters. Whoever had decided boots were a good idea for long hikes and runs hadn't tried them.

"You have two hours. You will be judged on how quickly you complete it. The sooner you're back here, the quicker we can head to the firing range." The private next to Tom moaned, and Tom jutted out his jaw, waiting for the attack. Sarge skewered him with a look, but held his tongue. He pulled the stopwatch out of his pocket and clicked the timer. "Go."

The men quickly closed ranks and jogged down the path. They'd run as a pack for the first quarter of the rugged course. Then the hills and rocks would take their toll on the heavier men.

The clump started to thin, but Tom kept his thoughts focused on the end. *I can do all things through Christ.* The verse pounded through his head in cadence to the beat of his feet on the hard, packed earth.

Sid jogged up next to him, breathing regularly with barely a drop of sweat on his forehead. "Hanging in there?"

Tom growled as rivers of sweat poured between his shoulder blades and the pack.

"That good? Think of our Class A passes waiting for this weekend."

"I might not still be alive."

"Yeah, you will. You'll do this if I have to drag your sorry carcass through the course."

Tom ground his teeth and grimaced. "With friends like you."

"You don't have to thank me."

"Great. Go encourage someone else."

Sid turned around and ran backwards a few steps. "Aren't we testy?"

"Show-off." Tom caught the rest of what he wanted to say. What had happened to his earlier attitude? Paul hadn't meant he could do all things through Christ including taking off a buddy's head with his words. "Sorry, Sid. I'm glad we're over halfway. This schedule is brutal."

"Just think, the guns are next. You're stealing the show with those."

Two hours later, his sweaty cheek pressed into his rifle's butt, Tom hadn't hit a thing. At this rate he wouldn't hit the broadside of a barn back at the fort.

They were hunkered down for crawl drills. He inhaled a slow stream of air and steadied his breathing against the rifle's butt. Dirt covered his uniform, and the pack pressed him farther into the sand. The grit had found its way between his teeth and his toes. Tom tried to force his mind past the discomfort to a zone that focused on the target. He knew how to do this. Years of hunting everything that moved in Wyoming had made him skilled with a rifle. Until people started scoring his shots, that is.

Almost half the guys in the first session qualified for marksmanship badges. He could do no less. Not in the one military skill he usually excelled at.

Tom blew out the breath and eased another one in. He sighted down the barrel of the gun and squeezed the trigger. The M1 Garand recoiled against his shoulder. There, that felt the way it should. Straight and true. He sighted down the barrel again and saw a hole in the target's chest. He squeezed off seven more rounds, emptying the clip. Each felt more natural than the one before it.

"Woohee! Look who's found his target." Sergeant Maxwell stopped and hunkered down next to Tom. "I'd begun to worry about you, but looks like that was misplaced."

"Yes, sir." Tom pushed himself up on his elbows, ready to insert another clip.

"All right, men. That's enough for today. If you all progress like Specialist Hamilton, we may win this war."

Sid war whooped, and Tom looked for a boulder to hide behind. Attention was the last thing he needed. He licked his teeth and grimaced at the grit. No, all he wanted was a shower and a slice of Mrs. Babcock's pie. On second thought, that only appealed if Lainie joined him.

CHAPTER 16

JUNE 18, 1943

*T*he sun sailed above the horizon even though it was after five o'clock.

"Night, Lainie. Have a good weekend."

"You too, Mary." Lainie turned from the window, looked around the now-empty office, and sagged onto her chair. Another week's work finished, yet the last place she wanted to go was home. She could always stay and head over to the USO, but it didn't appeal to her. No matter how she tried, she couldn't shake the funk she'd fallen into when she realized she could do nothing to free Mason. Isolation overwhelmed her when everybody—even Tom—refused to help.

Lainie searched the sky and weighed her options. Gray clouds looked like they'd been painted across the horizon. If she hurried, she'd have time for a short ride on Daisy. She might not be the world's best rider yet, but quick rides over lunch a couple of days had increased her comfort in the saddle.

She pulled her bag from beneath her desk and changed into the pair of pants she'd brought with her. When she reached the barn, Private Thorson was mucking out a stall.

"You're still here." Lainie smiled down at the man. "Would you mind terribly saddling Daisy for me?"

He looked out the window at the sky, then at her. "Only if you'll stay close. Storms can flare up quickly."

"I promise." Energy surged through Lainie at the thought of the wind blowing through her curls. She needed a taste of freedom and then she could refocus on life and its disappointments.

Private Thorson threw the rake to the side and whistled. Several horses perked up in the paddock, but only Daisy trotted toward him. Her black tail fanned behind her like a flag, and her ears twitched to the front as if she waited for instructions. In minutes Private Thorson bounced Lainie onto the saddle. "Remember to stick close to the parade grounds."

Lainie nodded and turned Daisy's head toward the road. They clipped to the end of the officers' quarters and continued down the road past more stables. Lainie let Daisy pick the path, and focused on the stark beauty of the land. Tom had led her in this general direction, and she trusted Daisy.

Daddy had called last night. Lainie couldn't shake how certain he'd sounded. She'd tried to tell him her concerns about Mason and how hurt she'd been when she'd learned he'd sent Mason to Dogs for Defense.

"Get over it, girlie. You're doing your part, and Mason will do hers." He had sounded hard, indifferent.

A chill shook Lainie, and she rubbed her arms. She examined the terrain and realized that, while she'd been lost in thought, Daisy had carried her past the fort toward the hills. Daisy picked her way up a hill, and Lainie grabbed for the saddle horn. She tried to time her movements to match the horse's but couldn't find the rhythm. Daisy's foot caught a dip in the ground, and she stumbled. Lainie grabbed her mane and hung on.

"Easy, girl."

The wind picked up and whistled through the pine trees. Lainie's skin pebbled. She eyed the sky, and her gut tightened at the angry clouds hiding the sun and forcing the temperature downward.

"We'd better turn around, Daisy." She pulled against the reins and waited for Daisy to comply. Before they'd traveled two hundred feet down the butte, rain-drops pelted her skin. The drops beat an raging staccato, and Lainie pushed soaked curls out of her face. "Find shelter, girl."

Lightning flashed, followed within seconds by thunder. Daisy forgot her gentle nature and reared. Lainie screamed and fought to stay on the horse's back. The mare danced as she tried to keep her feet. When more lightning zigzagged across the sky, Daisy bolted across the plain. Lainie tightened her grip on the saddle horn and mane. Her legs gripped the horse's flanks, and she tucked her head against Daisy's neck. She didn't know where they were and couldn't see through the rain even if she knew how to find the fort.

Fear gripped Lainie and squeezed. Her hair was plastered to her face, and she battled for each breath against the panic. Daisy had to find the stable, and soon. As the deluge continued, Lainie struggled to maintain her hold as shivers racked her.

* * *

"You have to let me go after her." Tom pushed past Edgar Thorson and grabbed Tornado's halter.

Thorson crossed his arms and planted himself in front of Tom. "You can't do that. This storm makes it dangerous for anyone in it."

"Especially a woman who hardly knows how to ride. That's why I have to go after her."

"Hold on there, private." Sergeant Lewis hurried into the stables. "She's one of my girls, but we can't go after her until the storm blows over. Soon as it does, we'll send dog teams out. They'll find her in no time."

Tom ground his teeth together to stop the flow of words. Didn't they understand? She didn't know what she was doing. What had she been thinking, to disappear with a storm coming in? He wanted to find her, and then Tom couldn't decide if he would shake her or kiss her. She had no business putting herself in this kind of jeopardy.

"I'll get a couple of the teams on standby." Sarge pulled his slicker's hood over his head and dashed out of the barn and back into the downpour.

"She doesn't know this area yet." Tom walked to the doorway and tried to make out anything through the dark storm.

Thorson stepped next to him. "She doesn't, but Daisy does. She knows where her food and shelter are. She'll return Miss Gardner."

Tom searched the horizon for Lainie and hoped Thorson was right. An hour later, Tom's stomach growled, but he refused to abandon his post. The rain eased up, and Tom hoped the gathering search teams would move out soon. If they couldn't, he thought he'd go crazy with worry.

Sarge took an item of Lainie's clothes that Mrs. Babcock had brought them and let each dog sniff it.

One of the dogs, a Lab, jumped to attention. His handler brushed his fur, encouraging him to relax, but the animal didn't budge. "Looks like Rocket has something."

Tom scanned the darkness, gut twisting with the need to see.

Other soldiers hurried to the door and joined him.

"I think I hear something."

Thorson perked up. "That's got to be Daisy."

Tom stepped into the rain, unable to hear anything above the downpour. But as he examined the night this time, he saw a wall of gray moving toward him. And on its back, a flash of white. Lainie.

Thorson raced past him and grabbed Daisy's reins. "Tom, get her off the horse."

Tom rubbed Lainie's hand. It felt ice cold. She hadn't dressed to get caught in a storm. "Lainie, honey, can you hear me?"

She stirred and moaned.

"I'm going to slide you off Daisy, okay?"

She barely nodded and leaned toward him. He caught her effortlessly, and another soldier wrapped a blanket around her.

"Take her to the hospital?" His chest pounded as he stared at her face. She was so still.

Sarge shook his head. "No. It's full and she's a civilian. She'll be more comfortable at Mrs. Babcock's."

Tom nodded and whisked her into the cab of a truck Sid pulled in front of the barn, cradling her against him. Shivers shook her thin frame, and her cheeks were pale as fresh snow.

He pushed his feet against the floorboard, willing the truck to move faster. The heater blasted warm air at them, but it didn't seem to reach Lainie. He prayed that somehow God would protect her, reach through the fog and touch her. Sid whipped the truck in front of Mrs. Babcock's, and Tom lurched forward, unable to brace himself while he held Lainie.

Sid jumped out and ran around to open Tom's door. He unfurled an umbrella and held it over Lainie's face as Tom hurried up the steps. Sid pushed through the door and hollered for Mrs. Babcock. They were met by Mrs. Babcock hurrying from the back.

Concern etched fresh lines on her face when she saw Lainie. "What on earth did you do to her? Well, never mind. Carry her up the stairs for me. Her room is the second one on the left."

Tom followed Mrs. Babcock as she hauled herself up the stairs. "Put her on the bed. I'll take care of her from here."

Tom watched helplessly as Mrs. Babcock turned her back on them and bent over Lainie.

"What are you waiting on? Go on. There's nothing you can do now, other than pray."

Even as he knew she was right, Tom hated the sinking sensation that engulfed him.

* * *

LAINIE FELT the weight of blankets pressing against her and the soft feather pillow cradling her head. She squinted against the sunlight streaming through the window. Something must be wrong if Esther let her sleep past breakfast. She shifted, and waves of pain rolled through her.

Daisy must have made her way back to the stable. Vague flashes of memory told her someone had cradled her as if she were a child. She'd had the sensation of being safe. Now she felt pounded by fever and aches.

"She's right through here." The soft murmur of Esther's voice filtered through the door. In a moment the doorknob twisted, and Esther peeked around the door. "Good. You're awake. Lainie, this is Doctor Gibson."

"Let's take a look at you, young lady." He eased onto the chair beside her bed. He looked young, with a minimal sprinkling of gray in his brown hair. Concern radiated from his kind expression. He pulled his bag onto his lap and examined her with a look. "Tell me what happened."

Esther slipped from the room, and Lainie told him what she remembered about the storm. "My joints are flaring up again. Could the rheumatic fever be back?" Her heart constricted at the thought of that pain.

He frowned and gently probed her arms and neck. "It's not uncommon for it to flare up in the first several years after the first attack. Did they treat you with penicillin in Kentucky?"

Lainie shook her head. "That was saved for the soldiers."

"Well, I don't have much, but we'll try that. See if we can't get this under control. I haven't tried it myself, but I read a journal article on the treatment. Bed rest for a week, too. Give your body time to fight the fever and let the antibiotic work."

"I don't think so. I've done this before."

"Then you know exactly why you have to obey my orders. Or you'll get sicker. The risk to your heart is greater with each attack."

CHAPTER 17

JUNE 20, 1943

*T*he last notes of the closing hymn lingered in the base chapel. The smell of paint touched the air, and sunlight played across the floor in rich colors filtered from the stained glass. The day stretched in front of Tom as he considered his options. After a full Saturday, he had time to relax before another week spent balancing basic training and teaching the new dog teams started. He'd struggled to focus on his tasks yesterday when he couldn't shake how cold and wet Lainie'd felt. Nor how small, tucked against him.

Had he done enough? Should he have violated orders and chased after her? He thanked God Daisy had found her way back. Mud had covered the horse past her fetlocks, but she'd looked beautiful when she arrived with Lainie on her back.

Tom walked to his car, waving at the guys who yelled but not stopping. A baseball game held no appeal today. He had to make sure Lainie was okay. Somehow during the last month she'd become important to him. He couldn't pinpoint where or how, but he couldn't fight reality. The fact she might not feel the same way weighed on his mind. Maybe today he could probe her thoughts.

Puddles dotted the sides of the highway, lingering traces of the storm. He'd found the dogs soaked but otherwise untouched. A few tree limbs strafed the road as he turned into town. He skirted around them, making a mental note to return and clean them up on his return.

The street in front of Mrs. Babcock's was empty. She never opened on Sunday, declaring the Lord's Day too precious to violate. He climbed the steps and knocked on the door. Minutes passed and he waited. He knocked again, this time louder. Finally, he heard the echo of steps on the wood floor.

A thin girl opened the door and stared at him. She looked all brown with her light-brown hair pulled back with a ribbon and a dress that matched. He'd seen her before in the dining room, so maybe she boarded here.

"Can I help you?"

"I wondered if I could see Lainie."

The girl stepped back. "Come in, and I'll check with Esther."

Tom did as told, hoping her words weren't meant to be as foreboding as they sounded. She showed him to a small parlor that sat to one side and disappeared. He paced the length of the small room and wondered when Mrs. Babcock would appear.

"Aren't you the picture of a nervous bull?" Mrs. Babcock marched to him. "You can't see her, Tom."

"I promise not to stay. I need to see she's okay."

"The doctor ordered strict bed rest. She's on that new drug, penicillin, too. This isn't the first time she's been sick, and we have to be careful. Doc says her heart could be damaged. According to him, she's lucky that didn't happen the first time."

"Is she going to be fine?"

"She thinks so. She's fighting the bed rest hard. Pray the drug works and we can keep her down until she's better." Mrs. Babcock shook her head. "The girl's stubborn to the core."

"She wouldn't be here otherwise."

"True. Come back in a couple of days." Mrs. Babcock shushed him and cocked her head to stare at the ceiling. "I hear her getting out of bed again. Go before she hears you."

Tom strained to hear whatever Mrs. Babcock had detected. A heaviness cloaked him. Things sounded more serious than he'd anticipated. He'd expected to find Lainie sitting downstairs, reading or playing a game with others. "Should I tell them she won't be at work for a few days?"

"Mary knows." Mrs. Babcock grabbed his arm and walked him to the door. "Good day, Tom."

Before he could say good-bye, he found himself staring at the door. He stood for a moment, hunting for a reason to go back in, but he couldn't. Not if her health was as fragile as Mrs. Babcock said. As he got in his car, he turned and looked up at the second story. Somewhere Lainie rested up there. The curtain of the window over the door fluttered, and a hand waved at him to stop. He paused.

The window opened, and Lainie ducked her head out. "Tom, watch Mason till I get back, okay?" Her voice rasped, and he struggled to catch her words.

"Sure, Lainie."

She disappeared from the window, and in a moment, it closed. Mrs. Babcock's disapproving figure replaced Lainie's thin frame. Tom turned on the car and hurried back to base before she could shake a finger at him. He liked her pie too much to get her riled.

That night he lay on his bunk in the barracks, arms crossed behind his head. It smelled nothing like the floral air at Mrs. Babcock's. Instead, the aroma of too many sweaty boots and men in one place never quite cleared the building. He'd pop the window near his bed, but another storm brewed.

Tom stared at the ceiling and tried to imagine a way to help Lainie. Once a family donated a dog through Dogs for Defense, it belonged to the military. If the Army no longer needed the dog or if it didn't meet the training requirements, the animal could be returned to the family if they'd requested. He'd examined Mason's paperwork, and Lainie's family wanted nothing more to do with the dog.

Dogs simply weren't returned without a military discharge.

Lainie would never accept that. She must be an only child or baby in the family. She expected the world to bend to her whims.

Only problem was the Army didn't work that way.

* * *

A MILLION FIRE ants burrowed into Lainie, and she bit back a scream. She drew in a ragged breath and released it slowly, counting against the pain. She tried to think of an ice cream sundae at Wahl's, an extra cherry decorating the whipped cream. Jumping into the Platte River on a hot day, the cool water splashing her fevered skin. Nothing worked. She was miserable, engulfed by heat burning from the inside out. She smashed her lips together as her muscles tightened, and a moan slipped from her mouth.

If she called for Esther, the doctor would be back with his negative diagnosis. Lainie would endure this attack. She had to. If Mama and Daddy found out how bad things were, they'd have her back home before Lainie could protest.

She couldn't let that happen. Not when she finally had a role, albeit a small one. Her legs jerked beneath the sheet, and a vise clamped around her chest. She struggled to catch a breath and groaned.

The door swung open. Lainie fought to cloak the pain as Dorothy slipped into the room with a glass and bottle of medicine. "Oh, Lainie." Dorothy hurried to the side of the bed, concern clouding her green eyes. "What can I do to help?"

Lainie couldn't answer as she felt like she inhaled through a straw.

Dorothy set the cup and bottle on the bedside table. She felt Lainie's forehead, and a frown marred her expression. "Your fever's spiked again. I'm going to get Esther."

Lainie shook her head , but Dorothy had already scooted from the room. So much for convincing Esther she was better.

The sound of a band—probably Tommy Dorsey's—floated up the stairs from the parlor radio. Normally, music like that would set her toes tapping and her thoughts swirling. She'd imagine dancing at the USO with a soldier, maybe Tom Hamilton. Not tonight. Even the thought of all he'd done for her couldn't distract her. She tried to remember his face, his compelling eyes. His image wavered in her mind's eye and then vanished.

God, help me.

The wardrobe started to move across the room in time to the beat of the song. She shut her eyes and burrowed into the pillow. She sank into the darkness.

* * *

Tom bolted out of bed.

"Where you going, Hamilton?" Henry Brighton rolled over to look at him.

"Checking something out for a friend."

"Keep it down next time you jump like that." Sid shook his head. "You'll have to hurry to return by lights out."

Tom pulled his boots on and nodded. "Thanks for the concern, guys. I'll be back."

He rushed out the door, ducking items pelted at him by the guys as he clumped across the concrete floor. He raced up the street, past the office building and war dog hospital, before veering left and up the hill. He paused at the rows of kennels.

The lines fanned in front of him. They had about thirteen hundred dogs right now, even though capacity was eighteen hundred. As many as four hundred fifty men could be on-site, most of those being matched with dogs for training. So how could he be so concerned about one animal? Especially when it was a dog?

Those kinds of questions had no answers other than one girl. Only a girl like Lainie could make him do something that could jeopardize his career if not his life.

He wasn't a doctor. He had no idea how to protect her until her body could heal. However, as he'd prayed tonight, he knew with a certainty that he could do something by caring for Mason. If only he could do that away from a thousand dogs who were unknown risks.

"Thought I'd find you here." Sid sidled up next to Tom. "You are over the moon for her, aren't you?"

"What do you mean?"

"You never voluntarily come here. Only a woman could motivate you."

"You don't know what you're talking about." Tom blustered against the knowing in his heart that every word Sid spoke was true. He scanned for Mason's kennel. He eased down the aisle until he saw her, laying in front of it, ignoring the rest of the dogs. He pulled a treat from his pocket, and her ears perked. "Here you go, girl."

Mason leapt to her feet and accepted the rawhide. She took it to her kennel and sat down in the doorway, chewing on it.

Seeing Mason reminded Tom that he couldn't lose Lainie.

Not when he'd just found her.

CHAPTER 18

JUNE 28, 1943

The lecturer stepped away from the podium and took his seat. He'd droned on so long about military jargon, that John Tyler, seated next to Tom, snored.

"All right, men. This is your last week of basic." Tired war whoops echoed Sergeant Maxwell's words. He glowered at them until quiet returned to the room, then nodded. "Attention."

Chairs screeched against concrete as soldiers bolted to their feet in the post theater. Tom tensed, staring ahead.

"Y'all think you're ready for war? We'll see what you feel after today. This is your introduction to the infiltration course. You must complete it in a satisfactory time before the end of the week." He stared down each man in the front row. Tom swallowed reflexively when Sergeant locked eyes with him. "There are many ways to soldier. But I guarantee you will not survive the war without the skills you'll learn on the course. Move out."

Tom joined the others in a retreat to the loading area for the transport trucks that would carry them to the course. His stomach clenched as a rush of adrenaline spiked through him. He climbed into the back of a truck, stories he'd heard from the first round of trainees cycling through his mind. This course would be a rush unlike any he'd experienced. Designed to simulate combat, it would require him to apply everything he'd learned in the countless lectures and demonstrations.

Sam Donahue leaned across Tom and whistled when a pretty WAC walked toward the truck. He stood, arms crossed on the wood slats. "You our driver, beautiful?"

She rolled her eyes, tossed her hair over a shoulder, and smacked her gum. "Honey, every guy here thinks I'm the girl for him. Get in line."

"Sit down, Romeo." Tom pulled on Sam's belt until he plopped down. The vehicle jerked into reverse, and the woman whipped the truck around before grinding into first gear and tearing down the road. The WAC acted like they were already on the front lines of a war and she needed to avoid enemy bombers. Maybe that was part of the training, too.

Tom bounced against Sam on one side and John on the other as the truck hurtled up hills to the course. It lurched over another rock and slowed to a stop. Tom twisted to look over the cab. "So this is it."

"Looks that way." John pulled on his helmet and squared his jaw. "Let's finish this."

Sam shrugged. "What's the rush? You know we'll do this again. Probably multiple times. Sarge is having too much fun convincing us we ain't real soldiers. Can't wait for him to head back to his real base."

"Knowing our luck, he'll get reassigned. Here. Permanently." Sid's long face would have made actor Donald O'Connor proud.

"Let's tackle this before we worry about where he ends up." Tom jumped from the truck and then walked over to where Sarge waited, beefy arms strapped across his chest.

"All right, boys. Here we'll learn who's a real soldier. The rest of you can play Army and hope you never leave Robinson. However, there's a war out there. One being fought across two oceans. This week you'll taste combat. Have fun." The glint in his eyes made Tom wonder how he defined *fun*.

Before he could spend too much time considering, the men separated into platoons with sectors to cover. Tom approached the course in a crouch, head swiveling as he tried to find the front of the attack. Surely it couldn't be as simple as a direct frontal attack.

A whistling noise pierced the air to his right. Tom turned to follow the sound in time for the explosion. Its concussion knocked him off his feet. As more bombs whistled across the sky, Tom tried to sort out the range and types of weapons. It wasn't as easy as indicated in the lectures. He gave up and began digging a foxhole with his helmet.

"Get that helmet back on your head, Hamilton!" Sarge barked in a tone that commanded Tom's obedience, even as he longed to burrow into the sandy earth.

* * *

LAINIE EYED the stack of books Tanya had brought from the library. Lainie couldn't focus on any of them long enough to read past the first chapter, not when images of the training Mason must be enduring filled her mind. Senseless romances weren't worth her time in the best of situations. Now, she longed for anything to hold her attention. Distract her from the pain and Mason. Over the last week, the pain had eased, but it still lingered if she did more than walk across her room. Traveling to the first-floor parlor caused her joints to scream in protest. Each spring in the couch seemed intent on gouging her skin. The blue and white floral striped wallpaper had transformed the retreat into a prison cell. If she couldn't get out of the house soon, she'd go crazy.

The screen door slammed, and Lainie looked up to find Ginny Speares waltzing through the opening. Her peaches-and-cream complexion was brighter than normal and her auburn hair damp around her face. "You've picked a good week to be confined indoors, Lainie." Her eyebrows jumped and she clapped a hand over her mouth. "Oh, I'm sorry. That didn't come out the way I meant. It's an oven out there."

"It's not much cooler in here." Lainie forced a small smile on her lips. "Anything interesting at the post office?"

"Oh, yes." Ginny reached into her pocket and pulled out an envelope.

Lainie grabbed it and stared at the handwriting. It could only be a letter from Roxie Ottman, her roommate in Kentucky. She fumbled with the flap. The envelope tremored in her grasp, and she tried to swallow but couldn't.

Ginny reached for her. "You okay, Lainie? Is it bad news?"

"I think I'll read this in my room. Thanks, Ginny." Lainie stumbled out of the parlor.

When she reached her room, Lainie set the letter on the table and eased onto the bed. A tornado of emotions tore through her. She hadn't expected the anger that pulsed through her. The passing months hadn't made her loss any less real. She tightened her jaw and squeezed her eyes shut. Even then, tears trickled down her cheeks. She rolled onto her pillow and buried her face in it as she sobbed.

Time passed, she wasn't sure how long and then shadows danced across her bed. Lainie watched them and wondered how long she'd slept. Her eyes felt crusted from her tears. And her soul emptied of hope. She turned toward the table and grimaced when she saw the envelope still sitting there. She'd wished it had been part of a dream. Why would Roxie write now?

She reached for the letter, then pulled back. Was she ready to read all about the adventures the girls found in Italy?

Squaring her shoulders, she grabbed the envelope and ripped the flap open. She unfolded the letter and brushed the folds smooth. Roxie's tiny script flowed across the page in even, narrow lines.

DEAR LAINIE,

We've arrived. You didn't miss much with the boat. Many of the gals spent days in their bunks as we bumped across every storm imaginable. I can't tell you how relieved I am to have solid land under my feet again.

We've only been in French Moracco a couple of days, but I had to write. This is nothing like I thought it would be. I know you wanted to travel with us, but I think the doctors were right. This terrain is too harsh for someone recovering from an illness like yours.

Now, don't hate me for saying that. I know how angry you are. As I've prayed these weeks, I've prayed Isaiah 43 for you. "Do not fear, for I have redeemed you; I have called you by name; you are Mine! When you pass through the waters, I will be with you; And through the rivers, they will not overflow you. When you walk through the fire, you will not be scorched, Nor will the flame burn you. For I am the LORD your God, The Holy One of Israel, your Savior ... Everyone who is called by My name, And whom I have created for My glory, Whom I have formed, even whom I have made."

LAINIE LOOKED up from the letter and swiped at her face. If only God felt that way about her. It was hard not to feel abandoned or overlooked. If God truly cared about her, why the pain of the last few months? Why the death of her dreams? Her heart ached at all she'd lost, and she rubbed over it, hoping to ease the pain.

DON'T YOU SEE, *Lainie? He created you and calls you His. He'll always be with you—no matter where you go or are sent. You are created for His glory. Don't you think you make Him smile just because? I love that thought. Especially on days it feels like there is so much more I should be doing.*

Write soon, okay? Fill me in on all you're doing. I can't wait to hear. Knowing you, it will be something wonderful. You have a way of transforming what would paralyze others.

The girls say hi. Miss you, roomie.
Roxie

LAINIE REREAD THE LETTER, trying to soak in the spirit behind Roxie's words. She could picture Roxie penning them, tongue tucked between her lips as she concentrated on getting them just right.

She reached for her Bible where it lay on the floor. There had to be more to Isaiah 43. Lainie felt a glimmer of hope. Maybe God did smile just because He'd made her and that was enough.

CHAPTER 19

JULY 5, 1943

octor Gibson pulled the stethoscope from around his neck and carefully shifted items around before placing it in his bag. Medical supplies bulged from the opening. When he finished, he tilted his head and stared at Lainie.

"Young lady, I'd say you're very fortunate. It appears your heart is unscathed, though we won't know for sure until you start your normal activities again."

Lainie slumped forward at the news. She'd braced herself for a far different prognosis. For the first time since the storm, she inhaled a breath and her lungs filled. His encouragement echoed freedom to her.

"Now you can return to work next Monday, but I want you to stop the moment you feel a flicker of weakness."

"Yes, sir."

"Do I need to send Mrs. Babcock with you to ensure you obey my orders?"

"No. I promise I'll follow your instructions." Lainie clutched the neck of her nightgown, eager for him to leave.

"No more riding in rain storms. In fact, you should avoid anything strenuous for a bit. At least two weeks. We'll ease you back into the world with church and your job."

Her pulse raced at the thought of returning to church. With the last week in bed and the parlor, she'd pondered Roxie's life-giving letter. She couldn't wait to join her voice with others Sunday as she thanked God for sparing her. She still didn't understand the whys, but she knew Who. And for now, she'd rest in His goodness. Even if He never showed her why she'd suffered, He deserved her love and worship.

Doctor Gibson grabbed his bag and stood. "Call me if you need anything else. Glad you're back on your feet."

"Thank you, Doctor." Lainie watched him go and wanted to twirl with her arms up in the air. Instead, she dressed and stumbled downstairs to the kitchen. Esther looked up from a pie she crimped.

Lainie leaned against the counter. "Which kind are you making today?"

"Strawberry rhubarb. I love the pucker of flavor the rhubarb adds."

Lainie grimaced at the memory of the last strawberry rhubarb pie she'd carried. Mason's image flashed in her mind. "Doc Gibson says I've recovered. Maybe I can find out what's happened to Mason. See if anything's changed."

Esther eyed her. "That's not exactly what he said."

"Maybe, but if I can leave, why not go there? Much as I like my room and appreciate your patience with me, I'm ready to see something else." Anything else, really.

"Then you can eat down here tonight." Esther's jaw set in a determined line, and Lainie sighed. This Esther she couldn't cross or persuade. She might as well accept that she was stuck here until next Monday.

Lainie smiled at the invitation. Maybe a special soldier would stop by. She'd heard Tom Hamilton came to check on her periodically. He'd been the only soldier to do so, and the action made her value him even more. He was unlike the other men she'd grown up with or met here. He cared and wasn't afraid to show it, yet somehow it didn't diminish him at all. Indeed, he seemed stronger because of it.

She wondered at her reaction. How could she care so much about a man she'd known less than two months? No man had ever caught her attention like Tom, yet many had tried. Somehow none had interested her enough to get a second or third look. No, she enjoyed dancing with and entertaining soldiers the best. Until she'd arrived at Fort Robinson, she'd never had to consider more than a fleeting moment with a man. Even here, most only stayed the eight to twelve weeks training with the dogs required. Then there was Tom and the rest of the cadre that stayed.

"You need something else right now, Lainie?"

She jerked, startled from her thoughts, and looked at Esther. The twinkle in Esther's eyes could power the lights in town tonight. Heat climbed Lainie's cheeks, and she shook her head. "No, I think I'll sit on the porch for a while. See you at supper."

"See you then." Esther's chuckle followed Lainie as the woman went back inside.

* * *

THIS WAS IT. Tom wiped a stream of sweat from under his helmet and then adjusted his pack. Even after six weeks, it rested heavy against his back and pulled at his shoulders. They were knotted tight as cords of wood.

Boots pounded the hardened trail. Scorching heat from the sun pounded against his helmet, and another trickle of sweat slipped down his face. He squinted up the trail to gauge the remaining distance to the Wood Reserve. Tom tried to focus on the trail and God's creation that dotted the path. Pockets of late-blooming sandwort stacked claims among the rocks. He stepped around a stand of plains pricklypear that had edged onto the trail. The bright-yellow flowers couldn't hide the long barbs of that cactus, one he'd learned the hard way to avoid.

The men entered a clearing and pulled to a halt.

"Ten-hut!" Sarge Maxwell strutted to the front of the group. "You're some of the sorriest excuses for soldiers I've seen, but I guess you'll do. You've completed basic training and are now free from the hikes and packs until sent elsewhere. But you're not quite free of me."

A murmur moved through the ranks, an echo of the relief Tom experienced. He'd earned his marksmanship badge and looked forward to getting back to the routine and avoiding senseless drills. Tomorrow, he'd wear his cowboy boots rather than the standard-issue ones he had the blisters to prove he'd worn the last six weeks.

"First, form up. Time to show us some drills."

The men marched in tight formation around the field until Maxwell grunted his approval. He stuck an unlit cigar between his teeth and grimaced. "Form up for inspection."

Tom swiped a drink from his canteen and then fell in between Sid and John. Maxwell dragged out the inspection until Tom's muscles tensed with fatigue. Maxwell seemed to delight in finding something, anything, to nag each man about. Tom wouldn't miss him one moment after the man finally left Robinson, taking his anger with him.

Eventually, Maxwell dismissed them, and Sergeant Lewis replaced him at the front. Sarge considered the ranks in front of him carefully.

"At ease." He paced in front of them. "I have to say I'm pleased with the way you have performed during basic. Despite Sergeant Maxwell's bluster, he's given me favorable reports of many of your efforts and improvements. Congratulations. Tomorrow, we'll return to our routine. Today, however, break into your platoons for field events." He grinned at them. "Don't forget, the winning platoon will be wined and dined by the rest tonight."

Tom groaned; he'd hoped to slip by Mrs. Babcock's and check on Lainie. He thrust his pack into the growing pile by one of the trucks and entered into the events. The balance of the day flew past in a series of races and contests. At the end of the competition, his platoon fell a bit short.

"The officers judging the long jump really need new glasses." Sid grumbled as he marched toward the roaring bonfire.

"And what about the dash? Come on, all you have to do is operate a stop-watch." John rolled his eyes. "Guess we'll have to remember I was the fastest man on the field today."

Tom walloped both men on the shoulder. "It's over now. Let's enjoy our freedom."

In no time, they joined the men gathered around the fire. Soon a soldier launched into a song, and others joined. Stress leached from Tom as he watched the hundred or so men around him kick back and celebrate. Now each was ready to serve wherever the Army determined they'd make the most difference in this war. He knew he would trust his life to any of them. They were trained and primed, even though many would serve out the war at Robinson.

The wood smoke filled his nose, and Tom's thoughts wandered to the many nights he and his father had sat around a fire, staring at stars too numerous to count. Dad had often been busy with his practice, but at least twice a year, they'd retreat to the mountains to hike. Each day had ended like this one.

"Hey." A voice cut across the singing. "We're under attack. Grab your weapons!"

Tom rolled out of the way as the men around him erupted to their feet. He looked through the lowering light. Where was the truck with his pack? He sprang up and dashed across the space.

He unfastened his rifle and tried to remember if it was loaded. There hadn't been any shooting drills today, so no need to load. He grabbed a box of shells from the pack and cast the pack aside. He loaded the gun as he ran to find the rest of his platoon. They formed a perimeter around one flank of the fire.

Tom searched the darkness for any sign of whoever assaulted their position. The sound of scuffling filled the air from pockets outside the light of the fire. Gunfire erupted, and Tom dove for the dirt and landed next to Sid.

"What?"

"I don't know." Sid's pupils were dilated, and his face held a crazed look. "Keep looking. We can't be the weak point."

Tom turned back to the perimeter. The explosion of an artillery shell shook the ground, and he started digging a foxhole with his bare hands. He scanned the horizon as he dug, throwing the dirt in front of him.

He stopped and the shadows rushed across the edge of the trees, but he couldn't find a clear line of sight. As the sun sank behind the buttes, the actions of the platoons became more organized as a messenger ran between them with instructions. Tom's blood pounded an intense beat in his ears, and his finger trembled on the trigger.

"I see someone." John Tyler bellowed in Tom's ear.

"I've got him." Tom followed the shadow's progress down the barrel of his rifle and then more shadows appeared. The gun was loaded with live ammunition, and he didn't want to injure a friend. This had to be part of a drill. Taking a deep breath, Tom considered his options, then aimed over the encroachers' heads. He eased back on the trigger and grinned when they startled and dove for the ground.

A shrill whistle pierced the air, loud enough to drown out intermittent blasts.

"All right, men." Corporal Hill's voice blasted through a megaphone. Tom's shoulders relaxed. The drill was over. "Congratulations on defending your posts and completing basic training. Enjoy the rest of your evening, but don't forget reveille sounds at 0530."

Groans mixed with whoops sounded as the men regathered around the fire.

Tom stowed his rifle back with his pack and then leaned against it as he watched the fun. Now maybe life could return to normal. Now he could show Lainie how much she meant to him. A smile grew on his face. He knew just how to do it, too.

CHAPTER 20

JULY 7, 1943

It looked like he had everything. Now Tom needed the day to end so he could launch his plan. He settled the picnic basket under the instructor's desk in the lecture hall. The space was empty as most men were in the middle of field drills with their dogs. Tom would rather be with them, enjoying the fresh air. Instead, he was shackled to the desk until he caught up on paperwork that he'd ignored during basic.

Mary, in the war dog office, had confirmed that today Lainie would be at work. He couldn't wait to see her. The last weeks had been too long, between basic and Mrs. Babcock's overprotectiveness. Maybe Lainie needed rest, but isolation?

Tom focused on the paperwork in front of him. He had dozens of evaluation forms to complete before he could leave. Then there were the stacks of examinations to grade. Those would be his excuse to drop by and see Lainie later. Not that he needed an excuse if she felt the same about him. If absence really made the heart grow fonder and all that.

He pulled his attention back to the record. Pepper and his trainer, Will Green, had turned into a good team. Over the last two weeks of war dog basic training, they had bonded into a unit. Pepper looked to Green for approval and obeyed without question. Green picked up the key skills in caring for and training his dog to obey and respect him. Tom filled in the Dog Training Record with *H*s to reflect Pepper's high degree of intelligence, willingness, energy, aggressiveness, and sensitivity. Flipping to Green's personnel record, he pulled out the practical tests and made sure all were completed and added a couple of remarks. Green, with his patience and quickness, would make a good instructor if needed.

He worked through several forms before looking up and stretching his arms over his head. Paperwork had to be the worst part about the Army. He rolled his neck and then turned back to the shrinking stack.

John burst into the room. "Why are you sitting there? Come on. You have to see this."

"See what?" Tom continued to fill in a form, this one on Rocky. Where did people get the names for their dogs? What did a dog have in common with a rock?

"The airfield. It's amazing to watch the engineers build it."

"Can't, or Sergeant Lewis will have my hide. See this stack? I've hardly dented it."

"It'll be there tomorrow. At the rate the strip is going in, it might be done by then." John's arms waved as he described the huge machines leveling the land and pouring out concrete. "You have to come."

Tom evaluated the stack. It had shrunk. And a few minutes wouldn't matter overall. Then he thought of Lainie and the picnic basket tucked under the desk. No, he had to finish. "You'll have to fill me in. Though, how are you finding the time to watch? You must be buried, too."

"Nope. That's the beauty of working in processing. The vets have to handle the paperwork. All I have to do is help with each animal."

"Get out of here." Tom shooed him away and shook his head. Some guys had all the luck. A job without paperwork. A beautiful bride. Maybe someday ... but not if he didn't get this done.

* * *

LAINIE WATCHED the clock on the far wall of the office all afternoon, praying the hands would spin faster. Instead, each minute seemed bogged down in the throbbing ache that settled over her. This morning she'd been so eager to escape the prison bars Mrs. Babcock's had developed. All she could think about was slipping between the sheets of her bed.

"Here, Lainie." Mary placed a steaming mug of coffee on her desk. "It's got sugar and milk the way you like."

A small smile pushed her cheeks up. "Thanks."

"Maybe it will help."

Lainie could only nod as tears clouded her sight.

"Hey, it's okay. You're here, and I, for one, missed you." Mary squeezed her shoulders and moved back to her desk.

Lainie scanned the room. Not all the girls felt the same as Mary. Kate had ignored her completely, while Rae Beth and Kitty seemed indifferent at best to see her back. Almost as if they thought the fever would spread to them. They should know the Army wouldn't let her back until both her doctor and the base hospital had cleared her. That had been a stop she didn't really need, but she'd been willing in order to check the box and get back to work.

Why waste her breath explaining? Either they understood or they didn't. Little she could say would change their minds. Part of her wished she could.

She flexed her fingers and wrists, trying to ease the stiffness and soreness. During the first hours she'd filed paper and had the cuts to prove it. Then, after lunch, the typewriter had demanded her skill. She picked up the warm mug of coffee and curled her fingers around it. Maybe the warmth would ease the tightness. She inhaled and then sipped at the brew. Mary had added enough sugar and milk to make it drinkable.

The steady beat of the clock ticking reminded her that the stack of correspondence wouldn't shrink on its own. Reluctantly she returned the mug to the desk and moved the first letter closer to the typewriter. She groaned as she read that another dog had died from distemper. She had to get Mason away.

Swiveling in the chair, Lainie began to type the standard letter.

It is with much regret that we inform you of the death of your dog, Bully, whom you so generously donated through Dogs for Defense for use by the armed forces. A war dog certificate is forwarded herewith. A mere certificate of death is, indeed, poor compensation for your patriotic sacrifice, and the Army is not unaware of it. We, too, are sorry to lose so prominent an animal and assure you that your generosity is sincerely appreciated.

TEARS TRAILED DOWN HER CHEEKS, but she typed anyway, determined to finish the letter and the next after it. She must prove she could handle the work.

Finally, the day ended. Lainie didn't think she could handle many more letters to owners about the demise of their dogs. Next time, she'd have to ask Mary to help her with them. With each move, she saw Mason's name even as she typed a different one. Maybe tomorrow she'd try to check on her, confirm she was okay. By now Mason must be past basic training and probably intermediate, too. What specialized training had the Army assigned her to? None of the options seemed good.

Lainie could imagine Mason's terror as she heard guns and artillery. Each day the instructors would bring the sound nearer and nearer, making the caliber of the gun larger, until all the dogs were inured to the sound.

The girls collected their hats and bags. Lainie stood to join them in the walk to the shuttle. She squared her shoulders and lifted her chin. No need to carry her fears with her. Rae Beth and Kate left ahead of her, so she locked up the building. She strolled out the door and stopped. The most beautiful sight leaned against the side of his car. The smile started deep inside her until it spread to her lips. "Hey."

"Hi, beautiful. Your chariot awaits." Tom gestured toward his car and then stepped toward her and offered a hand.

Rae Beth and Kate tittered as they looked back over their shoulders at Tom. For once, Lainie didn't care what they thought.

"I've missed you, Tom."

"Me too. Come with me?" The question in his eyes compelled her even as she nodded, her words swept away by his nearness. He opened the passenger door, then settled her in the car as if she were priceless china.

The aroma of ham and spicy mustard mixed in the air. Tom slid behind the wheel.

"It smells good."

"I thought we'd enjoy a picnic if you're up to it. Find a spot to watch the sunset and count the stars." He stared at her with such intensity that Lainie had to look away. "Lainie, I was so worried, and Mrs. Babcock wouldn't let me see you. Should you be back? Are you recovered?"

She touched her fingers to his lips and stilled his words. He held his breath. "Doctor Gibson and the base physician both say I'm fine. I'll need to be careful and have been warned to expect dire consequences if I let this happen again. But God sheltered me, and I don't know why though I'm glad."

Tom kissed her fingers. "I'm so relieved. The little that Mrs. Babcock told me painted horrible pictures in my mind." He turned, breaking the power building between them, and exhaled. "Let's find a place to catch up and eat."

Easy conversation filled the car, as Tom took them down dirt road after dirt road. Lainie didn't even try to figure out where they were headed. Instead, she enjoyed the mystery and the company.

As she watched Tom, she doubted anyone else could compel her focus. He was more than she deserved. Steady, unflappable, committed, with a heart that chased God's. She whispered a prayer of thanks. Only God could orchestrate a friendship like theirs. And maybe, just maybe, there was more. She'd only known him two months, but it was enough time to learn his character.

Tom pulled the car to the side of the road. "Here we are."

"I won't even ask where that is."

A wry grin creased his face. "If you're lucky, I'll find our way home."

"Hmm. I see your plan, bring the sick woman to the middle of nowhere. Feed her and then lose her. Sounds like a delightful evening." Lainie stuck her tongue out at him.

Later, Lainie lay on a blanket and watched vibrant colors paint the sky as the sun slipped below the horizon. The night had been perfect when she ignored the ache in her muscles. The evening had been worth it. She shivered as a night breeze blew, and Tom tucked a blanket around her.

"We should get you home."

She sat up and nodded. Much as she'd like to stay, he was right. He tipped her chin up. Heat traveled up her cheeks, and she froze. He leaned toward her and then waited, as if asking permission. She slid her arms around his neck, and his lips found hers.

In that moment, all she could long for was a future with Tom filled with nights like this.

He pulled back and searched her face. "I think I love you, Lainie Gardner."

CHAPTER 21

JULY 8, 1943

*L*ainie floated into the war dog office, a basket of Esther's muffins tucked under her arm. "Get them while they're hot, girls."

She watched the girls enjoy the muffins and knew the day would be wonderful. Her lips still tingled from Tom's kiss, and she didn't think she'd ever forget the feeling of being gathered so safely under his arm or hearing his words. While not a firm confession of love, they matched her feelings. This might be love. But they needed time to explore it.

The morning flew by as she prepared honorable discharge papers for dogs who had failed some aspect of basic training. Not every dog sent to the fort met the Army's requirements. Some were too short, others too aggressive, and still others too distracted by chasing anything that moved. Why couldn't wonderful Mason be any of those things? Of course she would take to the instruction like a prairie dog to the hills. It was decidedly unfair.

Lainie shook her head and forced her thoughts back to Tom. Time to think about better things. "You look far away." Mary leaned over the typewriter to see the stack of papers. "I know it's not the paperwork. Not with that smile."

"You're right. It's good to be back."

Mary chuckled. "Sure it is, honey. Don't worry. I have a feeling your soldier will be by soon. That man lights up around you."

"Let's just say last night was wonderful, and I hope he does come by soon. I already miss him."

"I think that qualifies for over the moon."

Kitty snorted. "Sappy's what I'd call it."

Lainie made a face and stuck out her tongue at the girl. Then she turned back to her typing and tuned out the girls' conversations. Not hard to do when her thoughts kept returning to a rock under the clear night sky.

* * *

TOM WATCHED another group of men parade their dogs through close-order drills. The men and dogs heeled like well-oiled machines. The dogs kept an eye cocked on their masters and followed the silent hand signals without a hitch. Time for the next challenge.

"All right, men. Close ranks for a minute."

The groups shuffled into position, forming straight rows. One dog growled in the back of its throat, and Tom searched the lines until he saw the animal. Brutus had an attitude problem that kept him in the program—barely. And only because Sergeant Prescott had firm control of the animal.

Prescott looked at him and nodded. "I've got him, sir."

Tom watched the dog another moment. Brutus's ears remained swiveled to the side, but his hackles had begun to settle. Satisfied, Tom did a quick inspection of the teams. Mason sat two dogs down from Brutus. Despite Lainie's concerns, Mason thrived in the Army. She'd picked up each new command quickly and showed an intelligence that would make her an asset wherever she served. She'd been paired with an Army Air Forces serviceman, so her destination was unsure.

"Since you've mastered the on-leash drills, we'll move to off-leash exercises. When I command, spread out and then release your dogs. Make them remain at your side. Then we'll run through some familiar commands to see how they do without the leash encouraging obedience. If all goes well, we'll reward them with a round of the obstacle course."

A cheer rose from the Marines. Leave it to Marines to love the idea of crawling through mud, leaping over obstacles, and running until you can't see through the sweat. From the odor blowing his way, it smelled like many of them had already run several miles.

"Separate." Tom waited until the men had spread out with enough space to keep each dog focused on its master. "Unleash your dogs and review *sit, stay,* and *down* with them."

He walked among the rows, checking for any signs that a dog had readied to bolt. The last thing they needed this week was another dog or two going AWOL. The last one had finally been roped down by a former rodeo star who now served with the Veterinary Corps. And that was only after several men on horseback had chased the dog all over the parade grounds and other side of the highway.

A deep, grumbly growl pulled Tom's attention back to Brutus. Brutus looked ready to attack. His ears were pinned against his head, his teeth bared, and he'd crouched. "Prescott, grab him." Tom barked the order and prayed.

Another growl rumbled, this one louder. The dog looked coiled to spring.

"Prescott!" Tom rubbed his scar. Nothing would happen to Prescott on his watch.

The man stood as if paralyzed, staring at his dog. Tom caught movement to Prescott's right and watched it out of the corner of his eye as he marched toward Prescott. Teams around the two put distance between them, all except for Mason and her owner. Tom grimaced. Airman Rush and Prescott had developed a friendship, and it looked like Rush wanted to intervene.

"Back away, Rush."

The man ignored him, easing toward Prescott. "Come on, buddy. Snap out of it. You've got to move. Now."

Prescott shuddered. Brutus followed his movements, then looked at Rush and Mason. Mason, still off-leash, followed Rush. The dog was too well-trained and obedient for her own safety. Brutus launched at Mason and wrestled her to the ground, teeth sunk into her neck.

"No! Rush, go get a tech. Now." Tom screamed the word and raced toward the two. How could he disable Brutus long enough to pull him away without shooting? Mason fought back, but her size was no match for Brutus. Tom froze, watching them war, flashes of a former dog fight blazing across his mind. He rubbed his scar again, then forced himself forward. Mason didn't deserve this mauling. He pulled his sidearm out of its holster and aimed.

A soft whistle whizzed past his ear and then a tranquilizer dart sank into Brutus's flank. His actions slowed, then he collapsed on top of Mason. Tom tore his eyes from the mess of dogs to the vet tech who raced up.

"Took you long enough to get here."

"I'm here now. Let's get these two separated and to the hospital stat. We may be able to save the black one."

Two more vet techs raced up in a Jeep. It took them several minutes to pry Brutus off of Mason and get her loaded. Rush and Prescott boarded the Jeep with their dogs and disappeared down the hill toward the vet hospital.

Tom rubbed his hand over his face. What was he going to tell Lainie? This was exactly what she'd feared since the moment Mason arrived. He didn't think he could tell her but knew he couldn't let her find out from somebody else.

He turned back to the remaining teams. The men waited, their dogs lounging at their sides. "Run through the obstacle course a couple of times. Nobody's hiding along the course, so focus on clearing the barriers." He followed the Jeep. The men would have to follow instructions without a babysitter.

When he reached the hospital a few minutes later, the techs had already whisked Mason away. All he could learn was she still lived. For right now that would have to be enough.

He stepped outside and took several deep breaths, trying to clear the heavy antiseptic smell from his lungs. He looked across the road. Less than a hundred feet separated him from Lainie. He had to tell her. Now. Even though he wanted to deliver any message but this one.

* * *

"Hey, Lainie. Look who's here." Kitty's voice pulled Lainie's attention from the file in front of her.

Lainie's heart skipped to a faster tempo. A smile curved her lips. "Hi, Tom."

He pulled his hat off and twisted it in his hands. He shuffled from side to side, and a bad feeling spread through Lainie.

"What is it?"

He just looked at her, emotions warring across his face. First a flash of concern. Then a tightening around his eyes and jaw. Followed by a visible effort to relax.

"Spit it out." She looked at her hands, surprised to see them trembling.

"Could you come outside for a moment?" He swallowed, then looked into her, through her. "Please, Lainie."

She glanced around the room, and Mary nodded, so she slipped from behind the desk and walked through the door Tom held for her. She wrapped her arms around herself and turned on him. "What happened? You're scaring me to death. Did you change your mind about last night?"

Relief lit up his face. "No, nothing like that. Last night was wonderful. It's about Mason." He spoke the last sentence so softly Lainie leaned toward him to catch the words.

"Did you say *Mason?*"

Tom nodded. Before he could say anything else, Lainie dashed in front of a truck and across the street. The driver honked his horn, but she kept running. She stumbled up the few steps to the door and pulled it open. "Please, God."

Tears tumbled down her cheeks as she whispered the words. Nothing could have happened to Mason. Not the sweet, obedient dog. She'd never done anything really wrong in her life other than chewing one of Mama's tables in a fit of boredom. But that was years ago now.

"I knew this would happen."

A man sat behind a desk in front of her. She skirted around it, but he stood to block her way. "Miss, you can't go back there."

Lainie pounded against his chest. "My dog is in there. I have to see her."

"You can't go back there." His gaze softened. "Take the chair over there, and I'll let you know when we know something. Which dog is yours?"

Which? More than one was hurt?

Her heart lurched.

Her handed fluttered to grasp her collar.

Her eyes smarted, and she covered her mouth.

She had to get Mason out of here.

CHAPTER 22

JULY 9, 1943

*L*ainie sat on her bed, staring at her reflection in the mirror on her wardrobe. Her face had a new brittle quality to it. It seemed to have settled there when she learned about Mason. She'd waited what seemed like hours for any word. At some point Tom had joined her, but she couldn't bring herself to acknowledge him. If he'd helped like she'd asked, Mason would be back in North Platte where she belonged rather than in some strange hospital.

Her mind replayed image after image of times spent with Mason. Each made her think of home and safety. Then the scent of bleach and other cleaners that had assaulted her when she entered the hospital overwhelmed her. She didn't know if she'd ever get rid of that awful smell.

This morning Tom had come by again to tell her the vets thought Mason would recover.

"Let me take you over there to see her." Tom had cajoled her, but she couldn't.

Her stomach turned at the thought Mason would recover, and she'd almost lost her breakfast. How could she explain to Tom that the last thing she wanted was Mason permanently injured. But if she was, then at least she'd be discharged. Instead, she'd recover and remain in the Army.

"I can't go over there now. Maybe over lunch." Fresh tears had washed her cheeks, and Lainie did nothing to wipe them away.

Tom had tried to pull her into his embrace, but Lainie pushed him away. Her emotions rocked all over. With one breath she had loved his sweetness. With the next she wanted to hold him accountable for what had happened. Even though someone had told her he'd been ready to jump into the fray.

"Please, leave me alone. I … I need some time to think." Time to prepare another plan to free Mason. There had to be a way before she was killed.

Confusion had clouded Tom's expression, but he backed toward the door, then he was gone.

Lainie had sunk to her chair and ignored the other girls' stares.

Mary had knelt in front of her. "Are you okay, Lainie?"

"No." She erupted into sobs. Mary hugged her as Lainie cried. What had she done? Would Tom abandon her now? She wouldn't blame him. Slowly she collected her thoughts. She straightened and sniffed while she dabbed her eyes with a handkerchief. "Thanks, but we both have work to do."

"Take a few minutes to see Mason. It'll do you good."

Lainie had, and now, as she looked in the mirror, she wished she hadn't. Mason had been sedated, the hair shaved from around her neck, and a large bandage swathed around one part of it. She'd whimpered in her sleep, her front legs jerking as if chasing a bunny or squirrel.

"Oh, Mason."

Lainie squared her shoulders and reached for the red dress that Audrey loved so much. A slight smile flitted across her face at the memory of Audrey trying it on and deciding it was too much for her red hair. Lainie had no such problems. A yoked waist and pleated skirt set off the cap sleeves and gathered bodice. It would be perfect when paired with her black pumps for the K-9 dance.

She didn't feel like a night out, but knew she couldn't stay home and mope. She reached for her new bottle of stocking lotion and brushed it along her legs. She eyed the color, pleased it looked so much like hose. When it dried, she slipped on her dress. She patted some powder on her face and reached for her lipstick.

Dorothy stuck her head around the door. "Ready, Lainie? The guys are here."

For a moment, Lainie wished Tom was the one taking her, but she'd turned him down. How much fun would she be tonight anyway, between an aching heart and body? She had to get her emotions under control before she could spend more time with Tom. She couldn't see him without seeing Mason, and that wasn't fair to him.

She swiped the lipstick on and hurried after Dorothy.

The tennis courts had been transformed. Someone had strung soft Christmas lights along the fence, providing a beacon. Chinese lanterns, streamers, and balloons festooned every surface. Tables were set up immediately outside the courts and loaded with finger sandwiches and desserts. The sun hung in the sky as if kissing the event with its warmth and light.

Dorothy and Tanya disappeared into the mass with their dates. Lainie smiled at the evolution in Tanya. She'd cut her hair and bought some new clothes. Even though they were from Sears, they'd wrought a change in her outlook, and that had enlivened her social schedule.

Lainie walked toward the food but was stopped by a soldier.

"Dance with me, miss?" The clean-cut young man had a youthful energy that radiated from him.

"I'd be delighted."

Song after song soldiers stepped up to twirl her around the floor. Occasionally, she accepted their offers. More often, she invited them to sit with her. From each she coaxed stories and loved to watch smiles light up their faces as they talked about home and sometimes the girl waiting for them. The music finally ended when the band took a break.

"Ladies and gentleman, if you'll clear the center of the floor, we will have a demonstration by Private Newman and his dog, Lucky."

Lainie watched with wonder as the dog ran through his tricks. The dog seemed to count as he tapped his foot on the court to answer questions from his master. Then they marched through a series of commands together. It was amazing.

All too soon the show ended. The sun had left a veil of darkness in its place. The sound of crickets filled the air now that the musicians and partygoers were silent. She searched the dwindling crowd for Dorothy and Tanya but couldn't find them. Lainie started walking the perimeter of the courts, looking for her ride. Tom leaned against his car as if waiting for her. She froze, then took a step toward him.

He looked good in his dress uniform with sharp pleats and buffed shoes, like he'd dressed up for the dance, yet she hadn't seen him there.

He pushed off the car and strolled toward her. "Can I give you a lift?"

Lainie swallowed against the fist of anger that had lodged in her throat. Was it only two nights earlier that she'd listened to him murmur that he loved her and prayed that it was true? That her heart had begun to race at such a pace that she'd wondered if it would calm? His blue eyes had a deepened to almost black, intensity pulsing.

A glance revealed her ride still hadn't appeared. With that, she had no option but to accept. "All right, Tom. Thank you."

He took her hand and settled her in the car. Awkward silence filled the air as Tom drove. He cleared his throat. "I've talked to Sarge about Mason. He says if she's going to recover, she has to stay in the Army."

"I know."

"I'm working on it, Lainie. Don't give up."

"I wish somebody acted before she's almost mauled to death."

The car slowed as Tom drove off the highway and into town. "I'm sorry, but I tried everything I could to stop the attack. Why aren't you mad at the folks who sent her here?"

She fought that question. How could her dad be so callous? She longed to throw herself in Tom's arms and listen to him tell her everything would be okay. Another part longed to lash out at him rather than her dad, even though Tom didn't deserve it. Instead, she counted houses until they reached Mrs. Babcock's. She opened the door before Tom could turn off the engine. "Thanks for the ride."

All night the picture of Tom's open-mouth surprise at her behavior plagued her. Why lash out at him? If adversity shows what one is made of, she didn't like what her sickness and the scare with Mason revealed about her. She swiped away another tear as she sat on the edge of her bed and stared out the window. She tried to number the stars, but her tears blurred her vision.

God, I need help. Please show me that You care about me, because right now I feel pretty over-looked.

* * *

SUNDAY MORNING LAINIE strolled with Esther and the other girls through Crawford's streets until they reached First Christian Church. She waited for the others to slide into a pew two-thirds of the way back in the sanctuary before slipping in. She smoothed her skirt and adjusted her beret. Hollowness seemed to choke her as she looked around the small room. She felt like a child who'd lost her daddy at a large fair. She could spin in a circle looking for him but not see him in the crush of people.

Pastor Stevenson stepped to the podium and gazed across the group. "A couple of weeks ago I talked about the passage in Isaiah 43 where God promises He has redeemed us and will walk through trials of all sorts with us. I think this is a hard concept to grasp, yet foundational to faith. Does God mean what He says? Is His Word the same in Isaiah's day and today? And why would God care enough to reassure us of His presence and redemption? Because without Him we are nothing. We are desperate creatures in need of God to save us."

Where had God gone when He chose not to save her? Since her illness in Kentucky, it felt like she searched for Him in a heavy fog, and He chose not to be found. She'd thought He cared about her. Now she wasn't sure. She mouthed the words to the hymns and went through the motions of the service, her heart desperate for an answer.

"This is a hard concept to grasp, yet foundational to faith. Does God mean what He says? Is His Word the same in Isaiah's day and today? And why would God care enough to reassure us of His presence and redemption? Because without Him we are nothing. We are desperate creatures in need of God to save us.

"If you feel abandoned by God, I assure you He is there. You may not see Him or sense Him, but it doesn't change the fact that He is still there."

Lainie felt a flicker of hope at Pastor Stevenson's declaration.

"Look for Him. Ask Him to open your eyes to His movement on your behalf. I am convinced that if you do, your perspective will be revolutionized."

Peace teased Lainie as she listened, seeming beyond her grasp. God was with her. She knew that in her head. He had to be since He promised. But her heart didn't believe it. So much had happened this year, good and bad. Would He reveal Himself? She'd been so sure after getting Roxie's letter. How could she reclaim that peace and hope?

CHAPTER 23

JULY 13, 1943

$\mathcal{T}$om rushed out the door of the training center and raced toward the K-9 office. He banged through the door without stopping to knock.

"Lainie, grab your purse and meet me at the vet hospital in ten minutes."

She stared at him with slack jaw, as did the other girls in the office. He couldn't wait to see if she'd take him seriously. There was too much to do if this was going to work.

Sarge had changed his mind over the weekend, and Tom wasn't going to give him time to reconsider. He raced to his car and checked the gas gauge. Full. Good, they wouldn't have to stop for gas. Next, he ran to the barracks and grabbed his duffel. He tossed in a couple of extra uniforms and other essentials before zipping it shut. He threw the bag over his shoulder and ran to the office to collect his pass. He had three days on a Class A pass. It would be crunched for time but they should make it. Now if Lainie would cooperate.

When he reached the kennel and hospital, Lainie waited at the door. He paused to stare at her after shutting off his car. Her hair was pulled back at the nape of her neck with a simple ribbon. Today she wore a blouse, sweater, skirt, and saddle shoes. A simple outfit that somehow managed to highlight her beauty.

He climbed out of the car and then reached into his back pocket and pulled out a sheet of paper. This was it. "Follow me, mademoiselle."

She looked at him quizzically, but twined her arm through his. "All right."

"I hold in my hot little hand Mason's Get Out of Jail Free card. We're taking her home."

Lainie squealed and threw her arms around his neck. She laughed and cried at the same time. After a minute, she pulled back from him. "Are you sure, Tom?"

"Absolutely, but I only have three days to help you get her home. So let's hurry."

The next hour passed in a blur of completing Mason's paperwork, taking Lainie to Mrs. Babcock's, and waiting for her to pack. Finally, they were all settled in his Chevy, Mason stretched out in the back and Lainie sitting next to Tom.

"Yesterday, I asked God to show me that He saw me. And now this. After everything I tried to do, all the people I talked to. Just like that, Mason is coming home." She tucked her head against his shoulder. "Thank you, Tom."

A warmth filled Tom. It wasn't often God used him and a dog to show His love. But God had changed him, too, in so many good ways. "My fear's gone, Lainie. I'm not necessarily ready to befriend any dog I meet, but I don't feel the need to keep an eye on Mason or defend myself from her."

"That's wonderful." Lainie bit her lip, but kept her eyes on the road. "I wish I could keep Mason here."

"Mrs. Babcock won't let you?"

"No. She's got a strict no-animal policy. Says she can't have them with the restaurant." She seemed to collapse inside herself, the excitement of getting Mason muted by something.

"What is it?"

"I with I knew how my family would react. I couldn't reach them on the phone, so our arrival will be a surprise. Daddy doesn't do well with surprises, especially when he thinks things are already set." A small smile touched her lips. "I guess I'll have to believe that this will work out somehow."

The miles disappeared as he got her talking about her family and then her friends. The afternoon melted away with a quick stop in Alliance, followed by another one for fuel in Ogallala. Just when he thought they would never arrive, they reached North Platte.

"Mama should be home, but Daddy's probably at the bank."

"Don't bankers keep regular hours? It's after five."

"Not Daddy. He has a hard time allowing someone else to take care of things. It's probably why the bank stayed solvent during the Depression, but it made for a lonely house."

Tom followed Lainie's directions to her home. He pulled the car into the circular driveway and stopped. The home had classic lines with a wide porch. The landscaping was lush even in the July heat. He'd known she came from a well-off family, but this was more.

"Let's get inside. I'm eager to introduce you to Mama. Then we can go down to Wahl's for a Coke, maybe see a movie." Lainie reached for Mason's harness and leash and helped her out of the car. Lainie's steps slowed as she approached the front door. She looked back at Tom. "Here we go."

Tom grabbed their bags and followed her. Ready or not, it was time to meet her parents.

Mrs. Gardner welcomed him warmly, through her surprise. Tom liked the vision of what Lainie would look like in twenty-five years. In fact, it looked like little would change other than a light touch of gray in her hair.

"Lainie, why don't you get Mason reintroduced to the backyard before your father gets home? I'll show Tom here to your rooms."

Lainie quirked an eyebrow at him as if asking if he'd be okay. He tried to shoo her on, but the bags hampered him.

"I hope you don't mind the visit, Mrs. Gardner. We had to jump when the Army agreed to release Mason."

"Not at all. You must be tired after that drive. I'm surprised you didn't take the train." She gestured into the room at the top of the stairs. "This will be your room while you're with us."

Tom tossed his bag next to the bed in the darkening room. "Thank you."

She appraised him, then nodded. "Yes. I think we'll enjoy your visit. This way, then."

Lainie's bedroom was past her parents', and then they took a back stairway down to the kitchen. Lainie returned with an unharnessed Mason, peace softening her features even as something kept her eyes tight. There was a hint of promise about her, too. Before he could ask her about it, the front door flew open. Tom caught his breath at the sight.

"Where's my little lady?"

Mrs. Gardner blushed as she rushed down the hall. A big bear of a man waited for her. Tom found it hard to believe he was dainty Lainie's father. Lainie caught his gaze and rolled her eyes.

"Someday they'll grow out of it, but for now they refuse."

"I hope my wife is that excited to see me twenty years after we're married."

"Try twenty-eight. It's almost scandalous." Her face formed into a mask of mock horror. "Let's slip out."

"Oh no you don't. I've waited to meet your father."

Loud steps echoed down the wooden hallway floors. "I see you've brought home a soldier and Mason. I must say I expected more of you, baby doll."

"What did you expect me to do, leave her with the Army after she was injured? I tried to tell you this would happen."

"Still all full of passion, aren't we? She's a dog. Sometimes you forget that. Come here." The man hugged a stiff Lainie, then shook hands with Tom and examined him. "Mr. Gardner, son. Mama, what's for dinner?"

And with that, Tom had a perfect understanding that he was not the man Lainie's father wanted for his daughter. He glanced at Lainie and knew she'd seen it, too. She shrugged and hooked her arm through Tom's.

"I'm taking Tom downtown tonight. We can only stay tomorrow, and then we have to return to Crawford. Mama, we didn't get a chance to warn you we were coming, so we'll slip out. You and Daddy have a great dinner, and we'll catch up with you later." She pulled Tom toward the front door. "Don't wait up."

Tom looked back and caught Mr. Gardner's face contorted in a grimace and Mrs. Gardner holding him back. "They'll be fine, Bob."

"Quit looking at them, and let's get out of here." Lainie's voice was pitched higher than usual. "Come on."

"We should spend time with them."

"We will. Later. We'll wait until Betty's a buffer. I'll show you bustling North Platte tonight."

Tom let her direct him the few blocks to downtown. They parked in front of a small diner and went inside. Over dinner, Lainie relaxed and regaled him with stories of growing up in town. Stories of dances at the city park, floating down either branch of the Platte River in the summer, and skating in the winter. After they ate, they strolled down the street, and she showed him the Canteen. They watched as soldiers rushed to reboard a waiting train.

"Maybe Audrey's here." Lainie pulled him to the brick building and through a door into a large room. Tables groaned under the weight of cakes and sandwiches. A coffee urn stood on a table, surrounded by miniature bottles of milk. Other tables were loaded with books and magazines, even a few Bibles. "Every troop train is met by volunteers. We've earned a reputation among the servicemen. The best twenty minutes they'll have crossing the country."

"It's impressive."

"You should see us get the men through." Lainie edged him toward a back room as she talked.

"Hey, Lainie. You back to help tonight?" A nicely plump older woman waved at them from a kitchen table.

"Not tonight. Is Audrey here?"

"No. Should be back tomorrow, though."

"All right. Thanks, Mrs. Edwards." Lainie scanned the kitchen, then drew away. "I guess she's not here. We'll catch up with her later. She and her husband live on a ranch north of town. She used to be here all the time." Her expression fell, and she stood still a moment as if not sure where to go next. "Guess we might as well look for a movie or something."

"Why don't we grab one of those cherry Cokes you talk so much about? Then we can head back to your house." Tom grabbed her hand and rubbed it. "It can't be as bad as you think it will be."

She searched his eyes for a moment, intensity turning hers brown. "You have no idea what my father is like."

"But I'd like to learn. And I can't do that while we hide here."

Lainie harrumphed, then shrugged. "Let's get that Coke."

When they returned to the home, Mason had curled in front of the fireplace, almost like she'd never left. Lainie's sister sat on the floor next to her, stroking the dog's glossy fur.

"Glad you could bring her home, Lainie. This house has felt like a museum while she was gone."

"It was nice." Mr. Gardner's deep voice echoed in the silence.

"No, I'm glad she's back, too." Mrs. Gardner patted his arm. "You're outnumbered. And I'd suggest you not try something like that again. Mason is part of this family."

He put on a fake pout, though Tom thought he detected a twinkle in the man's eyes. "A person knows when he's beat. Welcome home, Mason."

Mason pricked her ears up—probably at her name—then settled back on the hearth.

* * *

TWO MORNINGS LATER, Tom's stomach clenched tight as he sat with Mr. Gardner. The man had insisted they have lunch together before he and Lainie could leave. Mr. Gardner leaned away from the table and eyed Tom.

"Son, I can tell you care for my daughter."

"Yes, sir. Very much."

"That's all well and good, but she should never marry a soldier."

Tom sagged in his chair as if punched. "What do you mean?"

"Her mother and I did not raise her to become a widow at a young age. She's also used to the best we could offer. There's no way you could do that on military wages." He crossed his arms and jutted his chin out even farther.

"That may be so. But I'm unlikely to go overseas, and the war won't continue forever."

"And what are your prospects after that? Have a job lined up as a lawyer or doctor?"

Tom swallowed. He had no real answer, not one that would satisfy this father. "I think I understand."

"I certainly hope so. Nothing against you, but I only want the best for my daughter."

Tom heard the unspoken words loud and clear. *And that's not you.*

CHAPTER 24

*T*he ride back to Fort Robinson dragged on, and Lainie could hardly enjoy the scenery or the fact that Mason was safe. After talking to her daddy, Tom had crawled into a shell and refused to come out. She could only imagine what Daddy had said. He always knew best. Suddenly, Lainie realized that she didn't want him to chase Tom away. Instead, she wanted Tom welcomed with open arms. Based on the set to Tom's jaw and the distant look in his eye, that hadn't happened.

"Look, Tom, I'm sorry about whatever my daddy said. He doesn't speak for me."

Tom stared down the road. "I won't go against his wishes."

"But what about mine? Don't I count in this? Aren't I worth fighting for?" Her voice rose with each sentence until she almost shouted the last one.

He shook his head. "I can't, Lainie."

She shrank against the seat and turned away from Tom. She was worth fighting for. She was. And if he wouldn't, well, Lainie didn't want to imagine that.

* * *

TOM DROPPED Lainie off and then drove to the fort. He parked his car by the barracks, but rather than go in, he headed for the kennels. When was the last time he sought out dogs? He couldn't remember.

He walked the perimeter inside the fence. Thoughts raced through his mind. Mr. Gardner saying his daughter shouldn't marry a soldier colliding with Lainie insisting she was worth fighting for. Yes, she was, but maybe he wasn't the one to do it.

The week passed in an internal war. Occasionally, he saw Lainie across the yard, but he tried to keep a distance. He sent others to the K-9 office on errands. The sight of her sent him into a maelstrom of torn emotions. Fight or let her go? Which was best for her, regardless of his longings? *God, You have to help me.*

Tom started taking Tornado out for rides most nights. They'd go wherever Tornado wanted to explore. Tom held on and waited for the peace he normally absorbed in the wide-open spaces to find him.

He often took his Bible with him. When Tornado decided he needed a drink, Tom would hop off and pull his Bible out of a saddlebag. He'd munch on an apple and search the Scripture for something, anything that felt like direction. The rest of his life was too important to casually throw away. Marriage was also too vital to enter knowing that his future father-in-law would never accept him.

Thursday night Tom followed his new routine. After saddling Tornado, he pointed the horse toward the prisoner of war camp. They passed through the vacant camp at a canter and soon hit the plains beyond.

After twenty minutes racing the wind, Tornado stopped beside a stream. Tom ground tied him and grabbed his Bible and snack. He settled on a rock and bit into the apple. Wiping juice from his chin, he turned to the book. Today's devotional reading was Isaiah 43. "When thou passest through the waters, I will be with thee; and through the rivers, they shall not overflow thee: when thou walkest through the fire, thou shalt not be burned; neither shall the flame kindle upon thee."

He gazed across the land. Buttes pushed against the sky along the horizon. Last week, on the drive to North Platte, he'd passed Lake McConaughy and the Kingsley Dam for the first time. After seeing that body of water, he had a new perspective on what God promised. He would go with him through waters as vast as that lake. If the dam ever gave, water could spill out and overwhelm the north fork of the Platte. The river would lose its lazy quality as water rushed down and overflowed its banks. Even there God would be with him. If he received orders shipping him overseas and had to walk through the fire of combat, God would lead him.

Surely He would see him through this relationship with Lainie. *Lord, give me wisdom. I want to honor You in all I do. But I need Your help to do that here.*

Tom looked back at the Bible. "Fear not: for I am with thee ..."

That was pretty clear. Time to abandon his fear and walk into the future with God as his Guide. In all things. In all situations.

Tornado clomped up to him and pushed Tom's shoulder. He snorted and bumped Tom.

"All right, boy. Let's head back. I've got what I need now." Tom smiled. He did indeed.

* * *

LAINIE SAT in the rocker on Esther's front porch. August had arrived with a flood of heat and nary a breeze to ease it. She leaned back and let the rocker roll forward, her thoughts wandering.

Tom had disappeared since the trip to North Platte. She'd seen him occasionally, but never close enough to even say hello. She'd spent the time working and praying. She didn't want a relationship that wasn't part of God's will for her. Yet Tom set a standard she didn't think anyone else could match.

It had only been three months since she'd arrived in Crawford, but it felt like home. She'd gotten used to seeing people crammed into tiny apartments in little buildings and garages squeezed behind houses. The town had embraced her, and she couldn't imagine going anywhere else.

But she also couldn't stay if things didn't work out with Tom. It was simply too hard to see him and know that their friendship had changed. And just when she'd hoped it would become so much more.

I think I love you.

Those words continued to echo through her heart, even as her head argued that he should have emphasized the *think* more.

She closed her eyes and tried to form a response about everything God had given her.

The screen door slammed, and Lainie jerked up.

"Lainie, telephone." Tanya grinned at her. "Sounds like a cute one."

Lainie rolled her eyes. No one called her here, so it was likely her boss on the phone. She stood and went into the parlor to take the call.

"Hey, Lainie. This is Tom."

Lainie's heart jumped into her throat at the sound of his voice. She tried to speak but couldn't around the lump.

"Is it ... is it all right if I come over for a bit tonight?" He inhaled and released the air in a whoosh. "I've missed you."

"It's been hard to tell." She bit her tongue. Why had she said that? "I'm sorry. I'll still be up for an hour if you'd like to come. I think Esther has some pie left from supper."

"I'll be there in ten minutes."

Lainie raced up the stairs to freshen up. She brushed powder on her nose and laughed at the sparkle in her eyes. Didn't take much to resurrect her joy.

She'd returned to the rocker when he rolled to a stop. As Tom climbed out of the Chevy, she waited, unsure what to expect from him.

"Hey." Tom hesitated at the bottom of the steps, then squared his shoulders. He hurried up the steps and then sat at her feet. "Lainie, forgive me for being afraid."

"Afraid?"

"Of your father. Of your expectations. Of the future and knowing I can't guarantee what will happen." He grabbed her hands for a moment. "Please, Lainie. I'd like another shot."

"What happens the next time you're challenged?"

He pulled back a bit and searched her face. Heat climbed her cheeks, but she barely breathed as she waited for his reply. He rubbed his thumb over her fingers. Tingles shot up her arm, straight to her heart. If he didn't say something soon, she'd beg him to ignore her remark.

Slowly he nodded as he caressed her hand. "Lainie, I can't promise how I'll react in the future. I can only assure you are the most important person in the world to me. I want to give us a chance to build on that. Then we'll see what the future holds."

She nodded. "I really want to see what the future holds for us. Regardless of what Daddy said, Tom, you are a wonderful man and very special to me."

Lainie hesitated, considering saying she loved him. The rush of emotions she felt every time she thought of him or spent time with him had to be that. But she couldn't say the phrase, not until he could say that he loved her, without the *think* attached to it.

Tom stood and then pulled her to her feet. He caressed her cheek, searching her eyes. She caught her breath and stilled.

Was he going to?

She closed her eyes and tipped her head. For a moment that seemed to last for eternity, she waited. Then she felt his breath get closer and then he kissed her. She eased into the kiss, but he edged back.

"I think we'd better get inside and grab a piece of that pie."

Lainie opened her eyes and smiled. "That would be safer than kissing in front of all Crawford."

Though, as they shared a slice of apple pie, Lainie thought she wouldn't mind the extra attention if it meant he'd hold her again.

CHAPTER 25

*T*he sun lit up a cloudless sky on Wednesday, and Lainie rushed through lunch with her plans to ride urging speed. She had the afternoon off and couldn't wait to meet Private Thorson and Daisy at the barn.

Tom waited beside the private, and Lainie hurried toward him for a kiss on the cheek.

"Let me come with you."

"No, this is something I need to do. But you can come find me if I'm gone more than a couple of hours. The day is beautiful. Nothing's going to happen."

"Then let me join you."

Lainie shook her head. "I'll be fine." She stepped into the stirrup and threw her leg over Daisy's back. "Meet you at the pool in a few hours. I'll be there, Tom."

He stepped away and stuffed his hands in his pockets and hunched his shoulders.

Lainie squeezed Daisy with her knees and then blew Tom a kiss. "See you soon."

Daisy trotted away from the buildings, and Lainie pulled off her hat and let her hair blow freely in the wind. The trot jolted her too much, so she pulled Daisy to a walk. That didn't stop joy from bubbling through her as Daisy carried her over the plains and then picked a path up a butte. When they reached the top, Lainie stopped Daisy and slipped down, the reins clutched in her hand.

She led the horse toward the edge of the butte. Her breath caught as the expanse spread away in front of her. Off to her right was a ridge of hills that looked like God had taken a piece of paper, crumpled it, and then formed the hills to match. Sandwort and miner's candle grew in clumps around her feet, their white flowers brightening the dry landscape.

Lainie walked Daisy along the rim of the butte. Daisy stilled at a clump of creamy yellow flowers she'd never seen before. They looked like tiny fringed orchids with two stripes of red down the middle of each flower, but the flowers stacked like a snapdragon. She crouched to examine them and brushed one with her finger. The delicate fringe tickled. She leaned in, but couldn't catch a fragrance.

She leaned on her heels and smiled when Daisy nuzzled her hair. "Wait a moment, girl. We'll leave soon."

She sat and soaked in the sun. It felt like a kiss from heaven. All was right in the world at the moment. Sitting in the middle of God's vast and detailed creation, nothing felt like an insurmountable problem. No, as she examined the fringed flowers, it was clear He cared deeply about everything He made, even a flower no one but He would see and enjoy.

Closing her eyes, Lainie lifted her face. *I will believe that You walk ahead of me into the storms. Thank You for carrying me through this year.*

She inhaled the peace that saturated the air around her. A soft smile touched her face and then she stood. "Let's get back to that wonderful man who loves me."

That week the girls buzzed with talk about the new airstrip along the Glen feed area. The Army built the hard-packed dirt strip in one week, but its purpose remained a mystery since it was different than other airfields dotting the state.

"Maybe they'll bring the POWs in by plane?" Mary stood by an open file cabinet.

Kitty shook her head, then examined a fingernail she'd been filing. "No. I heard they'll come by train like everyone else."

"Then why build it? It's not like we're the next air base."

Lainie focused on the letter in front of her as the girls continued to chatter. Since it arrived yesterday, she'd dreaded opening it. The handwriting bore all the marks of her daddy's, but no return address sat in the left-hand corner. If it truly was from Daddy, she didn't know that she wanted to read it. Likely more words about how Tom wasn't the man for her. If only he'd give them a chance to show him the foundation of their relationship.

Some might call it luck or stars aligning in the right configuration, but Lainie knew the fact they'd even met bore all the hallmarks of the hand of God. Only He could have orchestrated every step of their friendship.

But how to make Daddy understand? The more she worried about it, the more she knew it was out of her hands.

"Lainie." Mary perched on the edge of Lainie's desk. "Are you going to read that or join us in our wild guesses about what's going on?"

Lainie tucked the letter in her desk and shrugged. "Personally, I think they built it as a landing strip for the Germans."

Groans filled the air, and someone pitched wadded-up paper at her. Lainie ducked and laughed with the others.

* * *

TOM WATCHED transport trucks roll onto base on August 5. He and the cadre had orders to get the arriving men anything they needed. Only problem was they still didn't know why they were here or where they were from. This operation was cloaked in secrecy so thick no one had penetrated it.

Friday night, as he and Lainie walked to a movie, he tucked her under his arm and listened as she told him about the speculation in the office. "No one's telling us what's happening. There must be some kind of maneuver."

"But why here?" Lainie leaned into his shoulder. "Fort Robinson isn't easy to find."

"I have a feeling we'll learn more only when we need to know."

Lainie snorted, the unladylike sound making him grin. "That's why you're in the Army, and I'm not. I have to know the why. Now."

* * *

TUESDAY AFTERNOON, the roar of airplanes filled the base. Tom rushed out of the classroom to watch. C-47 transport planes filled the sky, with wingspans of close to one hundred feet. Usually used to carry men and equipment, the behemoths flew east along Soldier Creek out of the Wood Reserve, pulling smaller planes behind them.

"I ain't seen anything like this before." Sid shielded his eyes.

Tom followed a plane across the sky.

"What are the planes towing?"

John Tyler joined them. "Gliders."

* * *

THE NEXT DAY the instructors got called into a meeting. Tom had heard the gliders were crashing all over the hay fields around the reserve. Sergeant Lewis stood at the front of the room, bouncing on his heels.

"War-training exercises are happening, and you get to participate. The observing officers want the dogs involved." He rubbed his hands together and grinned. "This is a chance to demonstrate what our dogs can do. Pick two of your teams. You'll go into the field and search for lost and injured soldiers. You'll receive maps when you're dismissed with your search zones. Good luck, and do us proud."

Tom knew exactly which teams to take. As his mind raced with plans, he rushed out of the room.

"Slow down, Hamilton."

Tom frowned at Sid. "Why? We've got a ton to do to get ready."

"Let's see which team can find the most stranded airmen." Sid slugged him in the arm.

"Deal." Tom couldn't hide his excitement. This is what all the training was about. The teams could demonstrate the value the dogs added to the war effort.

Before first light Wednesday, Tom gathered with his teams and the others to be transported to the drop zone. C-47s continued to fly across the sky, the parachutes dotting the sky like miniature clouds.

The dogs sniffed the air eagerly, tails standing at attention.

While in the truck, Tom reviewed the assigned sector again with his men. "Other teams will serve as sentries, but we're scouts. We'll give the dogs their heads. See what they find. We'll walk the perimeter and then walk in parallel lines until we cover it in a grid."

Privates Jensen and Mueller nodded, their eyes sweeping the map. As soon as the truck stopped, they bounded out with their dogs. Tom watched them start out, and followed at a distance. The men and dogs worked as a coordinated team.

Hours later, the sun pounded on Tom's back. As sweat dripped down the small of his back, he began to envy the remount guys left on base. Both dogs stopped and alerted. Tom scanned the horizon. "See anything?"

Jensen shook his head.

"Over there." Mueller walked with his dog toward a stand of trees. His dog raced the last few feet to the tree and started jumping up its trunk while barking. "We've got a live one."

A man, colonel by the eagle on his uniform, hung in a parachute from the branches of the ponderosa pine. As the dog leapt, he kicked his legs up. "Get that thing away from me."

Tom stepped forward. "Just a minute, sir. Mueller, pull back with your dog. Be sure to reward him for his good work."

Jensen hurried up with his dog. "Sorry, sir. Blitz got turned around by a rabbit."

"You'll get another chance. Get the dogs ready to continue the search." He put his knife between his teeth and climbed up the tree until he reached the colonel. "I'll cut you down."

"Not while the dogs are so agitated. What makes them so aggressive?"

"A little horse meat." At the colonel's twisted face, Tom sawed faster. "Grab hold of the tree, sir."

The man slipped to the ground as soon as he was free of the tangled parachute. The dogs jumped at him, and he leapt backward.

"Sit." The dogs immediately relaxed and obeyed.

The colonel nodded his thanks. "Point me to the nearest command center."

Tom pulled his cap off and scratched his head. Slapping it back on, he shrugged. "I'd tell you if I knew, sir. I'd hike that way if I were you." He nodded toward Mueller. "Jensen will take you in as his prisoner."

The colonel took off, muttering under his breath.

"All right, men. Let's see if we can't find another stranded colonel."

CHAPTER 26

AUGUST 11, 1943

*L*ainie strolled across the highway to the main section of Robinson, keeping one eye on the sky.

"Miss Gardner, a word with you?" The voice chased her back across the highway.

She turned and found herself face-to-face with Colonel Carr. "Yes, sir."

"It's my understanding you're trained as a nurse."

"Yes, though I haven't used those skills for a while."

"I've heard they're hard to forget. Tomorrow we'll need your services with the maneuvers. The hospital is already engaged with the airmen injured when their gliders crashed."

"Yes, sir." Lainie wanted to tell him that she hadn't enlisted so she couldn't be forced to nurse. However, she could tell by the glint in his eye that he expected his orders to be followed. He walked to his Jeep, and she determined to stay on her side of the highway as much as possible. It was far safer.

The next morning she rose after a restless night. She searched for any argument that she couldn't nurse. The doctors in Kentucky had told her she'd never have the strength to nurse. Her last attempt had ended in disaster when she couldn't keep up with the demands of the doctors. An orderly had physically removed her from the room as her roommate, Roxie, rushed in to fill her place. Her chest tightened and her fingers went numb at the thought of serving as a nurse.

No matter how hard she thought, there was no way around it. She might be a civilian, but she'd received orders. Lainie slipped beside her bed and prayed for strength to make it through the day. She got up and pulled on a pair of trim denim slacks, button-front shirt, and saddle shoes, wishing she'd brought her nurse's outfit to Crawford.

Concern edged Esther's expression as she handed a bag breakfast and lunch to Lainie. "Take it easy, you're still recovering from this last bout."

"Esther, you know I love you. It's been two months. I'll be careful, I promise. But I really am doing better."

Esther harrumphed, a touch of worry clouding her expression. "I suppose you're right. Don't overdo."

"I'll probably sit on a chair the whole time." Lainie inhaled the aroma of lemon poppy seed muffins. "Thanks for this. I have to run before the colonel sends someone after me."

Lainie kept glancing at the sky as she dashed to the shuttle pick-up. The large planes and parachutes filled the sky. Would many men be hurt when landing? She eyed the road, tapping her toes as she waited for the bus. She couldn't do any good here.

Once she reached Fort Robinson, she climbed into a waiting Jeep and was zipped to a staging area. She thanked the soldier for the ride and hopped to the ground. Soldiers hurried in all directions, purpose filling their strides, but none of the men looked familiar. Their patches indicated they weren't from Robinson. Scanning the scene, Lainie headed toward a tent with a painted white circle and red cross.

She pushed the flap aside and stepped in, giving her eyes a moment to adjust to the dim interior. A nurse slowed down.

"I'm Lainie Gardner. Colonel Carr ordered me to report here."

The woman relaxed and nodded. "We're expecting you, but you're supposed to be a nurse."

"I'm trained as one."

"I'm Nola Grable. Over there are supplies to organize before the rush of today's injuries."

Lainie did as instructed, delighted to work with familiar instruments. "Were there many yesterday?"

"I don't think many of those boys had flown a glider before. Most crashed. And who would think a hay field is a good place to hold maneuvers?"

"Only the Army?"

Nola laughed and shook her head. "You guessed it. Let's just say I hope these jumpers have more experience."

The first couple of hours were uneventful, so Lainie stayed in the background familiarizing herself with the set-up. A doctor sat, while two nurses readied twelve cots that lined the back in two orderly rows. Nola restocked the pharmaceuticals and then joined the doctor. An occasional solider hobbled into the tent, mainly with sprained ankles or twisted knees. Then two soldiers were carted in on stretchers. One had impaled his leg on a small tree, and the other had landed on some rocks and might have internal injuries.

The doctor barked orders at the nurses. One calmed the man who'd hit the tree, while the other three worked furiously on the second man.

Lainie moved to the front of the tent, praying God would guide the doctor's hands. Pounding feet hurried toward the tent, and she braced for whatever caused the race. Lainie jumped back when Tom rushed in.

"Lainie, we need the doctor quick." His breathing pulsed at a rapid pace, and he looked around the tent almost frantically.

"He's working right over there on someone else. What is it? Are you okay?" She reached for his arm, but he brushed past her. A sting of pain stabbed Lainie at his snub.

"It's John Tyler. He was attacked by one of the dogs who got too aggressive with a treed parachuter."

"Where is he?"

Tom pivoted and stumbled outdoors. Lainie rushed to catch up with him.

"Are you hurt?"

He ignored her and hobbled toward a group of men.

"Tom, look at me. What is wrong? Tom!" She pulled on his arm until he stopped and looked at her. She frantically inspected him but could not see blood.

"I twisted my leg when I pulled John away from the dog." He set his chin and looked away. "We're wasting time. John's that way."

Lainie waited a moment, then hurried ahead. Tom would only relax when John had the attention he needed. When she reached the cluster of men, she knelt beside John. He lay on his back, blood soaking the front of his shirt and covering his neck.

"What happened?"

Sid started to speak, then cleared his throat. "He got between an attacking dog and a soldier. The dog didn't stop and went for his throat. Tom separated them, but he'd already been bit."

Lainie felt a thready pulse on John's neck. "Grab that stretcher over there. We'll get him on it and move him to the tent." She jumped up and didn't wait to see whether they followed. She pulled the blankets off a cot and pulled a cart of supplies toward it. "Put the stretcher there."

She immediately bent over John's still form. "Stay with me, John." She grabbed bandages and started cleaning the blood so she could see the injuries.

"What have you got, Miss Gardner?" The doctor called from the table where he worked on a patient.

"A war dog trainer mauled by a dog. Looks like he was bit primarily on the neck, near the jugular."

The doctor whistled. "I'm stuck here, but I'll talk you through it. Have that man beside you apply pressure to the wound."

Lainie looked up to find Tom next to her.

"You didn't think I'd leave him." Tom reached for the gauze she'd ripped open.

Lainie turned her attention to John. "What next, doctor?"

"Is the vein intact?"

Lainie ran her hands through a basin of water and then doused them in alcohol. "Lift up for a second, Tom." As soon as he did, she probed the wounds. "I think it's intact."

"You think or you know?" The doctor barked.

Lainie closed her eyes and focused on what she could feel. "I'm certain."

"Okay, apply more pressure and clean the wound. When you're sure it's clean, call. One of us will suture him."

John moaned and began to thrash.

"Can I sedate him?"

"Give him a shot of morphine and get him closed up."

Lainie tried to still her trembling hands as she gave John a shot of morphine. She cleansed the wound and then called the doctor.

The doctor looked up. "I can't leave this man. You'll have to suture him."

Lainie nodded and took a deep breath. She threaded the needle. Her stomach clenched as she knelt beside John and the cot. "I'll be gentle." She nodded at Tom. "Lift off unless I ask you to add more pressure."

The metallic smell of the blood overwhelmed Lainie as she worked to stitch the wound together. John and Naomi deserved the best she could give. She tied off the last stitch and leaned back on her heels. She rolled the tension from her neck.

"How's he doing?"

Lainie jumped at Nola's voice. "Okay, I think."

"Good thing you were here. Looks like he's stabilized. Good work." She patted Lainie on the shoulder. "We'll take over."

Lainie looked up and found Tom staring at her, a strange look in his eyes. She tried to stand, but felt drained. Tom struggled to his feet and then helped her stand. He walked her to the basin where they both washed up.

"Let's get a breath of air."

Lainie gladly accepted his arm and followed him outside, feeling the after effects of adrenaline rippling through her. She tipped her face toward the sun and soaked in its warmth. The tremors slowly stopped. "Nothing I did in Kentucky felt like that."

"You saved John's life." Tom turned her toward him and pulled her into his arms. "Thank you."

"You saved him first, by getting the dog off him. And he's lucky. Since it wasn't his artery, he would have been okay without me." Lainie decided she wanted to spend the rest of the day like this, wrapped inside the shelter of Tom's embrace. Far from the stuffy hospital tent and the scent of blood. "John will be okay, you know."

Tom nodded, his chin tapping the top of her head. "I'm glad I could be there for John when he needed me today. Mason helped, too."

"She is a good dog." Lainie leaned into Tom's embrace for another moment, then pushed back. "Time to get inside. And we need to check your knee out."

Tom's eyebrows came together, and he grimaced at her.

She laughed and pulled him toward the tent. Her heart sang with the realization her training hadn't been wasted after all. If she'd shipped to Europe as planned, she wouldn't be here right now. And she couldn't think of anywhere else she'd rather be. Or anyone else she wanted to be with.

CHAPTER 27

SEPTEMBER 9, 1943

*T*om stepped off the train in Alliance. The town sat sixty miles southeast of the fort and offered more shops than downtown Crawford. He'd been sent to Alliance to retrieve another shipment of dogs from Dogs for Defense. He'd arrived early, because he had a bit of shopping to do, the kind he couldn't do in Crawford, where word would travel.

Things had quieted down after the glider wars with Sid's team winning, and he'd spent every free moment with Lainie. Each had only solidified the knowledge in his heart that she was the one. The only one he could imagine spending the rest of his life with.

Oh, she still had the ability to drive him crazy with her sharp tongue. But he'd also seen how deeply she cared about others. The tenacity and stubbornness that drove her when others gave up.

He glanced at his watch. One hour until the train arrived. He'd have to hurry but should have enough time.

* * *

THE OFFICE HUMMED with the usual backdrop of clicking heels, soft voices, and closing file drawers. Lainie leaned away from the typewriter relieved the day was almost over. She needed to correct the last mistake and finish the form. Thankfully her typing skills had improved, but she still kept an eraser handy in the middle desk drawer.

Lainie heard a crumpling sound as she tried to close her middle desk drawer. She frowned and pulled the drawer out again. She slipped her hand in the drawer and reached back, feeling for whatever might be caught. She groped until she thought her arm would fall asleep, but finally felt a piece of paper. Pulling it out, she sat back with a sigh.

She eyed the envelope. It was the one she had received from her daddy a month or more ago, but never read. She flipped it over and slid a letter opener beneath the flap. The letter was the first and only communication she'd received from her daddy since moving to Crawford.

Well, the only way to know what it said was to open it. Pulling out the single sheet, Lainie unfolded it.

Dear Lainie,

It was a surprise to see you last week with your soldier. Your mother tells me I was too short with him and you. I'd like to blame it on the shock. I only want the best for you. That has been my desire from the moment I first saw you.

Your mother and I trust you, and we trust your judgment. If you believe this man is the one you want to marry, we will not oppose that. Instead, we both feel peace about it. It helps that his superiors speak highly of him.

Come home soon. Mason misses you.

Your Daddy

LAINIE REREAD THE MESSAGE, wondering if her eyes deceived her. Did she imagine he'd penned the words? No, he actually was giving his blessing.

As she reread the letters, Lainie felt her heart lift. Now there was no reason she and Tom couldn't be together. She closed her eyes and imagined the next time she would see him. This time without any concerns about what her parents thought about him.

Her heart began to pound, and she wished Tom wasn't out of town transporting dogs.

* * *

SATURDAY AFTERNOON, Tom glanced at Lainie. He'd never seen her more beautiful than she looked now, hair bouncing as she cantered over the hills on Daisy. Tornado had no trouble keeping up, and Tom settled back to enjoy the ride.

Lainie had welcomed him into her life with an openness that pleased him. She'd sparred with him on the drive to the stables, yet it held a fun tone. There was no question. No one else caused this kind of certainty or knowing in him. He patted the saddlebags to assure himself that he had everything.

Daisy slowed, and Lainie slipped from the saddle.

Tom pulled Tornado to a stop. "Everything okay?"

"Walk with me?" Lainie looked up at him, an impish grin teasing him.

He jumped to the ground, and she reached for his hand. He loved the feel of her small hand tucked inside his. Their fingers twined together, and they ambled toward a butte, the horses trailing behind them. The silence between them was a comfortable one.

Tornado bumped his shoulder and snorted.

"Cool it, horse."

Lainie laughed. "Are you always so short with Tornado?"

"Only when he forgets his manners."

"He only wants a treat, you know."

"And rudeness is the way to get it?" Tom shook his head and pulled away from Lainie. "Stand still, Tornado." He unfastened the latch on a saddlebag and reached for the apples he'd tucked in there. He pulled them out, and his present with them. He tucked the gift in his back pocket and hoped Lainie hadn't noticed.

"What did you just hide?"

So much for that hope. "Nothing."

"Hmm. *Nothing* doesn't have to be denied. Come on, show me." She cajoled and tried to reach around him.

Tom danced away and held the apples out. "Don't you want to give one to Daisy?"

"Only after I know what you're hiding from me." She crossed her arms and stuck her lower lip out.

Tom rolled his eyes. "Fine, I'll give Daisy her treat." He slipped Tornado his apple, then turned toward the smaller animal. "Come here, girl. I've got a juicy apple for you."

Daisy tossed her head and whinnied.

"See, she wants to know what you're hiding, too." Lainie rubbed her horse's nose.

"Fine. I can't fight two stubborn women."

Lainie laughed and tried to slip around him.

"Now hold it right there. Here. Sit on this rock and close your eyes."

Lainie scrunched her nose and squinted at him.

"I'm serious. Close your eyes."

She shrugged and plopped on the rock. "All right."

Tom waved his hand in front of her face, looking for any flicker that she hadn't obeyed. His stomach fluttered liked he'd eaten too many slices of pie, and he took a deep breath to try and calm it. Couldn't go losing lunch on Lainie's shoes, nerves or not.

After pulling the small box from his pocket, he popped its lid and stared at the ring. It was simple. A gold band with a tiny diamond. He wanted her to like it. He sank to one knee and blew out a steadying breath.

Lainie bounced her legs and kept her eyes screwed shut. "Ready yet?"

That was his Lainie. Impatient as ever.

"All right, Lainie. Open your eyes."

When she did, they popped wider before she shut them again. She winked one eye and then the other. "What are you doing?" Her voice shook and her legs tapped even faster.

This wasn't the reaction he'd anticipated.

"Lainie Gardner, I've been captivated by you from that first moment you shouted in my ear. You are an amazing woman, and I love you." He reached up to wipe a tear from her cheek. "I cannot imagine my life without you in it. Would you do me the honor of marrying me?"

She nodded and opened her mouth, but nothing came out. She threw her arms around his neck, and he held her as they fell to the ground. Gently he helped her to a sitting position. She held out her hand, and he slipped the ring from the box and onto her finger. It fit perfectly, just like she fit perfectly in his life.

* * *

Lainie held the ring up and watched as the sunlight played with the diamond. She could hardly breathe as she tried to comprehend what Tom had offered her. Had he really asked her to marry him? In her dreams she'd imagined Tom and forever, but she hadn't expected the ring and the promise now. Especially since he hadn't seen Daddy's letter yet.

She searched Tom's face, desperate to find any indication he wasn't sure. Instead, all she saw was the quiet certainty and steadiness that he personified.

Peace also seemed to fill his smile, like he knew this was perfect. Her pulse fluttered and she pulled her gaze back to the ring.

This was real.

"I have something I want to show you, too, Tom." Lainie pulled the envelope from her skirt's pocket. "I got this over a month ago, but the unopened envelope got mixed into a pile of papers in a desk drawer. I uncovered it earlier this week, while you were gone. Here."

Tom looked from her to the letter, concern twisting his face.

"Read it." Lainie twisted the ring on her finger and smiled. He'd decided she was worth fighting for. Even without knowing her daddy agreed.

Tom pulled the letter from the envelope and read it. A slow grin spread across his face.

She threw her arms around Tom's neck and hung on.

"Are you sure?" she whispered against his neck.

"Absolutely. There is no question in my mind that God has put us together. Are you already having doubts?"

"Only that this is truly happening. I love you, Tom."

"I love you, too, Lainie."

And he sealed his words with a kiss that left her breathless.

EPILOGUE

OCTOBER 2, 1943

*L*ainie pushed back the curtain and looked out the window. She strummed her fingers against the pane. Where was the car? Any minute Tanya should whip in front of Esther's with Tom's car to carry her to the chapel on base.

It was hard to believe that tonight she and Tom would become husband and wife. A rush of excitement flooded her at the thought.

They'd drive to Ogallala and spend the night near Lake McConaughy before continuing to North Platte the next day. Her parents had accepted their decision to have a quick and small wedding, but insisted on a large reception at the Pawnee Hotel ballroom. That was tomorrow. Today, they'd have the simple ceremony.

All the girls but Esther had already left. They'd join Tom's Army buddies as witnesses.

Lainie turned from the window and smoothed the front of her gown. The pale-blue silk gown swept below her knees and fell in soft pleats. She'd brought the dress to Crawford, not knowing if she would have any occasion to wear it, and now it was her wedding dress. She twirled in front of the window and smiled.

Her bag already sat by the front door, ready to throw in the trunk.

"Tanya's here." Esther yelled up the stairs.

Lainie's dreams really were going to come true today. She flew down the stairs and into the car, Esther behind her. "Let's go."

It felt like they would never reach the chapel. Lainie was tempted to hop out and run to Fort Robinson. Finally, they arrived, and she hurried inside. Tom stood by the chaplain at the front of the small sanctuary. Tanya slipped up to join the girls and soldiers who stood in a semicircle up front. Lainie hurried to join them, unable to take her gaze from Tom and the love flowing from him. The ceremony passed in a daze as she stared into his eyes.

He wanted to spend the rest of his life with her. Lainie closed her eyes and could almost feel the pleasure of heaven.

"You may kiss the bride."

Tom leaned toward her. "Promise me forever, Lainie."

Lainie opened her eyes and smiled at Tom. "With all my heart, now and forever."

He kissed her, and Lainie knew that a dream, one that promises a thousand tomorrows filled with love had come true.

CAPTIVE DREAMS

To my mother, Jolene Catlett. Mom, did you have any idea all those days you home-schooled us and drilled grammar into me that someday all that diagramming would pay off in the books I write? Thank you for choosing to invest in us on a daily basis when you could have done any number of other things. I'm a stronger—and smarter—person because of you.

CHAPTER 1

MAY 5, 1944

"*P*apa, who on earth are those men in the fields?"

Anna Goodman swiped her hair from inside her jacket collar as she stared past her father's age sloped shoulder as he hunched in his chair to the kitchen window . She hated the feeling the burden for the farm outside Holdrege, Nebraska, had transferred to her, an encumberance she'd never expected to bear at twenty-one. The men working the fields reclaimed her thoughts. She didn't like the hardness they bore. Nor did she like the idea that German soldiers were the only option. Her spine stiffened until she stood as rigid as a fencepost. No matter that the time had come to plant the corn and the fields around Holdrege hummed with activity. Surely Papa hadn't hired prisoners of war.

Papa buried his head deeper behind the newspaper, huddled in his worn chair in front of the stone fireplace. Anna's heart tightened. She'd been gone only five days, yet he'd aged at least ten years.

"Papa. Look at me. Please." Her words whined until she tightened her lips against more.

The paper rustled, and Anna longed to rip the shield from him. Force him to look at her. Instead, she sighed. His hair might look grayer where it peeked over the paper, but he remained as stubborn as Betsy, the mule he refused to give away.

Mama's red-and-white checked curtains didn't bring a smile to her face this time. They were the only cheery thing left in the house now that Mama danced in heaven after a short battle against pneumonia two years earlier. The inside of the house could only be called a shambles, dirty dishes stacked all over the table and old papers strewn beside his chair, where Papa dropped them. Her nose wrinkled at the smell of stale sausage and spoiled food. Papa hadn't even scraped it into the slop pan.

Even Anna's brother, Brent, couldn't fill Papa's silence with his off-the-wall jokes since the draft board called his number. There was no escaping that the farm didn't feel like home but had morphed into her personal prison.

"Have it your way. I'll find out what they're up to on my own." Anna pulled her jacket around her and stomped out of the kitchen.

Anna stepped outside and wished for the freedom to leave Papa behind his impenetrable wall. He acted like he didn't need her. Reality shouted a different tune in her ears. The wind stung Anna's cheeks and sucked the air out of her lungs.

The home wasn't the only thing that needed attention. The closer she got to the fields, the more evident it became they needed care. The rows angled across the field in erratic lines. Weeds sprouted everywhere and, if left unchecked, would choke out the corn as it grew. If only the men in the field did not have Ps and Ws painted on their clothes. Even if Papa had requested the prisoners, she couldn't imagine the prisoners of war working her land when she came home after a long week at the Kearney airfield.

Her land. Her steps slowed as the thoughts ricocheted around her mind. It had never felt like her land. Indeed, most days it seemed more a ball and chain than blessing. Yet as the words rolled through, a steady peace filled her chest.

If it was her land, it was high time she treated it that way.

Time to take ownership of it.

If only Papa would.

As her thoughts returned to her papa hiding in the kitchen, she inhaled through her teeth in a whistle. A rush of emotions clamored into the spot peace had filled.

What are we going to do, Papa? I don't have the energy to shoulder this alone. And you don't have the will. Anna picked up speed and crossed the yard toward the barn.

Beyond that building a fence covered in peeling paint and missing boards protected fields of corn from something, though she'd never known what exactly. Deer could leap over it with ease to nibble the developing corn plants. It would take weeks, but all too soon the stalks would grow until their tassels touched the sky. Then the hard work started. Anna's shoulders ached thinking about the hours and days she'd spend walking the rows, separating the tassels from the corn. That job made even her sedentary job packing parachutes at the Kearney airfield endurable.

Anna lifted her face and released a slow breath. The sun kissed her skin with its warmth, and the weariness drained from her. Resolve cloaked her. Whatever the men were doing on the farm, she'd clear it up and get them on their way. She couldn't handle one more challenge at the moment.

She reached the fence and hesitated before climbing the bottom two wooden planks to get a better view of the action in the field. From her perch, she saw eight men walking among the rows. Her brow crinkled. The movements of most were unchoreographed and confused. One man strode among the others, pointing and appearing to give instructions as he went. He spoke to each man in turn and carried an air of assurance. By his uniform she could tell he was a guard sent with the men, probably a specialist. Yet he acted unlike the other guard who lounged against a truck.

A prisoner bent toward the ground and ran his fingers through the soil, crumbling it into smaller pieces. He lifted it and inhaled. A smile parted his face from ear to ear and then he patted the earth back into place and reached with energy for the seed resting at his feet. Then the seed corn flew through his grasp.

"No." She clenched her teeth as he seemed unable or unwilling to treat the precious seed with care. She'd worked long hours to pay for that corn. "Somebody stop him."

She jumped over the fence and marched toward the man that leaned against the government issue truck. His uniform hung on him in a rumpled mess. He didn't even glance her way, though he had to hear her. She splashed through leftover spring puddles, yet he still ignored her.

"Hey! What are you doing in our fields? They don't know what they are doing. There's seed everywhere." Her anger pushed her voice up an octave, and she struggled to rein in her temper.

The man turned to her. His hat was shoved on top of unruly brown hair that curled slightly around his collar. His shoulders were broad, and she almost stood nose to nose with him.

She stewed as his gaze swept over her body. He leered at her and stood taller. "Calm down, dame."

"I'll calm down when you get these men off my farm. Now."

* * *

THE YOUNG WOMAN'S shriek stopped the prisoners mid-action. Specialist Sid Chance stood from instructing the PW and arched his back. Even though he was only twenty-five, he felt the effects of all those hard hits he'd taken during high school football games. He hurried his steps as Pete pushed away from the half-tack he'd lazed against.

"Hey, Pete. What's the problem?"

"Just a broad who don't think we belong here." Pete's Jersey manners and words didn't seem to play well with the woman. Red flamed her tanned cheeks.

Sid shook his head. The little guy seemed to think he stood taller when he ordered everyone around. Only problem was he couldn't see the exact opposite occurred.

"Ma'am, I'm Specialist Sid Chance, and this lump of hot air is Private Peter Gurland. What's wrong?"

Her jaw tightened until he wanted to rub his own, ease the tension. "What's wrong is you. These men. Get off our land now."

Sid turned as Luka, one of the prisoners who enjoyed the outdoor work, approached the group with halting steps.

"Sir, I hate to bother, but men are unsure what to do."

"You certainly are." The woman stepped closer. "You get these men, these prisoners, off now, before I do something I won't regret."

"Pete, why don't you round them up? Ma'am, how will you plant the corn?"

"I ... I don't know yet, but I'll come up with something. You must be trespassing since Papa would never allow them here."

"Mr. Goodman signed a contract for the men, like the other farmers." He took a half-step closer to her and cocked his head. "He decided, like most, that the farm needed the extra labor to get the seed in. We can be done for now, but you really need help to get all the corn planted. I'll check back in the next week or so."

"Ya coming, windbag?" Pete's nasally voice jarred his ears.

"Please, don't bother. There's been a mistake. We've always handled the farm on our own. We'll do it again." She lowered her gaze and kicked at a clod of dirt. "We can't pay their wages."

"Where else are you going to get farm help? Many men are in the military, and everyone else works in industry." He took in her rumpled coveralls. "Like you. We'll work here at your father's request. Until he informs the camp commander or county agent differently, we'll be back. I always see a job to completion. And you might be surprised about the wages. They aren't as burdensome as you think."

"I think it's ridiculous to make us pay our enemies' wages."

"Ridiculous or not, it's what your dad signed up for."

The woman's eyes filled with tears. What had he said? He shuffled his feet in the dirt as he reviewed the words. He couldn't think of anything that should generate moisture. The horn blared behind him, and Sid turned and waved at Pete, for the first time relieved to have Pete interrupt him.

"Ma'am? You all right?"

She tipped her chin in the air and blinked rapidly. "Yes. And quit calling me *ma'am. Anna* will do."

Sid grinned as she stalked toward the house. She overflowed with spunk much like his kid sister, Pattie, had before she married that good-for-nothing Arthur Tucker, who tried to yell the life out of her. He shook his head and climbed into the truck. He'd make sure he made it back to check on things. He hadn't seen her the other times he'd come to the farm. She must work in Grand Island or one of the other larger towns.

He'd try to coordinate one of his trips to a time she'd be here. He had a feeling Anna was worth getting to know.

CHAPTER 2

MAY 5, 1944

*A*nna's pulse pounded in her ears as she stormed up the weathered stairs to the house. They screeched at her heavy steps. One more thing to add to the long list of items that needed attention. Maybe she should stop caring since Papa had. He used to take such pride in the appearance of the farm. Or maybe it was Mama who did.

She flung open the door and let the screen slam against the frame. Papa didn't even shift. She wanted to race to him and scream questions. Why allow the very Germans her brother fought to work here? The sons of the Germans who had held Papa captive?

He couldn't have invited them. Things weren't that desperate. He gave every indication he remained too proud, because a Goodman always cares for things on his own. Least that's what he'd always said. Before.

And where would she find the money to pay the wages?

Guilt nibbled at the edges of Anna's thoughts. Her father had ordered her to stay home and abandon her job in Kearney. Yet they needed the cash from her job. The Depression had stripped the family of all but the barest holdings, and the bank accounts had long sat empty of all but the smallest amounts.

The fight left her as she hung up her jacket. She longed to sink to the floor at Papa's feet, place her head in his lap, and feel him stroke her hair like he used to. Instead, she turned on her heel and opened the worn cabinets. Somewhere in here she'd find ingredients for supper.

"Papa, did you collect the eggs today?"

He grunted without getting out of his chair or turning toward her.

"I'll take that as a *no*. Fine. I'll be back."

295

Anna yanked her jacket from its hook by the door and pulled it on. She peeked out the window and felt a pebble lift from her shoulders. The government truck had disappeared, taking the men with it. She slipped out the door and hiked the short distance across the yard to the chicken house. The small wooden structure sagged beneath the weight of its tin roof. The chicken wire kept the chickens in and most of the predators at bay.

"Evening, ladies." Anna waited as the hens clucked and ruffled their feathers. "I hate to intrude, but I need some eggs if you don't mind." Mama always hummed to the hens to calm them. The more Anna talked to them, the more they danced with jerks. Yet the couple of times she remained silent, the chickens had attacked her. One nip at her fingers, and she'd decided to talk when she neared the door.

She cracked the door and slipped into the small space before letting the door close behind her. Her lungs filled with the dust of chicken feed, feathers, and waste. She coughed to clear the air, only inhaling more of the rank odor. Better make this quick. She stepped toward the stacked boxes. Reaching under one feathered rump after another, she scooped up the eggs. In less than a minute she'd filled the bottom of her basket with brown speckled eggs and slid back outside. "See you in the morning."

Indignant cackles were the only reply.

Anna turned away from the door and stopped. She leaned against the building and stared at the display in the sky. Stripes of rich color bled across the creeping darkness. Midnight blue topped lavender that sat on coral. The sun blazed orange as it touched the horizon. Awe filled her at the sight.

"Why do You do it, Lord?" War raged around the globe, yet He took the time to paint the sky each night. She shook her head. Switching the basket to the other hand, she continued to the house.

Silence dominated the dinner of biscuits and scrambled eggs. Her thoughts turned to the soldier, Specialist Chance, and his sympathy. How did he see into places she'd hoped to bury beyond anyone's reach? There short interaction left her unsettled and unveiled. With a grunt, Papa shuffled to his room as soon as he'd wiped his plate clean and shoved the last piece of biscuit in his mouth.

"Thank you for the wholesome meal, Anna. So glad you're home," Anna muttered, then threw her napkin on the table and stood. She busied herself cleaning the kitchen and trying not to wish she'd stayed in Kearney. At least there her friends wanted to spend time with her.

Reality dictated she didn't have a choice—each week Papa failed. The scent of alcohol followed him around the house, and his shoulders bowed more, she was sure of it. His eyes seemed a duller blue. They'd practically faded to gray. Soon, she feared, they'd turn translucent.

He'd stopped living. Somehow she'd carry on for both of them.

She flipped on the tabletop radio to fill the silence as she brought order to the chaos in the kitchen.

By Sunday Anna couldn't wait to return to Kearney and her life. Her days might consist of work at the airfield and sleep at the Wisdoms' home, but at least she had a purpose greater than gathering eggs, humoring a cantankerous old man, and milking the cow. She couldn't fight the entrapment that chased her from chore to chore.

That night, Anna planted a kiss on Papa's cheek, relieved her obligations had ended for the week. In an hour, she'd be back in her room, ready to return to her job at the airfield. A horn blared outside. Anna startled and grabbed her overnight bag. "See you on Friday, Papa. Don't forget to grab the eggs this week, okay?"

Dottie stood waiting beside her car when Anna skipped down the stairs.

"Way to keep a lady bored." A large smile creased Dottie's round face. "Let's fly."

Anna opened the passenger door and threw her bag in the footwell. "I'm ready to head back to sanity."

"I don't know that I'd call the Wisdoms' home full of sanity. Those kids could drive a girl batty, but we'll get you away from your vow of silence here at the farm."

Anna chuckled. "You have no idea. He seems to get worse each week. It's time to get some of his friends involved before he completely disappears."

"Next weekend, darling. Tonight we sail away to a new world. One filled with soldiers, many of them eligible bachelors."

"This whole thing is just about finding you a husband, isn't it?"

"Well, if that gets thrown into the mix, I won't complain. I think it's time I use the base chapel for a wedding, don't you?"

"I want more than a wedding."

Dottie turned and stared, pulling the car with her before correcting the steering. "Haven't you noticed all the eligible men are in uniform? You can work for whatever reason you want. Escaping the farm, your father, whatever. I'm here to find a man who'll take care of me. I won't share a room with you forever."

"Good. I've noticed you consume more than your share of the dresser, and someday I'll have to do something about that. What a relief if you married first."

Anna ignored Dottie's babble of information about her weekend as the miles flew by. Before Anna was ready, Dottie pulled the car in front of the Wisdoms' Victorian. The home overflowed with people. Between the five Wisdoms and six boarders, every spare nook and cranny was filled. The housing shortage caused by those working the airfield made Anna grateful for any bed. Maybe she should be thankful for the quiet on the farm each weekend, but Papa made it so hard.

She stumbled up the steps and through the front door Dottie propped open. The sounds of two boys fighting in the parlor assaulted her. Anna tossed her bag on the polished wooden steps, ignored the boys, and turned to follow the scent of spiced cider into the kitchen.

"Here. Let me grab your bag for you. I'd love to schlep it up to our room—no tip required."

"Thanks, Dottie." Anna turned back and caught the grimace on Dottie's face. Anna ran her fingers along the smooth chair rail as she continued down the hall. "Good evening, Mrs. Wisdom."

"Hello, dear. How was your weekend?" Bonnie Wisdom turned from the pot she stirred on the stove. Her turquoise eyes studied Anna with care as silence settled between them. "That good? I'm sorry."

"Maybe someday I'll enjoy trips home. Until then, I'll work hard during the week and endure days on the farm. Life and fun used to fill the place. That hasn't been the case for a long time."

"Grief takes time to ease, Anna."

"Isn't two years enough?"

"There's no magic time. Some people move on quickly, others linger with the one who has passed." Mrs. Wisdom settled at the table next to Anna. "Do you think you should go home?"

"I can't do that. It's too hard." A lump filled her throat. Anna sagged in her seat and played with the edge of the tablecloth. She willed her eyes not to fill with tears and then winced when one escaped. "I've lost everybody dear to me. Even my father is disappearing in his own way."

"You have." Mrs. Wisdom stood and turned down the flame under the pot, filled a mug with cider, and joined Anna at the table. She reached across the cloth and handed Anna the cup. "But you have time to reach your father. And your brother may still come home. Until that happens, we must ask God to protect them and bring them safely home."

As Mrs. Wisdom prayed aloud, Anna bowed her head and tried to join. The only words that filled her prayer begged for her faith to be restored before it disappeared with her hope.

CHAPTER 3

MAY 10, 1944

*R*eveille echoed through the air. Sid pulled the scratchy wool blanket over his head before facing the inevitable. The Army waited for no man no matter how tired or the dreams haunting his sleep. He'd wanted to hug the image of a petite, blonde dynamo to his dreams. Instead, bleary-eyed, he stumbled onto the floor and into the chest at the foot of the bed. A howling wind had chilled the air in the barracks overnight to the point even the three coal stoves placed down the middle of the large room couldn't heat it. Through his socks, the concrete floor felt like ice.

He grabbed a fresh uniform from the chest before heading to the washroom. In minutes he dashed out the door and across the compound to Camp Atlanta's mess hall. The facility was much more thrown together than the buildings at Fort Robinson. His stomach growled as soon as he entered the hall and the smell of powdered eggs scrambled in bacon grease reached his nose.

"Sounds like you need to cut to the front of the line."

"Thank you, sir. I mean, no, sir." Sid's words tangled to a halt when he realized his commanding officer spoke to him. "I'll be fine, Colonel Smith." He never used to be tongue-tied. Now any time he saw his CO, it made him remember the fiasco at Fort Robinson. He wanted to slam a hand over his mouth before more inane words escaped.

Colonel Smith nodded and proceeded through the line. Sid groaned.

"Sound like an officer in training. 'Yes, sir. No, sir. Right away, sir.'" Larry Heglin sneered as he shouldered past Sid into the chow line.

At times like this it was hard to turn his cheek and walk away. It would be so much easier to put a guy like Heglin in his place. Sid couldn't figure out why

Heglin had it in for him, but it was clear the private second class despised him. Sid slouched and screwed his eyes shut.

"Wakey, wakey, bud."

Sid opened his eyes as the scent of coffee swirled beneath his nose. Trent Franklin stood in front of him, sipping a cup of coffee while offering another to Sid.

"Thanks." Sid accepted the cup and yelped when the hot liquid scalded his lips. He touched the tender spot with his free hand. "This should come with a warning. So what's today's agenda?"

"First, get some food. Then back to the prisoners' side of camp. I don't think any groups are heading to farms today." Trent grabbed a tray. Throwing a fork and knife on it, he slid into the line.

"Nothing like passing time in a guard shack."

"Yep. Another exciting day."

Sid stepped up to the line and waited as soldiers slopped food onto his plate at each station. His mind wandered to the spitfire he'd met at the Goodman farm. Something about her intensity and emotion had caught his attention. Something the other gals he knew failed to do. Something had caused all that depth of feeling, and he wanted to learn what. He also wondered what she was like on a routine day when fatigue didn't pull her down. If her smile matched the fire that danced in her eyes.

"Hey. You still with me?"

"Yep."

"Sure you are. Maybe I should replace you next time you head to the Goodman farm."

"Why would you do a crazy thing like that? It's just another farm."

"Your mind's lived somewhere else since you got back. You didn't even join us at the USO this weekend."

Sid shouldered Trent. "A guy needs an occasional break."

"From good times?" Trent shook his head and pushed through the tables to a vacant one. "You'll come back. This war could last for years. You like the girls too much to stay away."

Sid slid onto a seat and unease settled on him. He'd always liked his life, but now he wasn't as content as he'd thought.

Trent's prediction came true. The day dragged as Sid sat in a guard tower. In an effort to pass the time, he fiddled with a broken searchlight. The bulb had shattered inside the fixture, and he had to pull the glass and metal out piece by piece. The task took time, but not nearly enough to fill even the morning.

Once the light worked again, he paced around the rim of the tower. His gaze swept back and forth across the camp in front of him. Camp Atlanta housed around nineteen hundred prisoners of war at any given time. The tiny town had grown into the fields to support the camp, administrative buildings, and soldiers' quarters.

Row after orderly row of twenty-by-one-hundred-feet frame buildings spaced thirty feet apart spread across the camp. Barbed wire fences surrounded the prisoners' section, clearly delineating the line between compounds. He looked over the eleven buildings that formed the hospital complex, then to the bakery and the administration buildings. Small groups of prisoners, guards, and soldiers circulated around the camp, but nothing unusual happened.

A stiff breeze snaked past his jacket collar and down his neck. The sun had dived behind a cloud, taking the warmth with it. With a shudder he walked back inside the tower. The glass windows didn't provide enough protection from the Nebraska weather, but they were better than the alternative.

Trent huddled over a cup of coffee when Sid walked in. "Seen enough?"

"Yep. There's so much to see today. The dead wire's where it's always been. The prisoners are still glad to be here and not in the war. And we're bored as usual." Sid leaned against the doorframe.

"Isn't this why we enlisted? See the world—or Nebraska. I'm sure that was in the Army's materials."

Sid shook his head. "I don't mind Nebraska so much." Between Fort Robinson and Camp Atlanta, he'd seen more of Nebraska than he'd intended. Europe had been a little more what he had in mind. He'd hoped to serve with Patton or someone equally brilliant rather than work as military police at a home-front base. "At least the people are friendly."

"Yep." A goofy grin stretched Trent's face. "You should have joined me. The gals were extra friendly this weekend."

Sid studied Trent, not sure he wanted to dive too deeply into what Trent meant. "How about the base theater? What's showing?"

"Doesn't matter, you'll come whether it's John Wayne or Laurel and Hardy."

A siren pealed across the camp. Sid lunged off the wall and then rushed outside to the platform. "Man the gun, Trent. Let's see what's going on."

The phone inside the guard shack rang. Sid turned to see Trent grab it with one hand while keeping the other firmly on the gun's handle. Trent would let him know what was going on as soon as he knew anything, so Sid turned back to the prisoners' section. Wherever he looked, nothing appeared out of place. The prisoners outside had frozen in spot, probably too scared to move. Next, he scanned the dead man's line. As far as he could tell, no one had strayed there. He reached for his riot gun just in case he'd missed something. There were blind spots behind buildings.

Other soldiers rushed toward the interior compound, guns at the ready. Sid prayed no one pulled a trigger unnecessarily. The last thing he wanted to witness was the slaughter of unarmed men. To date, nothing like that had happened at Camp Atlanta. He didn't want today to be the first time. Especially not when he and a small unit of men manned the guard towers.

The window rattled behind him, and Sid whipped toward it, his glance darting between the guard tower and the perimeter.

Trent gave him an OK sign and motioned him in.

Sid pushed into the inside of the small tower. "What was that all about?"

"Someone leaned on the siren by mistake."

"Sure. It's so easy to hit the button on top of the machine and so hard to find the button to turn it off." Sid made a mental note to find out who it was and give him a talk that would ensure he'd never be so careless again.

"Maybe we aren't the only bored ones today."

"Right. Here's hoping they punish the fool."

"Don't forget you get to be a part of that with your new duties, Chance."

Sid nodded. His new duties as a Specialist would take a while to get used to, but he'd enjoy this one.

Things settled down in the compound. Sid's thoughts wandered as he watched nothing happen. In the coming days, he'd escort prisoners to local farms where they could fill the desperate need for labor. He stifled a groan at the long days filled with emptiness. The prisoners didn't want to escape. And he didn't sign up to be a taxi driver for POWs. The only variety in his days came from locals who decided they didn't want the Germans around after all. Like one particular blonde.

Maybe he should stop by the Goodman farm, make sure everything was okay. Find out how to contact her. He didn't want to rely on stopping by. And it wouldn't hurt if he could get a better sense of the underlying story. As he closed his eyes, he knew he would.

He'd find a way to bring a smile to Miss Goodman's face.

CHAPTER 4

MAY 12, 1944

*F*riday afternoon Anna glanced back at the Wisdoms' home before inching inside Dottie's car. She tossed her bag into the backseat and collapsed next to her friend.

"Ready for another weekend?" Dottie's grin tipped to one side.

"At home? Have I ever?" Anna flipped her blonde, bobbed curls behind her ears. "I wonder what crisis Papa will create."

"He only wants to keep you home."

Anna stared out the window and watched Kearney slip behind them. Part of her understood that's what Papa wanted. Her at home. All the time. But the thought of staying in that too-quiet farmhouse pulled the air from her lungs. And they couldn't sacrifice her income, could they? Without it, there was never enough money on the farm. Much as Papa might want to avoid the reality, cash remained a necessity.

So she'd balance her job at the factory and helping at the farm. Though the image of the crooked rows of corn made her wonder if twenty-four hours a day, each day of the week would be enough time. Too much work existed for two people who gave their all, let alone two fragmented people.

She had to pull Papa out of his depression. Keep him out of the bottles that had turned into his only friends. Somehow. The miles rolled by in silence as Anna's thoughts flitted from idea to idea.

Dottie turned the car off the highway and onto the rutted driveway leading to the farm long before Anna had a plan or felt ready. Dottie turned toward Anna. "You know how to reach me if you need anything."

"Thanks." The town girl forgot that, to reach her, Anna had to walk to the neighbor's farm to use the phone. "See you Sunday."

"Yes, ma'am."

Anna grabbed her bag and slipped from the car. The house looked desolate with light shining from a single window. She squared her shoulders and marched to the door. Ready or not, another two days at the farm awaited her.

"Who's there?" Papa stumbled through the kitchen. "Annie, that you?"

"Yes, Papa. I'm home."

"Harrumph. About time. I'm tired of eating scrambled eggs three meals a day. The chores need you, too."

Welcome home. Anna stilled the words that wanted to explode from her mouth. Every lesson she'd ever heard about honoring her parents raced through her mind. She unclenched her hands and forced a smile on her lips. "Let me drop my bag. Then I'll get started."

He grunted and turned back to the kitchen radio and his chair.

Anna threw her bag on her bed and sank on to her mattress. The twin frame creaked in protest. She held her head in her hands. She'd spent the week working full days at the airfield, sewing and packing parachutes and patching airplane wings. Long twelve-hour days. Exhaustion tempted her to lay down, rest for just a moment. But if she allowed herself to relax, she doubted she'd get up before morning. And then what would the poor cow do as her udder threatened to explode?

With a groan, Anna pulled herself off the bed and pasted a smile on her face.

"Anna?" Papa's voice bellowed down the hallway. "Where'd you go, girl? Time's wasting. Where's my dinner?"

She headed toward his voice, the knot in her stomach tightening. She had to survive … somehow. She'd make sure there was a farm left for Brent to come home to if it killed her. As Papa continued to yell, she braced against the thought that it might.

* * *

SID SHRUGGED out of his jacket, keeping one hand on the wheel, and threw his jacket on the truck seat next to him. The truck slid around a large pothole as he traveled the back highway toward the Goodman farm. The week had been jammed with activity. He hadn't swung by and checked on the fields as promised. That inability to follow through grated on him. The moment his duties ended Friday afternoon, he'd known exactly where he needed to go.

Now he neared the farm. Compared to the other fields lining the county roads, Goodman's acres showed neglect. Enough neglect to make him wonder how on earth the spitfire from last week thought she could handle the land alone.

Maybe Anna had a hidden solution, but he doubted it.

The image of Mr. Goodman's face flashed through Sid's mind. He'd only interacted with the man once, but his features had twisted into a mask of bitterness. He'd argued with the county extension agent in charge of assigning prisoners to work groups that he must have help. No one had stuck around on the farm, and he couldn't maintain the three hundred acres on his own. Sid had hustled his team to the farm, only to have Mr. Goodman refuse to open his door or leave his house.

The man seemed filled with contradictions. Griping passionately for help one day, and ignoring the same the next.

Sid pulled down the narrow lane that led to the farmhouse and barn. If Anna'd come home tonight, her sharp tongue would make it interesting. He'd been serious when he told her he'd keep an eye on the place. Someone needed to. She reminded him so much of Pattie before she married Peter and he sucked the spark of life from her. The similarities hurt.

He stopped the truck in front of the barn. He walked to the house and banged on the back door. A shuffling sound neared the door. The curtain on the door's window swept to the side, and Mr. Goodman peered out. He cracked the door.

"What you need, boy?" The hint of something sour carried on his breath.

"Wanted you to know I'm here checking the fields."

"Why waste your time?" Mr. Goodman's face twisted.

"The Army intends to fulfill its contract with you." Sid tried to peer around him to see if Anna'd made it home. He stepped back when it became clear Mr. Goodman wouldn't invite him in. "Good night."

The door slammed in his face. "All right." Sid spun on his heel. He walked the edge of the nearest field and started to cut through it. The sound of a booming voice carrying on the wind through a window halted his progress. He strained to hear the words.

"Girl, you're one to sass me. Home an hour, and I get nothing but disrespect. Get over here and clean up this mess."

The yelling tapered off, and Sid hesitated. The cause wasn't his business. Maybe the man lived life angry. That would explain why everyone had left. Which developed first? The leaving, the anger, or the drinking?

The thought of his brother-in-law and the way he harangued Pattie left Sid's blood boiling. He couldn't protect Pattie across the miles, but he refused to let anyone treat another woman that way. He started across the yard to the house.

A door bounced open and then slammed shut. Sid looked toward the sound and saw Anna leave the house, muttering under her breath. Her head was down, shoulders hunched as if protecting herself from the next shell her father would lob.

She scooped up a bucket, where it listed against the side of the house, and hurried toward the barn. Headed to do chores? Her face looked pale with splotches of color in the middle of her cheeks. He followed in case she needed help. Though he could imagine her response. He surveyed the fields. There wasn't much he could do about them until he returned with his group of POWs.

Anna disappeared around the corner of the barn, and he picked up his pace. A small shack stood tucked in its shadow. The cacophony coming from the ramshackle hut indicated it was a chicken coop. Her steps slowed as she neared the door, then slipped inside.

Five minutes later Sid lounged against the side of the barn when she stepped outside. "Need help with the chores?"

She startled and juggled the basket, mouth open as she stared at him. "What are you doing here?"

A lazy grin creased his face. "I told you I'd keep an eye on the farm. I'm a man of my word."

"We can't pay. Anything."

"The United States Army takes care of my pay, ma'am."

The tightness around her eyes eased, and the redness to her eyes almost disappeared in the tinge of laughter. "So they have. I imagine you have other tasks than keeping an eye on a failing farm."

"Not once my prisoners are assigned." He reached for the basket, and their fingers brushed. Electricity flowed between them, and he swallowed hard. "Let me help you with that, then we can get to anything else that needs to be done."

She chewed on her lower lip as her glance darted toward the house then around the yard. She seemed determined to look anywhere but at him. Finally, her gaze landed on him, and she squared her shoulders as if reaching a decision. "I'd like that, but only if you quit calling me *ma'am*."

He dipped his head. "All right." He considered her a moment. "Who does the work when you aren't here?"

"I don't know. Papa must drag himself out of the house most days. But sometimes when I get here, the poor cow looks so miserable I wonder when he milked her last." She pushed a blonde curl behind her ear, but it refused to stay in place. His fingers itched to reach out and brush it back. "He milks and does the other chores when he gets thirsty or hungry. He wasn't always like this. But now he's unbearable. I dread coming home but feel like I have to or there won't be anything for my brother to return to when this war finally ends." Her hand covered her mouth probably to stop more from escaping.

Sid slipped a hand into a pocket and rocked back on his heels. "Look, instead of standing here in the yard, let me take you to dinner. Give you a break for a bit." Her forehead crinkled as she frowned at him. "Think of it as a chance to educate me about the farm. What works best. What to avoid. Between us we'll keep the farm running."

She opened her mouth, then closed it. "There's a lot to do, and I only have until Sunday."

"All the more reason to accept my offer. And give me some way to contact you during the week if I have a question." He quirked an eyebrow at her in his best Clark Gable impression and waited.

"What's keeping you, girl? I'm starving in here." The bellowing carried from the house to their position. Anna squared her shoulders and set her chin.

"I accept. But on one condition."

"What?"

"You milk the cow while I make a quick supper for Papa. I need to know he gets at least three days of good meals a week." She hurried toward the house before he could stop her or claim that contact information.

He entered the barn's interior and waited for his eyes to adjust. He eased down the aisle toward the cow standing in her pen. He stared at the large animal, then swallowed when he spied her bulging udder. Was now a good time to mention he didn't know the first thing about milking a cow? Guess he'd learn the old-fashioned way, good ol' trial and error. If he was lucky, he might just have the task completed before Anna joined him.

He grabbed the empty pail he'd carried in and eased into the stall. The cow stamped her feet impatiently and kept her eyes on him.

Then again, he might be branded by the cow's hoof.

CHAPTER 5

MAY 12, 1944

*T*he sound of Nellie pounding the stall with her hooves sent Anna running back into the barn. All thoughts of fixing a meal for Papa were pushed aside by the image of Nellie kicking Sid. She turned the corner and found Sid cowering in the stall as far from Nellie as he could get. The docile cow had backed him into the corner. Her hind feet tap-danced, while her tail twitched his side like a switch. He clutched the milk bucket in his hand and grimaced when he caught her watching.

Anna tried to wipe all expression from her face as she eased into the stall.

"Here, Nellie. That's a good girl."

Nellie approached her, freeing Sid.

"You can come out of the corner now."

Sid hurried around the edge of the stall until he stood next to Anna. "You didn't warn me she's violent."

"Oh, she's not. You must have riled her. What did you do?"

Color flushed Sid's cheeks, and Anna wondered if she'd somehow pushed too far. "I'll have you know I didn't do anything. Just sat down and started pulling on those … things … trying to get the milk to come."

"You haven't milked before?" Anna laughed at his expression. "Here, stand next to me, and I'll show you how. Next time she won't back you into the corner." He settled behind her while she explained milking as she stripped Nellie dry. The cow mooed in relief, and as the bucket filled, Anna could understand why. Papa simply wasn't getting the poor cow milked often enough. Keep that up and her milk might dry up.

Once the pail was filled and covered, Sid carried it to the porch. He stared at

309

Anna as she paused with her hand on the door. "Still want to have dinner with me?"

Anna looked at the house. Anything sounded better than going inside. "I still have to get Papa supper. I'll fix him a quick sandwich, and then we can leave." She made the food, then followed Sid to the truck. The meal passed full of awkward pauses. He asked questions about the farm interspersed with requests for her phone number. She finally gave it to him to end that conversation thread. The more questions he asked about the farm, the more she revealed how much she didn't know.

"I don't want to talk about the farm anymore."

"Why? Afraid you'll find something I know more about than you do?"

She refused to rise to the bait. Instead, she sat with arms crossed, looking at him. "Why did you decide to be mean?"

"You put me in a stall with a crazy cow."

"She's sweet. You didn't know what to do with her."

Sid shrugged. "And your dad doesn't have a problem with alcohol."

Her mouth dropped open as her eyes widened. "What did you say?"

"He stumbles around and always has the telltale smell on his breath, or aren't you home often enough to notice?"

"He does not have a problem with alcohol." She pulled her napkin from her lap and threw it on the table. Even if he did, that was her responsibility. She didn't need some soldier to act better than her because of Papa's struggles. "I'm ready to go home."

"Fine." Sid stalked to the counter to pay. The drive home was filled with terrible silence.

All week she couldn't get their argument out of her mind. Why should she care what he thought? She'd hardly known him a few days. Over the next few days, she tried to force her thoughts to anything but Sid Chance as the bus rattled to a stop outside the gated entrance to the Kearney Army Airfield. Each time she passed the guardhouse, Anna thought one good puff from the Big Bad Wolf or other enemy would blow the structure over, removing any deterrent to entering the complex. If the Germans ever made it to Nebraska, the guard shack certainly wouldn't stop them.

Why couldn't she get that obnoxious serviceman out of her mind?

A soldier waved the bus through, and Anna stifled a yawn. Ever since her weekend home, she'd struggled to regain her normal routine in Kearney. This morning she'd met the bus on time only because Dottie prodded.

Usually, returning to the daily cycle wasn't a problem. The hard work on the farm filled her days at home as her job at the factory did in Kearney. Her evenings evaporated in slow minutes in the Wisdoms' parlor with the other boarders. This week, though, the Wisdoms' youngest son, Andy, came down with something and barked through the nights. It felt like his bed stood next to hers, separated by only a paper-thin wall. No matter how she tossed and turned, Anna couldn't block out his coughs. And Sid invaded the dreams that peppered her erratic sleep.

A cloak of helplessness followed her steps. The intricacies of farming eluded her. Papa had trained Brent on those, fully intending him to partner with Papa until he took over. A sigh escaped at the thought of Brent being so far away when he should be here. If he was, life and Papa could return to routine.

"Earth to Anna." Dottie pinched Anna's shoulder.

"Ouch. What was that for?"

"You disappeared somewhere. Didn't want you to miss our stop."

The driver ground the bus's gears until the vehicle chugged to a stop in front of the warehouse that housed the parachute packers.

Anna rubbed the sore spot and frowned. "I can think of less painful ways to catch my attention."

"Sure, but not nearly as enjoyable."

"You and your warped sense of fun."

Dottie grinned and grabbed her purse. "Spend a day with my family, and you'll understand why." She stood and inched her way down the aisle. "Come on, slowpoke. Time to get to work saving all our airmen."

Dottie's flippant tone grated. Anna prayed over each parachute, asking God to protect the man assigned to it. And invariably Brent invaded those prayers. He piloted a B-17 like the ones processed at Kearney. The big bombers served as a daily reminder of the danger he flew into with each mission.

"Wow, you're even more morose. Don't worry about him." Dottie linked arms with Anna as they walked to the warehouse. "Brent's fine."

Dottie knew her too well after rooming together for a year. Anna worried her bottom lip between her teeth. "We haven't received a letter in weeks."

"That you know of."

"True." Surely Papa hadn't forgotten to show her any of Brent's letters. "No word must mean everything's okay. That he's busy. But …" Her mind filled in all kinds of alternatives.

"Let's focus on what we can do. And that's pack these parachutes so the boys are as safe as we can make them."

Anna stashed her lunch bag, purse, and jacket into the locker next to Dottie's. Time to concentrate on what mattered right now. That meant doing her job thoroughly and well. One mistake could have far-reaching consequences she didn't want to consider.

The day eased by, and Anna fought to stay focused on the intricate pattern she folded into the silk. Some days the work felt mindless though demanding precision, perfect to ponder other issues. Today, that routine propelled her thoughts back to the farm.

Somehow she had to figure out a schedule for cultivating the crops. They couldn't afford another off year. She couldn't imagine paying the mortgage and taxes plus surviving on what she made at the base. A solution existed. Somewhere. Maybe one of the men from church would help. If she could only get Papa to join her, she knew his friends would ease him from his cave.

"Miss Goodman."

Anna's head snapped up as Corporal Robertson's voice sounded close to her ear.

"Yes, sir?"

"You haven't moved in fifteen minutes. Are you feeling well? Or do you think the war is in hand and we no longer need to work hard to stay ahead of Hitler?"

Anna opened her mouth, coherent thoughts abandoning her as they flew through her head. She caught Dottie's grimace and counted to ten instead. "I'm sorry, sir. I didn't realize I'd stopped."

"See that you work. Too many men depend on the job you do."

He strode between the rows of women, and Anna relaxed as his attention diverted to other unfortunate gals.

"Have you heard from Specialist Chance?" Dottie leaned toward her with an eager light in her eyes.

"No. You'd know if I had. Goodness, you're my roommate and best friend."

"I hoped I'd missed a note or a call. He's so good-looking."

Anna rolled her eyes. "You need a new pair of glasses, then." Sure, he was nice enough, but she'd always gone for the tall blondes. Sid was average height with dark hair creeping out from under his cap. She fully expected that the next time she saw him, if there was a next time, some Army barber would have shorn his hair back to the scalp again.

"Looks are fine, but there's something deeper in him, too."

"Now wait a minute, Dottie. When have you seen him?"

Dottie blushed and looked down at the silk overflowing her lap. "I may have bumped into him at a USO dance or two."

"And you never introduced us?"

"Why would I do that? Besides, you aren't interested, remember?" Dottie's grin telegraphed that she saw through Anna's protests.

Anna clamped her mouth shut before she said anything she might not regret but should. One thing about having a best friend, she knew how to dive under the layers and protections Anna'd developed. Was Dottie jealous? Sid was a nice man, but he certainly hadn't done anything to indicate he'd focused on her in more than a helpful manner. And they hadn't parted on good terms.

Whether she wanted to admit it, she needed his help. The farm required the prisoners' labor to continue.

She'd simply stop spending anything beyond the bare necessities so she could pay the prisoners. Pressure built behind her eyes. That money should pay the property taxes, but without crops there'd be no reason to pay. If only she could delay payment. What had Papa been thinking? They didn't have the money and they didn't have a way to transport the prisoners. Did the Army charge extra for that?

Her stomach tightened at the image of prisoners on the farm. Papa could take care of himself. But Germans there felt unsafe. It felt like bringing the war squarely to their corner of Nebraska. Not just this war, but the Great War, too. The fact remained that no other source of labor existed. Not while most young men wore uniforms and all other able bodies worked in the war industry.

Maybe a neighbor could deliver the prisoners to the farm every other day for awhile. If only a couple of them worked there consistently, the money might stretch to pay the forty-cents-an-hour wages. She'd have to play with the numbers and cut back her expenses, but it might be enough to turn the farm around. More men more often wouldn't cost as much as a large group once a week. And the results might be better.

A spark of hope warmed her. She'd have to talk to Papa, but maybe she could pull this off and save the farm after all. Even if it required working with Specialist Chance.

CHAPTER 6

MAY 19, 1944

Silence filled the truck as the eight men jostled against each other. Each day this week, Sid had transported prisoners to the Goodman farm. The prisoners rocked, serious expressions painted on their faces. Franz usually loved the chance to get out of the camp and into the open air for a day, but today he sat slumped in the seat, the brim of his hat pulled over his eyes. Next to him, Otto sat, back ramrod straight as if condemned to a firing squad. Five other prisoners bounced around the bed of the truck. He'd drop them off at a neighboring farm after Franz and Otto were settled at Goodman's. It still surprised some civilians that the prisoners didn't require a guard, but the prisoners were grateful for the work and variety. It helped that they were even paid.

"All right. Someone explain the long faces."

Both looked straight ahead. Franz's Adam's apple bobbed up and down as he swallowed. Hard.

"Either of you sick?"

More quiet.

"Unable to work?"

Their stoic looks didn't falter.

"Fine. I can get to the bottom of this now or after the others are settled at the Berkeley place. If you lose time, it's not my fault."

Otto looked at him quickly, then glanced back to the road. "We not like the man."

"Shhh!" Franz nudged Otto into the door.

Sid looked at them, then back at the road. "Which man? Mr. Goodman?"

Franz's chin dropped in a quick nod. "It true."

"Why? There has to be a reason."

"He yells when we there and you are not. Blames us for ..." Franz whirled a finger in the air as if trying to find the right word. He shrugged. "He not nice. Not like you."

"His farm needs the labor, and you two are the perfect fit. This will be where you work three days a week. More as we get closer to harvest or detassling."

"Not mind hard work." Otto rubbed his hands together and then held them to his nose and inhaled as if taking in the aroma of dirt. "I love land. Much better than battle."

Franz nodded.

"If there's a problem, let me know. I'll take care of it."

The men nodded, but their faces made Sid wonder if they'd follow through.

The program of prisoners helping as labor on farms was still in its infancy. Some counties and communities had embraced the program as the answer to the severe labor shortage. Other farmers and towns resisted the idea of having the "enemy" on their farms. After Anna's reaction that first time, it didn't surprise Sid that Mr. Goodman fell in the latter category.

That didn't change reality. The man needed assistance. Especially if he wanted to keep the farm a going concern until his son returned.

Sid dropped off Franz and Otto before continuing up the road. The two trudged toward the barn as if to a torture chamber. Sid continued to the Berkeleys'. Unlike their reticent neighbor, this family embraced the extra help. He often had to turn away as they invited the prisoners to the house to eat lunch and other violations of the rules. If more families treated the prisoners like men and valued human beings, it would do more to end the threat of future misunderstandings and wars between the countries than anything else.

The prisoners jumped out of the truck as soon as it pulled into the Berkeleys' farm and hurried to the barn. Sid waited until he caught Tom Berkeley's eye. "I'll be back to get these men around four thirty. That okay?"

"Sure. I can keep them plenty busy until then."

"All right. Let me know if there are any problems."

Tom patted the shotgun that leaned next to him against his rusted pickup. "This girl and I have it covered. I don't expect trouble."

Sid turned the truck around and headed toward Goodman's.

Before he saw the house at the end of the lane, Sid heard screams. Instead of slowing the truck down, he whipped it next to the barn and braked hard. The motor coughed and went silent.

A bird sang its song somewhere nearby, but otherwise, a cast of silence covered the farm. What happened to the yelling he'd heard?

Sid scanned the distance between the house and barn, but saw nothing unusual. Might as well check on Mr. Goodman first. He climbed the steps to the porch and then pounded on the door. "Mr. Goodman?" He waited a moment but heard no answering call or footsteps. "Mr. Goodman, Specialist Chase here. Everything okay?"

It felt strange yelling at the man through the door. As he knocked again, the door slid open. Sid slipped inside.

"Is that one of you Krauts?" The slurred words filtered from a room behind the kitchen. "Show yourselves, cowards. Couldn't even fight like men, could you? Had to go and get captured. No wonder we beat you in the last war."

The insults trailed off, followed quickly by what sounded like a snore. Sid eased down the hallway, checking the rooms he passed. The kitchen and living area stood empty. When he reached the first bedroom, he found Mr. Goodman slouched over in a chair, an empty bottle of liquor next to him. Sid monitored him to make sure he still breathed before rousing him.

"Let's get you to bed."

Mr. Goodman mumbled something but staggered beside Sid as he led the man to the double bed. Once Mr. Goodman lay safely on the bed, Sid stepped back and watched him awhile. How often did the man allow himself to descend into a drunken stupor like this? If frequently, no wonder the farm stood in its current state. And if he yelled consistently, he understood why Franz and Otto cowered at the thought of working here.

Something had to be done, but what? He wouldn't fail Anna like he'd failed Pattie.

* * *

THE WEEK PASSED QUIETLY for Anna. Days filled with work, followed by nights at the Wisdoms'. Some evenings, everyone gathered around the cleared dining room table to play games. Others, Anna escaped to her room. Until Dottie slipped in, she'd have a few minutes to escape and pretend the war had ended and life somehow returned to normal.

As Anna sat in the hangar patching the silk wings on a plane Wednesday morning, the thought of routine made her snort. It felt like decades since her family had been together and eked out a living on the farm. That time had required hard work, too, but it hadn't seemed as daunting when they'd all gathered around the dinner table at the end of a long day.

Now Mama was gone, Papa had a drinking problem, and Brent fought somewhere in Europe. There was nothing she could do about Brent or Mama, and Papa was a puzzle. She longed to help him but didn't know how. She ran her thumbs over the pads of her fingers and winced at the thick calluses. Life had certainly changed. Anna dropped her needle and rubbed her hands up and down her arms against the sudden chill that engulfed her.

A bell sounded, startling her from her thoughts.

"Lunchtime. Come on, Anna." Dottie bounced from her seat and pulled Anna with her. "I think Mrs. Wisdom sent us sandwiches and fruit."

"She usually does."

"But today's might have real meat."

"Not a fan of Spam?"

"Think positively with me." Dottie's bright smile coaxed an answering one from Anna. "Maybe there's pheasant tucked between the bread."

"In May?"

"So? Nothing wrong with wishful thinking."

"You take it to an extreme, but I like the thought." Anna grabbed her lunch from her locker and followed Dottie into the lunchroom. Heat brushed over her as she passed the cafeteria line. Her nose wrinkled at the stale aroma of over-cooked hamburger surprise. "Let's find a table far away, okay?"

Dottie looked at her, concern filling her eyes. "You feeling all right?"

"I will once we eat."

"Let's do something different. You work too hard, and I have a remedy."

Anna stilled, the unwrapped sandwich partway to her mouth. This should be interesting.

"The USO's holding a dance tomorrow night. It would be good for both of us." A knowing grin creased her face as if she'd uncovered a winning argument. "It's our patriotic duty, you know. Spend time with the boys before they ship out. What does it hurt to forget about things like farm responsibilities for awhile? What do you say?"

"Thursday night?"

"Right. I'll even get you back to that prison of a farm Friday. You can still be the ultra-responsible daughter."

The idea actually sounded fun. Anna wouldn't mind an evening with the soldiers. Most were nice and wanted someone to spend a few minutes with while they talked about their girls back home. Sure, some prowled for prospects, but she easily spotted them.

"I guess it is my civic duty." Anna laughed at the thought. "Imagine Papa's reaction to that argument."

"Who cares? We'll put a spring in your step before you retreat to the farm and him."

The next night, Anna prepared with care. It felt good to spend time playing up her curls rather than pulling her hair out of her face. She appeared down-right feminine in a dress that swirled around her knees rather than work clothes. Dottie was right. Too much time had expired since she relaxed and had a diversion. She touched up her crimson lipstick, then followed a giddy Dottie to her car.

As soon as they pulled into the makeshift USO parking lot, Anna heard the wail of a saxophone and pounding of drums. Her toes tapped as the musicians poured out their tune.

"Wait until we get inside. This will be a good night." Dottie linked arms with Anna and pulled her through the door. "Can't you feel it?"

Anna sashayed into the large hall. Spring flowers decorated the windows and tables that lined the walls. A piano stood crammed in a corner and surrounded by a hodgepodge of players. She inhaled the aroma of flowers mixed with the press of bodies. Her shoulders relaxed, and knew Dottie was right. Tonight would be a good night.

Then her gaze landed on Specialist Chance. A lazy grin creased his face as he nodded her way. Was he pulling his dance partner closer? Anna gasped as he winked at her over the shoulder of the girl he spun around the floor. She turned her back and flounced to the refreshments table. She could hear Dottie's heels clack against the floor as she followed.

The music ended, and Anna didn't wish to see him after that display. Someone tapped her shoulder. Anna stiffened and resisted turning, until curiosity got the better of her.

"Dance with me?" Sid stood there, same easy grin on his face.

The insufferable man saw nothing wrong with what he'd done. Anna thrust a cup of punch at him. "Clutch this. It's the closest you'll get to holding me."

She spun and walked toward the entrance. Where had Dottie disappeared? Her friend had disappeared, but Anna had to get away from Sid and the laughter that chased her.

Why did he have to be so unbearable and easy on the eyes at the same time?

CHAPTER 7

MAY 25, 1944

*A*nna shimmered in the light, her blue dress skimming her figure as she hurried away. Sid couldn't take his eyes off her. She wouldn't disappear that quickly. He followed her to a corner, where she grabbed the arm of a gal who looked vaguely familiar, but then most of the gals here did. "Let's start again. Good evening, Miss Goodman."

She startled as she turned and met his gaze. "Specialist Chance. You don't give up, do you?"

"Not when it involves a beautiful woman."

The gal with her looked between the two of them, then unhooked arms with Anna. "Your first dance arrived. Told you it'd be fun." With a wave of her fingers, she headed toward the refreshments table, leaving the two of them alone.

Anna stared after her, a subtle stiffening to her stance.

The first notes of "Boogie Woogie Bugle Boy" filled the air, and Sid bopped his head to the beat. He cleared his throat and reached for her hand. "Join me?"

"What, the other girl won't dance anymore?"

"I'm not asking her."

"Maybe you should." She blew out a breath. "I am not another girl to add to a long list of conquests. If that's what you're looking for, then kindly leave." Sparks lit her eyes. She had no idea how enchanting her anger made her.

"No. You're the girl I want to dance with this evening." He offered his hand, and her chin tipped as if to challenge him, even as her hand slid into his.

"You really don't want to dance with me." A shadow of something like fear darkened her eyes.

"I can't imagine why not."

"I've danced with Clark Gable. He sets a high standard."

"That's funny. I've heard he has two left feet."

"Merely a rumor from *Gone with the Wind*." A smile softened her lips with a hint of promise that left him wondering.

He led her to the floor, and they started a quick jitterbug. By the time the song ended, color tinged her cheeks. The stress and worries that burdened her when he saw her on the farm evaporated before his eyes. Something about her captured him, made him want to learn more. The band slid into a beat that had some swing to it, and she followed his lead as if they'd practiced many times. It felt like they were in a Fred Astaire and Ginger Rogers movie as they glided around the floor with the other couples.

He lost track of time as the song melted into another. After three or four, he pulled her to the side. "How about some punch?"

"Sounds wonderful." She fanned her face. "I'm a bit out of practice."

"So how did I do?" He led her to the table and offered her a cup of the red liquid.

"What?" Mischief filled her eyes. "Well, I didn't jitterbug with Mr. Gable, so I can't compare. I'd say you held your own, soldier."

Sid wiped sweat off his brow. Anna took a drink, then placed her empty cup on a tray. Before she could say anything, a soldier approached her.

"May I have a dance, ma'am?"

Anna glanced at Sid, and he shrugged. Much as he'd like to keep her to himself, he didn't have the right any more than she should have been angry when she saw him with someone else. Even so, as she walked away on the other man's arm, his chest tightened. Maybe he'd need to change their status.

* * *

THE NEXT WEEK dragged as Sid wondered when he could see Anna again. The image of her from the USO filled his thoughts. She'd been so full of life. He wanted to learn how to bring the butterfly out of her self-imposed cocoon. She lived like she'd forgotten how to enjoy life.

He walked the perimeter of the Shivelys' sugar beet field. The denim shirts of a dozen POWs dotted the field, easy to spot among the low crop. Sid stifled a yawn. The morning had begun earlier than usual in order to get the men to the farm with plenty of time to work.

Word had spread. The demand for labor had him driving all over southern Nebraska.

At noon, the farmer's wife and children lugged out baskets filled with sandwiches and well water for the men. They dug in heartily, while Sid and Trent counted noses on their rounds checking on the prisoners. With so many here, it helped to have Trent along.

Sid stopped and counted again. "Tell me I've missed someone. We're short one."

"Impossible. Where would he go?"

"Get the list out of the truck. We should have a dozen men but don't."

Trent hustled to the truck and returned with the clipboard. "I double-checked. Twelve prisoners are on the roll."

Sid shoved his hands deep in his pockets as he struggled to explain how they had eleven. He couldn't imagine the flak if they lost a prisoner or one escaped.

"I count eleven, too." Trent tossed the clipboard at Sid, his face white as a sheet.

Trent stayed with the eleven and interviewed them without success while Sid spent the next hour scouring the farm .

Sid hung his head in his hands. "How does a prisoner disappear?"

"Do you want me to rouse the alarm at Camp Atlanta?" Trent looked at him like the answer better be *no.*

"No. I'll handle that and take the other prisoners back. I don't believe any of them saw anything."

Trent shrugged. "Maybe their jobs absorbed them."

"No, they're covering for their buddy." Sid scanned the horizon again. Nothing but fields surrounded them, with an occasional farmhouse visible on the horizon. "Round them up."

The drive to camp passed too quickly, and then he'd returned the prisoners to compound A and stood in front of the camp commander and tried to explain.

Commander Moss sat behind his desk, a dark scowl on his face. The man prided himself in running a tight ship without problems. "Where's Private Franklin?"

"Searching the farm, sir." Sid stood at attention, back stiff, as he waited for the verdict. Kitchen patrol couldn't be too terrible, right? His mom made sure he knew how to use a potato peeler. He'd survive KP.

Commander Moss ran his hands over his thinning hair, his eyes fixed in the distance as if developing a course of action. "You were at Fort Robinson with the war dogs, right?"

"Yes, sir."

"All right. Take five men and the bloodhounds. Sniff out the prisoner."

Sid swallowed and considered the task. He'd worked with many dogs but never bloodhounds. "Are they trained search dogs?"

"Consider this a training exercise. One that can't fail."

"Yes, sir."

"I'll notify the sheriff and town police. We have to find this man before he gets away."

Sid saluted, then collected five men from the barracks. A vague uneasiness filled him at the thought of using bloodhounds. He'd prefer any dog he'd trained at Fort Robinson instead.

None of the men he'd found had experience with war dogs, though a couple of them hunted. Hopefully, those skills would transfer to a search like this. "Either of you worked with dogs when you hunted?"

Blank stares met his, until one soldier nodded. "We had a mongrel who went with us. She was pretty handy at bringing back the fowl. She never treed a man, though, if that's what you mean."

"I'll take any experience. We'll pick up a few bloodhounds, then head to the farm. Private Franklin and I noticed this prisoner missing at lunchtime." Sid glanced at his watch. "It's now four. The other prisoners claim they didn't see him slip away. Since we can't pinpoint a time, he could have quite a head start on us. We'll begin on the farm, see what the hounds pick up. We'll fan out from there."

"And when we find him?"

"We bring him back. In one piece. We don't know he tried to escape."

"Sure. He wandered off."

"Maybe. Our job is to find him, not try him. Let's head out."

The men climbed into the bed of the truck, and after picking up the hounds at the barn, Sid returned to the Shively farm, which stood within a mile of the Goodman place.

Mr. Shively met the truck as it pulled to a stop at the barn. His overalls strained to contain his stomach as he marched toward them. "It's about time you got back. Private Franklin's searching the hills, while you're off gallivanting."

Sid took a deep breath and tamped down the flare of heat filling him. "Where is Private Franklin?"

"Off that way." Mr. Shively waved in a northerly direction. "You'd better find that German before something happens. Maybe he's headed to Kearney to sabotage the air base."

"Then he'll walk a long way." Sid turned and found himself face-to-face with seven other men. Some looked familiar, because they had prisoners at their farms periodically. "We'll find him."

The men stared at him with hard eyes, broad shoulders set in firm lines. One clutched a shotgun. Sid looked from man to man, taking each's measure. This situation could turn ugly in an instant, and he didn't want the fallout. He had to find the prisoner before the word spread to the locals and they turned into vigilantes. He hurried back to the soldiers and Mr. Shively where they waited by the truck.

"We'll break into groups of two each with a dog and head into the field the prisoners worked today." He watched the bloodhounds mill around. He didn't have any way to alert the dogs to the scent they should track. Without that, he doubted they'd help at all, even if they were trained. "Let's move. Private Franklin is somewhere in front of us. Keep your eyes open."

Hours later, as the sun sank low on the horizon, Sid wiped perspiration from under his cap brim. His feet were sore, his skin itched, and he hadn't the first clue which direction the prisoner had gone. The only good news was they'd found Trent.

"Any thoughts?"

Trent gulped a swig of water from his canteen. "We covered this farm. Unless we move to the next ones, we're done. Problem is which direction to explore. There's nothing to track."

"I'll head back to the farmhouse and call the command post. Maybe somebody had better luck."

Trent snorted. "This land's too wide open. There's nothing to stop him from walking to Kansas or hopping a train."

"But where would he run? His clothes are clearly labeled. He has no papers to get out of the country. And he's one of those who barely speaks ten words of English."

After checking with the camp, Sid told Trent that none of the search parties had found the prisoner yet. He also hadn't shown up in his barracks or anywhere else.

Sid returned to the group of men waiting on the ground around the truck. "Nobody's had any luck. We're to check the nearby farms. Trent and I will take his Jeep." He tossed the truck keys to another soldier. "You can drive the rest of the men back to Atlanta. Take the east road and check the farms on the way back. Don't forget the barns and out buildings."

After stopping at another farm, Trent pulled into the Goodmans' driveway. "You get to talk to Goodman."

Sid nodded and jogged to the door. Knock, ask his questions, and leave. It wouldn't take long, and they'd be off. Though, if Anna'd come home, he'd love an excuse to stay. One look inside the kitchen, and he forgot about Anna. The prisoner sat in a tall kitchen chair, Mr. Goodman leaning over him with a gun.

"Look what the wind blew in." Mr. Goodman limped toward Sid. "I was about ready to walk him to Camp Atlanta for you boys."

"I'll escort him to camp, sir." Sid approached the prisoner. He appeared unharmed, though an unusual glow filled his eyes. Sid eased between the two men, a knot forming in his belly that this prisoner might be a rare, hardcore Nazi. He'd return the man and let the commander sort out the prisoner's status.

Mr. Goodman pulled his gun to his chest, then nodded. "Get him off my property. He's the kind I fought in the last war. I don't like him on my farm."

"Come with me." Sid grabbed the prisoner's arm and tugged him to his feet. He looked Goodman in the eye. "Thanks for your help."

Mr. Goodman walked away without a word, then sank onto his chair and grabbed a bottle. He took a swig from it, clearly ignoring them. Maybe lost in a sea of memories from the earlier war.

Sid backed the prisoner out the door and into the Jeep. Trent raced back to Camp Atlanta while Sid kept his gun at the ready while he watched the prisoner carefully. Sid whispered a prayer that God would free Mr. Goodman and his family of the effects of the Great War.

CHAPTER 8

JUNE 1, 1944

*T*he day had worn on Anna, and exhaustion quickly pulled her into a deep sleep.

Round multicolored balls hung from the tree, and the scent of fresh-cut pine mixed with apple cider. Mama snuggled next to Papa on the couch, her hand tucked firmly in his. A soft expression crossed his face as he gazed at her. Anna watched from the chair beside the fireplace. Brent rolled on the ground with Patches, the Australian Shepherd that roamed the fields with the guys during the day and curled up in the kitchen at night. Strains of Bing Crosby crooning "White Christmas" cackled from the old phonograph.

Anna relaxed into the dream, reluctant to release the memories. Had only two years passed since love overflowed in her life?

"Good morning, sleepyhead."

Anna groaned as something or someone bounced onto her bed. She squinted up at Dottie. "Can't you let a girl sleep?"

"Not when we have to get to work. Come on. You'll miss the bus if you don't hurry."

"But I have a secret weapon."

"Oh?" Dottie cocked an eyebrow at her, tapping her fingers on her arms. "What could that be, pray tell?"

"Your car."

"Good ol' Stude." Dottie frowned even as she mentioned her beloved Studebaker. "He's low on gas, so if we want to get home tomorrow, we'll have to bus it today."

Anna rolled out of bed and reached for the coveralls waiting on the bedside chair. "These don't get any more glamorous."

"Nope. Each day they look the same."

"Good thing I'm not planning on turning any guy's head."

"Definitely won't if you don't hustle."

Anna tuned out Dottie's babble as she rushed to get ready for the factory. After running to catch the bus, Anna puffed out a breath of air. The morning held the promise of a hot day that could turn stifling in the parachute-packing area. Crates loaded with supplies for the jungle packs lined the room when they arrived.

Grabbing a canvas pack, she joined the line of women. First, she stuffed in a pair of leather gloves, then a large knife, compass, and fishhooks in a plastic container. She stepped to the next series of boxes and prayed that if a soldier ever used this pack, God would keep him safe. Field rations, mosquito lotion, matches, and a red fuse joined the other items. After adding several packets of medicine, Anna sealed the kit and added it to the growing stash. The supplies ran out before her prayers did.

The work didn't tax her, yet by the end of the day, she felt ready to crawl into bed and pull the covers over her head. Despite her prayers, the papers were filled with casualty lists.

Rumors flew that the big push to reenter the European continent would come this summer. She hated to imagine the loss of life bound to accompany such an assault. And Brent's crew lived and flew somewhere near the coming combat. He tried to keep his letter light, but Anna could sense things he couldn't write. Her heart clenched at the thought of the danger he faced each time his B-17 joined a bombing run. Too few crews experienced the success of the popular *Memphis Belle*. That B-17 crew's angels had worked overtime to bring them home after twenty-five missions.

If only Brent lived under the same protection. Anna wanted to hope. But reality forced her to be honest with herself.

No wonder her mind sought happier times during her dreams.

* * *

BETWEEN CHORES ON SATURDAY MORNING, Anna walked the periphery of the farmyard. The place looked worse than only a week earlier. Signs of neglect abounded from the peeling paint on the house to the loose boards in the fence around Nellie's pen. Good thing the cow was too old to run far even if she wanted.

God, I need some help here. Some fresh ideas to get Papa moving again.

As she walked, several options ran through her mind. Maybe she should quit her job at the air base. But what would they do without the cash? Maybe she could find someone to live here during the week. She thought of her purse balance and knew she couldn't pay anyone enough to put up with Papa.

The weight pressed into her until she feared she'd topple forward into the dirt. She didn't have the strength to pretend Papa was okay. But she also didn't know how to change anything. Life wouldn't change because she wished it.

Gravel spun under tires. Anna didn't recognize the pickup truck headed down the drive. It looked government issued. Her stomach churned at the idea that Specialist Chance brought a load of prisoners with him. She couldn't imagine who else would stop by the farm. Papa had pushed away all of their friends since Mama's death. She ran her hands across her pants, then pushed her hair behind her ears at the realization it must be Specialist Chance. She'd enjoy sparring with him, but Papa's mood wouldn't allow prisoners to swarm the fields.

She held her breath and shielded her eyes as she waited to see if anyone joined him.

Sid opened the door of the truck but didn't wait for anyone. "Morning."

Anna stepped back at the distance in his tone. He wasn't here to see her, and she tensed, waiting for him to explain his presence.

"I ..." Sid cleared his throat and shoved his hands in his pants pockets. "Anna, we need to talk about your father."

She hugged her arms around her middle. "What do you mean?"

"He didn't tell you about what happened?"

"You'd better explain what you mean."

"A prisoner wandered away from the Shively place. We tracked him here." Sid widened his stance as if to brace against her reaction. "Your father had him cornered in the kitchen with a gun at the ready."

A throbbing filled her temples. She tried to rub it away, but it only pounded harder. "I'll take care of it."

"How? You aren't here during the week."

"Sorry, I can't be here and do my part for the war effort. Maybe you should focus on keeping track of your prisoners. Seems that's the easy solution."

The silence stretched as red crept up his neck. Maybe Sid hadn't done anything to lose the prisoner, but she didn't care.

"I have work. As you pointed out, I'm only here on weekends." She hurried into the barn before he could see the tears pooling in the corners of her eyes. She waited until she heard the slam of the truck door before venturing toward Nellie. Even then, her hands trembled. She'd find a way to do something about Papa. She had to before he did something crazier than trapping a prisoner in their house.

* * *

SID SLAPPED his cap on the seat next to him. That woman could raise his blood pressure faster than anyone else. What gave her the right to walk away without finishing the conversation? Then again, what gave him the right to barge onto her farm to tell her everything she did wrong?

It wasn't her fault her father acted crazy. Nor did she have anything to do with the prisoner escapade.

He pointed the truck back toward Camp Atlanta. Much as he might wish to be anywhere else right now, his duty lay there. The ribbing from the guys hadn't stopped since he and Trent brought the prisoner back. What bothered him was that he still didn't know how the guy slipped away. Post intelligence had spent time with him, but answers weren't any clearer than Wednesday.

The system had built-in slack. Only so many soldiers stationed at Camp

Atlanta could serve as guards. Most farmers checked out their prisoners as needed, with no supervision at all. Mid day checks weren't even required, but if Sid and Trent hadn't checked it could have been days before they found the prisoner. It had to happen at some point. With almost three thousand prisoners, sooner or later one would disappear or try to escape. The next escapee would learn from this attempt. The Goodman farm required a wide berth if you wanted a change of scenery.

He'd learned too. Not to

Maybe Sid would get lucky and get moved to one of the satellite camps springing up across the state. Then he might escape the reputation as one of the only soldiers to lose a prisoner.

He glanced at his watch and pressed down on the accelerator. Commander Moss wouldn't appreciate him arriving late to the policy-and-procedures meeting, an emergency conference in response to the fiasco.

He pulled into a spot in front of the administration building and hopped out. The building mirrored the others on base. The Army Corps of Engineers had spread a concrete foundation of roughly 25 by 150 feet and thrown up tar-sheeting walls and a roof.

The camp wasn't designed to last more than a few years, just till the war ended. A far cry from the permanence of the brick buildings and barns that lined the parade grounds at Fort Robinson.

Sid opened the door and took a chair toward the back of the lecture room.

"Nice of you to join us, Specialist Chance." Commander Moss frowned at Sid. "Approach the front and update everyone about the escape."

Sid hesitated as he tried to collect his thoughts. He stood and briefed the assembled officers. "Any questions?" When there were none, he sank onto his chair.

"Here's how procedures will change." Commander Moss's voice carried easily across the assembled men. "We haven't had trouble to date, and frankly, we've been fortunate. I've already assigned men to work more closely with each camp liaison as we screen prisoners to detect troublemakers. We'll also watch for homesick blokes now." Moss paced the front of the room. "Our job is to get these men safely through the duration so we can send them home to their country and families." He paused and pierced Sid with his stare. "We can't end the prisoner program on farms. Their labor is too valuable, and it keeps them occupied in productive endeavors. We'll have no more than ten prisoners to every two guards. As soon as the prisoners become proficient, we'll lower the number at each farm.

"The key: remain vigilant. We don't want this to happen again. Let's work with the community to keep the prisoners content. Hopefully, we won't face many more of these situations."

Sounded great to Sid, but how would it really work? There were too many prisoners to monitor. Too many needs to meet.

CHAPTER 9

JUNE 4, 1944

The smell of bacon sizzling on the stove filled the kitchen. Anna hoped it would pull Papa out of bed. She'd leave for church in an hour, and he needed to make the trip with her.

Her mind and heart continued to seesaw between disappointment and hope. Yesterday's announcement that the invasion of France had started had sent her hopes and fears skyrocketing as she whispered prayers for all the boys in uniform. Then, the news that the attack hadn't started flooded her with relief, followed by anxiety that the battle would come.

How could she focus on Papa when so many other crises erupted all over the world?

Nobody else would take care of Papa, and he certainly didn't care. All week she'd prayed about what to do. All she could think was he needed to get out of the house and focus on something or someone other than the grief he clung to. What better place to start than with a worship service? He hadn't attended one with her since Mama's funeral. It was high time he focused on important matters and relationships.

Anna tucked an errant strand of hair behind her ear. Getting him out of bed before noon would be challenge enough. She'd let the bacon talk for her.

Twenty minutes later, the eggs and bacon had cooled, the toast toughened.

"I won't give up that easily." Anna marched toward his bedroom door. She squared her shoulders and knocked. "Papa, time to get up. Breakfast is getting cold."

A noise like a grunt served as his response.

"Now, Papa. You know you like a hot breakfast. Come on. It's after nine, and I finished the chores hours ago."

"Go away."

"Not until you talk to me." Anna stamped her foot. Why was he so insufferable?

Curses echoed against the door as he stomped around his room. He threw open the door, and Anna jumped back. A dark cloud covered his features, contorting them into a mask. "What do you want?" With each word, his voice rose until he yelled the last.

Anna tipped her chin up and stared. "If you'd care to put your robe on, breakfast is served."

"I ain't hungry."

"Well." Anna floundered. Where had her conviction fled? Somewhere into the anger boiling in his eyes. He had to change, and she'd do whatever she could to force the subject. "Papa, I'd like you to go to church with me."

He sputtered. "What gave you a crazy idea like that, girl? I vowed at your mama's funeral that I would never darken the door of a church again. God didn't care for her, and she was a good woman."

"That's not true. He loves us all. Papa, something is eating away at you. It'll destroy you if we don't do something. I can't stand to watch that happen any longer. Please."

A flicker of pain flashed across his face. He shouldered past her as if pushing the memories and emotions behind him. "I think I'll eat some of that breakfast now."

Anna sagged against the doorframe. She wouldn't give up; he meant too much to her. He flopped onto a chair at the table, then shoveled food on his plate. By the mound heaped there, he'd be eating long after she left.

"I'll be back after service."

Papa didn't bother to answer as she grabbed her hat and purse and headed out the door.

The old, unpredictable Ford practically laughed at her when she tried to start it. That's why she preferred to walk most places, but she wouldn't get to church in time if she did. After several false starts, it roared to life. She glanced at the gas gauge and hoped enough remained to get her to town and back. The white clapboard Cornerstone Community Church building finally came into view. The church nestled in the heart of Holdrege, across the street from a gas station. If only the station were open. Papa would have to find gas next week.

Gus Powell and Teddy Whitaker stood by the front door, opening it for the families hurrying into the sanctuary. Salt and pepper colored their hair, and their shoulders sloped, evidence of the long days each had worked throughout their lives. The two used to sit by the fire at her house for hours in the winter, playing checkers and chess with Papa. Maybe they'd come today.

Anna's steps quickened at the thought. Help might be that simple to arrange. They'd known her papa since grade school. The long tales they liked to weave might help him forget his troubles and pull him back into the thick of life.

"Well, hello, Miss Anna." Gus wolf whistled. "Don't you look smart."

Anna held out her navy polka-dot skirt and twirled. Her hand touched her chin as she curtsied to the two.

"Lovely as a picture." Teddy offered his arm, which she accepted. "Let me escort you in to the service."

"I'd love that. I have a question first."

"Shoot."

"Could you join Papa and me for dinner after church?"

"I don't see your daddy anywhere." Gus frowned as he pretended to search the sidewalk.

"I know." Anna shrugged. "I don't know what to do anymore. I thought your visit might ease him from his moods."

The large bell atop the church rang. Anna jumped at the loud sound that boomed from directly overhead. Teddy patted her arm.

"Let's get you inside. I'll bring this lug with me to dinner."

Tears pricked her eyes. "Thank you."

"Don't worry." Teddy's eyes clouded over, maybe with thoughts of his own dear wife in heaven. "Your daddy'll pull out of this funk he's in. It takes us all different amounts of time and prayer to move on. Besides, we'll help push him out if he's stuck."

Gus chuckled. "Pushing him'll be like convincing a pheasant to go where you want. Sounds like a good challenge to me."

Teddy walked Anna through the doors and toward a back pew. She settled in between Mrs. Manahan and the wooden arm. She shifted as she tried to find a comfortable position between the ledge and Mrs. Manahan's wide girth. The frown she shot Anna stilled her efforts. Mrs. Manahan had been her mother's best friend, but she disliked disruptions of any kind, especially those that didn't fit in the life-or-death category.

While Pastor Reynolds intoned the announcements, Anna tried to create a menu for lunch. Gus and Teddy were simple men, widowers who'd walked the road Papa now lived. Anna hoped they could reach him where she'd failed. The organ burst into life, and Anna stood with the rest of the congregation. The men would be happy to eat anything they hadn't cooked. If only the cupboard weren't so bare. She shook herself. She'd think of something. This meal would be worth every bit of effort.

The service passed in a blur as Anna's thoughts ping-ponged between prayers for Papa and Brent and flurries of fear that Papa would reject his friends. She hated that possibility, but what else could she do?

After the service, she lingered toward the back of the church while she waited for Gus and Teddy. Gus seemed intent on greeting every person who'd attended ... again, and Teddy straightened the abandoned hymnals and Bibles. Anna tried not to rock, even though she knew how antsy her papa would be getting.

Finally, Anna glanced at her watch and headed toward Gus. She waited, hands clutching her purse, while he greeted Mr. and Mrs. Conway. "I'm heading to the farm unless you and Teddy need a ride."

"Oh no, we'll be fine." He turned his broad smile on another family. "See you next week."

What would the pastor do without Gus to welcome everyone? Anna smiled in spite of the vise that gripped her stomach. "All right. Come as soon as you can."

Gus scanned the emptying sanctuary. "Shouldn't be much longer." He whistled sharply, causing Anna to jump. "Right, Teddy?"

"What?" The man stopped collecting the Bibles he was placing back in the pews and frowned at Gus.

"We'll be at the Goodman place soon."

"Sure, sure." Teddy shook his head and muttered as he returned to work.

Anna slipped out before anyone could stop her. As soon as she reached the house, Papa started grumbling.

"Where have you been? I'm downright starved."

"At church. I'll have dinner ready in a minute."

"Church? This long? This is exactly why it's a waste of time to attend."

Anna's heart clenched at his harsh words. She grabbed one of Mama's aprons. "Could you grab some potatoes from the cellar?"

Mumbing under his breath, he shuffled from the room in the general direction of the cellar.

Anna rubbed her forehead, trying to ease the pain that pounded whenever Papa came near, then set to work slicing ham. A few minutes later Papa returned with a handful of potatoes and one onion.

"Thank you." Anna set to work cleaning and dicing both. By the time Gus and Teddy pulled into the yard, the room smelled like ham, potatoes, and biscuits.

"Papa, you've got company."

"What on earth?" He looked up from the paper, a frown etched on his face.

"Come and see." Anna peeked out the window, a new hope rising in her as her father's old friends climbed from a pick-up.

She hurried to the back door and when she opened it Gus and Teddy stood on the step, faces wreathed with grins. Papa glared at her and then his friends.

Gus entered, strode to the table, and stuck out his hand. "Where you keeping yourself, stranger? We've missed you at the café."

"I'll be. Have a seat."

Papa seemed to relax as the men chatted about nothing at the table. She leaned against the sink and soaked in the sound of his laughter. It'd been so long since she'd heard the once-familiar sound.

Soon She set the platters of food on the table and served the simple meal. Then she walked into the living room, tears streaming down her cheeks, and listened.

Maybe God had heard her prayer for help.

Three hours later, when Dottie picked her up, Anna wasn't so sure. Papa shut down the moment Gus and Teddy left. Then, he turned on her, rage mottling his face.

"I don't like you interfering, girl." He stormed around the kitchen, then flipped on the radio with a force that had it rocking on the counter. "Leave Gus and Teddy out of this."

She'd backed into a wall in an attempt to stay out of his reach. She didn't want to think what Papa would have done if Dottie hadn't arrived. Anna had never seen him like this. And after he'd been friendly with his buddies. She didn't understand the mood swings.

All she knew was she didn't think she could come home again. But if she didn't, who would ensure there was a farm left when this war ended and Brent finally came home?

As Dottie's Stude rattled down the road away from the farm, Anna realized Sid hadn't appeared all weekend. Had Papa scared him away, too?

CHAPTER 10

JUNE 5, 1944

A knock rattled the door to Anna's bedroom at the Wisdoms'. She cracked her eyes but couldn't see anything. She groaned and rolled over. Why would anyone pound on their door in the middle of the night?

Dottie elbowed Anna when the door shook again. "Go see what's up."

Anna stifled a yawn. "Why me? You're the night owl; you get it."

"Oh no. It can't be good news." Dottie's voice sounded strangled.

Reaching for her robe, Anna slid out of bed. "Who is it?"

"Mr. Wisdom. I think you'll want to come downstairs, ladies. There's news on the radio."

Anna tied her belt and hurried to open the door. She cracked it. "Thank you. We'll be right there." What could be so important after FDR's fireside chat earlier that day about the fall of Rome?

Hot cups of peppermint tea sat on the kitchen table when Anna and Dottie shuffled into the room. Anna wrapped her arms around her stomach, desperate to still the tremor. The Wisdoms and other boarders sat huddled around the kitchen table and the radio.

"Someone tell me what's happening." Dottie's voice cracked on the words.

Mr. Wisdom motioned her to a chair. "General Eisenhower launched the invasion of France."

Anna relaxed. "Probably another false alarm. You know how the rumors have flown."

"No, the reports sound real, but we're only hearing random details." Jessica Ferguson hunched in a chair. Anna wondered if Jessica's thoughts focused on her fiancé, who'd shipped to Britain months ago. As part of the infantry, he'd surely participate in the real invasion.

Anna glanced at the wall clock. Almost two a.m. She wished an announcement, any announcement, would come. Was the invasion real? How was it going? Were the casualties high?

The murmur of voices soon overshadowed the radio broadcast.

"Shh." Mrs. Wisdom smiled as she waved everyone down. "I know we're all anxious, but no one can hear if we're all talking."

Uncomfortable silence settled on the room. The strains of an orchestra flowed from NBC. While it sounded nice, it wasn't what she wanted to hear.

"IN A FEW SECONDS, we will take you to London for the first eyewitness account of the actual invasion of France by sea—of the landing of Allied troops on a French beachhead. War correspondent George Hicks saw those landings from the bridge of an Allied warship, and thru the ingenuity of radio wire recording, the National Broadcasting Company is able to give you the story as witnessed by George Hicks in a pool broadcast. So, now, NBC takes you to London for the first eyewitness account of the actual invasion of Europe!"

ANNA HELD her breath as nothing but static came across. The seconds ticked by while Dottie chewed on a fingernail. The subdued voice of George Hicks filled the room. Anna released a breath as the noise of planes passing overhead served as a backdrop to his narrative. In mid-sentence, static again interrupted, and everyone groaned.

The group stayed glued to the radio through the early morning hours, no one able to tear themselves away from the sporadic updates. Yet the musical interludes drove Anna crazy. It didn't seem right to have swing music playing when the infantry attacked the beaches of France.

"It's really started." Anna's heart constricted. Where was Brent? Did he man one of the bombers paving the way for the infantry? She tried to pray for him and all the other boys she knew fighting somewhere around the world.

God, help them. Help them all.

THE NEXT MORNING dawned much too early. Anna buried her head under the pillow, wishing for the oblivion of dreams. There war didn't exist, Mama still lived, and life felt normal. Reality intruded with the sun's rays.

"Do you think anyone will work today?" Dottie's sleepy voice tugged at Anna.

"Until we know, we have to treat it like every other day."

Dottie propped herself up on her elbows. "Are you kidding? We're finally doing something offensive in Europe. That doesn't make today like yesterday or last week."

The image of American boys scrambling to reclaim French soil from the German Army flooded her mind. Anna tried to block out the accompanying sight of bombs exploding and bullets flying. "What else do you want to do? Curl up here and pretend nothing happened? Or get back to work and do something that will help all those soldiers? Maybe today some of the men are wearing the parachutes we packed." She sighed and wiped her hands across her face. "We have to go to work until they tell us to go home. There's too much left to do."

"I hate this feeling." Dottie threw back the covers. "It's like I'm sitting on pins and needles, waiting to see if the assault worked."

"We won't learn anything staying in bed."

When the bus reached the air base, a buzz filled the air, this one not caused by the B-17s flying overhead. Instead, nervous energy seemed to consume everyone, as if they couldn't decide whether to work harder than ever for the boys invading the beaches of France or run to the nearest church and pray.

* * *

SID EXAMINED his group of men. In the aftermath of the Normandy invasion beginning, Commander Moss had each group running through their paces. They'd be well-oiled units either to avoid a repeat of a prisoner disappearing or to join the battle overseas. Each time Sid thought about the fiasco, he wanted to head straight to the nearest battle. France would suit him just fine.

"Ten-hut! To the lecture hall." Commander Moss wanted the rank and file to hear more about the escape, disappearance, loss, whatever you wanted to call it. Sid called it embarrassing.

An hour later, Sid was more than ready to get away from Camp Atlanta for awhile. He accepted the assignment to deliver a load of prisoners to the Kearney air base with a grin. Trent joined him for backup, and they rounded up the skilled carpenters from among the prisoners.

The wind whistled through the truck's lowered windows as miles rolled along. The drive took a little over an hour, then Sid popped the truck in neutral and presented the paperwork at the guard station.

"Do you know where you're headed?" The baby-faced soldier hardly looked old enough to carry a gun, and he served as the first line of defense? Guess sabotage wasn't a big concern.

Sid glanced at the papers. "Nope. Want to point us in the right direction?"

"Head down this road and turn left at your first chance. Follow that road till you see the signs."

"Thanks." Sid put the truck in gear. "We'll be there in no time."

Trent eased lower in the seat and leaned against the backrest. "So what do we do while the prisoners work?"

"Keep an eye on them."

"And any pretty girls we spot?" Trent let out a wolf whistle. "Those girls look like they could use some new friends."

"Focus. We've got a job to do."

"Babysit a few prisoners who'd stand out like a sore thumb if they tried anything? Give me a real job." A sour frown sagged Trent's face. "Days like today I want to join the fight overseas."

"You and me both. But Uncle Sam, in his wisdom, has us stationed here. So let's complete the assignment. Our day could still come, but only if we do what's needed now. Besides, someone has to take care of all the prisoners."

"Not what I signed up for."

"Maybe, but you get to follow orders."

"Can't blame a guy for wishing."

Sid thought about the guys trying to gain a foothold on the beaches of France. When would Camp Atlanta know more? The world was too big at times like this. The snatches of radio broadcasts Sid had heard only let him know the fight was real.

"Hey, isn't that the girl from Goodman's farm?" Trent poked Sid in the ribs.

Sid swerved to keep the truck on the road. "Watch it." Once he knew the truck wouldn't roll, he looked in the direction Trent pointed. "Looks like it. Let's get these prisoners dropped off."

"Then you can track her down and take her to lunch. You'd have better luck if you stopped and asked her now, while you know where she is."

Sid watched her walk the direction the truck had come from. For once Trent had a good idea. Finding her later could be impossible since he didn't know which building she worked in. And the idea of asking around for her did not appeal to him. He eased the truck into an open space on the side of the street. "Watch the boys."

"Yes, sir." Trent winked as he saluted. "Good luck, sir."

Sid slapped him with his cap before pushing it back on his head and hopping out of the truck. He glanced down the street and saw her about a block behind the truck. He hustled after her. "Anna."

She stopped, then eased toward him. A frown creased her face like she didn't like being stopped then the light of recognition dawned. "What are you doing here, Sid?"

"Wondering if you'd like to have lunch with me in a bit." He stood at ease while he waited. The seconds ticked by as she considered him.

"I still don't understand why you're here."

"Delivering some prisoners. Thought if you had time we could grab a bite."

A smile started in her eyes and spread to her lips. "I'd like that."

"Where can I meet you?"

"The mess hall is fine. I need to finish this errand. Can you meet me there in thirty minutes?"

Sid had no idea where the mess hall stood, but could find it if it meant spending time with the woman in front of him.

As if reading his mind, she stepped back. "See you then."

A honk interrupted his thoughts as he watched her walk away. After one more glance , he hurried back to the truck. Time to get the prisoners delivered.

After a few wrong turns, Sid pulled the truck in front of the building housing the post engineer. He and Trent turned the prisoners over to the corporal on duty and were told not to come back until five p.m.

They returned to the truck, and Trent leaned against it. "Guess you have plans for lunch."

"Want to join us?"

"And be the third wheel? No thanks. I'll find someone else to entertain with my charm. Meet you here at five." Trent walked away, whistling with his hands stuffed in his pockets.

Sid left the truck and headed in the general direction of the mess hall. He asked for directions a couple of times before finally locating the correct building. Like so many structures on base, the engineers had built it quickly and it already showed signs of wear from the harsh Nebraska weather. He didn't care what it looked like as long as the food was decent and he shared it with Anna.

She stood inside the door, foot tapping.

"Have you waited long?" He swiped his hat off and shoved it in his back pocket.

"No." Circles he hadn't noticed earlier shadowed her eyes. Even with her canvas work coveralls and fatigue, she carried herself like royalty.

He offered her his arm. "Let's feed you before you have to get back to work."

"I don't know that there's a rush today."

He quirked an eyebrow at her.

"Everyone seems distracted by the news, or lack of it, about the invasion. Have you heard anything?"

"Only what's on the radio."

"You'd think we'd have access to better information, working at military installations." She shrugged.

They traveled the cafeteria line, loading their trays with food, and then he led the way to a table. Time passed quickly as he told her stories of growing up in St. Louis. Their backgrounds were so different. Big city versus small-town farm. Large family versus small. Yet, as he watched her laugh at an indicent, he knew they could build a solid friendship. And if he could keep her laughing, maybe it could turn into something much more.

CHAPTER 11

JUNE 8, 1944

Sid watched as Luka and Otto worked alongside several other prisoners in one of the Goodman fields. The prisoners were getting the rhythm of pulling the weeds that grew between the wavy rows of corn. They'd come a long way since their first visit to the farm. Even so, it'd take several days to eradicate all the weeds that had sprung up since the last round of rain.

The sun beat down on Sid's head. He looked for shade but couldn't spot even a shrub to provide some relief. The prisoners had to feel the heat, too. The corn wasn't tall enough to provide even sporadic shade.

He glanced at the house. At many other farms, the prisoners would be invited in for lunch despite regulations. In turn, he'd disappear for a bit so the prisoners could break and interact with the families. The visitors had an intense curiosity about the American way of life. So much of what they'd learned in Germany didn't match the farms' reality. The exposure could only help in the post-war days.

"Specialist Chance?"

Sid turned to Luka. "Yes?"

Luka looked pale under his white cap. "May we break for water?"

"Grab your canteens from the truck."

Luka whistled, and the other prisoners gathered around him. As the weeks passed, Luka had stepped into a leadership role. He translated Sid's instructions accurately, making it easier on the prisoners and guards. In a few more weeks, Sid thought he could trust Luka to keep a small group of prisoners in line without a guard. Even with the escape attempt, the commander had decided the requests for labor plus sheer number of prisoners compared to the smaller group of soldiers stationed at Camp Atlanta and the satellite prisons made it critical to get as many prisoners as possible ready to work on their own. The administration clerks worked hard to match trusted prisoners with cooperative farmers.

Mr. Goodman wouldn't make that list anytime soon.

* * *

FRIDAY NIGHT, an Army truck sat next to the barn when Dottie pulled her car into the Goodman yard. Anna looked from the house to the truck. Hadn't Sid heard any of her arguments for why they couldn't afford any extra labor? Or had he come to see her? Heat climbed her neck at the thought. Since their lunch, she'd looked forward to seeing him again.

She eyed the house, a clamp of dread gripping her. If Papa remained in the same foul mood she'd left him in, she couldn't stay.

"Are you getting out or coming home with me?" The concern in Dottie's eyes softened the edge to her words.

"I'm sorry." Anna grabbed her bag and turned to Dottie. "I just hope Papa's ready for some company."

"You can always call, and I'll come get you." Dottie pulled her close for a hug. "It'll be okay, and you're only here until we can find some soldier to sweep you off your feet."

If only it were that simple. Dottie deliberately forgot that the farm didn't have a phone—or electricity, for that matter. The lines hadn't made it that far. And she refused to understand the depth of responsibility Anna carried. Maybe Dottie's multiple siblings at home made it easier for her to slide in and out of her homelife. She could work in Kearney and come home for fun. Anna came home to hold everything together for another week.

"Don't look now, but here comes your soldier."

Anna grimaced. "I do not have a soldier."

"Uh-huh. That's why you get a funny look on your face when you're thinking about him. Not to mention the rosy color in your cheeks." Dottie shrugged. "Whatever he is, he's headed this way. And I need to get home. Call if you need anything."

"Thanks for the ride." Anna squeezed a smile out and opened the car door. When she turned around, Sid stood there, a peaceful presence. She tapped down her irritation that mixed with a bewildering urge to run into his arms. "What are you doing here?"

"Nothing. Thought I'd come see if you need anything."

"I've told you we can't afford to pay the prisoners. Please take the men and leave." She fought the urge to cringe. Where had those harsh words come from?

His stance stiffened and his eyes hardened. "And I've reminded you your father signed a contract with the county extension agent." Sid crossed his arms. "Until that contract is cancelled, we'll keep coming."

"Wonderful. And what am I supposed to pay you with? Last year's leftover potatoes? The sugar beets nobody wants? No, I know. How about one of the cows we no longer own?" She sucked in a breath and held it a moment. "We don't have anything. And as long as Papa hides in the house, that won't change."

She fought the prickle of tears that tickled her throat. She would not cry in front of him. She crossed her arms and set her jaw.

Sid held up his hands, palms out. "Hey, I'm not the enemy. We're here to help. And if I could trust your father with the prisoners, I wouldn't come anymore."

The pain that assailed Anna at the thought of Sid not returning almost dropped her. Who would make sure she was okay each weekend? It wasn't his job, but he'd seemed to adopt her as one of his responsibilities. Or was it a duty? She cringed because s he wasn't anyone's duty. Not even a soldier who cared for no reason at all other than he wanted to.

Anna opened her mouth, but couldn't turn her thoughts into sentences. She must be more tired than she realized. The screen door slammed behind her. She turned to see Papa standing on the step, arms akimbo. From a hundred feet away, she could see the tight set to his eyes. He stood, legs splayed and back ramrod straight.

"I have to go," Anna whispered. She reached to pick up her bag and startled when Sid's fingers brushed hers.

"Let me carry that to the door for you."

Anna nodded and backed out of his way. She hurried toward the door without stopping to see if Sid followed. "Hi, Papa."

He looked at her with an expression that let her know she'd hear from him soon enough. Hopefully, he'd wait until Sid returned to the prisoners. She grabbed Papa's arm and pulled him into the house. She heard Sid set the bag on the floor of the kitchen. "Thank you."

Sid looked at her, eyebrow quirked in a question. She mouthed *go*, and he nodded. With a second look, he slipped out the door.

"What do you think you're doing, girlie?"

So much for waiting until Sid returned to the fields.

"I don't want you mixed up with some soldier. Especially one who fraternizes with the Krauts."

"He doesn't fraternize. It's his job to guard them."

"Nobody should enjoy it as much as he does. Doesn't he remember they're the enemy? I don't like anyone who gets that friendly with them."

"What's this really about, Papa? The Germans in our fields? Or the war you fought in? And if you're so against having them here, why on earth did you sign a contract inviting them?" Anna took a deep breath, trying to stem the rush that flooded her. "You know we have no way to pay them."

Papa glared at her, standing stiffly to his full height of six feet. Any other time that could intimidate her, but Anna faced him squarely now. He needed to answer some questions. Without those she didn't know how to proceed.

His jaw tightened, but he didn't respond.

"You don't have to respond, but I will talk to Specialist Chance. He's been nothing but kind to us from the first moment he stepped on this farm."

* * *

Sid STARED at the house from his vantage point by the barn. He rubbed at the knotted muscles in his neck. Why did he feel such an urge to protect Anna?

There had to be more to it than his failure with Pattie. After all, Anna had handled her father fine for years without him.

Even as he thought the words, he wondered if they were true. Had she really been safe, or had she lacked options? She had opportunities, yet chose to come home every weekend. He didn't know if he could do it with a dad like hers. The old codger could be mean. Though Sid had never seen the man get physical, he threatened his daughter more than any man should.

Why did Anna have to remind him so much of his sister? Every time he looked at her, he saw the bruises lining his sister's arms. That was a different situation. Pattie had made a poor choice in her husband. Anna's father wouldn't beat her; fathers didn't do that. Not even grumpy, drunk old men like Ed Goodman. Right?

Even as Sid wanted to know the reason, he knew there was nothing he could do in this situation than he'd done for Pattie. A woman had to desire freedom from the abuse. Otherwise, all of his intervention wouldn't mean a thing. She'd just return to the relationship.

He really should get back to the fields and make sure the prisoners were on task. He couldn't tear himself away from his post. He had to wait and ensure nothing happened between Anna and her father. Regardless of whether she wanted his help, she had it. Until God released him from this burden for the Goodmans, Sid would be here as often as he could make his duties overlap with his concern.

Nothing filtered through the open windows except a curtain flickering in a light breeze.

"Specialist Chance?"

The voice sounded like Luka's. He wouldn't call unless someone needed Sid. Sid looked at the house one more time.

Anna knew how to find him as long as he was here. He'd have to trust God with her safety. Surely God would hear and answer this prayer.

CHAPTER 12

JUNE 20, 1944

*T*he days slipped by with a speed that left Anna clinging to each. The news that filtered out of Europe in the days after D-Day kept a tight feeling around her chest. Why hadn't her father received any word from Brent? Anna sat on her bed in the small bedroom she shared with Dottie, clutching the thin stack of letters she'd received from Brent since he'd shipped out. Several had worn edges from constant reading. If only he would write more often. Answer each letter she sent to him. Even a short note that he'd survived the assault was better than the silence that often dragged on for months.

As a pilot, wasn't he based at an airfield like Kearney? The post office here handled more than five thousand pieces of mail each day. Any base he lived on must have similar facilities. Mail would come in and out unless Brent lived on the front lines. And that didn't make sense. Not for a member of a bomber crew.

Anna glanced at her Bible, where it rested on the chair next to her bed. She grabbed it and clutched it to her chest. *Father, I need some peace. And it has to come from You. Nothing else will get me through today.*

That prayer circled through her mind throughout the day. Something was wrong. She couldn't shake the cold clutch her heart no matter how often she entreated.

Later that morning, as her needle passed up and down through the silk fabric on a damaged plane wing, she wondered where her faith had gone. She used to believe that she could move mountains if she believed. Now, her prayers didn't seem to float any farther than the ceiling. Her faith must be much smaller than she had thought.

"Miss Goodman?"

Anna looked up to see Corporal Robertson standing in the doorway, watching her with a closed expression on his face. Anna glanced down at the wing in front of her. Had her fingers stopped working while she agonized? No, she'd continued to work.

"Please grab your things and come with me. I've been told you won't be back today."

Dottie shot her an encouraging smile as Anna grabbed her purse and followed Corporal Robertson out of the repair area. Anna tried to match her friend's grin but failed. The clasp on her heart squeezed until she had to rub over the spot in an effort to ease the pain.

"Yes, sir?"

"You're wanted in the administration building."

"Any idea why?"

"I'm not at liberty to say."

Her fears for Brent disappeared as she tried to identify what infraction she'd violated to get called into the office. She double-timed to keep up with Colonel Robertson's long strides as they crossed the base. Too soon they arrived at the office.

"Good luck, Miss Goodman."

Anna scanned his face, looking for any encouragement. Instead, all she found hiding in his eyes was a hint of compassion. Compassion? From Corporal Robertson? While he strove for fairness, he'd never displayed emotions. Anna tried to propel her feet to move, but they remained frozen to the sidewalk as if a sea of ice encased them.

Colonel Robertson watched a moment, then opened the door for her.

"Thank you." Anna swallowed and entered the room.

Several desks were lined in shallow rows across the room. She watched the activity a moment and wondered who she should approach. Corporal Robertson could have given her some more information.

"Can I help you, miss?" A young woman from a far desk stood and approached her.

Anna's smile wavered. "Corporal Robertson told me to come here."

"Your name?"

"Anna Goodman." She'd choke if someone didn't tell her what was going on. Soon.

"Oh. Please come with me." The young lady escorted Anna to a door next to the office. Anna felt huge compared to the woman's dainty form that wasn't hidden under a bulky pair of coveralls. The thought of working in an office hadn't appealed to Anna before. Now she wondered if the guys wouldn't be more interested if she looked feminine each day instead of like one of them in her work uniform.

She stopped. Where had that thought come from? Since when did she care about what men thought about her? Especially when the job she did was important to the war effort?

Maybe she'd eaten something funny yesterday and that's why everything seemed out of kilter today. Unquestionably, she'd worked herself up over nothing.

"Right this way."

Anna startled. The gal held open the door. Anna approached the door and looked inside. Sid stood there, hat in his hands, shoulders bowed as if under some great load.

"Sid, what's wrong? Did something happen to Papa?" The words tumbled over each other as she ran into the room. "Please tell me he's okay." He might be insufferable some days, but he was all she had left. *Please, God.*

Sid reached out to steady her. "He's okay. He asked me to get you when I dropped off the prisoners today."

Anna searched his eyes, desperate to believe him. But his sentences did not change the reality that everything wasn't all right. If it was, Sid wouldn't stand here in front of her now.

"You need to come back with me, Anna. He wouldn't tell me anything other than it's an emergency."

She nodded, then followed him to a Jeep. After ten minutes of quiet, Sid thumped the wheel. "Anna, how would you like to accompany me to dinner on Saturday? We could slip into one of the USOs or attend a show some prisoners are putting on for the officers at Camp Atlanta. Some of those have been pretty good."

Anna tried to pull her mind from the fears tangoing around. "All right. I can do that."

"Come on. Don't make it sound like it's a chore." He took his eyes off the road for a second to pull a face at her. "You might even have a good time. It's okay to relax, you know."

"Make it Friday night. I'd like that." Her fingers twisted the handles of her purse as she tried to focus on their date rather than the unknown that awaited her at home.

The rest of the ride to the farm passed in a silent blur. Anna couldn't calm her thoughts that spiraled in a myriad of directions before returning to a central fear. If Papa was okay, then something had happened to Brent. What would Papa have to live for if her fears were true?

Before she'd prepared herself, Sid pulled the truck in front of her house. Anna stared out the window at the home that was nothing more than a shell. Mere walls constructed of wood and covered by a roof. The heart of love had died.

She needed to get out of the vehicle. March into the house. Face head-on whatever awaited her.

But all she could do was sit there like a statue. Trapped by her fears.

"Do you want me to come in with you?"

She started to nod, then stopped herself. She couldn't depend on Sid. Maybe Papa was right about him. He remained a soldier who'd disappear like the rest when new orders arrived.

"No. I'll be fine."

"You don't have to face this alone."

Yes, she did. That was her life. One disaster after another to handle without help or support. She turned to open the door, but Sid hopped out and ran around the truck. He swung the door open and offered his hand.

"I'm praying for you. God can help you whatever waits in there." Sid nodded toward the house. He chucked her under the chin, then stilled. Her breath caught at the intensity in his eyes. His gaze trailed to her mouth, then back up. He stepped back but continued to pierce through to her soul. "Let me help. I won't push, but I'm not disappearing either."

How had he read her thoughts? Anna sucked in a breath, ordered her heart to calm down. Now wasn't the time to act like a schoolgirl. She let him help her down, then released his hand.

"Thank you for the ride." She closed her eyes and prayed for strength to accept what lay behind that door.

Steps slowed by dread, Anna climbed the stairs to the front door and pushed through.

"Papa, I'm home." Her voice echoed in the stillness.

She walked from the kitchen to the living room, but Papa didn't recline in his favorite chair or on the sofa. She looked back into the kitchen, expecting to find she'd overlooked him at the table.

"Papa?" Her tone rose as she continued to call for him. Anna slipped down the hall to his bedroom. The door was closed, but she knocked anyway. "I'm here like you asked, Papa. Please let me in."

The silence dragged on so long she feared he'd slipped out of the house.

"Anna?"

Her knees trembled from relief. She twisted the knob and eased the door open. "Yes?"

Papa's face sagged under the weight of new wrinkles that had appeared in the couple of days since she'd returned to Kearney. A tremor shook his hand as he reached for her.

She froze. When had he last reached to her? Tears welled in her eyes. "What is it? Please, you have to tell me."

Instead of answering, he reached for a yellow paper on the bedside table. Anna ran to the bed and sank beside it as she grabbed the slip of paper. Her mind refused to absorb the simple message:

REGRET TO REPORT your son Brent Goodman is missing in action over France.

ANNA SUCKED IN A SHUDDERING BREATH, then tried to read the sentence again through tears that streamed down her cheeks. She looked up to find moisture trickling down Papa's face. He reached for her, and she leaned into his embrace.

She absorbed the news and wanted to cling to the hope that Brent wasn't confirmed dead. There had to be possibilitiy in that.

But reality wouldn't release her from its grip. Brent served on a B-17. If his plane had gone down, he'd either died or become a prisoner.

She hugged Papa tight. What was left to fight for? Brent. Until the Army changed his status from MIA to KIA, she would work hard to keep the farm. He would need somewhere to return when he came home. And she would struggle to prevent Papa from disappearing inside himself during this latest battle. She had to, or she was afraid she'd join him in his pit of despair.

CHAPTER 13

JUNE 23, 1944

id eyed his reflection in the mirror. He looked standard military issue. Nothing that stood out in a crowd unless you counted his slightly off-center nose. It had never recovered from that fight during basic training.

He straightened his tie and splashed some cologne on his neck. Time to go collect Anna.

He hopped into Trent's Ford. It wasn't Cinderella's carriage, not with as many years as it had run up and down the roads. Neither was it a government-issued truck. He wanted tonight to feel like a special event. Focus on getting to know her beyond the surface level of their interactions on the farm. When he caught her away from the farm, she delighted him with her stories and wit. Only on the farm did they have confrontations rather than conversations.

Tuesday when he'd invited her, it had seemed like the right thing to do. She'd agreed without much reluctance. Now if she could muster up a bit of excitement, the night could be great.

Sid whistled as he drove the miles from Camp Atlanta to the Goodman farm.

As he ran to the door, Sid wondered what had happened after he'd dropped Anna off Tuesday. He'd waited as long as he could before taking the prisoners back to camp. The poor men had looked wrung out from their day in the fields. And Sid couldn't tell if the fields had benefited from their labor. They'd returned the next day, and he'd monitored the men carefully, pleased with their progress. The only disappointment came when he learned Anna had returned to Kearney early that morning. How had she made it back?

Now he knocked on the door, a grin he couldn't restrain spreading across his face.

The door opened, and Mr. Goodman stood staring at him.

"Good evening, sir. I'm here for Anna."

The man grunted a reply.

"Is she ready?"

"I don't like the idea of my girl going out with you."

Sid felt the edges of his grin fall. The sound of footsteps running reached his ears.

"If this fool girl'd listen to me at all, she'd stay right here where she belongs rather than run around with a soldier who's just gonna get killed."

Heat flamed up Sid's neck as Mr. Goodman yelled. Sid tried to swallow the urge to explode, then caught a glimpse of Anna. Her face had turned white as snow, and her mouth hung open.

"Papa." Anna sputtered as if trying to catch a breath. "That's enough."

Mr. Goodman turned toward Anna."No, you need to hear all this. Maybe it'll sink in this time. Spend time with a man in uniform, and he'll break your heart. If your mama still lived, she'd tell you that exact thing." Mr. Goodman's voice broke on the last sentence but then he caught himself. He thrust his finger in Sid's face, forcing Sid down a stair. "You leave my girl alone."

Sid looked from Mr. Goodman to Anna, unsure what to do. Should he leave? Or should he fight for the right to take Anna out for an evening? What did Anna want? He searched her face but found nothing in her blank face to indicate her desires. He balanced on the balls of his feet while he waited for whatever Mr. Goodman would throw his way next.

"Papa, please let me through." Anna's voice barely reached Sid's ears yet held strength. "Mama told me she loved you and never for one moment regretted marrying a soldier. She would encourage me to spend time with a man like Sid. Especially after the way he's cared for the farm."

Uh-oh. Now Sid could feel the heat climb to include his ears. Marriage? He only wanted to spend an evening with Anna, not the rest of his life. At least not until he knew her better. A lot better. He ran a finger under his collar. Maybe he should leave, before someone said anything else that would make his temperature rise higher.

Mr. Goodman sighed and stepped back. "Don't say I didn't warn you. And remember what happened to your brother."

"How can I forget?" Anna slipped past her father to Sid's side. "Take me away, soldier."

He held out his arm, and she grabbed it like a lifeline. Her hand tremored against him, and he covered it with his own. "Are you sure you want to come?"

She bit her lip and nodded, gaze on the ground in front of her.

A snort behind him made Sid turn. Mr. Goodman remained in the doorway, watching them like a hawk.

"Don't look back," Anna whispered.

"Why?"

"He'll take pleasure from knowing you care what he's doing. Papa's become a great manipulator in recent years."

Sid opened the car's door and helped Anna in. He walked around the car and slid behind the wheel. "Let me make a suggestion. Since you still want to spend the evening with me, let's drive to Holdrege and the diner there. After that, if we have time, we can go to Camp Atlanta for the prisoners' show or for a movie. Or we can stay in Holdrege for a dance in the park. Whichever sounds good to you."

Anna sniffled.

Sid felt a spike of alarm course through him. No, not a woman crying. Anything but that! He glanced at her, but she turned toward the door and he started the vehicle.

"So you don't like my plan. That's okay." Sid reached for something that would distract her. If only he knew what had set her off. Where had his wit disappeared when he needed it? "How about a trip to Kearney?"

A sniffle answered him and he pulled from the driveway onto the road.

"Or a trip to Omaha. We could really make your dad crazy with the idea we ran off and eloped." Did he just say that?

The next sniffle mixed with a giggle.

Okay, this worked. "I know. How about a run south? We could slip into Kansas and drive until we hit Mexico. I'm sure no one would miss us. We could pretend you were a princess, and I'm your escort whisking you away to a magical world."

A watery laugh filled the car. "No, let's drive west until we hit the mountains. We can find a corner of Colorado no one's claimed. Pretend the world is simpler."

"Or we could go into Holdrege and have dinner."

He glanced over and watched Anna's cheeks curve. "I'd like that. It'll work until we can run away without the military chasing you across the country."

Sid waved her off. "No worries. What's one lowly specialist in a sea of enlisted men? I am the one who lost the prisoner after all. I'm sure they'd find my disappearance a huge loss."

"They must've forgotten."

He thought of the pranks that dogged his steps. "It's probably written up in my file. My kids will someday discover the wonderful fact that their daddy lost a German. In rural Nebraska." He heaved a sigh. "The price of notoriety."

Anna wiped her eyes, and a comfortable silence filled the car. They reached the outskirts of Holdrege, and the small homes whiz past. Soon he turned the car onto Main Street. It wasn't a long road, and most of the businesses looked shuttered. Fortunately, Rosy's Diner blazed with light.

Sid made a big show of inhaling. "Smell her famous biscuits?"

Anna followed suit and started coughing. "All I smell is exhaust."

"Then we'd better get you inside. Can't have something happen to you on my watch."

"No. Wouldn't want to become like the prisoner."

He nearly choked as she scampered out of the car and up to the café.

"Come on, slowpoke."

Her emotions had definitely improved. He shook his head. What was it with women and feelings that changed like the weather? He'd get whiplash around her if he didn't watch out.

After a few minutes he had Anna settled at a table tucked in a corner halfway between the door and the kitchen. Stains dotted the once-white tablecloth, but the lit candle in the middle of the table pulled his attention from those to Anna's eyes. While a smile now touched her lips, it didn't reach her eyes. Shadows filled them.

They talked for a few minutes before the waitress came for their order. After she left, Sid placed his hand over Anna's.

"Will you tell me what's wrong?"

Anna looked away, scanning the room as if for an escape. "What do you mean?"

"Something more than your father has you distracted."

She tugged her hand free from his. A mask settled over her features, and he wished he could retract the question. Then again, maybe not. Someone needed to climb beneath the surface with her. See what caused the hurt that shadowed her expression.

The waitress placed their plates in front of them. "Can I get you anything else?"

Sid shook his head, and she sashayed away. "Can I pray before we eat?"

Anna nodded without a word.

"Father, join us tonight. I ask You to comfort Anna. You know her inside and out. Please give her whatever she needs tonight. Amen."

She eyed him and then picked up her silverware. "Do you always pray like that?"

"Only when I don't know what else to say or do."

"Hmm." She took a bite of her vegetables and chewed. "We had a telegram Tuesday."

Sid looked up, trying to read her expression. Telegrams rarely contained good news anymore. "What did it say?"

Tears slid down her cheeks. He reached across the table with his napkin and wiped one away.

"Brent's missing in action. The military probably presumes he's dead. It likely happened with the assault on Normandy."

He longed to take her into his arms and hold her until everything was okay.

"I'm sorry Papa turned so mean when you came tonight. He wants to protect me. All I need is Brent home with us." She buried her face in her hands as her shoulders shook.

Sid noticed the patrons at the tables around them starting to stare. "Would you like me to get you out of here?"

A nod indicated she'd heard him. He strode to the cash register at the front of the dining room and handed over some cash and ration coupons.

"Want me to package your meals?"

Sid glanced at the table where Anna sat wiping her face. "Yes. Thanks."

The waitress wrapped up the fried chicken and sides, then handed the containers to him.

Once Sid had Anna in the car, she leaned against the seat and closed her eyes. He reached to crank the engine, then stopped. "What would you like to do now? Go somewhere to talk or back home?"

"Take me to the park."

Sid turned the car toward the park and, when they arrived, parked at the edge of the lot for the dance.

"Have you ever felt like God abandoned you?"

The quiet question filled the car like a bomb exploding. Sid prayed for an answer but remained silent.

"Why is God so mad at me? He's stripping everything away from me. First, Mama. Now Brent." She curled into herself against the door of the car. "I haven't done anything to deserve this. All I know is every time I try to hold things together, something else gets pulled away. I'm ready to stop trying altogether." Her hand covered her mouth as if stifling any more words.

Sid turned toward her. What could he say to penetrate the walls of hurt? Should he even say anything? Quiet settled on the car, and Anna turned to him before he could formulate anything profound.

"Please take... me home... now." Her voice shook.

He looked at her, smelling the fried chicken, and tried to read whether she really wanted to go home. Her features were shuttered. He'd missed an opportunity she might not hand him again, but he had to try. "Look, let's go sit over there on the bench and eat our dinner. The moon's out, and it's a beautiful night. If you want to go home after that, I'll take you."

She nodded.

He hurried out of the car and around to open her door before she could change her mind. "Here you go, milady."

"Thank you." She leaned into him as they walked to the bench. He held her tight against him with one arm while he juggled the meals in the other.

"Here's we go." He eased her down onto it, sat beside her, and watched her pick at the meat. After the first bite, she ate her portion quickly. Sid wiped his mouth on a napkin, then turned to her. "I'm sorry about everything that's happened, Anna. I wish I could fix this. All I can promise is that I'm here if you ever need me."

She snuggled closer and nodded. "I know. Can you take me home now?"

As he drove her home, he sensed her trying to push him away. She couldn't so easily distance herself. Somehow he'd find the way into her heart.

CHAPTER 14

JUNE 28, 1944

*T*he strains of "Swinging on a Star" filtered through the parachute room. Anna had stopped counting how many chutes the Army could cram into the room at a time, but in the late-June heat, the room felt stifling. She wiped a trail of sweat off her forehead with one hand while keeping a firm grip with the other on the lines she'd untangled.

News continued to trickle from the front in Europe. Each shipment of fresh B-17s matched with their crews from Kearney had lost the air of celebration. These men would fly straight into Europe and the fight.

She wavered between reminders that Brent had disappeared, likely presumed dead, and the thought that, while she couldn't help him, she could help these men. She stifled a yawn. She'd slept fitfully this week. The smell of food turned her stomach. All she wanted to do was curl up in a corner and hide from the world. Instead, she plugged on, because that's what Goodmans do, or did, until her father decided to distance himself from life.

Chin up, Anna. Goodmans always face their troubles head-on.

How many times had he said those words when it looked like they'd lose the farm? Then the war started and things looked up until Brent enlisted. Then Mama died. Now Brent had gone missing.

Dottie walked to her and stood like a shield between Anna and the rest of the room. "Are you okay?"

"Yes. Why?"

"You might want to wipe the tears off your cheeks, then."

Anna touched her face, surprised to find wetness on her cheeks that wasn't sweat. "I didn't realize I'd started crying."

"I know. Finish that parachute, and let's take a break."

As Dottie and Anna walked back from their coffee break, Anna's gaze landed on the chapel. Something about the simple white structure drew her.

"I'm going to stop in there."

"Take your time. I'll cover for you." Dottie squeezed Anna's hand, then continued toward the repair hangar.

Anna stood looking at the chapel. She'd passed the building numerous times in the past, yet never felt this urge to walk inside. "Just for a minute." The stacks of tangled parachutes called to her, but maybe she could give her full attention to the job after spending a few moments soaking in the quiet of this place.

She pulled open the door and slipped into the foyer. It took her eyes a moment to adjust to the dim interior. Anna hesitated. Now that she stood in the building, she didn't know what to do. No sense of peace enveloped her. No presence whispered hope to her soul. Instead, she felt just as empty here as she did anywhere else. The questions, the sense of abandonment that followed her through the days and nights, still lingered. Trailing her hand along the back of the pews, Anna walked to the front and sank onto one. The windows in this chapel were modest, without stained glass to delight the eyes.

"What do You want from me, God?" The question bounced off the wooden floors and carved pews. "Haven't You taken enough?"

She pounded toward the altar. "You've taken Mama, Brent. Might as well have taken Papa. The land's left, but there's no money to keep it. Nobody to run it."

Is that true?

The question whispered in her soul, generating even more questions.

Different images filtered through Anna's mind like snapshots, many of them filled with people. Chasing Brent around the barn during morning chores years ago. The Wisdoms and the warm way they had opened their home and hearts to her. Dottie and her solid friendship through the ups and downs. German prisoners laboring their hardest in the fields. Gus and Teddy laughing with her papa at the table. The pastor standing in front of the church, expounding on Sunday mornings. Sid watching over her and the farm.

She took a deep breath. Okay, maybe she hadn't been abandoned. Then, why did she feel, so ... empty ... isolated ... drained.

Words from Sunday's sermon filtered through her mind. Pastor Reynolds had examined Deuteronomy 31 and the principle that God would not fail nor forsake His people. He'd set a specific job in front of the Israelites but promised to go with them. And because of that, the Israelites were to walk in courage and strength.

What was the job God had for her? At the moment, she wasn't doing anything well. So many things pulled on her for time and attention. And she couldn't pretend to handle it all.

Good.

Good? How could it be good that she couldn't manage everything in front of her?

Rest in Me. I'll provide as I did for the Israelites.

The thoughts soaked in to her heart. Maybe she didn't have to carry the burden alone. God could provide everything she needed. She certainly hadn't done a good job on her own.

Anna tipped her head toward heaven and lifted her hands. "Okay, Father. I don't even know if I can do this, but help me turn my fears and anxiety to You. Here's Brent. Take care of him if he's still alive. Help him find his way back to us." She shuddered and covered her face with her hands. She had to do this. "And here's Papa. Help me, Lord. I don't understand everything that's going on in him. But I know my life is meaningless without You."

The sound of footsteps reached her, and Anna lowered her hands and turned to find a man approaching her.

"Can I help you?" Though hooded with fatigue, his eyes crinkled at the edges. Peace radiated from his gaze.

"Is it okay that I came in?"

"It's why I leave the doors unlocked. Come any time." He settled next to her on the pew and stared at the cross behind the pulpit. "I've been thinking about the evening service."

Anna tried to look interested. Where was he headed?

"I spend much of my time talking to different soldiers and airmen. Do you know what their biggest concern is?"

She shook her head as a long list filled her mind. Fear of the unknown? Concern for those they left behind? Apprehension about doing their jobs well? The questions seemed endless.

"For those who have faith, they want to know that God will go with them into battle. For others, it's fear of death. What wonderful assurance that God promises to never leave us even when He sends us into battle." He leaned against the pew. "That's an amazing promise. Now if we could learn how to live like we believed it." He studied her closely. "That's the challenge I have. To present that truth in such a way that it transforms lives."

The bell on top of the chapel tolled out the new hour. Anna eased from the pew. Time to get back to work. Time to see if she could live. Time to see if she'd relinquished her fears like that promise was hers. She needed God to go with her in order to survive the battles with her father. An uneasiness filled her that Papa would take out all his pent-up rage against the prisoners someday. Having them at the farm brought out the worst in him. She needed to talk to Sid about that before something happened.

"Good luck with your sermon."

The chaplain smiled at her. "Remember, the door is always unlocked."

"Thank you." She returned his smile, then walked down the aisle and out of the chapel.

Anna wound back to the repair hangar. She took her time since she'd already missed an hour. For the first time in awhile, she noticed the base around her. Outside one administrative building, someone had taken the time to plant a flowerbed. Purple coneflowers mixed with pure-white daisies. Honeybees buzzed between the plants, collecting the precious nectar.

Soldiers and civilians raced past her, but for once she didn't join them. A bomber crew walked by. One of the group wolf whistled, and she nodded in acknowledgement but didn't stop. He must be desperate if he thought her attractive in her work garb.

She and God had a few issues to work through. Then, maybe she'd be ready to consider a relationship with someone. But it wouldn't be with someone who whistled indiscriminately.

No, it would be with someone who made her feel sheltered and protected. Someone like Sid.

CHAPTER 15

JUNE 30, 1944

The fields that lined the road showed the benefit of rain. The winter wheat stood ready to harvest in another week to ten days. The corn reached toward the sky, feet yet to grow but well on its way. Even the soybeans had started to take on their bunched forms.

Sid braced himself for the conflict he would walk into when he reached the Goodman farm. Not the way he'd planned to end his week. However, the wheat needed to be harvested in a matter of days, but Mr. Goodman had refused to pay the prisoners.

The county extension agent shifted on the seat next to Sid. "Are you sure I need to be here?" Jude Rosen looked as uncomfortable as a hen surrounded by foxes.

"Last time I checked, your job as county extension agent included collecting the prisoners' wages. I transport them."

"But I told you Ed Goodman won't see me." Jude lifted his hands as if to ward off blows. "Last time he threw me out."

"That's why I'm here. Think of me as your protection."

Jude scrunched down in his seat.

Looked like Sid might have to pull him from the military Jeep. "Look, this farm will go under if we don't get this resolved. The wheat crop will rot in the fields without prisoner labor. You know it, and I know it. Mr. Goodman will before we leave."

"You haven't known him as long as I have. That man is more stubborn than the most obnoxious bull."

Sid decided he'd take Jude at his word; he had no desire to test that theory.

But the Goodman farm would be in serious trouble if the crop didn't get out of the fields. And after the wheat came the corn, but that wouldn't be ready to harvest until mid-October. One battle at a time.

The two men approached the house, and Sid couldn't detect any signs of life. He knocked on the door and waited for any sound to indicate Mr. Goodman headed their way to answer it. After a minute, he rapped again.

"Well, guess he doesn't want to talk to us." Jude headed toward the Jeep.

"You can't leave without me, so you might as well stick around and do your job." Sid stood firm.

A storm passed over Jude's face, and he shook a finger inches from Sid's nose. "Do you understand how mean that man can be?"

If only Jude knew Sid had found Mr. Goodman holding the prisoner at gunpoint. Or how many arguments Sid had overheard. Yep, he had a good sense of the bile in that man's mind.

Sid reached out and knocked again. "We'll leave when we know Mr. Goodman isn't here."

A moment later the door flew open. "What do you think you want?" Mr. Goodman stood in the doorway in his undershirt and jeans, a scowl plastered across his face.

Jude froze slack-jawed in front of the man.

Sid elbowed Jude, then took over when the county extension agent remained immobile. "We're here to discuss the farm labor you've used this year."

"What about it?"

"You're behind in payments, and the prisoners can't return until you're current."

"So?"

"You have anybody else lined up to help with the harvest? Planning to do it on your own? One man and a machine?" Sid tried to keep the derision from his voice. The man might not be honorable at the moment, but Sid had heard enough stories to know Mr. Goodman hadn't always lived like this.

Mr. Goodman crossed his arms and stared at Sid. "Now why would I pay for Nazi labor? I think they've taken enough from me."

"You don't know Brent's dead."

"Maybe, but he's either dead or a prisoner. And you can bet they ain't treating him as soft as you treat the prisoners."

"The Geneva Convention applies to the Germans, too, sir."

"You didn't fight in the last war. Mark my words, you're too good to these prisoners." He spat out the final syllabols. "We're done."

Sid pushed against the door to keep it from closing. "No. You need the men for the harvest."

"I'll make that girl of mine come home."

"She wouldn't know what to do even if you made her come home. Did you ever teach her how to harvest?"

"Well, no." Mr. Goodman looked away. "She's always helped around, but not with the actual farming."

"I know she's a smart gal, but you'll need able-bodied men if the wheat's to get harvested in time."

Mr. Goodman turned from the door and hurried deeper into the house. Sid stared after him, wondering if he should follow or stay.

Jude stepped inside. "Guess he wants us to follow him."

The two made themselves at home at the kitchen table. Mr. Goodman returned down the hall and threw a coffee can at Jude.

Jude fumbled with it a moment. "What am I supposed to do with this? It feels empty."

"Look inside." Mr. Goodman stood tightly in front of them, arms crossed and a taut expression on his face. "That is the sum of cash I have. That's it. All I have to get me through until I sell the crops. It's earmarked for taxes, not that either of you care."

All at once, Sid realized the man in front of him stood broken. Life had overwhelmed, and in his mind, he'd done all he could and still lost. No wonder he acted defeated all the time and took it out on anyone who had the misfortune of getting near him. Sid watched Jude count the money. "How close is he?"

"About two dollars short."

"But close enough, right?"

"Sure." Jude looked like all he watned was to leave the house in one piece.

"Thanks, Mr. Goodman. I'll have my best group here in a week to start the harvest." Sid stood and offered his hand to the man.

After a reluctant shake, Mr. Goodman nodded.

"We'll leave you alone now. Have a good evening."

Jude hustled out of the kitchen and to the Jeep.

Sid followed at a slower pace, climbed in, and turned the Jeep around. He had to stop as another car drove down the lane. He stilled, then looked at his watch. It was only four p.m., early for Dottie to drop Anna off. As his heartbeat surged, he had to admit he'd scheduled the trip out here for now, hoping to see her for a few minutes.

Anna climbed out of the car.

Jude sighed. "Guess we won't be going anywhere soon."

"Why?"

"The reason you're so concerned about the farm isn't Mr. Goodman. Nope, it's that lovely young lady over there." He gestured to where Anna watched his Jeep, a smile on her lips.

Sid shrugged. Why deny the truth? "Maybe you can get a ride to town with Dottie. I'm sure she wouldn't mind." Sid couldn't leave before he knew everything was okay with Anna and her father.

* * *

ANNA's HEART raced in her chest as if she'd run the length of the farm with a message. How could the sight of Sid Chance do that to her? Her eyes drank in the sight of him while her feet refused to move.

"Go on. I can't leave until you step away from my wheels." Laughter livened Dottie's words.

"How can I be so mad at a man and so drawn to him at the same time?" Anna sighed and leaned against the car. "I am such a mess."

"I do believe most people call it 'flashes of love.'"

361

Anna snorted. "That is the last thing I would call what I feel toward him. Animosity. Friendship, maybe."

"And it's natural to hate someone you're friends with? When you're ready to admit the truth, I'll try not to tell you I told you so."

The horn honked, and Anna jerked away from the car. "You didn't need to do that."

"Maybe not, but it was fun. Don't forget I need to pick you up tomorrow night."

"I'll be ready."

Dottie tapped the wheel, then muttered. "Looks like I didn't leave soon enough."

Jude Rosen strode toward the car. His face hung long like that of a condemned soldier.

Dottie climbed out of the car and nailed him with a glare. "Let me guess. You think you'll ride with me." At his miserable nod, she snorted. "Hop in if you're brave enough."

They pulled out of the drive, and Anna shook her head. "I hope they both survive the trip to town."

Sid walked to her then stood next to her, arms crossed while he rested at ease. "Why do you say that?"

"There's a lot of history between those two, and none of it's good. Surely you had a good reason to put them together."

"Jude and I came out to collect the wages your dad owed."

Heat crept up Anna's face. Times like this, she wished her skin was bronzed by the sun to better hide her emotion. "I told you we didn't have the money."

"He came close, though he wasn't happy about it. Pulled out a can filled with cash."

"That money should pay the taxes." Anna stamped her foot. "Do you know how hard it is to get cash money? Farmers don't get a steady salary like you soldiers. No, we have to scrimp and save every penny we find because who knows when the next will arrive. First, the Depression. Then, the Dust Bowl. Now, things begin to improve, and Papa stops working."

"He had to pay." The muscles tightened in Sid's jaw as he spoke. "If he didn't, I couldn't bring prisoners here to harvest the winter wheat. What's your plan? Hitch that old mare to the wagon and do it all yourself? I don't see a tractor around here to help with the work."

"Of course not. A tractor takes money. Lots of it." Anna swallowed hard against the lump that had developed in her throat. She would not cry in front of this insolent man. She looked around, desperate for an escape.

Sid placed a hand on her shoulder.

The gentle action nearly undid her.

"I'm not the enemy. I'm trying to help."

Anna nodded, not trusting herself to speak. She stared at Sid's hand on her shoulder, wanting to shake it off, distance herself from him before he got too close. Before he saw how scared she was, how isolated she felt.

Sid stepped away, taking his support. He shoved his hands in his pockets and looked at her as if he could see right through her.

Anna stiffened and then raised her chin. She would not let him in that far.

"Look. Be careful when you go inside. I'm not sure what kind of mood your dad will be in. He seemed sober when we left, but that was fifteen minutes ago."

Anna rolled her eyes. Surely he hadn't returned to that tired path.

"Fine. Consider yourself warned." Sid took a breath and glanced around the farm. "July 4th is coming up."

"Yes." Where was he headed with that change of topic?

"Why don't you and Dottie, and any other gals who would like to, come down and join us at Camp Atlanta? We're having a big celebration."

Why would she spend more time with this overly opinionated soldier who had no shortage of ideas about how she and Papa should live their lives? "I'd like that. I'll see if Dottie can join me." Anna shut her mouth before any other unintended commitments escaped. What would she say if he asked her to marry him right now? She shuddered at the thought.

Sid straightened taller, a puppy dog grin slapped on his face. "That's great. I'll call you at the Wisdoms' on Monday to confirm details. I think the camp is sending a bus to Kearney to collect folks. See you then."

Anna watched him stride to the Jeep, wondering what on earth she'd agreed to.

CHAPTER 16

JULY 4, 1944

Someone pounded on the bedroom door, and Anna stirred. Dottie mumbled something in her sleep and then rolled over. Her twin bed creaked in time with her movements. Anna pulled the blanket over her head and tried to slip back to sleep.

"Anna, you have a call."

Anna flopped over and grabbed the alarm clock from the bedside table. 5:30. What was so important at this hour of the morning? The night had passed slowly as she tossed and turned from dream to dream. Papa, Brent, even Sid took turns starring.

The pounding echoed off the door.

"We're up." Anna slid out of bed and grabbed her robe. Her thoughts flashed to the last time someone had woken them up. The war couldn't be over already, could it? Talk about wishful thinking. She pulled open the door. "Mr. Wisdom. What's wrong?"

"Phone's for you, Anna." His brow crinkled as he spoke, like he felt concern for her.

"Thank you." She slipped out of the room and followed him down the hallway and stairwell. The family's phone was hooked up in the kitchen. Anna braced herself before picking it up. The news couldn't be good this early in the morning. "Hello? This is Anna."

"It's about time."

"Good morning, Papa."

"I don't know what's good about it." Though his words were gruff, she heard something in his voice that made her wait. "I couldn't find your number last night. Really hid that, didn't you?"

Anna rolled her eyes. She had pasted the Wisdoms' number in Mama's old address book. "Sorry. Why call this early?"

"Well, I thought you'd like to know Gus and Teddy came for dinner last night."

Were his sentences slurred, or were her ears merely tired? Anna hated the fact that, between her fears and Sid's accusations, she analyzed every nuance of Papa's speech patterns. Maybe he'd always rolled his *r*s, and she hadn't noticed.

"I'm glad to hear that, Papa. Is there anything else?" If he got off the phone soon, she could get a few more minutes of sleep before heading to work. And she still had to pack a change of clothes for the celebration at Camp Atlanta.

"Are you listening to me? I told you I had folks over. Thought you'd be more enthusiastic than that after your harping about getting on with living."

"You're right. I'm not used to getting wakened for a phone call."

"If you were home where you belong, you'd already be up and the cow milked."

"But I'm here, Papa. Doing my part for the war. Saving men's lives."

"And when was the last time you did that?"

The sound of her pulse filled her ears at his challenge. Why did he have to be so mean?

"Before you go back for your beauty sleep, you should know I got another military telegram."

Anna's heart stopped, and she rubbed her chest where it ached. She opened her mouth to ask what it said, but couldn't get the words out.

"It's about your brother."

A gasp escaped Anna's throat. Her knees quivered, and she grabbed the counter.

"He's alive, thanks for asking. But he's a prisoner of the Germans in some place I can't pronounce."

The sense of relief fled at his abrupt words. A prisoner? Anna covered her mouth with a hand to stifle her tears. Papa was too upset to deal with her grief.

"You listening, girl?" His gruff tone ground into her ear.

She nodded, then cleared her throat. "Yes, Papa. You're sure he's alive?"

The rustle of paper sifted across the line. "That's what it says here."

"That's better than we feared."

"But he's a prisoner. Of the Nazis. They don't coddle the prisoners like we do." He snorted. "We treat the Germans too well."

"Papa." Anna pushed warning into her voice. He didn't need to think that way again. She didn't want to imagine what he'd do if he let that thought develop. "Tell me about dinner. And where are you calling me from?"

"Thought it was too early to bother you with details like that."

"I'm awake now. Who did the cooking?"

Papa harrumphed. "I did, and then made them clean. I've got to get to the chores. Bye."

Before Anna could respond, he'd hung up. She replaced the handset, but didn't let go. "I wonder how many neighbors listened to that exchange."

"Everything all right, Anna?"

She startled and turned to find Mr. Wisdom leaning against the doorframe, worry filling his gray eyes. "Yes. Sorry he woke you. Papa wanted me to know Brent is no longer missing. The Germans captured him."

"Need anything?"

Anna swallowed and then shook her head. "I'll be fine."

"I'll let Mrs. Wisdom know."

"Thank you. And thank you for waking me." Anna dredged up a smile and then stepped around him and up the stairs. When she entered the room, Dottie sat in the middle of her bed. She opened her arms, and Anna slid next to her.

"Brent's a prisoner."

"I'd ask if you'll be okay, but I know the answer to that."

Anna stared at her, unsure if she knew the answer.

"You'll walk around in shock for a day, then you'll square your shoulders, pray for Brent, and get back to work." Dottie squeezed Anna. "So here's the question: Are you working today and going to Camp Atlanta?"

Anna rubbed her hands together, trying to warm them, as she considered the question. "I can't do anything for Brent by moping. I think the distraction would help."

"That's my best friend. You'll be happier if you're doing something." Dottie bounced out of bed and grabbed a bar of soap and towel. "I'll go get cleaned up first."

Anna watched her go and pondered her advice. She'd always had to carry on, bear the load for other people. Now she couldn't do anything for Brent. Nothing but worry or pray. Somehow she'd pray and release him into God's hands.

The morning evaporated slowly as Anna let the other gals' babble flow around her. She couldn't make herself care about how hard it was to buy food, even with ration coupons. Or that Darling's Shoe Shop had received a shipment this week. Instead, she kept a constant prayer running through her mind, first thanking God that Brent was still alive, then asking why he had to be a prisoner. She knew to the core of her being Papa was right. The Germans wouldn't treat Brent as well as all the men held at Atlanta. But God could still protect him.

At two, Dottie and Anna joined the rest of the gals heading to Atlanta. A bus waited for them outside the gates. Anna ran a hand down the front of her navy skirt, almost expecting to feel the rougher material of her coveralls. She'd brushed her curls out and tried to freshen her face, but she had a feeling Sid would see right through her. The idea made her feel exposed.

The forty-three-mile trip slid by in a blur of chatter. The other girls seemed excited about the chance to attend the celebration.

"I heard they're having fireworks, too." A cute redhead bounced on her seat.

"And a cookout with all the trimmings." Another licked her lips. "I can taste the hamburger now. The military doesn't have rationing, you know."

Anna tried to join into their anticipation, but didn't want the food.

The chaperone, a thin, tired-looking woman in her forties, stood at the front of the bus as it approached the gates to Camp Atlanta. "Remember, ladies, we are here as guests to join in the celebration. Find a lonely soldier and help him experience the fun. Make conversation. Do not leave with a soldier, but stay with the group. Also, be mindful that the bus will leave at the close of the fireworks show. No lollygagging. Most of all, remember to have a good time. If you do, the boys will, too."

The bus pulled to a stop, and Anna scanned the men assembled outside. It didn't take long to spot Sid. He stood slightly to the side with his hat in his hands. He wore his dress uniform and looked so handsome. Why would he bother with her? Someday she needed to ask him . As she watched his face light up when he saw her, she decided today she'd enjoy the reality. For whatever reason, he'd decided to become her friend. And for today, she'd overlook the way he inserted himself with Papa. She wanted to forget about the farm and family burdens and pretend for a moment she was like these other girls. Here to have a good time, without a care to weigh her down.

Sid rushed up to her after she stepped off the bus. "Hey, beautiful."

"Hello."

"Ready to enjoy the celebration? You look worn out."

"Papa called this morning. The Army located Brent in a German POW camp."

Sid picked her up and spun her around.

She tried to catch her breath as he squeezed her tight.

"That's fantastic news, Anna." He set her back on her feet but didn't loosen his embrace.

"Yes, it's wonderful to know he's alive. I just wish he wasn't a prisoner." Anna straightened her skirt, then glanced up at Sid. "Thanks for inviting Dottie and me. I need a good distraction."

"I plan to do more than distract you, Anna." His cocky grin made her step out of the circle of his arms as heat raced up her throat. "Come on."

He led her through the crowd. An easy silence fell between them as they walked among the tents that dotted the field. The smell of charcoal drifted on the breeze. Enough watermelons to fill a field loaded one table. Men in uniform walked with women wearing Sunday dresses. Everyone had donned their best to honor the country's birthday.

"Different footraces are taking place to the west." Sid turned that direction. "And over there"—he pointed east—"is where the fireworks will shoot off at dusk. They shipped them in from New York, so it should be a great display."

The hours flew by. They started by munching on juicy burgers and slices of sweet watermelon. Then, Sid tried to talk her into a three-legged race.

"We could beat everyone here."

Anna eyed the couples assembled and grimaced. "I've never been athletic."

"That doesn't matter. It's a field race. How hard can it be?"

Five minutes later, Anna laughed until she felt breathless. "This is why I'm not athletic."

"Nah. I'd call it uncoordinated." Sid collapsed next to her and untied the strips of cloth binding them together.

Anna stuck her tongue out at him. "I'm not sure that's much better. Besides, what do you expect when I'm handicapped by this skirt?"

"Let's head over to the parade area and get a good seat for the fireworks."

"Isn't it early?"

"Never too early to sit down with a beautiful woman and get to know her better."

Anna let his voice wash over her as he told her stories about his early days in the Army. Tale after tale about basic training and the shenanigans he and the other drafted men developed.

"So how many of these pranks did you instigate?"

Sid shrugged, color rising in his cheeks. "One or two. Somebody had to create ways to keep the new guys on their toes."

"And how often did you get KP duty?"

"Not often enough. I kept coming up with innovative ways to get the fresh recruits involved."

"What was your favorite?"

"Favorite joke? I don't know. I've left those days behind me. Currently I'm a fine, upstanding citizen who never does anything crazy."

Anna arched her eyebrows. "I'm supposed to believe that?"

A glint filled Sid's eyes.

Had she pushed too far? "On second thought, don't answer that question. I'm sure you've outgrown that."

"I guess I'll have to prove it to you."

Before she could respond, the initial flurry of fireworks launched. The explosions filled the sky with color and the field with waves of smoke. His arm slid around her shoulders and she found herself relaxing into the comfort of his shelter. She felt so safe tucked next to him and didn't want the moment to end.

When the display ended, Sid walked her to the bus. "Will I see you this weekend?" He held on to her hand, his fingers laced through hers, as she stood at the base of the bus's stairs.

"Only if you bring prisoners to help with the detasseling." She sighed. The work was hot and miserable no matter how you looked at it. The wheat was barely in, and now the corn demanded attention. "If I were you, I'd take an assignment that moves you anywhere but toward our farm."

Sid leaned in closer, and Anna found it hard to concentrate. "I'll be there with plenty of help. Haven't you figured out that I care about you?"

CHAPTER 17

JULY 7, 1944

*L*ong days occupied the rest of Anna's week as she made up the extra time off on the Fourth. By Friday, all Anna wanted to do was crawl into bed for the weekend. Instead, she knew the time at home would be packed with physical labor far beyond the normal effort of cleaning the house and catching up on chores.

Destasseling corn was an essential yet dreaded part of summer. Every year it arrived like clockwork. It threatened to sap every last ounce of her energy. She'd felt that way even in years she didn't work in a factory more than forty hours a week.

This year she couldn't imagine where she'd find the strength to endure the grueling labor.

As Dottie prepared to turn into Anna's driveway, Anna longed to tell her to keep driving, that she'd spend the weekend at her house instead. Dottie wouldn't mind. However, much as Anna loved her roommate, she looked forward to closing the door at the end of a long day and being alone. That happened far too infrequently.

"Do you want me to come back tomorrow and help?"

Anna grimaced at the thought. Dottie had never worked that hard in her life. "You've put your time in. Go home and relax. Do that for me, too."

"I'd come."

"I appreciate it. No reason for both of us to be covered in cuts and blisters on Monday."

Dottie's eyes danced despite the frown she plastered on her face. "Fine, keep all the enjoyment to yourself. See you Sunday night. I'll come around six."

Anna climbed out of the car and waved good-bye. She turned and stared at the home, trying to talk herself into the battle that likely awaited her inside. A curtain fluttered back in place, and she knew Papa must have seen her. No time like the present to enter the fray. With an air of determination, she trudged toward the house.

The night passed with a minimum of conversation as Papa wolfed down his food then retreated to his chair and radio shows. Anna was grateful for the uneasy peace as she worked through the week's worth of dirty dishes in the kitchen and newspapers piled around the living room.

The détente ended Saturday morning when Papa pounded on her door. She groaned and rolled over to look at the window. The faintest light seeped through her curtains.

Anna stretched. "I'll be there in a minute." She stifled a yawn and walked to the window. Pushing back the curtain, she saw the first hints of dawn painting the sky. Heaviness cloaked her at the thought of the day. *Father, help me survive today. And help me find a way to serve You in the midst of it.*

Anna slipped outside at five forty-five and stopped to appreciate the sun cresting the horizon. Colors glowed across its lower sweeps. While such sights used to be routine, it had been months since she'd risen this early, even when she came back to help with chores. She shivered in the chilled air. Tires crunched against the gravel driveway. She turned to see two trucks entering the farmyard. One bore the marks and coloring of a military truck. The other looked like Gus's old beater. Her heart jumped at the sight of Sid climbing out of the first vehicle.

Half a dozen prisoners descended from the back of the truck, clad in their jeans and denim shirts. They didn't carry any sort of jackets, which they'd need until the sun burned the dew off the corn. Then they'd swelter the rest of the day under the glaring sun without any covering to shield them.

Gus, Teddy, and a few of the older men from church climbed out of Gus's truck. They'd come prepared with rain slickers. They eyed the prisoners, then ambled to the back door to join Papa. He looked wide-awake and ready to tackle the task. Something hard but resigned entered his face when he looked at the Germans.

"Who's going to teach them?" He thrust his chin in their direction.

Anna shrugged. "You."

"I haven't taught them a thing."

That explained the undirected activities she'd seen them undertake on other trips to the farm. "Someone has to make sure they know what they're doing."

Papa crossed his arms and stared at her. The other men refused to meet her eyes.

She rubbed her face and groaned. "Fine. I'll take care of that." She turned and headed into the house knowing that somehow in the next fifteen minutes she had to remember everything she'd ever seen her dad do in the fields.

"Where are you going, girl?"

"If these men are headed into the fields, they're going to need some bandanas. Don't worry, I'll let them use yours, Papa."

In a minute she came back out, loaded down with bandanas and hats. She thrust them at Sid. "Make sure they wear these. You don't want them to get corn rash if we can help it."

"Corn rash?" Sid looked at her with a blank expression.

"Trust me. It's bad." Anna returned to Papa. "Which field do you want them in?"

"We'll take the middle field. They can work the south. And don't forget we'll need a big lunch."

Anna rolled her eyes. Of course they would. "I'll see what I can pull together while teaching these men what to do." Before she said something she shouldn't, she turned and headed toward the field. After a moment, she put her hands on her hips. "Are you coming?"

Sid stared at her. "Coming where?"

"Time to get these men to work." She took off again, satisfied when she heard the sound of footsteps behind her. When she reached the edge of the south field, she waited for the others to catch up. "Tell them to relax. It'll take a minute to explain what they need to do."

Once the men crouched on the ground, Anna took a bandana and hat from Sid. She put them on, the bandana tied securely around her neck. "Tell them to do the same."

He pantomimed what she had done, and Anna tried not to laugh. "Know much German?"

"Nope. They do know some English. Franz, here"—he gestured at a rail-thin, blond man—"does a decent job interpreting if you keep the words simple."

"All right." Anna walked along the edge of the field. "You'll each take a row. Pull the plant down, remove the tassels off the top, and drop them on the ground." She pulled down a plant and grimaced as dew sprayed her face. "You'll repeat to the end of the row. Then start again. We've got one hundred-some acres of corn, so it'll take a couple of days if we're lucky."

Sid watched her motions as she demonstrated detasseling more plants. "Are you staying out here with us?"

"For awhile."

"Doesn't look like you're tall enough to do this."

She stared at him, mouth agape. Was that a challenge? Sure sounded like one. "I've detassled corn for years. My father just likes to forget all the times he dragged me out here to help. Where there's a will, there's a way."

He looked her up and down, and she stood tall on her toes. A twinkle filled his eyes. "All right, sprite, let's see who reaches the end of a row quickest."

It really wasn't a fair contest. Her experience would beat his height any day. She pulled her gloves from the back of her waistband. "Fine. Let's go. You take that row, and I'll grab this one. Get the prisoners started and then we're on."

He eyed her gloves. "Have any more of those?"

"Sorry. You should have brought your own." It wouldn't be a fair fight if he didn't have them. His hands wouldn't last twenty plants without protection. "Did any of you bring gloves?"

Sid glanced at the truck, then shrugged. "Don't think so."

The prisoner named Luka raised his hand. "We bring gloves."

"Let me borrow a pair."

"Sure thing, boss."

"Guess you're here to supervise." Anna smirked at him. Soon all the prisoners but Luka were in their rows and pulling tassels from the corn. "Showtime. Take your row."

Sid tugged the gloves on and took a ready stance.

"Go."

Anna entered the row. It felt like she'd stepped into a shower. In moments the dew drenched her, and her shoes stuck in the mud. Her arms and shoulders ached as she switched from side to side, grabbing tassels on the plants. Some plants were her height, others she had to stretch as far as she could to reach the tops. Her legs throbbed from plodding through the mud as she marched methodically down the row.

Amid the rustling of corn stalks and leaves, she heard an occasional grunt from Sid. He really shouldn't have laid down the challenge. She'd lived on a farm her entire life, and until he'd reached Camp Atlanta, he'd never stepped foot on one. Poor city boy.

There. She could finally see the end of the row. How were Papa and his gang going to hold up? They were too old for this. This was a young person's job. Her neck twinged. A much younger person. If the soldiers couldn't work, maybe she'd hire kids from church.

She pushed through the last plants and stopped.

Sid lay on the ground, arms spread, chest heaving. "Looks like I won."

"Humph. I think I'll check your row on the way back."

He waggled his eyebrows at her.

She couldn't help laughing. "So your height is an advantage."

"Maybe."

"I'll walk your row and then you need to make sure all the prisoners are doing a good job. If one plant is missed it can ruin the whole crop."

"Why?"

"It's a hybrid crop, and detasseling's the only way to keep it that way. I'll stick around for a bit, then I have to make lunch."

The morning slipped by quickly with the prisoners working steadily across the rows. As she checked their work, she found they'd done a thorough job and only needed minimal redirection and clean-up. This would work.

She hurried back to the house and stoked the fire on the stove. Biscuits and gravy with applesauce and green beans would have to do the trick. It was all she could find to fill the quantities needed. She finished the meal, then rang the bell on the side of the house. The men and prisoners trickled into the yard.

Gus limped to a stop next to the door. "Can I help with anything, Miss Anna?"

"Please rest. I've got everything ready."

Teddy and the other men from church didn't look much better than Gus. Teddy kept a hand anchored to his back. Leroy sank to the ground with a sigh. Only Papa looked like he had any energy for the afternoon. *Probably because he hasn't done anything for months.*

She served them at a table she'd pulled to the yard. The men dug into the bowls of food and filled glasses with water or milk. Anna hoped enough would remain for the prisoners. The prisoners and Sid walked into the yard. While quiet, they looked ready for more work that afternoon. Anna pulled out some blankets and handed them to Sid.

"These can go on the ground." She collected extra bowls from inside and placed them in the center of the blankets once they were spread out. She tried to ignore the storm cloud gathering on Papa's brow. "Here. Have the men sit down and eat. They've earned it."

Sid stepped in front of her. "Anna, the prisoners aren't supposed to eat with you."

"Why on earth? They worked as hard as everyone else."

"It's against regulations."

"Yet another reason not to have them here. If I can't provide for them like other hired help, then you can keep them at Atlanta." The murmured sound of German filtered toward her. She stood with arms crossed, staring down Sid.

He hesitated, then waved the prisoners forward. The prisoners collapsed on the blankets and filled bowls with food.

Papa stood with a roar. "Get these men off my lawn. Ain't it bad enough what they've done to my boy? You insist on feeding them, too?"

Anna's mouth fell open. She tried to speak, but couldn't find her voice.

Papa spun and disappeared inside the house. A moment later the screen door slammed against the side of the house, and Papa barreled out with a shotgun. "Get them away."

"Papa, you don't mean that."

The prisoners stopped eating and stared at the gun.

"Get them off now." Papa aimed the gun at one prisoner, then swiveled it to another.

"How will we finish without their help?"

"I don't need Krauts to do that." The shotgun quivered in Papa's grip.

Gus stood and approached his friend. "It's okay."

"No, it ain't. Nothing about this situation is right."

"Let's go inside." Gus forced Papa to join him in the house.

Anna stared after them, unsure what to do next.

"Maybe I should pack them up and leave." Sid joined her, standing shoulder to shoulder with her.

"Maybe." But if he did, how would she get all the detassling done? Her muscles quaked from the row and clean-up she'd done. That was nothing compared to doing row after row. She turned so Sid couldn't see her chin tremble. She would not cry in front of him. She couldn't. Once she started, she didn't know if she'd ever stop.

CHAPTER 18

JULY 8, 1944

*S*id stared at Anna, wanting to take her in his arms but unconvinced she'd let him. Instead, he stood, arms hanging at his sides, shifting from foot to foot, as she fought for control. Would she ever realize she could depend on him? That he didn't see her as a burden? That he wanted—no, longed —to help?

After a minute he cleared his throat. "Will you finish the detasseling without help?"

She shook her head. She stayed still a moment longer, then sucked in a deep breath. "Don't worry about us. I'll get us through this."

"Maybe you don't have to."

She whirled on him, eyes blazing extra bright. "What? Have a plan up your sleeve to keep the prisoners here without Papa shooting them? I've carried this place for more than a year. I'll keep doing it."

"All I'm saying is you don't have to do it alone. We can keep your dad away from the prisoners. Keep the reminder out of sight." Sid pulled his hat off, then raked his fingers through his hair.

"You think I can't handle this." The set of her chin matched the tone of her words.

How was he supposed to respond to that? No, he didn't think a woman could handle a three hundred-plus-acre farm on her own. Especially when she worked four to five days a week in a factory. He didn't know many men who could do that.

"Look, you don't have to do anything to convince me you're an incredible person. But everybody needs help." He glanced at the prisoners.

The six men had finished their lunch. They clustered at the edge of the field, a cautious alertness to their postures, as if ready to bolt at the next attack. Luka eyed Sid, a stiff air about him, as if he understood the tension that crackled in the air. Luka gestured to the men. "Time to get back to work?"

Sid nodded. He'd get the men back into the field. Too much work remained to waste time talking about things he couldn't fix. Anna's father wouldn't change unless he wanted to, but the acres of corn remained to be detasseled.

"We'll be in the field if you need us." He went to where his men stood before Anna could protest. She might not like his methods, but better to get back to the fields now while her father couldn't tear into a German.

The afternoon stretched out in a slow succession of hours. Anna avoided him like he had a contagious disease, but she hadn't order them to leave. She needed the labor and kept her father inside and away from the Germans. Sid missed her teasing presence rom the morning.

At the end of the day, Sid gladly hauled himself into the truck. With a few groans and mild complaints, the prisoners collapsed in its bed. Once they'd settled, Sid headed back to Camp Atlanta. It had been a long day. Already his shoulders and back ached from the work. He had a feeling by morning he'd feel all kinds of other muscles he'd forgotten. Anyone who thought farmers had an easy life hadn't spent a day like his.

Problem was that, after a full fourteen hours in the fields, they'd barely covered a third of the crop. Sure, the men were became proficient at the work. But it had taken too long to reach that point. Tomorrow had to go faster. He'd attend the early chapel service, then head back. Luka promised he'd have the men ready.

The old men had creaked through their rows. Sid supposed their help was better than nothing, but he didn't avoid the fact they needed more hands. He'd bring more prisoners tomorrow except he needed approval. The prisoners were spread thin between the local farmers and branch camps. With the fields planted and crops growing, work wasn't in short supply. No, the farmers needed and valued the prisoners' labor. Even by folks who felt like Anna's dad. Fortunately, he hadn't come back out after Gus led him inside.

Soon as he reached his barracks, Sid dropped onto his bed and kicked off his boots. In minutes he fell asleep.

Sunday passed in a blur of repetitive motion. Anna remained aloof until Sid decided she'd pouted long enough.

As the prisoners marched to the truck that evening, he stalked up to her. "Be ready in an hour."

"For what?" She crossed her arms and stared at him.

"I'm coming back and getting you away from here. We've worked hard, and it's time to relax."

"But Dottie will be here soon."

"When?"

"Around six."

Sid frowned. "Tell her to wait. I'll bring something back for all of us." He squared his jaw. She couldn't put him off that easily. "Don't go anywhere until I get back."

He turned toward the truck but could swear he caught her sticking out her tongue in his peripheral vision. If he weren't so tired, he'd smile. Crazy girl had spunk.

After returning the prisoners to their compound, Sid flew through a shower and into clean clothes. He pulled out of Camp Atlanta and drove to Atlanta. He reached the little café in town thirty minutes before it closed and grabbed a quick picnic of fried chicken and potato salad.

When he pulled into the Goodmans' lane, Dottie's car stood next to the house. He released a breath at the realization Anna had waited. Maybe she wasn't as angry with him as she acted. He hopped out of his car and hurried toward the house.

"We're over here."

He found the girls lounging in chairs next to the barn. Anna looked wrung out, her face pink with sunburn, short curls tucked behind her ears. Her eyes were closed, a tired smile on her lips. Even exhausted she stole his ability to think. He tried to rein his thoughts in. The important thing was discussing how she'd make it through a week in Kearney after the weekend she'd had. And how the detasseling would be finished while she did.

Dottie smiled at him, a hint of Mary Martin flashing in her grin. "I'd begun to think Anna lied about you coming back." She looked over his shoulder. "Bring anyone with you?"

Sid shook his head and then shrugged. Hadn't crossed his mind to grab someone like Trent.

"I'll entertain myself while you guys enjoy your dinner."

"There's plenty here."

"Thanks, but I don't like playing third wheel." She stood and patted Anna lightly on the cheek. Anna opened her eyes and glanced up at her. "We leave in forty-five minutes."

"Sure you don't want to eat with us?"

"Certain. I'll be over by the apple trees."

Sid watched Dottie head off. Why hadn't he thought to bring Trent with him? Anna shifted in her chair, and he pulled his attention back to important matters. "I brought some chicken."

"Thank you."

Sid pulled out the meat, salad, plates, and silverware. Once they each had a plate of food, he said a quick grace. Silence settled between them as they ate. When he'd cleared his plate, he set it aside and focused on Anna.

"I'll bring the prisoners back until the job is done. Hopefully, we'll finish before Jude reassigns them."

"He's never liked Papa much."

Sid could imagine. If her father had always been this prickly, it was easy to understand. But Gus and Teddy seemed to genuinely like him, so something at the core of the man had appealed to others at one time.

"Maybe Papa's right." Anna's sigh resonated with heaviness. "Perhaps I need to quit at the air base and stay here for awhile. There's no way he can handle the farm. Yesterday made that clear if I hadn't already known it."

"Do you like your job?"

"It's fine, and I'm making a difference. The boys need those parachutes packed properly. I've gotten good at it." She set her plate on the ground. "The problem is, if I come home, I don't know how I'll stand it."

"Do you like the farm?"

"Doesn't matter."

"Yes, it does. You seem to come back week after week because you feel a sense of duty. But I haven't seen you enjoy it."

Fire sparked in her eyes. "What about my life am I supposed to love right now? I have a father who is angry all the time. I have a job that requires long hours. I live in a small room in a boarding house with my best friend. I come home on weekends and work until I'm past exhausted. What part should I enjoy? The part where the Germans are holding my brother? Or the part where they're working my fields?"

"The fact you're alive. That you live in a free country. Maybe the fact that God loves you. That He's given you a job to do, whether it's in Kearney or here." Sid stopped, counted to ten. Where had this rush of words erupted from? "When I look at you, I see a beautiful woman who has a lot to offer, but you're held back by cares you carry alone."

Anna stared open-mouthed at him, color flashing up her face.

Sid raked a hand through his hair. How could he explain what he saw in a way that she would accept? "Frankly, I think you're needed here this week. There's a lot that must happen to maintain the crops. You said yourself if the detasseling isn't done, it could ruin the entire crop of corn. But if you don't want to stay, go. Whatever you choose, you need to decide in your heart that you're going to find a way to release the load. You can't carry everyone else's burdens for them."

Her mouth shut like a trout pulled out of a stream, desperate for water. She snapped her lips together and hurried away from him.

Sid's shoulders sagged as she got into the car without a word to him. Guess she'd made her decision about what to do. He watched her go and wondered if he had ended any hope of more than a tentative friendship with her.

He turned toward the fields. The corn waved in rows across the land, seemingly unending.

If he wanted to bring more prisoners to work tomorrow, he needed to return to camp. He'd bring as many men as he could. Get the job done and move on. Anna had made it clear that she didn't want his help or his friendship. And her father didn't hide his feelings.

Walking to his car, Sid caught Mr. Goodman watching him through the kitchen window. Sid waved at the man—sooner or later he had to soften. And maybe his daughter would join him.

CHAPTER 19

JULY 13, 1944

"*A*nna Goodman, I have had enough. It is time to stop moping." Dottie plopped down on the bed across from Anna's, a mock frown plastered on her face. "Get dressed in your prettiest skirt and blouse. We're going to the USO tonight."

Anna stared at Dottie with her mouth hanging open.

"What? Aren't you tired of sitting here, long in the face? I know I'm sick of watching you. Time to get your focus off yourself and onto somebody else. Who, I don't care. Anybody will do." Dottie launched off the bed and scurried to the wardrobe. She pulled a skirt off its hanger and threw it at Anna. "Here. Put this one on."

"I'll pick out my clothes. First, you have to tell me where you think you're taking me."

"The USO. Didn't you listen to me?" Dottie heaved a dramatic sigh. She playfully pushed Anna to her feet. "Come on. You'll have fun. Might even meet some nice people and get a life beyond me."

A very unladylike snort escaped before Anna could stifle it. "I doubt that. Then you would need another person to order around."

Dottie's eyes sparkled, and she tapped her toes.

Anna might as well give in to the inevitable. "Give me fifteen minutes, and I'll be ready."

"With bells on your toes."

"Yes, ma'am." A melody hummed out of Anna. It would do her good to forget about everything for a bit. She pulled out a dress with a bodice that crossed in front with a beautiful drape. The large flowered print always brought a smile to her face. She slipped into the dress, then a pair of baby doll heels. She added a veiled beret to her curls, then adjusted it while looking in the mirror. She already felt better, more positive about the evening. It had been too long since she'd dressed up like this.

"Ready?"

"Just a minute." Anna grabbed an eyebrow pencil and ran it up the back of each leg. She twisted but couldn't tell if she'd gotten them right. "Does that look straight?"

Dottie eyes the lines, then nodded. "Let's scoot. The guys'll be here soon to pick us up."

Anna stopped and gaped at Dottie. "I didn't sign up to go with somebody. I'm not in the mood for a date."

"It's not like that. One of the soldiers is a pal of mine. He's grabbed a buddy, and they'll escort us. We won't be tied down to one person, and neither will they."

Sure. That's what she'd said the last time she got them into a situation like this. Anna plopped down on the bed and removed the pins from her hat. "I'm not interested."

"You don't have to be. Didn't you hear a thing I said? Some days it feels like your ears don't work." Dottie flopped down next to her. "They're our ride. I'm not made of gasoline rations, you know. But it's important to get you out. I suppose we could ask another boarder to go with us and drive."

Anna shuddered. The other gals were nice enough, she supposed, but Anna hadn't made the time to know them beyond basics. Sometimes she wondered what had happened to her. She used to love getting to know new people. Now she didn't have the energy.

The doorbell's ring echoed up the stairs.

Dottie stood and thrust her hands on her hips. "You can stay here and sulk all you like. I'm going out tonight. If I can encourage a few soldiers, I'll consider the night a success." She grabbed her flap bag and left.

The walls closed in on Anna as Dottie clunked down the stairs. Anna needed to go. She'd already dressed for the evening. No need to waste that effort.

"Wait, Dottie. I'm coming." Anna placed her hat back on her head and flew down the stairs. Two soldiers wearing their dress uniforms waited inside the door.

"Anna, I'd like you to meet my friend John Chester and his friend Thomas Reynolds. Gents, let's hit the road." Dottie linked arms with John, leaving Thomas looking at Anna through narrowed eyes. She tried not to squirm under his intense scrutiny.

Anna nodded toward the door. "Shall we join them?"

He tipped his head. "After you."

The USO hummed with music and the conversation of at least one hundred people. The air stifled Anna. Add all the bodies to the residual heat, and the room seemed very closed. Thomas tried to lead her to the dance floor, but she resisted.

"I'm not ready to dance yet. Why don't we sit down and chat for awhile."

He answered each question with a monosyllable. His eyes darted around the room until she looked over her shoulder to follow his glance. She grinned at the realization he watched the girls at the food tables. Color climbed his neck when he caught her. He stood abruptly. "Can I get you something to drink?"

"That would be great." She watched him walk away. This exchange reflected why she hated coming to these events. Stilted conversations with people you didn't know and didn't care to know. Some people had the gift of gab, but she didn't think she wanted it either. Why couldn't more men be like Sid Chance?

She stilled.

Where had that thought come from? Many of their interactions ended in near arguments.

"May I have this dance?"

Anna looked up into eyes that were so deeply blue they almost matched the hue immediately after the sunset, but were filled with a twinkle that had nothing to do with stars. He smiled as he held out his hand.

"Private Trent Franklin, at your service."

Anna stood and accepted his hand. He eased her onto the dance floor as Bing Crosby crooned some tune. It sounded like "White Christmas," which didn't make much sense in the middle of July.

Private Franklin was a quiet man, but Anna didn't mind. She closed her eyes and enjoyed the moment. Before she knew it, the dance with him led to others with different soldiers. Most wanted to dance, and those who talked didn't expect her to do anything other than listen. That she could do. Then she found herself back on the floor with Private Franklin, a dance she enjoyed because there was no need to make small talk but to simply enjoy the moment and music.

"Anna."

She turned from the circle of Private Franklin's arms to find Dottie waving for her from near the door.

"We have to leave."

"Thank you for an enjoyable dance, Private."

"My pleasure. I don't think I caught your name, though."

"Now that seems odd. We've spent several dances together."

"If you leave now, I'll have to call you my mystery lady."

Anna smiled. "I like the sound of that. Good night." She slipped away before he could say anything else.

The next morning her duties at the air base seemed less tedious. It felt like new energy had infused her. Dottie had been right. She needed to get out and forget about herself for awhile, focus on others and making them smile. It hadn't been that hard once she got into the swing of it.

She caressed the silk parachute she held. Would this parachute save a soldier's life someday? Maybe somebody like her brother? Then all the struggles, the work would be worth it.

* * *

By Friday morning, Sid decided farming wasn't the life for him. He'd had it after a week of taking the prisoners around the Goodman acres, stripping the corn of its tassels and weeding after that. The only good news was they'd finish today. The other field at the far end of the farm contained regular corn rather than seed corn, so each of those plants kept their tassels. Today, he felt grateful for the small things.

Trent Franklin walked back from getting the last prisoner settled in his row. "Looks like you're all done in."

"Feels that way." Sid leaned against the truck and closed his eyes. The sun beat down on him.

"You should have come with me last night."

"After working like a dog all week? Franklin, I don't know where you get the oomph, but I'm glad I fell into bed."

Trent leaned against the truck next to him and stuck a stalk of wheat between his teeth. "There was this girl I danced with. You would have liked her, though I'm glad you weren't there to compete with me. I'll never understand why gals flock to you when I'm standing right here with my good looks."

"If you like Danny Kaye."

"Exactly, lean, lanky. That's me." Trent pulled the stalk from his mouth and struck a pose. "Not tall and rugged like you. Anyway, this gal was a looker. Short, blonde curls. Perky little nose. Come to think of it, she looked a lot like Miss Goodman. And she wouldn't tell me her name. What do you think of that?"

"Sounds like she wanted to play and not get involved."

"See, that's what I'm thinking." He shrugged. "You know, I think she could serve as Anna's twin. Even sounded like her. Not giving me her name, like she thought I already knew it."

Sid fought the heat that enveloped his gut. He'd spent the week slaving in her fields. And she danced the night away? He couldn't decide whether to be angry with her or glad that she'd loosened up.

Trent pushed off the truck. "I'll go walk the rows a bit. Check on the prisoners. You stay here and rest. You need it."

Sure he did. All because he worked hard for a gal who didn't notice or care. Well, he'd finished being her lackey. He'd find someone who appreciated him without letting him work to the bone.

Even as the thoughts assaulted him, he wondered if he could be happy with anybody else.

CHAPTER 20

JULY 14, 1944

*T*he door to Commander Moss's office stood open, and Sid spied him sitting behind his desk, working on paperwork. If that's how officers spent their time, Sid would stay at his current rank. He'd rather invest in people. He rapped on the doorframe.

Commander Moss looked up. "Come in, soldier."

"Specialist Chance reporting, sir." Sid remained at attention in front of the desk.

"At ease, Specialist." Commander Moss shifted some papers on his desk until he found what he wanted. "I've got orders sending you to the Grand Island satellite for a week. We've got a group of prisoners who need transport. You'll oversee that, then report back on the camp's status. I hear rumors of trouble and want it taken care of now."

Sid reached for the paperwork and swallowed. If he could pick, he didn't want to leave. Anna and he had some issues to work through. Unfortunately, the Army didn't bother iteself about such personal issues. "When do we leave?"

"Tomorrow morning. The prisoners report to work Monday. Take enough time to evaluate the situation. I need eyes and ears on the ground."

"Yes, sir."

"That's all." Commander Moss turned back to his work.

Sid snapped a salute, then spun and exited the room. There went his plans for the weekend. At least he wouldn't spend the next few days surrounded by corn. His skin itched at the thought. He'd never been so glad to end a task in his life.

The only drawback came from missing Anna. He'd planned to spend time with her while on his A pass. He'd earned that much. Guess he'd pocket the pass for another time. Maybe he'd find someone to spend time with at the Grand Island USO. The idea didn't excite him like he'd expected. There'd been many a day when the mere thought of spending time with a pretty gal would bring a lift to his mood. Today that didn't happen. Anna had crept further into his mind and heart than he'd realized.

Should he take the time to pray about what to do with Anna? She remained a complete puzzle to him. A frustrating one, but one he couldn't shake.

* * *

ANNA WATCHED Dottie throw a couple of blouses in her bag. For once, Anna would stay in Kearney for the weekend. The thought of spending the days right here, in her room, sounded wonderful.

"Sure you don't want to come see a certain soldier?"

"There's no guarantee he'll come to the farm."

Dottie snorted. "Sure. And cows are purple."

"He didn't seem very happy with me last weekend, anyway. Based on that, I'd be surprised if he came around while I'm there." Anna fluffed up her pillow, then leaned against it. "I need some time alone. Time to think and pray. Figure out where I'm supposed to focus my energy and attention."

"You mean you've finally heard everything I've said?" Dottie zipped up her bag and plopped next to Anna. "If that's what you're going to do, stay. Just make sure you don't have fun without me."

"Yes, mom."

"I should stay and supervise."

Anna shook her head. "No, I need solitude. At least as much as I can get in a boarding house. If I slow down awhile, maybe I'll hear something."

"You don't need me for that." Dottie hopped up and grabbed her bag. "Ta-ta. See you on Sunday."

The door closed behind Dottie, and Anna relaxed. If she let herself, she could sleep the entire weekend. While that might feel fantastic, she really needed time to think. Could she feel so out of sorts in recent weeks because she hadn't taken time to care for herself? The very idea seemed odd, but the more she'd prayed this week, the more she'd sensed the need—at the core of her being—to stop and reconnect with her heavenly Father.

Anna startled awake. Long shadows filled the room, and her stomach growled. She glanced at the clock. 8:00. Too late to ask Mrs. Wisdom for supper. Anna grabbed her clutch and hat and headed outside. She'd walk the couple of blocks to the café, see if they still served supper. Skipping meals hadn't been part of her agenda.

She strolled into the café, a hole in the wall tucked between a shoe store and small grocer. Couples sat at two of the tables, and a waitress stood at a counter, smacking gum while reading a copy of *Life*. Anna took a seat at the counter.

"Can I help you?" The waitress didn't look up from her magazine.

"Are you serving dinner?"

"Not anymore. Pie or coffee?"

Two slices of pie rested in the display case. "I guess I'll have the apple."

"Pear?"

"Fine. With a cup of coffee, please."

The waitress slapped the pie on a plate and slid it, with a cup of coffee, to Anna. "Enjoy."

This hadn't been how she envisioned starting her free weekend. As the piecrust melted on her tongue, she decided it wasn't a half-bad way after all. She paid and then walked back outside. The night felt mild, with a breeze to ease the earlier heat, as she strolled toward the Wisdoms' home.

Images of Papa filled her mind. Without a phone at the house, she couldn't tell him she wouldn't come home. By now, he'd probably figured that out, if he even missed her.

She savored the freedom Kearney offered. Papa couldn't yell that she was terrible or lazy. He would never understand how it felt to listen to his words day after day. But his silence was worse, leaving her wondering what she'd done wrong.

The thought of spending more time at home with him made her want to curl into a corner and hide. Yet, the more she prayed, the more that seemed the only solution.

Saturday Anna spent the morning in her room, reading her Bible and praying. By noon beads of sweat rolled down her cheeks. Her mind wandered as the blanket of heat weighed down on her. No matter how hard she tried to quiet her thoughts, they refused to cooperate. Instead, her ears seemed tuned to the sounds of the building. As the morning passed, her heart sank that Sid hadn't called for her.

"Enough." Anna threw her Bible next to her on the bed. "Time to do something."

If she walked around a bit, she could regain her focus. Work off the malaise that sapped her strength. She pulled on her loafers and headed for the stairs.

"Anna, you're in time." Gillian Turner clapped her hands together. "I wanted to knock on your door, but you were so quiet I was afraid I'd wake you."

Anna snorted. Like she'd ever slept to noon in her life. Shows how little Gillian knew her. "What did you need?"

Gillian turned to the soldiers with her. "We were headed to the USO for awhile. There's a lunch and afternoon activities there today. Join us? We need a fourth." She implored with eyes wide.

The two soldiers stood at ease, looking everywhere but at her. She'd seen the shorter one with Gillian before. But the taller, lanky one was new. It couldn't hurt anything to spend time with them. Anna wondered briefly about returning to her room, but after a morning locked inside, she couldn't stomach the idea of spending the rest of the day there.

"All right. Let me grab my bag." She scooted upstairs long enough to get her purse and touch up her lipstick.

Gillian introduced her to the two soldiers, and they headed to the USO. Anna's escort, Sammy Kersh, sat next to her in the car. The USO burst at the seams with soldiers and local girls. Anna wondered if she'd ever see it any way but packed. How could she feel so alone when surrounded by so many people? She caught the eyes of several soldiers watching her, but each took one look at her escort and turned around. "Do you mind giving me a little space?"

He locked his deep-brown eyes on her and grinned. "Mind?"

"I'm feeling a bit cornered." Anna crossed her arms and met his gaze with a glare.

"I don't know why."

"You're stuck to me like a burr to a steer."

Sammy threw his head back and laughed.

Anna bit the inside of her lip to hide the smile that wanted to escape.

"How about I do something about that?"

Anna held her tongue and hardened her expression while she waited for him to elaborate.

Sammy held up his hands. "Listen, the band's started. Let's take a whirl around the floor. Then, we'll grab a plate of food and eat outside, where we can find a quiet place to talk."

He tugged her after him onto the floor. He led her through the steps with self-assurance.

Anna tried to concentrate on him and the moment, but Sid's clear-blue eyes kept invading her mind. "What brings you to Kearney?"

"What brings anyone?" Sammy shrugged. "My crew is collecting our B-17. We'll ship out in a week or as soon as we've completed all the flight checks."

The song ended, and he led her to the tables loaded with sandwiches and salads. The conversation continued while they filled their plates. In a few moments, they settled in the shade of a large oak tree. It stood in a secluded location behind the building. Anna looked around, surprised to find no other couples had ventured out, away from the closed air of the hall.

Sam edged closer until their legs touched. She pulled her legs beneath her and eased some space between them. Sam eyed her over his meal, almost as if he wanted her for dessert. She tried to swallow a bite of her chicken sandwich, but it tasted like sandpaper.

"Come here, Anna."

"I think we're quite close enough." If he got any closer, she'd leave. Coming along to the USO looked like a worse decision with each minute.

Sam siddled toward her. "Never close enough."

"You are no gentleman."

He laughed at her. "I never said I was."

"I'm not interested in being any closer." Anna pushed her plate of food in his lap and stood. "You can find someone else to spend the rest of your afternoon with."

She shook and felt sick to her stomach as she walked to the street. Gillian could catch up with her at the Wisdoms'. Thank goodness, the walk wouldn't take all day.

As the blocks disappeared, her heart returned to its normal patterns. One thought cycled through her mind. In all her interactions with Sid, he had never once treated her with anything less than complete respect. She rubbed her arms, trying to bring some warmth, wishing Sid were here.

CHAPTER 21

JULY 17, 1944

$\mathcal{G}$rand Island, though larger than Holdrege or Kearney, didn't fit the bill for Sid that weekend. Even when the other soldiers headed out to explore the local scene, Sid stayed behind. Then, he wanted to check his temperature, see what was wrong. By Monday, he couldn't wait to get to work, discover what concerned Commander Moss, and return to Camp Atlanta.

Anything would be better than spending every waking moment wondering what one young woman was doing. He hated the fact that Anna Goodman had crept under his guard.

His style was to enjoy whatever woman he found himself matched with. Now, he mooned over a girl who drove him batty. A gal who forever surprised him. And a woman who made him want to drop everything and protect her.

What magic had she worked on him?

Monday morning, Sid strode into the satellite headquarters and introduced himself to the officer in charge. He tried to cover his surprise when he learned Larry Heglin filled that bill. "Commander Moss asked me to spend some time with you this week and see how we could better support your opereations in Grand Island."

Heglin sneered at him from behind his desk. "We're just fine, Chance. I've got things humming along without any interference from the bigwigs." He kicked back and stared down his nose at Sid. "Why would Moss send someone like you here, anyway? You're the one who lost the prisoner. Still trying to get in Moss's good graces?"

Sid stiffened his back. Heat climbed his neck, and he tried to force it away with a deep breath. "I'll spend the day with the prisoners at their assignment and check their quarters tonight."

"Waste your time all you want. I don't know what you think you'll find. The prisoners are fine, the employers pleased. That's all the Army can want."

Sid marched from the room. Of all the people who could command the post, he had to deal with someone as incompetent as Heglin. Yet another reason to get in and get out. It would have helped if Commander Moss had told him anything about why he was here. He hadn't picked up anything over the weekend. But most of the soldiers were on passes, with just a couple left to guard the prisoners.

Sid strode around the compound. The Army had retrofitted the old Dodge School to meet its needs. An eight-foot fence towered around the school with a few men and dogs patrolling the perimeter. Directly across the street stood the German American social club at Liederkranz Hall. The polka music had blasted from the facility over the weekend, but nothing that concerned Sid.

A bus waited outside the front door, and a steady line of prisoners boarded it. They stood with heads high, and quiet conversation flowed among them. From all outward appearances, they seemed content … at least as much as they could for people thousands of miles from home.

Sid made a mental note to learn who served as prisoner liaison and spend time with him. Until then, he'd circulate among them, see what he could pick up. He hadn't heard of aggressive Nazis being relocated from this group, so he didn't expect that to be the challenge.

The bus rumbled over the road until it reached the beet fields, where the prisoners worked. The day passed with Sid talking to the prisoners or their guards and finding each group equally unwilling to cooperate.

At this rate he'd have to spend a year here to learn anything.

Sid kicked back on his bunk that night, trying to stay as quiet as possible, as the soldiers bantered around him. Maybe they'd forget he was there.

"Did you see what Heglin did today?" A skinny soldier with a Bronx accent spoke from the doorway.

A soldier lying on his bed snorted. "You mean he actually left his desk? That guy likes to sit and look important rather than do anything."

"Sure, but today he strolled around surveying his kingdom after you left. I thought he acted kind of funny, so I kept an eye on him. He headed into the prisoner section. When he came out, he had a odd look on his face and loaded pockets."

"So? What's the big deal with that?"

"I don't know. Thought it interesting since he avoids the Germans like they've got some a disease." He pushed away from the door. "I'll never understand why someone like him was put in charge."

"That's the Army for ya. Always makes perfect sense."

The men chortled, then wandered into topics that held no interest for Sid. He couldn't imagine what Heglin could have found in the prisoners' quarters.

The next morning Sid stayed behind when the bus left. He decided to keep an eye on the prison and see if he could learn anything. If he could stay out of Heglin's way, maybe the man would forget him and repeat his actions from yesterday. Although, in a corner of his mind, Sid wondered if Heglin had put the soldiers up to that conversation last night. Surely, if theft were the issue, Commander Moss would have mentioned it.

Sid strolled through the prisoners' section, and everything seemed in place. The beds were neatly made and the aisles clear of clothes and other personal belongings. As he reached the end of the first room, Sid was surprised to see a prisoner asleep under his covers. Nothing appeared wrong with the man other than he lounged in bed rather than worked his job.

Sid neared the bed, keeping his steps light. The man sprang from his bed and grappled with Sid until he held Sid in a neck hold.

"You looking for something?" The words hissed into Sid's ear. "I told you come today. You take nothing more from my men and will return what you stole."

Sid pulled down on the arms locked around his throat. The man was stronger than he looked, and Sid grew light-headed. Someone said he'd been here? And he stole? That had Helgin's fingerprints all over it. But he couldn't get to the bottom of this while in a choke hold.

He tried to slide his foot behind the prisoner and knock him off his feet, but the man only pulled harder while lifting him off the ground. Sid scratched at the man's face and arms, but he seemed oblivious to any contact.

The man was a brute.

Why would Heglin set him up? What was he trying to cover up?

Sid licked his lips and tried to force some words out. "Stop. You'll be executed for killing an American soldier."

"I accept the punishment if it ends the stealing."

The man was beyond reason. Sid arched his back and lunged backward with everything in him. The prisoner grunted as Sid's full weight toppled on top of his, carrying them both to the floor. Sid felt the whoosh of air that left the man's lungs as they collided with the floor. His choke hold eased. Sid rolled to the side and rubbed his neck, keeping a wary eye on the prisoner.

Sid pulled a piece of rope from a bed frame and used it to tie the prisoner's hands together before he came around. The prisoner groaned and attempted to roll over. He eased to a sitting position and hung his head.

"Who told you to wait for me?"

The prisoner shook his head, lips squeezed in a tight line.

"I will get to the bottom of this, so I suggest you tell me before I decide you tried to kill me." Sid's heart pounded. If the prisoner didn't decide to talk soon, Sid didn't want to know what he'd have to do to get answers. He took a deep breath and prayed for control. He needed some. Fast.

The prisoner stared at him, his face a mask. A muscle twitched in his jaw, but his eyes remained set.

"All right. You get to come with me." Sid hauled the man to his feet and dragged him up the stairs and to the office. Heglin had disappeared, so Sid marched into his office, shut the door behind them, and settled the prisoner on a chair. He slipped around the desk and grabbed the phone.

"Commander Moss, please." Sid tapped his foot as he waited. What should he tell the commander? Someone used a prisoner to try to harm him? That he didn't have any proof of who, just a series of bruises?

"Moss, here."

"Good morning, sir. I'll bring one of the prisoners back with me." The conversation spooled out quickly. "No, sir, I don't have any concrete answers yet. Yes, there are some strange things happening. But the prisoners seem well cared for. I'll stay another day or two and then return. Yes, sir." Sid hung up and stared at the prisoner. "What am I going to do with you for another couple of days?"

The man continued to ignore him.

"Guess you're my new shadow." Sid stood. "Let's get back to work."

The door opened as Sid reached for it. Heglin stood there, face rigid. "What are you doing in my office? With one of my prisoners?"

"Checked in with Commander Moss. And this prisoner is no longer yours. He attacked a U.S. soldier and will return to Camp Atlanta with me. I wonder about your security, Heglin. He shouldn't have stayed behind."

"The doctor determined he was too sick to work."

"Seems healthy as a horse now." Sid grabbed the prisoner's shoulder and pushed past Heglin.

The next days passed without learning anything new. He hiked over to the German center across the street and ate with some of the locals, met with the doctor who checked the prisoners, and generally kept his eyes and ears open. While things felt off, nothing jumped out as wrong.

He drove back to Camp Atlanta with one prisoner and a truckfull of questions, feeling like he'd somehow failed.

Once he'd turned the prisoner over to the camp brig, he marched toward Commander Moss's office. He waited and waited and waited. Thoughts of what he'd rather do filtered through his mind. And a feisty blonde kept pulling at him. Regardless of what happened next, he knew he needed to find Anna. Too much time had expired since he'd seen her.

That feeling seemed strange. What happened to the guy who enjoyed the company of everybody? When had she snuck so far under his radar that she demanded more from him? Yet, he knew she would never actually do that.

No, she'd wait for him to make a decision and approach her. And if somebody else stole her affection during that time, it would be Sid's loss alone. He couldn't let that happen. As soon as he was done with Commander Moss, he'd have to try to reach her at the Wisdoms'. The sound of her voice would have to be enough today.

But it wouldn't be forever.

CHAPTER 22

JULY 20, 1944

*T*hursday afternoon, nausea roiled Anna's stomach as she approached Corporal Robertson. She hoped he'd be in a good mood since remnants of his lunch sat on his desk. Though everything in her fought what she had to do, she had no choice. Maybe if she did this, the knot that continued to tighten her stomach would finally ease.

"Corporal Robertson?" Her voice squeaked, and she cleared her throat.

He looked up, his mouth pressed into a slight frown. "Yes, Miss Goodman?"

"Could I speak with you a moment?" At his silence, she swallowed and rushed on. "I need a week to go home and make sure everything's okay. My papa isn't well, and it's a crucial time at the farm. If he's not caring for things, the crops could be lost."

"You've made a commitment to work here."

"Yes, sir. And I'll return. I need this time to take care of business at home. I'm not asking you to hold my job long. One week should be plenty of time." Anna crossed her fingers behind her back and waited.

He shuffled through some papers on his desk. "To keep your job, you'll need to be back by the following Monday."

"Yes, sir. Thank you." She slipped from his office before he could change his mind.

That evening the still July heat pressed Anna deeper into the chair she'd curled into. The Wisdoms' parlor stood empty, and usually she'd soak up the solitude. Instead, tonight the book she'd picked up couldn't hold her attention. Her thoughts kept returning to the conversation she'd had with Corporal Robertson that morning. She'd actually done it. She'd made the decision and now she had to find a way to survive the time. It would be easy to count down the days until she returned to her job and her steady existence here at the Wisdoms'.

She shook her head. It was too late to second-guess herself now. And what harm could come in nine days at home?

No, this was the right thing to do. That she knew full well. If only her mind would quit arguing with her heart.

One good thing about going home was she might actually see more of the captivating Mr. Chance. Warmth cloaked her from the inside out and stole up her cheeks. She liked that thought. Very much.

By Friday afternoon, even the idea of seeing Sid couldn't control the shivers that coursed through her body. Staying all that time—alone—with her father would drive her crazy if she let it.

Dottie eased to a stop in front of the farmhouse. Anna tried to move, but every muscle in her body refused to obey. Sheer determination kept her lungs pulling air in and pushing it out.

"You don't have to do this." Dottie's soft voice tugged at Anna. "We can turn around and go back to Kearney. You know the Widsoms won't mind."

Anna stared at the back door. If she didn't move, Papa would barge through it, yelling orders and curses. She couldn't tear her eyes from it any more than she could fly away. She slowly shook her head.

Dottie reached for her hand and held it tight. "I will pray for you. And you know Sid will come running the moment you ask."

A tear trickled down Anna's cheek. If only he were here. She'd searched for the truck that often waited next to the barn on Friday afternoons, but the yard was empty.

She took a deep breath and pulled her shoulders back. "Thanks for the ride." Anna leaned over and kissed Dottie on the cheek. "See you in a week."

"You can't get rid of me that easily. I'll be by Sunday ..." Dottie shrugged. "In case I miss you at church."

"Of course. Don't worry. I'll be fine." Maybe if she said them enough she'd eventually believe the words. *Okay, Lord. I'm trying to do what You asked. Please be with me and give me the strength I'll need to survive the next week.*

Anna grabbed her bag out of the backseat and waved as Dottie pulled out of the yard. This time Dottie missed the flowers as she backed out. Maybe it was a sign for the rest of the week.

After plopping the bag by the door, Anna walked toward the fields. She needed to see the progress. At least that excuse worked if needed. From the outside rows, it looked like the prisoners had completed detasseling. The wheat looked ready to explode from the kernels. She pulled a head off one stalk and popped the kernels out. She chewed on pieces until they gelled together and turned the consistency of gum.

She'd noticed that many surrounding fields that once held rows of winter wheat were now bare. Not one row at the Goodman farm had fallen. She'd need to get a ride to town and make sure the county extension agent knew she needed help. Now.

As she eyed the crop, she prayed they'd have time to get it in before a summer storm blew through.

* * *

SID GLANCED at his watch and winced. Everyone seemed to move slowly through the thick heat. A blast of humidity filled the air, adding to the discomfort.

While no one else was ready for the weekend, he was. A Class A pass waited for him, and he knew exactly what he would do with it: head to Holdrege, with a stop by the Goodman farm. He'd missed Anna each time he called the Wisdoms' this week. He'd explode if he didn't talk to her soon.

That unsettled him. But he couldn't deny it.

As he'd prayed this week, he'd decided he had two options. One, run from any possible deepening of their relationship. Or two, surrender and see what God might have in store.

He longed to fight surrendering. How could that be what God had in mind? Yet, he couldn't shake the idea that was exactly what God wanted him to do.

The line moved forward, and finally Sid walked out with his pass in one hand and keys to Trent's vehicle in the other. The miles rolled by in a blur as he raced the Ford to the Goodman farm. He didn't know what he'd say to Mr. Goodman if Anna wasn't there. Since the detasseling was completed, Sid didn't have any business stopping by except to check on the wheat. And he didn't think Mr. Goodman would welcome his company, not that he looked forward to seeing Mr. Goodman either.

He flipped on a blinker and eased onto the driveway. No vehicle waited, so either Dottie had already dropped Anna off or Anna wasn't coming home.

A small bag leaned against the house by the front door. He parked and hopped out of the car. A flash of color caught his eye, and his heart lifted. She'd come home after all.

* * *

ANNA TURNED BACK toward the house. She couldn't delay the inevitable any longer. A rumble caught her ear, and she spotted a Ford coupe pull in front of the house. Her hand fluttered to her neck as she waited to see who sat in the vehicle.

A tall soldier sauntered from the car toward her. Her breath caught in her throat. He'd come after all. Her thoughts jumbled, and she stood as if struck dumb. How could one man have such an effect on her?

A lazy grin carved Sid's face as he approached. "Hey, Anna."

"Hello."

"I didn't know if I'd see you."

She nodded. "I needed to come home for awhile. Make sure the crop got in."

"Your dad will be glad to see you."

"I don't know about that."

"He'll be glad to see anyone but me and the prisoners." Sid stood toe to toe with her.

The scent of his cologne reached her, and she could almost taste the cloves.

He grabbed her hand and rubbed a thumb across her fingers. "Come have dinner with me?"

Anna nodded, and warmth exploded through her. "I'd like that. But I have to check on Papa and see to the chores first."

"You might be surprised."

"Why?"

"I've actually caught him outside the house a few times."

She tried to focus on what he said even as her attention wandered to their interlocked hands.

"A couple of his friends came out and had him doing all kinds of things. They seemed to be a good influence on him."

She chuckled. Who would do something like that? She couldn't picture others leading Papa to do something he didn't want to do. "So who were they?"

"Who?"

"These two miracle workers."

Sid shrugged. "Teddy and Gus, I think. They did a good job with him." His Adam's apple bobbed. "So will you have dinner with me, or are you delaying?"

Warmth engulfed Anna. The usually self-assured, almost cocky Sid Chance stood almost undone in her presence. She grinned at him. "Race you to milk Nellie. The winner chooses our dinner location."

Anna sprinted toward the barn and laughed over her shoulder when she caught Sid languishing behind. "You're supposed to race, silly."

"Oh, I'm all too happy to let you milk the cow." The goofy look on his face warned that he had other things on his mind. Heat crept up her cheeks, and she hurried to the barn. He could play whatever games he wanted. They were too old for silliness.

The chores were done in a flurry of laughter and games, and Anna wondered if maybe she'd forgotten how to have a good time. The fight to keep everything going could have stolen the joy from her days. The words of Psalm 103:2 washed across her mind. *Bless the Lord, O my soul, and forget not all His benefits.* When was the last time she'd taken the time to consider everything He'd done for her rather than count up a laundry list of things she needed to handle? And when had she invited Him to help her with that laundry list? Why did she feel such a need to take the burden on her shoulders?

Sid approached her and grabbed her hands. "Where did you go?"

She lowered her gaze. "God was reminding me it's okay to celebrate the little things. Like beating you at chores."

His eyebrows arched. "I think it's time you picked your dinner spot."

She tugged, trying to free her hands. "All right. Let's head up to the house. Don't forget the basket with eggs."

Sid reached for the basket but refused to let go of one hand. "So we're staying here?"

"Simple fare on a simple farm." If he wanted to tease her like that, he would do it on her turf. And with Papa around, that would keep Sid in check.

"Then I'll have to steal my kiss now." Sid pulled her closer to him, and she found herself staring into his eyes. One could get lost exploring their depths. Expression flashed through them before a guard fell. "You aren't playing fair, Anna."

"What?" Confusion clouded her thoughts as he pushed her away.

"Why do you insist on knowing me?"

"Isn't that how it's supposed to be? You know my fears and joys, and I know yours?"

He grunted. Then pulled her back into the circle of his arms. "This is what I want you remembering." His lips closed on hers, and Anna sank into it for a moment.

When she almost couldn't breathe, she placed her palms against his chest. "You can't do that, Sid. Either you want to know me or you don't. You have to choose." She spun on her heel, grabbed her bag, and entered the house, cheeks flaming.

CHAPTER 23

*T*he truck ground across the country road, its bed loaded with prisoners. The county extension agent had assigned this group to return to the Goodman farm for harvesting the winter wheat. Days like this, Sid longed to return to Fort Robinson and the simplicity of training men and dogs. That job seemed so much easier than navigating farming on the fly and the mind of a certain young woman.

He hadn't known whether to laugh or groan when the powers that be determined he should return to that farm. He'd spent the days and nights since Friday plagued by Anna Goodman. Her blonde curls and pert nose haunted him. Why did she impact him this way? And why did one kiss make him feel like such a louse?

She was a puzzle that could drive him crazy. He couldn't determine how he felt about that.

"So are you turning or driving all day? Gas is a premium product, you know." Trent's teasing pulled Sid from his thoughts.

"Maybe I'll let you drive next time."

"And the moon will turn green. You aren't willing to give up control. Even to someone dependable like me."

Trent's words hit him in the chest like a machine gun blast. Was that his problem? He couldn't give up control? He wanted things his way or not at all? The thought settled on him like a spotlight illuminating a corner of his heart he didn't want to examine.

"Yeah, well, I suppose it's time to get these fellas to work."

"Another day, another wage. I'll never understand how grateful they are to work."

"Eliminates boredom and let's them do something important."

Trent snorted. "Not so sure why doctors and engineers think farming is important. Especially when it's for the enemy."

Sid held his tongue. While he enjoyed hanging out with Trent, there were times that his opinions bordered too closely with that of some of the other guards. The prisoners were men. As such, they deserved respect. Most of the time they received it, but the biases boggled his mind. Those biases traveled over to the civilians. Nebraska had a large German population, immigrants who were now in the second or third generation. Yet many of them had taken to hiding their German heritage in fear of reprisals like the Japanese Americans experienced.

Sid pulled the truck to a stop in front of the Goodman barn. Three men stood in a semicircle, watching. Looked like Mr. Goodman had decided today made a good day to get out of the house. His cohorts waited on either side of him. Gus and Teddy, the men working a miracle in the old bear.

"Mr. Goodman." Sid reached out to shake his hand. "Good morning, sir. Gus, Teddy. I've got prisoners ready to bring in the wheat."

"We could have used you a week or two ago."

"Yes, sir. We finished the detasseling, and the prisoners were assigned to another farm last week. The county agent didn't assign us until this week. The prisoners go where he indicates." No need to mention where he'd been last week.

"Harumph." Mr. Goodman turned to his friends. "Do you think these men can be taught?"

"Now, Ed, you know they can. You've seen how hard they work and eager to learn they are. Don't you think it's time to forget what happened to you in the Great War?"

Mr. Goodman's face soured. "I'm out here, ain't I? What more do you want?"

"An attitude change, but we'll take what we can get." Gus rubbed his ample belly. "Let's get to work while there's daylight."

Teddy nodded. "I've got the threshing equipment all set up."

Sid watched the two older men get the prisoners settled into groups. Mr. Goodman viewed their actions from his position to the side. Sid wondered if he'd ever learn the full story behind Mr. Goodman's animosity, but at least he had left the house and wasn't holding a gun to the prisoners' heads. He also hadn't sensed any alcohol on the man's breath. Come to think of it, he hadn't noticed that for a few visits. It was a start.

He looked to the house, noticing the curtains billowing out through the open kitchen windows. The scent of something sweet and spicy drifted on the wind.

"She's still here, boy."

Were his thoughts that transparent? Based on the grin covering Mr. Good-man's face, they must be. Looks like more than his attitude toward the Germans had softened. Sid wasn't sure what had caused the difference, but he liked it.

Mr. Goodman studied the house. "Anna said she's here through the harvest, so you might want to drag things out a bit."

Or speed them up. Sid didn't know how many more encounters with her he'd survive.

The morning rushed by in the fields, and when the sun stood high in the sky, the bell by the back door pealed. The Germans straggled out of the fields, many looking drained by the heat and labor. They perked up when they reached the backyard and found blankets spread in the shade of the oak trees. A table stood by the backdoor, laden down with sandwiches, apples, and glasses of fresh milk.

The men loaded chipped plates before collapsing on the blankets. In minutes, the food disappeared, followed by quiet snores, as the prisoners lay down. One pulled a slim book from his pocket and flipped its pages.

Sid leaned against the truck, watching Anna avoid him. Any time she caught him looking at her, color bloomed across her face. She had no idea how beautiful she was as she served the men. She seemed to have settled whatever had weighed her mind down about having the prisoners on the farm. Maybe the money issue had been resolved. It must have if she chose to stay here rather than hurry back to Kearney and her job.

She disappeared into the house with the last empty platter. He stepped away from the truck, ready to follow her until Gus stood and roused the prisoners. Time to head the men back to the field.

"You got them, Trent?"

"Sure, lover-boy. Don't take too long." A gleam sparked in Trent's eyes as he laughed.

Sid strode to the door and knocked. He opened it and slipped inside.

Blonde curls had escaped her headband and ringed her face, begging to be touched. She froze when she saw him.

"What can I help you with, Specialist Chance? Need more food?"

He shook his head. "I wanted to see you."

She leaned against the sink and crossed her arms. "Not sure I want to see you."

"Sure you do. Your face turn a beautiful shade when you see me." He edged closer. "Can we start again?"

"Why would we want to do that?"

"Because you are a beautiful woman that I care about."

"You have interesting ways of showing that, mister." A twinkle filled her gaze, and he relaxed in response. She might be mad, but she'd play along.

"So maybe I stepped out of line Friday."

"Maybe?" She exhaled. "Definitely."

"So give me another chance." He tugged one of her hands free. "I promise to be a perfect gentleman."

"Frankly, I don't think you have it in you." She considered him carefully, searching his eyes until he thought she must see every last corner of his soul. "If you can manage to be a gentleman the rest of this week, then we can go out on Friday or Saturday. But you might want to make sure the wheat's in by then."

"Why?"

"If a storm blows up while it's in the field, that will end any chance of a night out."

"All right, young lady. You win. I'll hurry back to the field and bring the wheat in myself if I have to."

"See that you do." She came closer. "I'd like that time with you very much."

He leaned in for a quick peck on the cheek. "See, I can be a perfect gentleman."

She shooed him away with a towel, but he left whistling a wordless tune filled with promise.

* * *

THE WEEK FLEW FOR ANNA. Caring for the chores and providing food for the men filled her days. Fortunately, they appreciated the sustenance no matter how many times she offered hard-boiled eggs, apples, and fresh bread.

The crop came in as big as it looked, giving the farm a chance to turn the corner this year. The knots of tension lining Anna's neck eased each time she thought of that. Maybe next year could start with a little money in the bank rather than robbing Peter to pay Paul. And the corn remained in the field where it stood tall, soaking in the sunshine.

By Friday, the prisoners had cut down the wheat, threshed most of it, and stored the precious kernels in the silo. Next week a truck from the co-op would come collect the crop.

Another year or two like this, and the farm might join the 1940s with a tractor. Gus had managed to sweet-talk one of the neighboring farmers out of his for a couple of days, and it had amazed Anna to watch the wheat fall in short order.

Looked like Sid would get his night out. And she had to admit she looked forward to it. Maybe he'd even act like a gentleman. No, she kind of liked him with his rakish air, like Rhett Butler. She had a feeling it remained an act, but she'd play along as long as he honored her lines.

It felt good to slip into a dress after a week in work clothes. It would be nice to have a job that allowed her to dress up each day. Until then, she'd enjoy every moment of the rare nights like tonight.

Sid's whistle announced his arrival through the open window. Anna pinched her cheeks in the small vanity mirror and then hurried to the living room. Papa was welcoming Sid with a sturdy handshake. She marveled at the change that had come over Papa in the last week. The more time he spent with the prisoners, the less they seemed to bother him. Could he have determined the time had come to let go of the pain from twenty-seven years earlier. His limp even seemed less pronounced. She paused outside the living room to enjoy their interaction.

"So where's that beautiful daughter of yours, sir?" Sid teased Pappa and her father seemed to enjoy it.

"Primping in her room." Papa turned and saw her. "Ah, there she is. You'd better be good to her, son. She's all I've got left."

Sid's face softened when he saw her. His eyes widened, and he stretched out a hand for a chair. "I'll do that. Yes, sirree, I'll take very good care of her."

Papa chuckled. "Be sure that you do. She'll demand nothing less from you."

"We'll be back soon, Papa."

He smiled at her. "See that you are. There's still plenty of work to do tomorrow."

There always was, but as she looked into Sid's eyes and saw the deep appreciation hidden in them, she didn't care. Right now, she would enjoy every moment of their time together.

He took her hand, and a jolt shot up her arm. She almost pulled back. The last thing they needed was more energy between them. No, time would prove whether their relationship was grounded on more than goose bumps.

As he led her to the car, she couldn't wait to explore the future.

CHAPTER 24

AUGUST 1944

*J*uly melted into August, the heat unrelenting, interrupted only by short periods of rain. Anna had returned to Kearney, safe in the knowledge that Papa seemed well on the road back to himself.

While she'd been home, one of the prisoners approached her about helping with costumes for a musical. Now, one corner of her room bore the results. Bolts of cloth tumbled in the area next to her wardrobe. Sid had promised to help her, but unless he could find little elves to sew costumes in the middle of the night, she didn't know what he could do.

A sigh slipped out, and she slumped on the edge of her bed. Someday she must learn to say no.

"Staring at that lump of material won't turn it into whatever it's supposed to become." Dottie leaned, arms crossed, against the door.

"You must think I'm crazy."

"Maybe a little. Did they do that great a job with the harvest?"

"I was a little grateful. We'll make it through the winter thanks in part to their work." Anna shrugged. "Staring it at won't make it go away. Let's cart the first bolt downstairs."

Before long, fabric covered the dining room table, and several boarders gathered around to help. Anna was glad it didn't bother anyone that the costumes were for the prisoners to use in one of their plays. Instead, the gals treated it like a social event. Mrs. Wisdom brought some of her famous snickerdoodle cookies and lemonade from the kitchen. That week afer the table was clear and Anna brought down the fabric and patterns, the evenings flowed by filled with laughter and flying needles. Then together they sewed the pieces together into the costumes. By Thursday, the bolts of cloth had turned into costumes needing only buttons and other finishing details.

Thursday Sid called with the message he'd pick her up Friday night to take her to Camp Atlanta to deliver the costumes. Her heart fluttered at the thought of dinner afterward. Then, back to the farm for a weekend interrupted only by the show on Saturday evening. Somehow, it sounded like a perfect two days.

As Anna was preparing her bag the next evening, she glanced at her room-mate. "Dottie, do you mind me going with Sid?"

"Don't be silly. I think I'll relax here." Dottie lounged on her bed, arms locked behind her head. "It seemed to work well for you, and I can't stay if I'm carting you home."

Anna's mouth dropped open, and she grabbed the pillow from her bed and threw it at Dottie. "I can't believe you said that."

Dottie's eyes flashed as she launched to her feet. "Time for you to stand on your own two feet, darling. I think Sid will be good for helping you do that."

"You are impossible." Anna stifled nervous laughter. "Time will tell what becomes of the two of us."

"Just remember to invite me to the wedding." Dottie flounced out of the room with a big grin.

Anna shook her head, grabbed another shirt, and thrust it into her bag. Before she was ready, Dottie ran back upstairs to tell her Sid waited. Together the girls wrestled bags of costumes down and dropped them at his feet.

"Think you can get them in your Jeep, soldier?"

Sid's eyes got big as he looked at the piles. "How many costumes did you make?"

"As many as they requested. Let's get going. I can't wait to see their faces."

The expression on Sid's face indicated he couldn't either. Anna pushed the thought from her mind as they hopped in the car. As the miles ticked by, Sid loosened up. Conversation flowed, and before she was ready, Camp Atlanta came into view, and Sid slowed the car.

"Don't be surprised if the prisoners are … hesitant around you. They aren't used to seeing many civilians here."

"It will be fine. They asked for my help, after all." Anna bounced out of the car when it finally pulled to a stop in front of a long, narrow concrete building. She glanced around. All the buildings had the look of standard government-issue structures built in a hurry.

This particular structure had posters on the outside in German and English. Looked like a community hall. A prisoner exited, dressed in his denim outfit with the painted Ps and Ws. He stopped in his tracks when he saw Sid.

"Sir?"

"Luka. Miss Goodman has a carfull of costumes for you." The funny look returned to Sid's face as he spoke.

Luka cocked his head and looked from Anna to the car. "Costumes?"

"Yes, one of you asked her to help. She took that to heart."

Luka disappeared into the building and came back out with several men. In no time, they had the car unloaded. Quiet German comments passed between them as they worked, but Anna couldn't understand any of it.

"Thank you for your help." Luka nodded in a bow. "Please come to show."

"You're welcome." Anna looked at Sid. "Can I come? To the show?"

"I can bring you if you like. Tomorrow night, Luka?"

"Yes, sir. Six." Luka bowed again and slipped into the building.

Anna linked arms with Sid. "Sounds like we have a date, then."

"How did I get lucky enough to spend so much time with you?"

Sid settled her in the car. Anna marveled at the change only a week had brought into their friendship. Maybe more was possible between them. Her heart skipped at the hope she felt at the idea.

* * *

Sid tried hard to wipe the smirk off his face before he climbed back in the car. Who in their right mind thought the prisoners would need twenty costumes for their plays? Sid had no idea what entertainment the men planned for tomorrow night, but this would be interesting to see.

The evening passed quietly at the Goodman farm. Anna and Sid had fallen into a routine over the last weeks of completing the chores together and then enjoying a quiet meal with her father. Friday night Mr. Goodman even brought out checkers when they'd finished the meal. Sid kept an eye open for alcohol, but it looked like Mr. Goodman had put it away. Maybe getting back to the work of the farm had been the cure all along.

"Mr. Goodman, thanks for the game of checkers. It's been awhile since someone trounced me."

Mr. Goodman grinned. "You can always learn something from your elders, boy."

"Yes, sir. I need to get back to camp. See me to the door, Anna?" Sid stood and reached out for Anna. Her soft smile stilled a place deep inside him.

"I'll be back in a minute, Papa."

Mr. Goodman nodded and picked up his paper. Sid must have made progress if the man didn't feel the need to watch them through the window.

The screen door slammed behind them, and he pulled Anna against him. "I'll be back tomorrow late afternoon to pick you up."

She relaxed next to him. He tipped her chin up, searching her eyes in the glow from the kitchen windows. Her gaze was filled with gentleness and a spark of something. He leaned toward her and waited, but she didn't pull away. He closed the distance for a tender kiss, then stepped back, taking a deep breath. "Till tomorrow."

She smiled and then stepped back and waved as he pulled out of the driveway.

Saturday afternoon Sid collected Anna and took her into Holdrege for an early dinner. They strolled the streets of downtown, enjoying the cool breeze. The sounds of a violin's tender wail drew them to a store.

Anna peeked in the window of the pawnshop. "Let's go in."

Sid pulled open the door, and they stepped inside. Stale cigar smoke mixed with mint and tickled his nose. Old Mr. Gustave, the proprietor, leaned against the counter, fingers tapping a beat on the counter. Two Germans stood in the shop with a guard behind them. One of the prisoners held a violin and played the instrument with a passion that made it sing.

Anna leaned into Sid and sighed. "That's beautiful."

Sid had to agree. The man had turned a lump of wood into a songbird. After listening a few minutes, they returned to the car. They made it back to Camp Atlanta in time to catch the show. The prisoners had used the costumes to add humor to their vaudeville-style act. Sid watched Anna out of the corner of his eye. She soaked in the show with enthusiasm. Did she ever do anything half-heartedly? He hadn't seen any evidence that she did.

They strolled out of the building, Anna humming one of the tunes. He looked down at her, and his heart stopped. Why could he now imagine walking like this until they were hunched and gray? He rubbed her hand with his thumb. "How would you like to have dessert at the officers' club?"

Anna stopped mid-hum and nodded. "I'd like that. Am I dressed appropriately?"

"Hmm. Let me check."

She twirled in front of him, hand posed under her chin. Her skirt swished around her knees, and the color enhanced her eyes.

"I can't think of anything better."

A soft blush tinged her cheeks, only heightening her beauty. "Thank you." She reclaimed his arm. "Lead on."

It took a few minutes, but too soon they reached the officers' club. He opened the door, and she glided past him into the entryway.

"Looky here. If it ain't the German-loving soldier."

Sid stopped inside the doorway, trying to decide how to respond. Should he let it go? More and more of these remarks were fired his way, and he'd grown weary of them.

Anna held her breath by his side. Her fingers tightened on his arm, and when he looked down, he saw her knuckles had whitened.

"Cat got your tongue, Chance? Or do you only understand German?"

Sid drew his shoulders and tugged Anna to follow. "Let's go find a table away from the rabble."

She pressed her lips together. She bobbled on the first step, and he held her firmly.

"Guess he's too good to talk to us. Maybe if we were POWs that would change." Larry Heglin stood in front of Sid, an ugly leer on his face. What was he doing here? "So is she German, too?"

Sid fisted his hands to keep from punching Larry. It took every ounce of control not to jump the man. "Don't ever speak about Miss Goodman that way again, Heglin. You can say whatever you want about me, but leave her out of this."

"Ever the noble one, aren't you? Someday you'll slip, and I'll be there spreading the word." Heglin brushed by Sid as he pushed through the door.

Sid glanced at Anna. "Are you okay?" She nodded, but her chin trembled. "Let's get you in and settled. Don't worry about Larry. Men like him are all talk. You learn to ignore them until they have something meaningful to say."

Anna relaxed when she sank onto a seat.

Sid started talking, regaling her with stories until the shadows left her gaze. He'd shelter her for a lifetime if she'd let him.

CHAPTER 25

SEPTEMBER 3, 1944

*T*he sunlight pulled Anna from a dream she didn't want to leave. In it, Sid defended her from others, eyes alight with love and concern. She squeezed her eyes more tightly and curled around her pillow.

The clock ticked a metronome's beat in her ear until she finally groped for it. She squinted at it and groaned. Time to get up and ready for church. She'd join the Wisdoms at their community church today, then head to the air base for the Labor Day picnic. She'd mentioned the picnic to Sid, but he hadn't taken the hint. Guess she'd go alone.

The pastor preached on Psalm 103:2. Everywhere she turned, it seemed God reminded her to pay attention to everything He'd done for her. With each day, she could see His movement in her life, and gratitude bubbled inside her.

The Wisdoms dropped her off at the air base after the service.

"Will you be able to get back home all right?" Mr. Wisdom pulled Anna's picnic basket from the rumble seat and handed it to her.

"I'll catch the bus. Thanks again." Anna set down the basked and adjusted the beret resting on her curls then waved as the Wisdoms pulled away from the gate. Picking up the basket, she smiled at the guards and strolled to the other side of their barricade.

The grounds buzzed with more activity than usual as cars zipped to the parade grounds. Anna joined the flow of people, feeling incredibly isolated.

"Anna, over here."

Anna scanned the crowd, trying to locate the person yelling for her. Finally, she spied someone waving. She raised a hand to shield the sun. Gillian Turner waved from a group of Anna's coworkers. Anna waited for a car to pass, then hurried across the street.

"Morning, gals."

"So you ventured out for the shindig." Gillian smiled and hooked arms with Anna.

Anna nodded. "It was a good weekend to stay in town."

"Let's find a place to settle down and eat. I'm starved." In no time, Gillian had the group of girls relaxing on a couple of blankets. They broke into their baskets and spread the food out, a buffet of choices.

Once Anna had filled her plate with fried chicken and potato and other salads, she sank down and enjoyed in the carefree banter. A military band struck up a rousing march, and the crowd clapped along. Local politicians and officers took turns making speeches. As the afternoon wore on, Anna's eyes grew heavy. If things didn't change soon, she'd fall asleep to the droning voices.

She slipped her hat off her hair and fanned her face with the hat. Anything to wake up.

Corporal Robertson stepped up to the podium, and the microphone squealed. He tapped it and then shrugged. "Good afternoon, ladies and gentlemen. It is a pleasure to add my personal welcome. As we celebrate Labor Day, I wanted to take a moment to recognize one individual who works in my department.

"In the parachute department, we have instituted what I like to call the Cocoon Club. It is an exclusive club. Only people who have packed a parachute which later saved someone's life can be inducted into this group. To date, about one dozen of your fellow residents have had the honor of saving someone's life by completing their jobs diligently and competently."

He rubbed a hand across his cheek and shrugged. "None of the members strive for recognition, and that certainly remains true of the newest member. She works hard every day and focuses completely on the task at hand.

"Two weeks ago, I received a letter from a captain, thanking me for the excellent job with his parachute. He flew a bomber behind enemy lines hours before the attack on Normandy launched. However, the Germans hit his plane with shrapnel and antiaircraft fire. As a result, he and the rest of his crew were forced to bail out over enemy territory. A parachute of a crew member failed to open, but the captain's performed as expected.

"He spent two months as a prisoner of war before escaping and rejoining American troops three weeks ago. The first thing he did was post a letter to us expressing his appreciation. Captain Brent Goodman's parachute was packed by his sister, Anna Goodman. Anna, please join me up here as we welcome you to the Cocoon Club."

Anna tried to pull in a breath of air, but her lungs had frozen at the mention of Brent's name. He had escaped from the Germans! All this time Papa and she had thought him a POW, and he'd fought to find his way back.

The crowd erupted into applause. She clamped an arm around her stomach in a desperate grip as she covered her mouth. A veil of tears tried to blind her. "Anna." Corporal Roberson tapped his foot as he stared her direction.

She didn't have the strength to stand, let alone walk in front of the crowd. A strong hand covered her shoulder. She could tell by the strength it offered that

Sid had found her. Tears poured down her cheeks, and her colleagues wrapped her in warm hugs.

"I'll help you up there." His voice held a cord of strength mixed with compassion.

At his words, her tears turned into sobs. She leaned into Sid's shoulder and cried as if her heart would never recover. He ran his fingers over her hair and whispered words she couldn't understand. The applause slowed, and the rustle of people standing to their feet took its place.

Sid brushed a strand behind her ear. "I think they're determined to see this dynamo who saved her brother's life."

Anna nodded and wiped the tears from her face. She could do this. All it entailed was walking to the podium and shaking Corporal Robertson's hand. Sid helped her to her feet, then guided her through the crowd. Anna kept her gaze fixed on his shoulder, sure that if she looked at anyone, she'd erupt in fresh sobs. God was so good! Her brother had returned, though after she got through giving him grief for letting her find out like this, he might wish he'd stayed hidden a bit longer.

"Come on up here, Anna." Corporal Robertson helped her onto the stage. "Congratulations on saving a man's life. Keep up the good work." He leaned close and whispered. "Take tomorrow off if you need to. I didn't realize you didn't know he'd escaped."

"Thank you, sir." She hurried off the stage before he could ask her to do anything else. All she wanted to do now was go home and make sure Papa knew. She turned to Sid as soon as both feet were on solid ground. "Can you take me home?" She sucked in a shuddering breath as tears skimmed down her face. "I need to tell Papa."

Sid studied her face a moment, then nodded. "Follow me."

With Sid navigating her through the field of well-wishers, they reached his car in short order. The trip to the farm passed in a cloud of conflicting emotions. Thankfulness dominated her jumbled thoughts. Only God could have protected Brent through everything and helped him find his way to the Allies.

She stumbled from the car before Sid braked. "Papa. Papa! Come here."

Did she run to the barn to look for him? Or was he in the house? Her mind couldn't get instructions to her legs. She couldn't decide whether to sink into Papa's arms or spin and shout the good news.

The slamming of the screen door caught her attention.

"What is it, girl? You aren't hurt are you?"

"No, Papa." She gulped in air, but felt like she gasped it through a straw.

"Well, spit it out."

"Brent. He's ..."

"He's what?"

She let the joy explode inside her. "He's safe! He's with the Allies."

Papa pulled her into his arms, then slapped Sid on the back. "My boy's coming home."

As Anna watched his exuberance, she knew everything would be all right.

* * *

Camp Atlanta seemed mundane after watching Anna tell her father that Brent lived. Yet, Sid tried to focus on the task at hand. With the corn harvest a few weeks away, the farmers needed the prisoners less, so more of Sid's time drifted by watching prisoners who didn't want to escape. He supposed he should be grateful he had a posting like this when so many experienced battle firsthand. But boredom brought its own struggles. The lone highlight on many of his days was a call to Anna in the evenings or the occasional opportunity to see her at the farm. Unfortunately, now that her father had come alive, she didn't spend every weekend at home.

The September days felt mired in molasses. One evening late in the month, Sid joined the soldiers in their barracks. Trent sprawled across the bunk next to Sid's, and they played a game of cards using the floor between their beds as a table. Before long, someone turned the lights out, and Sid tried to settle in.

He woke when something foul smelling reached him. It smelled like someone had set a campfire outside the building. The smoky smell made his stomach grumble, and he thought about nights spent around a campfire. Maybe someone could find some marshmallows, graham crackers, and chocolate.

A pounding caused Sid to sit up.

"What's with all the racket?" Trent's raspy voice penetrated the Sid's fog.

"Looks like someone wants us up."

"Well, you go check. I'm in the middle of a great dream." Trent rolled over and pulled the covers tight against his chin.

The pounding continued. "Get up! You must get out now!" The voice bore a heavy accent, and one of the soldiers cursed.

"If this is some kind of joke, someone will pay."

Sid sighed as he climbed out of bed. "And if it's not, you'll be sorry you didn't respond." He plodded to the door and opened it. He paused when he saw one of the prisoners standing there. "What do you need, Oskar?"

"Hurry. Must get out. Fire on building." He gestured wildly around the corner. "Come. Now!"

Sid hurried to follow the man. He turned the corner and spotted a dozen prisoners in a line of sorts, throwing buckets of water on a fire that lapped at the building. Dashing back into the barracks, he ran up and down the aisle, pulling blankets from the men.

"Everyone out! The barracks are on fire."

The men launched out of their beds and hopped into pants or pulled on shirts. An hour later the water had quenched the fire. A bedraggled group of prisoners and soldiers collapsed on the ground. Other soldiers straggled out of their barracks.

"What happened here?"

Sid looked up to see Commander Moss approaching. Even in the middle of the night, he wore his uniform and looked ready for an inspection.

"There was a fire, but a group of prisoners smelled it and came to put it out. They also alerted us, so we were able to get out. It looks like the building will be fine, though we'll need to sleep somewhere else until the smoke clears."

Commander Moss turned to the prisoners. "Thank you for what you did tonight. I won't forget it." He turned to one of the officers. "Please escort them back to their building and make sure they are allowed to sleep late into the morning."

"Thank you, sir." Oskar spoke for the others. "We do anything for Officer Chance."

Sid felt warmth spread through him. The prisoners appreciated his efforts on their behalf. The occasional ribbing from other soldiers amounted to nothing compared to what the prisoners had done. He couldn't wait to tell Anna about this. A yawn stretched his face. First, he needed some sleep. Then, he'd find her.

CHAPTER 26

LATE SEPTEMBER 1944

*T*he first nip of fall tinged the air, but the hint of a looming Indian summer promised autumn hadn't officially arrived. Anna sat on the Wisdoms' front steps and hoped it would arrive in time for the corn harvest. She'd already arranged to spend that week home, helping with meals and anything else Papa needed.

She marveled at the changes in him. Since she'd told him Brent had escaped, he'd returned to his work with the farm. He didn't need her there on weekends to hold his hand and finish chores. Instead, those days were often filled with good-natured ribbing when Gus and Teddy came for dinner. They'd josh and tell tall tales with Papa until long after Anna gave up and went to bed.

With one breath she felt nothing but relief. Other times she wondered if he needed her at all anymore. She couldn't imagine finding her only purpose at the air base. Little remained for her at home, and a curious emptiness gnawed her.

The screech of the front door opening pulled Anna from her thoughts.

"Anna." Anna turned to see Mrs. Wisdom step onto the porch. "You've got a phone call. Sounds like your soldier."

Warmth replaced the uneasiness that had surrounded her. It amazed her that the mere thought of Sid could do that. "Thank you." Anna followed Mrs. Wisdom inside and into the kitchen.

"Hello."

"Anna, are you free tonight?"

She paused as if checking her full calendar. "I could squeeze time in for you."

How was it possible to hear him smile across the phone?

"I won't have long, but let's grab a piece of pie somewhere." The hope in Sid's voice made her want to agree to almost anything he would ask.

"I think we have some left from dinner. Mrs. Wisdom won't mind if we eat it."

"Sounds even better. I'll be there in thirty minutes." Sid rang off.

Anna rushed up the stairs to her room.

Dottie lounged on her bed, reading a book. "What's the hurry?"

"Sid's coming over."

A knowing grin curved Dottie's lips. "That explains it. Let me try to do something with that impossible hair."

Anna sat down on the floor and handed Dottie a hairbrush.

"Do you think Sid feels for you anything close to what you feel for him?"

Anna sighed. That was the question that plagued her when they were apart. She hoped, even prayed, that he did. If he didn't, she wasn't sure what she would do. Her heart felt entwined with his.

* * *

SID DROVE the truck across Kearney to the Wisdoms'. His heart raced at the opportunity to see Anna. Any time with her was valuable, and he wondered if that was good. She filled his thoughts and drove him to distraction. He couldn't imagine living the rest of his life without her. Spending time with her made him want to be a better man, someone she could honor. No one else drew that out of him.

Maybe she was the one. He'd prayed about it. But he'd also decided they needed to spend time together, build their friendship, and see what their relationship contained. Would she forever think of him as a nice soldier that she once knew.

That wasn't enough for him. He wanted more. But he wanted it in God's timing.

And no matter how he prayed, he hadn't received the freedom to move ahead. Not yet. Hard as it was, he'd wait for that release.

That didn't mean he had to stay away, though. As he pulled up to the Wisdoms' home and saw Anna waiting on the front porch, his heart caught in his throat.

He only wanted to be with her gazing into those amazing eyes and hearing her heart.

* * *

SEPTEMBER ROLLED INTO OCTOBER, and Anna returned to the farm for the long week of the corn harvest. Storm clouds threatened on the horizon, and the radio carried word that the fields to the south were pounded by rain. Anna prayed the storms would keep to the south or disappear altogether until after harvest. She hated hearing the rain devastated any crop.

Papa paced the house, pausing at each window to swipe the curtain aside and stare at the sky. Occasionally, a curse would escape his lips, followed by a quick apology and prayer for protection.

"Please sit down, Papa. You're driving me crazy with your constant pacing." Anna pulled the coffeepot off the stove. "I've brewed some fresh coffee. Sit down, and I'll pour you a cup."

"I don't need something to add to my jitters." Papa harrumphed and took a seat. Anna handed him a mug, then watched as his fingers laced and unlaced around the cup. Back and forth in a gesture that telegraphed his fear.

She settled down next to him and placed a hand over his. "Papa, we can't do anything about the storm but pray. Maybe God will send it around us."

"Or maybe He'll send it right through here." His head bowed, and Anna didn't know if he'd ever seemed so defeated. "Girl, we can't survive many more hits."

"God has seen us through so much, He won't leave us now. And we'll fight to keep the farm for Brent. If we have to let it go at some point, God will have something else in mind for us. You have to believe that."

Papa shook his head and stood. "I'm going to walk the fields."

Anna watched him leave and prayed that God would push the storm away. Papa might not endure another test.

The next morning the sound of large raindrops pounded the windowpanes jerked Anna from sleep. She hurried out of bed to the window and brushed the curtain aside. Puddles stood in the yard. How had she not heard the storm during the night? She grabbed her robe and hurried to the kitchen.

Papa sat at the table, head in his hands, bottle of whiskey next to his mug of coffee.

Anna scurried toward him and grabbed the whiskey before he could look up. "Papa, no."

A dark scowl covered his face as he stared at her. "Leave it be, girl. What else am I supposed to do?"

"It's rain. It'll end, and the clouds will clear. Soon we'll be in the fields."

"This is Nebraska. It's practically Columbus Day, and we could have a hard freeze before we get back in those fields."

"Can we do anything about it?" She waited. "I didn't think so. Your choices are to start drinking again or trust God."

Papa sagged against the table. "I can't do this on my own."

"Good. That's exactly where God wants us. Recognizing that life is more than we can handle on our own without Him." Anna took the bottle to the sink and set it down. "Papa, I can't worry about you when I'm in Kearney. You have to choose to stay sober. Mama would want it, but you have to do it." She sighed. "I'll go get dressed and handle the chores."

Anna slopped through the rain and puddles to take care of the cow and chickens. By midmorning the rain had stopped. It would take days to dry, and soon as it did, they could hurry into the fields.

She returned to the house with hesitant steps. What if Papa had picked up the bottle of whiskey after all? Instead, she found him pouring over material.

"Maybe it's time to try something new. I've heard good things about soybeans."

Anna nodded. "Could be a welcome change for the land."

"Don't worry, Anna." He looked at her with hope in his eyes. "We'll make it.

Gus came out to tell me that we'll have his corn harvester as soon as the fields dry. I was afraid we'd lost our window, but he'll take care of it."

"Then we won't need prisoners to get the crop in?"

"We'll let the machines do the heavy work, but we'll need the men, too. It'll be a record harvest once the water drains." Papa plotted out plans on a piece of paper as he poured over the brochures.

For the first time in a long while, Anna believed him. The farm would make it regardless of the weather. And if Papa was fine, she should start preparing for her future.

CHAPTER 27

OCTOBER 15, 1944

*T*he congregation sang the closing words of "Trust and Obey" when Sid slipped into the pew and settled next to Anna and her father. The corn harvest had kept him driving the surrounding counties. Some had endured rain, while other fields sat dry, waiting for the corn pickers and men.

As a result of all that driving, Sid had plenty of quiet time to think and pray about the future. With each day, he felt more certain that God would honor his desire to pursue Anna. Sid still didn't know what she would say—he hoped she'd say yes—but he knew he could ask.

He tried to ignore the soft scent Anna wore and forced his attention to the pastor. The sermon came from Hebrews 6, with the pastor focusing on anchoring to God. "Sometimes God asks us to follow Him without a clear plan or direction, but He will honor our faith."

Sid leaned forward, eager for that kind of bedrock faith. *Lord, I want to follow anywhere You lead. Become my heart's true desire and passion. I want to trust and obey whatever You ask.* It would be hard to trust God that completely, but he'd learn. He knew he'd mess things up if left to his own devices.

No, he needed Someone bigger and wiser to direct his steps.

The service closed with another hymn, and all too soon, he stood in the aisle, looking down at Anna. Despite the week's setbacks, she seemed calm. He liked the look. A lot.

"Will you join us at the farm for lunch?" Her eyes twinkled as if she knew he couldn't turn her down.

He toyed with the idea of saying no, but discarded it. He wanted to spend every moment with her he could. And once the new morning came, he'd be busy as ever and she'd return to Kearney. "All right."

"Good. It'll be simple, but Papa can beat you at checkers to make up for that."

Sid followed them to the house, surprised by the lightness that filled the home. It was as if a heavy burden had lifted from it in the week since he'd last stopped after the harvest. He watched Ed closely and decided the root of the change came from him. Ed walked and talked with a new freeness and openness. He'd wrestled with his demons and killed them. The change was wide-reaching.

After a filling meal and a game of checkers, Sid grabbed Anna's hand and tugged her to him. She leaned into him, gazing at him with trust.

"Yes?"

"Let's go for a walk."

"The farm hasn't changed since you were here other than some mud."

"Put on some boots, and let's stroll."

Anna raised an eyebrow at him, then nodded. "I'll be right back." She returned a minute later, having traded her church dress for a practical shirt, pants, and boots. He wished she hadn't changed, except the shirt matched her cornflower-blue eyes, making them sparkle even more.

He took her hand and pulled her out the door. Once outside, he tugged her out of sight behind the barn.

A mischievous light filled her gaze. "What do you think you're doing, Specialist Chance? Stealing a kiss?"

He studied her sweet lips and liked the idea. "Maybe in a minute. First, I need to ask you something."

Anna waited against the barn. He loved the way she didn't rush to fill silence.

"I've thought a lot lately about us and what happens after the war ends." He rubbed a hand through his hair. Why was this so hard, even after rehearsing it continually on the drive to church and here? "What I'm trying to say is I love you, Anna Goodman. I adore your heart. The way you fight to protect those who are important to you. The way you live life intently. And I want to share the future with you." He groaned. "Maybe I will take that kiss."

He hesitated, saw her take a breath and collect herself. He eased nearer. "I love every single bit of you, Anna Goodman. Will you be my wife?"

She threw her arms around his neck and pulled him down until they stood eye to eye. "I will, Mr. Chance." She closed her eyes. "Now you can kiss me."

* * *

THE NEXT TWO months flew by for Anna. The harvest made it in, Papa had settled back into farming, and they'd even received a couple of letters from Brent. Christmas Eve dawned bright and clear, with a thick layer of snow on the ground. Anna rolled over in bed, wanting to hold every moment tight.

"Come on, sleepyhead. Today's your day!" Dottie bounced up and down on her bed at the Wisdoms, already dressed in a beautiful suit. "If you don't hurry, we'll be late to the chapel." She sighed dramatically and threw her hand to her head. "I can't believe you get to use it before me."

Anna smiled. Guess she'd have to capture the moments as she lived them.

Dottie wouldn't give her any peace until she was dressed in her white suit. After Anna was ready, Dottie tried to corral the curls around Anna's head, until Anna finally pushed her away.

"Sid won't recognize me if you restrain them." Anna took one last look in the mirror, touched up her lipstick, then grabbed Dottie's hand. "Let's go get Papa and head to the base."

Christmas Eve probably wasn't the best day to get married, but Sid had insisted he could imagine it no other way, that she was the best gift he'd ever received and he wanted to always remember the day. Fortunately, the chaplain had worked with them, squeezing thirty minutes into a day already packed with services.

Papa stood at the bottom of the stairs near the Wisdoms' front door, yanking on his tie. "Don't know why I have to wear this thing."

"Because your only daughter only gets married once. Come on, Papa. Don't be a bear on my day."

He grunted, then helped her into her coat and the car. The Wisdoms had already left, and Anna couldn't wait to get to the church.

* * *

Sɪᴅ ᴘᴀᴄᴇᴅ the small foyer of the chapel. He tried not to look at his watch, but where was she? He'd waited what felt like an eternity, but couldn't have been more than a half hour. Last night she'd seemed sure before she shooed him away. Maybe he'd misread all the signs. What did he really know about women and serious commitments, anyway?

"Calm down, soldier." Trent lounged against the wall, laughing at him. "She'll be here. You have to be patient. Isn't this what women do? Leave men waiting?"

"I suppose you're right. This is harder than I thought."

Trent pushed off the wall and straightened Sid's collar. "Don't worry. You look great. She'll be blissfully happy. And then you'll have to find a place to live in Holdrege."

"We'll be on the farm, at least as long as I'm stationed at Camp Atlanta."

"Now, that sounds like a recipe for newlywed bliss."

Sid socked Trent in the shoulder. "And what would you know about that?"

"Nothing." Trent looked toward the opening door. "But you'll know all about it very soon."

Dottie popped through the doorway, followed by Anna and her father. Sid's mouth dropped. Anna had never looked more beautiful than she did right now. Why had God chosen to bless him so? His heart slowly began to beat again, and he smiled at her.

"I'll let the chaplain know you're ready for him." Trent slipped into the sanctuary.

"Ready for this?" Sid whispered the words in Anna's ears.

"Absolutely." The promise of years together shone in her eyes.

Trent ran down the aisle. "The chaplain's waiting."

Sid smiled. He'd never been more ready for anything in his life. "Let's go."

EPILOGUE

SIXTY-THREE YEARS LATER

*W*armth flowed from the fire crackling in the fireplace. The laughter and pounding feet of children running up and down the stairs brought a smile to Anna's face. On those rare occasions when the whole family gathered, she couldn't help counting her blessings. God never ceased to overwhelm her with His goodness.

Since that day so long ago, when Sid took her hand in the small white chapel at Camp Atlanta and they'd recited their vows, God had walked with them. Through the joys of the birth of each child. A daughter just like her. Two sons, each as different as could be. A second daughter who brought such joy to Anna's heart with the close friendship they shared.

But the story didn't stop there. No, by God's goodness, they'd walked through their share of valleys, always toward the peek of the sun's rays on the other side. There was the child they buried before his time. The layoffs at the company that had employed Sid. The uncertainty of his next job, and Anna's return to work long enough to make ends meet. The loss of Papa and their eventual move back to the farm.

Yet, through it all, God had walked each step beside her. She'd even seen His hand prepare the way for them on occasion. How else could she explain the wonderful men and women who had joined their family by marrying the children? And the blessings when those unions added grandchildren to the family.

The grandchildren delighted her heart. They'd filled her days with joy in her sixties as she chased seven little ones all over the farm. Now, they'd magnified the joy by marrying and having children of their own.

Today, the pounding feet that beat a rhythm in her heart came from the nine great-grandchildren. And next year, if God allowed her to live so long, there'd be two more. His goodness knew no bounds.

"What's putting that sweet smile on your face?"

Anna looked up to see Sid standing beside her. Age had pushed his shoulders forward, and his knees didn't cooperate like they used to, but he was every bit the proud solider she'd met in 1944. "Counting my many blessings."

He chuckled in a gravelly voice. "Let me guess. Four children and spouses, seven grandchildren and their spouses, and nine great-grandchildren."

"Yes. He's been so good to us."

Sid pulled her to her feet. "He has indeed. All right, everyone. Settle down for a moment."

Anna watched him, uncertain what Sid was up to as she snuggled into his shoulder. They hadn't discussed any grand announcements. One thing about Sid, even after sixty-three years, was he continued to surprise her.

The noise calmed down as their children and grandchildren found seats. Their younger son, Bruce, stood at the stairs to prevent the little ones from coming up from the basement.

Sid cleared his throat. "Your mother and I agreed we wouldn't exchange gifts this year. When you reach our age, there's not much left that you need."

Soft laughter filled the room.

"Sixty-three years ago, I first saw this lovely woman. She wore her blonde curls in a short hairdo, and she had the perkiest nose and sweetest smile of any woman I'd ever seen. I decided right then and there that I had to get to know her. Over the summer of 1944, she pushed me away and then I pushed her away. We chased each other. Finally, I caught her, and I haven't regretted it for one moment. The white rose, please."

Anna's eyes widened as she saw their oldest granddaughter, Catherine, coming toward her with a single white rose. Tears pooled in the corners of Anna's eyes when Sid took the rose and handed it to her.

"You were pure as this rose when we married. And the wonder of our love has carried us through many years."

Anna buried her nose in the rose, inhaled its fragrance, hoping to hide her emotion.

"But our love didn't stop in 1944. By God's immeasurable grace, our family has grown until we almost don't fit in this house anymore. Each addition to the family has been perfect. Each loss poignant. But through it all, my love for you never faltered. The red rose, please."

This time Catherine brought forward a single red rose. Sid took it and gently handed it to Anna. "Know that I have loved you for sixty-three years and will continue to love you for as many days and years as the good Lord chooses to give us."

He leaned toward her, hesitated. He wiped a tear from her cheek with a work-worn hand. Then, he kissed her, and she responded to the depths of her soul. Catcalls and clapping filled the room, until she pulled back from Sid.

"I love you, Sid."

"I love you, too."

She surveyed the room and knew that every moment, every challenge had been worth it as she watched the evidence of their love.

ABOUT THE AUTHOR

Cara C. Putman, JD MBA, the award-winning author of 25 books, graduated high school at 16, college at 20, and completed her law degree at 27. *FIRST for Women* magazine called *Shadowed by Grace* "captivating" and a "novel with 'the works.'" *Beyond Justice* is being called a page-turner that can't be put down.

Cara is active at her church and a full-time lecturer on business and employment law to graduate students at Purdue University's Krannert School of Management. Putman also practices law and is a second-generation home-schooling mom. She serves on the executive board of American Christian Fiction Writers (ACFW), an organization she has served in various roles since 2007. She lives with her husband and four children in Indiana.

Connect with Cara online:

www.caraputman.com

CPSIA information can be obtained
at www.ICGtesting.com
Printed in the USA
LVHW010123150620
658043LV00002B/528